# THE BOLLYWOOD BRIDE

**Sonali Dev's** first literary work was a play about mistaken identities performed at her neighborhood Diwali extravaganza in Mumbai. She was eight years old. Despite this early success, Sonali spent the next few decades getting degrees in architecture and writing, migrating across the globe, and starting a family while writing for magazines and websites. With the advent of her first gray hair her mad love for telling stories returned full force.

She lives in the Chicago suburbs with her very patient and often amused husband and two teens who demand both patience and humor, and the world's most perfect dog.

Sonali's novels have been on *Library Journal*, NPR, *Washington Post*, and Kirkus's lists of Best Books of the year. She won the American Library Association's award for best romance 2014, and is a RITA® finalist, RT Reviewer Choice Award Nominee, and winner of the RT Seal of Excellence. She was hailed by NPR.org as a "stunning debut".

# THE BOLLYWOOD BRIDE

SONALI DEV

HarperCollins *Publishers* India

First published by Kensington Publishing Corp. in New York in 2015

First published in India by
HarperCollins *Publishers* in 2018

Building 10, Tower A, 4th Floor, DLF Cyber City, Phase II,
Gurugram Haryana – 122002, India
www.harpercollins.co.in

2 4 6 8 10 9 7 5 3 1



P-ISBN: 978-93-5277-931-4
E-ISBN: 978-93-5277-932-1



Printed and bound at
MicroPrints India, New Delhi

*For Manoj, for seeing me with your heart and for steadfastly holding on to your vision. This is why seven days were enough.*

# Prologue

How do you explain losing your words to someone? When it's the words that are gone, what would you even use? If Ria could, she would have told them it was like trying to cook without ingredients, paint without color, laugh without air. But there was nothing to tell them with.

They'd given her paper and a pen. As though it was her voice that was lost and not her words. They'd given her other things. . . .

A ruler on her knuckles. *Talk.*

Hours in the punishment room. *Talk.*

Pills that made her sleep all day. *Talk.*

Baba's tears. *Please, beta, why won't you talk?*

If she could've done it, if she could have touched with her tongue all the things the monster had broken inside her when it broke her bones, if she could've spoken them without screaming so loud they burst Baba's eardrums, his tears would have done it. But the thing that took your words in the first place could hardly be what brought them back.

In the end what brought her words back was not being asked.

And him.

The day he arrived at the foreign house, he had grabbed her hand and dragged her off the couch where she wept, unable to stop. Out the door and into the sunshine, he pulled her along as they ran and ran, hand in hand.

"It's a magic tree," he shouted, the way people shouted when they ran as fast as they could. "It's like a castle, with bridges and towers and a moat."

She sped up, racing him as though she ran across grass in her bare feet every day.

It wasn't a castle at all. Just the biggest, tallest tree she'd ever seen.

"I'll race you to the top," he said, his hand still in hers.

She snatched it away and flew. Up on the bridge. Branch to branch to branch, rough bark scraping her soles, smooth leaves slapping her cheeks, higher and higher. Her feet clasping, her hands grasping until there was no higher to go. Until sunshine and wind kissed her face and she was all the way at the top of the world where there was no one else but her, and a boy she'd never seen before today on the branch below.

"Wow! Can you teach me to climb like that?" he said, beaming at her with eyes exactly like the kaleidoscope Baba had given her back before her words went. Blue and silver, stars and sparkles. Remnants of bangles and beads, opening and closing and pulling her in. But it was the wonder in his eyes that changed everything.

No one had ever looked at Ria that way—no tentativeness, no pity, no fear. None of the things she sought out in eyes. Nothing that jumped out and demanded words and stole them. Nothing but a spotless invitation letting her in, and it let her out.

Standing up there on the frailest branch at the top of the tree, looking down at the face that would change her life, Ria's tears stopped. After a week of leaking down her cheeks incessantly, they dried up just like that. For the first time since Baba had thrust her at the flight attendant and broken into a run without turning around to wave good-bye, her tears were gone.

"Who are you?" The words slipped out, her first after a year of silence.

"Vikram." He said his name like it was a badge of honor. "Vikram Jathar. You want to be friends?"

# 1

*Mumbai*
*Twenty years later*

Ria would have given anything to be left alone, but she knew being left alone was not in a Bollywood star's job description. Not even if you were universally acknowledged as a freakish recluse and rather aptly nicknamed The Ice Princess.

Did ice princesses battle beaded fabric? And lose?

Ria tugged at the dress pulled halfway over her head and struggled to free herself. But the stubborn thing grabbed her breasts in a vicious grip and tied her up in a knot of hair, arms, and pure frustration. Somewhere to her left her phone continued its relentless ringing.

Folding over with the skill of a contortionist, she squeezed down her breasts—a photographer had called them "magnificent" today—maybe the blasted things had swelled with pride. She put all her strength into the next tug. The dress flew off, throwing Ria back on her substantially less magnificent behind. Thank God for the rug that pooled beneath her. Standing up, she used her foot to straighten the flaming orange silk that jarred against the white minimalism of her bedroom, mimicking her mood perfectly, and grabbed her cell phone off the nightstand.

"Yes, DJ?" she said in a voice so cool no one would ever know that she'd just been sparring with her clothes. If only acting in front of the camera were as easy as acting in real life.

"Isn't that your sleazeball agent?" Her cousin's beloved all-American drawl instantly melted Ria's irritation. Her tensed-up muscles relaxed. Then just as suddenly they went into a panicked spasm.

"Nikhil? It's two in the morning! What's wrong?"

"Ria, sweetie, everything's okay. Calm down. *Jeez.*" Nikhil's bratty smirk—the one he had perfected on her growing up—flashed in Ria's mind. "Shit, is it really two in Mumbai? Sorry, I'm not used to Malawi time yet." Nikhil and his girlfriend had just moved to Lilongwe for a medical mission. "You sound wide-awake. Are you at a shoot? Or did someone finally drag you to a party?"

Ria rolled her eyes and pulled her slip back in place. "Yeah. I decided it was time to come out of my shell." Nikhil knew better than anyone else how dearly she valued said shell. She carried the dress into her closet and hung it in its color-appropriate spot and grabbed her oldest pair of shorts off a meticulous stack, adjusting it so its meticulousness stayed undisturbed.

"Good, because there's somewhere you need to be." Excitement simmered in Nikhil's voice like the soda cans he liked to shake before he popped them open. Ria's heartbeat sped up. "Jen and I picked a date," he said, and the tiniest shadow of tentativeness crept into his voice.

Ria squeezed the phone between her ear and her shoulder and pulled on the shorts, her hands suddenly clammy.

"They're giving us time off next month. After that we won't be able to get away for another year. So we're getting married in two weeks. And there's no way we're doing it without you."

She grabbed the phone off her shoulder and clutched it to her racing heart for a second before bringing it back to her ear.

"It's time to come home, Ria."

*Home.*

The word caught in her throat. Exactly the way her breath had when she'd ridden her bike full speed into a low-hanging branch and hit her head so hard she hadn't been able to scream or cry or breathe until she hit the ground. And then her lungs had filled so fast she thought they'd explode.

Home.

For ten years she hadn't let herself think the word out loud.

Nikhil cleared his throat. "Ria?"

She had to say something. But her breath was still trapped in her lungs. There was no way she could go back to Chicago. It had been ten years since she'd been home. Ten years since she'd pushed it away to where not even her dreams could touch it.

Nikhil sighed. "Listen, sweetie, will you at least think about it?"

She needed air. She crossed the room, the marble floor cold beneath her bare feet, and pushed past the French doors onto the balcony. The sweltering Mumbai night slammed into her as she left the air-conditioning. She sucked in a huge humid lungful and let it out. "Nikhil, I'm in the middle of a shooting schedule." A lie. She'd sworn never to lie to him again.

He let out another sigh, heavy with disappointment. "It's okay, Ria. I understand."

Of course he understood. Every decision she'd ever made he'd stood by her like a rock, no questions asked. And here she was ready to miss his wedding. His *wedding!*

Wrapping an arm across her belly, she leaned into the railing. The rough-hewn sandstone scraped her elbows. Fourteen floors below, silver moonlight danced over the bay, the restless waves all turbulence under the steady rhythm. "Actually, you know what? I might be able to throw one of those diva tantrums and move things around. Give me a day to figure it out?"

"Oh, thank God!" he said with such relief that shame flooded through Ria. "You have no idea how badly I need you there. Jen's going nuts with the traditional Indian wedding thing. She wants the vows around the fire, the henna ceremony, all sorts of dances and dinners. I swear she's making some of those rituals up. She's even talking about me arriving at the wedding on a damn horse!" His voice squeaked on the word and Ria couldn't help but smile.

Jen was fire to Nikhil's earth. Despite his whining, love colored his voice.

"You poor baby. Deep breaths." Ria attempted one herself.

"And Aie's not helping at all. She's doing everything she can to encourage Jen."

Of course Nikhil's mother would support Jen explicitly. Ria knew only too well how fiercely her aunt loved. Uma Atya was the only mother Ria had ever known. All she wanted to do right now was crawl into one of her jasmine-scented hugs and block everything else out the way she had done as a child. "A horse isn't that bad, Nikhil. In my last film, the groom used an elephant—it's the latest craze."

"Yikes!" Nikhil said. "Have Aie or Jen watched that one yet?"

"It isn't out yet. But if you give them a hard time, I'm sending them a DVD."

"Traitor," he mumbled, laughing. Then he got serious again. "Ria, Just come home. Everything will be all right. Trust me."

And with that impossible promise he was gone, leaving Ria leaning over the railing, suspended over the world, memories squeezing out of her heart with the force of seedlings breaking through concrete at the first sign of a crack. And idiot that she was, instead of pushing them back, she clutched at them the way a starving street urchin snatches at food.

She was going home.

To him.

*Viky.*

No, just Vikram. Not Viky. Not anymore. Only she had ever called him that. He'd been her Viky since she was eight years old. Been as much her home as the redbrick Georgian that had changed her life once. He would never let anyone call him that again, not after what she had done to him.

The bay gleamed onyx in the moonlight. In a few hours the sun would paint the waves the palest gray-blue—an entire ocean the exact color of his eyes.

Great, now she was acting like one of those lovesick drama queens she played in her films. Next she'd be grudging them their absurd hope and their contrived happy endings.

No, she couldn't go back.

But how could she not? Nikhil wasn't just her cousin, he was her brother in every way that mattered. Maybe Vikram would choose not to come. But that was just as ridiculous. Vikram couldn't miss Nikhil's wedding any more than she could. Nikhil and his parents, Uma and Vijay—Ria's aunt and uncle—were as much Vikram's family as they were hers. Not to mention the fact that Vikram had never backed away from anything in his life. Except her.

She, on the other hand, had backing away down to an art.

The phone buzzed in her hand. A text from her agent. Trust DJ to be up at two in the morning texting her. Usually she had no trouble indulging his compulsive excitement about a new script, but right now she couldn't think about work, not before she slipped back into Ice Princess mode. The press couldn't have come up with a better nickname for her. It was perfect. Hard and cold and unbreachable. And she needed it now more than ever.

Instead of reading the text she reached behind her, gathered the heavy curtain of hair that hung down to her waist, and slung it over one shoulder in a loose twist. The movement hurt. But the familiar soreness in her muscles anchored her in the present, which is where she needed to be. This was her life. Two hours at the gym before a twelve-hour shooting schedule. Focusing on her body was the only way to keep the mess that was her mind buried deep, the numbing exhaustion the only way to put her to bed every night. Except tonight, there would be no sleep.

She leaned into the railing and stretched her back, arching up, then down like a cat. Rickshaws whirred in the distance, cars honked. Even at this hour, there was no silence in the city, no peace. Billboards and streetlights threw a twilight glow over the tightly clustered buildings and sparkled off the water like stars shooting out of an inverted sky. An intense urge to flip it the right side up overwhelmed her. She thrust her body over the railing and twisted around, letting her hair spill into the night.

The cell phone slipped from her hand and landed on something hard with a crack. She straightened up, frowning, and glanced around to find it. But it was gone.

*Bloody hell.* Her entire world, all her contacts, it was all in that phone. For a split second she considered not searching for it at all. It had disappeared and maybe she could disappear too. Go back home as though the past ten years had never happened.

But then the fluorescent screen flashed at her from the outer ledge of the swirling balusters and nipped her flight of fancy in the bud. There was no escape. She had to retrieve it. In one easy movement she pulled herself onto the railing and swung herself over it.

Her legs were too long for her body. They had always made her feel awkward and gangly. But now they made her lithe, almost graceful, as she landed on the wide cantilevered overhang. She picked up the phone and shoved it into her pocket. Her low-slung shorts slid even lower down her hips. A gust of wind caught her hair and lifted it into a flapping cape behind her. She faced the ocean. The old heady freedom of being so far away from the earth wrapped itself around her. She threw out her arms and let the unrestrained beauty of the sparkling night sink into every pore.

Suddenly a spark shone too strong, too bright, and broke through her trance. Then another. Then another. Blinking, Ria followed the flashes to the rooftop terrace of the neighboring building.

A hooded figure shrouded in black leaned over the concrete wall and reached into the meager space separating the two buildings. A giant bazooka-like contraption projected from his hands and he had it aimed straight at her.

A lens.

The realization slammed into Ria, the force of it turning every cell in her body to lead and locking her in place, as the rapid flashes went off incessantly.

Suddenly they stopped. He moved the camera aside, looked directly at her, and made a bouncing, diving action with one hand.

He was signaling her to jump.

# 2

The doorbell gave a loud clang. Ria sat up in bed panting, memories thrashing around inside her like rabid things kept locked up too long.

She pulled her knees to her chest, pressing them against the name slamming inside it.

*Viky.*

Had she screamed it out? Or had it stayed trapped inside? All she knew was that she wanted to hear it again. Wanted to say it again so badly she had to swallow to keep it inside.

The doorbell clanged again.

She dragged herself to the door. Every joint in her body felt like it had come unhinged from being rolled up like a fetus all night. Tai, her day maid, who cleaned and cooked for Ria, stood on the other side of the door, both hands planted squarely on her hips, her face scrunched up with disapproval for being kept waiting. One look at Ria and her glare turned to alarm. Apparently, the Ice Princess mask hadn't held up to last night's events.

"Who will believe you are a *filum shtarr*, babyji?" Tai pulled the door shut behind her and took her street slippers off by the door. "You look like my friend when her husband whacks her twice and her eyes swell into slits this small." She narrowed her own eyes, simulating her friend's abuse with her usual matter-of-factness. But the concern in her voice was so heartfelt that Ria attempted a smile to put her at ease before heading off to the bathroom to assess the damage. Tai tucked her sari around herself and followed close on Ria's heels.

Tai was right. Smudged mascara and kohl painted twin black eyes into Ria's throbbing head. Leaning over the sink, Ria flicked on the lights that outlined the mirrored wall and studied herself in it. She couldn't remember the last time she had gone to bed without stripping her face of every last bit of makeup. She turned on the faucet and splashed her face. Time to snap out of all this self-indulgent moping about. The cold sting felt so good she kept splashing until Tai nudged her shoulder and handed her a towel, staring at her the way one stared at a pathetic, hungover drunk.

"You know, babyji, my friend just started doing cleaning for that new girl who lives down there." She pointed at the bathroom floor. "On the second floor. You know the one who acts in TV *sherial?*"

A tiny smile nudged at Ria's heart. She loved the way Tai peppered their native tongue, Marathi, with English words like *film star* and *TV serial*, turning all her *s*'s into *sh*'s. Ria nodded and started rubbing globs of aloe extract into the soreness around her eyes.

Tai put down the commode cover and lowered herself on it. "*Arrey*, you should hear the stories my friend tells. Day and night they do *party*." Again, she said the word *party* in English and rolled her eyes one full circle to make sure Ria knew exactly how despicable the partying was. "*Bottle* everywhere. Even *ciga-rette. Shi!* And men? All times of the day there are men."

The smile broke through to Ria's lips.

Tai went on. "I told my friend, not my babyji. Never. Never a party. Never noise. Never nothing!" She shook her hands to indicate the nothingness of Ria's life. "And men? Not ever. Not one. And you are a real *shtar*. Not just some TV *shtarlett!*" She spat out the word *starlet* with such disgust that Ria paused in the middle of rubbing circles up and down her cheeks and turned to her. Tai didn't deserve all this worry.

"Thank you, Tai." Ria had always used the endearment that meant "big sister" for her. She was much older than Ria, so using her name was out of the question and Ria hated the standard *Bai* reserved for maids. "When do I have time for parties? And you know there's no alcohol in the house. It's just that there was a little problem last night and I didn't get much sleep." As understatements went, this one was ridiculously over the top.

Ria grabbed a tissue and wiped around her eyes. The naked, violated feeling that had made her hands shake when she tugged the drapes shut after running in from the balcony last night spread through her in an unbearable throb. She eased the pressure of her fingers. Some desperate paparazzo wasn't worth gouging out her skin for. Especially not just before a shoot.

A frown creased Tai's forehead. But Ria didn't respond to her silent question. Tai's curiosity would be satisfied soon enough. The pictures were going to be all over the media. Ten years of keeping her private life off the media's radar, and she had potentially blown it all in one fell swoop.

She turned back to the mirror, her spine so straight it made her feel ten feet tall and lifted her away from the problem. Blowing it wasn't an option. After spending ten years guarding her private life with everything she had, she wasn't going to let one stupid impulsive moment ruin it all. Silence was the only defense against the press. It was the best antidote to scandal. And Ria Parkar did silence better than anyone else.

Tai shook her head, giving up on a response, and straightened the stack of the *MindBender* magazines Ria special-ordered from England and solved obsessively. "Come on, babyji, I've worked for you for five years, you don't think I know you are as straight as an arrow?" She pulled her arms apart and shot out an imaginary arrow. "Look at you. Who else has a face like that? Those almond eyes the color of honey." She widened her own eyes. "That skin like churned cream!" She rubbed her own cheeks with both hands, jangling her glass bangles. "What is the use, babyji? I ask you, what is the use? You don't eat, don't sleep, don't have any friends. That family of yours visits you every few years like some strangers. When I was twenty-eight like you I had five children. Five!" She held up five work-worn fingers and pride flashed in her eyes at the mention of her children.

Ria crushed the blackened tissue into a wad and swallowed the sharp edged lump that stuck in her throat like a mangled ball of nails.

*You will have to find someone else to have crazy children with. It will not be my Vikram.*

Even today, ten years later, the memory of his mother's words was as fresh as a bleeding wound. It cut her off at her knees and in the space of an instant turned her into the helpless girl she'd been.

"Babyji?"

Ria found her fist pressed against her belly—a womb she would never allow to fill. This curse of hers would go no further than her. She pulled her hand away and tossed the tissue in the trash. Enough. If the idea of going home was going to undo all the distance she had traveled, she really had to think of a way to get out of it.

She forced her mind back to Tai's concerned face.

"But I have you, Tai, don't I? You take such good care of me." She conjured up her best smile, making her dimples dance, her eyes twinkle, shamelessly wielding her weapons with the skill of a hardened warrior.

Tai's worry dissipated. She touched the wooden door to ward away evil spirits. "With a smile like that, no wonder that Kunal Kapoor was willing to kill himself for you in *Jeena Tere Liye*," she said, the smile back on her face, her eyes at once bashful and shining with mischief.

"Thank heavens he didn't," Ria teased her. "How would I ever live it down if I hurt your favorite heartthrob?"

"*Ish!*" Tai giggled into her sari like a little girl, blushing furiously. "Such a jokester you are, Babyji! Those stupid press-walas should see you like this." She picked up the laundry basket. "When was the last time you ate?"

Her tone reminded Ria so much of Uma Atya that for one moment the intensity of her need to go home squeezed the breath from her lungs.

"How about you make me a chapati?" she said, ignoring the pang. "And give me some yogurt with it. And don't you dare sneak ghee on my chapati. I have to be at a shoot in two hours."

Tai snorted and switched on the water heater so Ria would have hot water in the shower. "Who eats a chapati and yogurt for breakfast when they could eat just about anything they wanted? It's nonsensical, that's what it is," she mumbled under her breath as she left the bathroom. And it almost turned the smile on Ria's face real.

Even today, ten years after her first time, being in front of the camera felt like being stripped naked and held down against her will. Ria let the gush of relief wash over her as she stepped away from the blazing set lights. The forced synch-sound silence dissolved into the din of pack-up that erupted around her. Her mind turned back on and slid back into her body just as it switched back into itself. Years of practice made it easy to use the rituals of pack-up to reorient herself. She relaxed and adjusted her sari so it didn't show quite so much cleavage.

"Excellent shot, Riaji!" Shabaz Khan, her hero in the film, followed her as she walked away from the set and beamed at her with all his newcomer enthusiasm. "Thank you so much for all your help."

Ria nodded politely. Five minutes ago he'd been holding her as though she was his life's blood and it was a huge relief that he was able to drop the character just as quickly as she did.

"You too, Shabaz." She should have asked him to dispense with formality and call her just Ria. But she liked the distance the *ji* tacked on to her name provided. This was his first film. Between his small-town upbringing and his eagerness to please, she doubted he would have called her just Ria even if she asked him to. Truth was, his newcomer reticence made her own social ineptness in the industry seem less awkward. It was one of the reasons she always agreed to act with new heroes when none of the other established heroines were willing to take that chance.

She hated the usual hugging and kissing in the industry and her greatest horror was one of those sets where everyone acted like it was one big party with the pranks and the spontaneous get-togethers. Fortunately, her reclusive reputation preceded her and all she got for hiding away in her room was a few sniggers and some name calling behind her back.

She returned Shabaz's smile and was about to walk away when he took a step too close and reached for her hand. "The film is done now and we don't have to pretend anymore," he said, his smile turning suddenly heavy lidded and far more bold than she'd ever seen it.

Ria stepped back, so startled that for one second she forgot how to hide it.

His mouth tightened along with his grip. "Oh come on, you don't really think I buy the "benevolent senior actor" bit, do you? It's not like I haven't heard what they say about you."

In a rush of cold, hard fury Ria's composure returned. With all the calm befitting an Ice Princess she looked around the set. Everyone appeared to be absorbed in packing up, and there wasn't a journo in sight. Good. Without a single word she turned her glare on his hand, which was still gripping her wrist, until he dropped it. He stepped back, both hands raised as though it was her reaction that was completely irrational and not what he'd just said.

She regained her polite smile and gave him a second to return it before walking away. And when he mumbled the words "frigid bitch" behind her, she blocked them out just as she blocked out the sting of his fingers on her wrist.

"*Fun*tastic shot, Riaji." The lanky unit boy caught up with her as she made her way to the dressing room. He held an umbrella over her head to keep the harsh sun off her face and handed her a bottle of water, smiling at her with such sincerity, the useless anger that had flared inside her calmed.

She took a long sip. "Thank you, Rameshji." She presented another rendition of the signature Ria Parkar smile.

His eyes lost focus, his mouth fell open in a besotted "O," and Ria quickly dialed it back.

"You'll kill someone with that smile someday." How her agent knew the exact wrong thing to say in any given situation, she would never know. He strode up to her in his all-black ensemble. Quintessential DJ in all his intimidating glory. The boy cowered.

Ria frowned at DJ. He ignored her and snapped his fingers, signaling for the boy to leave. "We need to talk."

She turned to Ramesh again. "Did you get Choti's board results?"

He brightened. Brotherly pride turned him larger, older than he was. "She got eighty percent, Riaji!"

This time Ria didn't have to make herself smile. She patted his head. "Excellent! I told you she would do well. Remember what I said about marriage? Wait until she finishes college, okay?"

He nodded shyly before running off.

"You can barely remember your costar's names and you know everything about the unit hand's family?" DJ said as though it were somehow an accusation.

"You needed something?" Ria turned and headed for the cottage that served as her dressing room in the sprawling studio complex. She had steadily refused to buy a trailer. Too many bad memories.

DJ fell in step next to her, but didn't answer. Ria could hear the cogs in his brain turning. DJ was never at a loss for words. Everything about DJ was out in the open, and what wasn't was barely contained. He was one of those small men who cast a large shadow. Everything about him, except for his height, was huge. Huge hair, huge mannerisms, huge ambition. And amazingly, for someone most women had to look down at, he also had a huge reputation that suggested he wasn't called Big DJ for nothing.

As they approached the cottage, a uniformed security guard who had been smoking under a tree ran up and unlocked the door for them. Ria thanked him, but instead of his usual cheery greeting, he gave Ria a formal smile and DJ a stiff salute and stepped away quickly.

"How is it they only smile at you, never at me?" DJ asked, one of his spectacular frowns darkening his face.

"Maybe because I don't glower at them and scare them half to death."

"Yeah, you save your glowering for your costars and the press." DJ signaled the guard to bring them chai, his dark mood perfectly in synch with his black muscle shirt, black jeans, and chunky black elevator shoes. The only speck of color on him was the scarlet prayer thread on his wrist and the scarlet *tilak* etched across his forehead.

He was probably coming from one of the many *poojas*—the prayer ceremonies he attended almost every day as part of his job. Religious rites to invoke favors and give thanks were standard fare in the film industry. Success was elusive—no one knew what brought it on or how to keep it from slipping away. So divine intervention was universally accepted as the only explanation and everyone rushed about to lay claim to whatever divinity they could intercept. They changed the spellings of their names and rebuilt their homes to follow feng shui and *vastu shastra* to open up their energy centers and let in light and peace and the one thing that made all that light and peace worth having—money.

Ria settled into the leather sofa and slipped off her silver heels before placing them neatly in their box and stretched her feet under the heavy *zardozi* border of her sari. Must be nice to be able to believe that destinies could be reversed by something as simple as prayer.

DJ noticed her looking at his wrist thread. "The Kapoor *satya narayan*," he said, doing a quick thing with his fingers, touching his head, then his heart, and the restless set of his shoulders relaxed for a few seconds.

Ria nodded and arched one eyebrow at the oversized manila envelope he pulled out of his shoulder bag.

He handed her the chai and biscuits the security guard brought in. "Eat first." He tapped the envelope with a finger. "These aren't going to help your appetite."

She took a sip of the chai and put the biscuits on the coffee table. "I thought you liked it when I didn't eat. What happened to 'There's no such thing as too thin'?" She reached for the envelope.

He moved it out of reach. "Babes, if you get any thinner, we'll have the eating disorder police to deal with on top of everything else. Fat bunch of frustrated journos and their fucking sour grapes. Talk about destructive Western influence." He lowered himself onto the arm of the sofa.

"On top of everything else? I thought I was your easiest client." She wasn't much of an actor, but she knew what the audience wanted and she gave it to them, always looking her best, working hard at her dances, and following the director's directions to a T. Having learned to separate from herself at such a young age had its advantages. Even the critics followed along, calling her *nuanced* and *ethereal* if the film clicked, and *robotic* and *plastic* if it tanked. She was also his most scandal-free client. He'd never had to clean up a single mess for her. DJ had absolutely nothing to complain about.

Usually, he would've responded with a cocky comment. But his frown didn't budge. He held up the envelope when she reached for it again and opened and shut his mouth a few times in a ridiculously un-DJ-like gesture, before his words finally tumbled out. "My guess is you haven't posed semi-topless while trying to kill yourself. So this has to be some bastard who got lucky and caught you doing something incredibly stupid."

The milky chai curdled in Ria's throat. The paparazzo had worked faster than she'd expected. But why had he sent the pictures to DJ? She swallowed and snatched the envelope from his hand. It opened, spilling pictures on the tightly stretched black leather of the sofa.

There were four of them. All sepia-toned with the hue of night. All surreal.

Her hands were spread-eagled. Hair billowed in a tangle around her face. Her bare toes clutched the edge of the concrete, and her body leaned forward like it was about to go flying to its death. He had even managed to capture a hollow maniacal gleam in her kohl-smudged eyes.

To make things worse, her sheer slip strained against the heavy globes of her braless breasts and the powerful flash turned her nipples into dark darts poking through the thin fabric. The filmy hem of her slip had ridden up, exposing her midriff and throwing into stark relief everything from her bare ribs to the hipbones jutting out of her low-slung shorts. She looked like a complete lunatic trying to put some sort of dark, erotic end to her life.

It looked like a bloody poster for mental illness.

Anger so violent exploded in Ria's chest, she wanted to scream into his face and shred the pictures until the abomination on them disappeared into nothingness. Instead she didn't let her tone so much as falter. "They're completely out of context, Big. Plus, they're clearly Photoshopped."

He looked utterly unconvinced and the sympathy that flashed in his eyes made her control stretch at its seams. He sat down next to her, his posture commiserating. "Talk to me," his face said. "I can help you."

"Oh for God's sake, DJ, really?" She wanted to spring off the couch to get away from all that sympathy, but she refused to give him anything that would reinforce the direction his thoughts were taking.

He shook his head dolefully and reached into his shirt pocket, pulling out a business card and placing it on top of the envelope. "I knew you wouldn't talk to me. But this guy comes highly recommended. The highest level of discretion. You won't believe his patient list."

Ria didn't look at the card. She didn't need to. She knew exactly what DJ had just offered her without looking at it. It was right there in his eyes. He had never looked at her this way, as if she teetered on the edge of madness and he wanted to help, but he didn't know if she could be helped or if it was easier to just slowly back away before she snapped. That look was a snapshot of her childhood. Her teachers, the girls at her boarding school, that look captured all she had been to them.

*The Girl Who Came From Insanity.*

Ria sprang off the couch, unable to bear the weight of that look, and strode to the other end of the living room. She had worked too hard, given up too much, in order to wipe that look off people's faces. Now it reached inside her and tugged at a part of her she had sworn never to let anyone draw out again.

"I don't need a shrink, Big." She struggled to stay calm, to not let him see how much this meant. An Ice Princess. She was an Ice Princess.

"You were on a ledge. On the fourteenth floor. That's a sheer drop to death, babes!"

"My cell phone fell. I was just getting it back. It really was that simple." Oh God, please let it be that simple.

He stared at her. Just stared. It was that look again. She refused to let it overwhelm her. "It's not a very narrow ledge." She kept her voice even. Perfectly level. Perfectly sane.

He didn't respond.

"I'm just not scared of heights, okay? Is that a crime?" She loved heights. Higher and higher. As far away from the earth as she could get.

DJ continued to skewer her with that look. Her words sank down her windpipe, racing out of reach as her tongue grew heavy. But she couldn't lose her words now. This was not the time for the solace of silence. She grabbed them with her voice and threw them at his skeptical face. "It was a crazy day, DJ. I wasn't thinking. And I most certainly was not trying to kill myself. Why on earth would I?"

He didn't react.

She made her voice even calmer. "If anything I was trying to save myself. You would have killed me if I had lost my phone." She even smiled at her lame joke.

His frown turned positively gargantuan.

"Okay, I'm sorry. That was not funny. But seriously, that's all it was. And I'm fine. Nothing happened."

He shook the pictures at her, their roles reversed. Him silent and her babbling.

She walked back to the couch, regaining control with every step. "Okay, so something happened, but don't you dare make some bastard journo my problem." She picked up the pictures and stuffed them back into the envelope.

Instead of softening, DJ's expression stayed as dark as ever. "I don't think you understand how bad this is."

Oh, she knew exactly how bad this was. He was the one who didn't know just how much worse it could get. A reclusive Ice Princess the public couldn't get enough of. Those comedy sketches where they mimicked her were funny enough. But an unstable star careening toward full-blown madness like her murderous mother—that was something they wouldn't want to touch with a barge pole. The public wanted their darkness in bite-sized chunks, small enough to be entertaining. For real tragedy they had the terrorists, the rapists, the natural disasters. Film stars were for entertainment purposes only.

For the first time since Ria had got off that ledge, instead of feeling violated and cornered, fear stirred inside her.

Hard negotiator's curiosity flashed in DJ's eyes as he weighed all the pieces of the catastrophe at hand. "The only reason we got to see these pictures before they went to print is that my contact at Filmistan called me instead of printing them. I was able to track the photographer down. He's the worst kind of bastard, all sleaze and greed. He says the pictures aren't all he's got."

Ria clutched the back of the couch. The floor beneath her seemed to tip to one side. What else could he possibly have? No one, not even DJ, knew anything about her past. Not even her real name. "He's lying. I've got nothing to hide." Her tone stayed cool, but the blatancy of the lie scalded her tongue like a too big gulp of steaming coffee she could neither spit out nor swallow.

"I don't know. But do we want to find it in the papers? Can we really call his bluff?"

We? Was he the one who would lose everything if anyone started asking questions? She wanted to scream at him to do his job, to make this go away. But she didn't, because that would make her sound as terrified as she felt. And because it would make her sound crazy.

"Can't we take legal action?" she asked instead. The man had, after all, photographed her in the privacy of her flat, without her consent.

Tea spurted from DJ's mouth. The man had a law degree and the mention of legal action made him spray milky brown liquid all over the spotless marble floor. It took him a few moments to stop sputtering. "Legal? You mean like calling the police? Like filing reports and restraining orders and shit? Babes, this is Mumbai, not LA. Sometimes you're so naïve, I forget how long you've been around."

She threw a bunch of napkins on the tea and soaked up the mess.

DJ paced the room. "We should call the police. So they can arrest you for attempted suicide. Then this could turn into a real media circus. Money can't buy this kind of publicity. We could stretch it out for months if we play it right. Why doesn't this happen to clients who want it?"

Something warm prickled in Ria's eyes. It had been ten years since she'd let herself cry off camera. The last time she'd cried she had been Ria Pendse, an eighteen-year-old on her back in Ved Kapoor's bed in his fancy trailer. India's biggest superstar had been excited by her eighteen-year-old tears. They had made him wild as he rammed into her. *Don't forget you're getting the better end of this deal, girl,* he'd told her. He had been right. Not only had he given Ria a new name and her first role, but he had pounded every last remnant of hope and innocence from her heart, and every last memory of Vikram from her body.

Crying because some bastard wanted to make a quick buck off her was an insult to those last tears she had cried. None of this trivial shit was worthy of tears.

She tossed the napkins in the trash and turned to DJ. "Fine. Find out what he wants. Pay him off. I don't care how much. I don't want these pictures to go public. And I do not want him digging around."

"You got it." DJ didn't even bother to hide his triumph. This was the exact outcome he had been working toward from the very beginning. "I'll take care of it. You go enjoy your cousin's wedding. It's the first time you're taking time off in ten years, get some rest." He sank back into the sofa, his body finally relaxed. The disaster averted for now.

Ria, on the other hand, was too aware of what lay ahead to feel any relief at all.

# 3

*Chicago*

Ria struggled with the zipper on her halter *choli* blouse. Yet again her designer had ignored her and made the heavily embellished garment far too snug. She sucked in a breath and gave the tiny metal zipper another yank. This time it complied and slid into place under her arm. She adjusted the *choli* so things weren't pushed up quite so much, hooked the halter straps around her neck, and then pulled on her *ghagra*. The full ankle-length skirt of cream silk was much more obliging and slid easily around her hips.

Another wave of music and laughter seeped in through the door and her already-nervous heartbeat sped up. The party was in full swing downstairs. The celebratory sounds had shaken her awake an hour ago. She must've looked really pathetic when she arrived that morning because no one had come up to wake her when the party started.

She'd almost wept with relief when she'd seen Nikhil at the airport that morning. It had been the journey from hell. Some psycho terrorist had brought all of Heathrow airport to a standstill and it had taken twice the usual eighteen hours to get from Mumbai to Chicago. At home her aunt had fussed and fed her while Nikhil teased her mercilessly about being such a wimpy traveler. The sound of their beloved voices reverberating against these familiar walls had kneaded all the tension out of her and she had fallen asleep right there on the couch.

She vaguely remembered Nikhil leading her up the stairs. It reminded her of the countless times her uncle had carried her up after she'd fallen asleep in the car driving home from all those weekend dinner parties.

She blew the hair off her face and threw herself back on her bed.

*Her* bed. Uma Atya had gone overboard with the girly furnishings when Ria had first come to spend the summer with them when she was eight years old. Until then Ria had never seen so much pink. The house she had once shared with her father in Pune, the home he had banished her from, was overridingly gray. Her boarding school was grayer still. The color of Ria's childhood had changed from gray to pink in this house. These brightly colored walls had held within them enough warmth to heal even the most broken child.

She stared at the frilly canopy that floated above her. Tiny wrinkles crisscrossed the faded pink flowers and Ria knew her aunt had washed and reattached the canopy in preparation for her visit. She crushed the matching comforter against her nose and sucked in a deep, drugging breath—lemons and lavender and sleep.

She had craved this smell, this bed for so long she never wanted to leave it. But Nikhil was waiting for her downstairs. Today was the engagement ceremony—the kickoff to the wedding celebrations that had reduced her fearless hero of a cousin to a nervous wreck. She remembered the relief in his voice when she'd agreed to come home for the wedding and kicked herself for the hundredth time for having hesitated in the first place.

"Just come home. Everything will be all right," he had said on the phone that day.

She trusted Nikhil with her life. And he worked miracles every day, treating children no one else would go near, in places most people wished didn't exist. But even he couldn't pull off a miracle like that.

She dug her elbows into the mattress, pushed herself off the bed, and dragged herself to the bathroom, ignoring the pull of the bed and her weak-willed legs that wanted nothing more than to succumb. She had already washed her hair, twice. And dried it. Now she flat-ironed her already straight hair, one section at a time, until it took on an unnatural sheen.

Vikram had loved her hair. Loved to tangle his fingers in it, press his face into it, tug at it when he teased her.

She rolled it tightly into a bun, and poked in pins to keep it in place. *Keep your mind where your hands are,* her aunt always said, *and the future will take care of itself.* It wasn't working. The future she'd been dreading since Nikhil's phone call was here and it was far from taken care of.

She looked around for something else to do and found the long-handled brush that stuck out of her giant makeup pouch. Her eyes were too tired for makeup, but she grabbed the brush and swept bronze shadow across her lids. Then on went a thin line of kohl, then a coat of mascara. Ria Parkar, Film Star, stared back at her from the mirror and she tried to follow her lead. An Ice Princess wouldn't be a terrified mass of jelly, and even if she were she most certainly wouldn't show it.

Ria reached for the chiffon scarf and tried to drape it across her bare shoulders, but it took her shaking fingers a few tries. She closed her eyes and imagined the cameras turning on, felt the heat of the set lights on her skin. It didn't quite create her usual disconnection, but she felt distant enough from her body to squeeze a few thin gold bangles around her wrists and sling a chain around her neck. By the time she had adjusted the diamond teardrop to fall precisely in the center of her throat her hands were steady enough. Finally, she pushed a pair of tiny hoops into her oversensitive earlobes.

*Why do you wear those damn things?* Out of nowhere his whisper blew into her ear. The memory of his breath on her bloodstained lobes so stark and fresh she almost pressed back into him. Earrings had always hurt too much and she had never worn them as a child. But Uma had given Ria her grandmother's earrings the summer she turned sixteen and Ria had wanted to wear them no matter what. Even when Vikram hid them away she had made him give them back.

Ten years of wearing outrageously large earrings and her ears, like everything else, had adjusted to the pain.

She closed her eyes and stepped away from the mirror. So much for Ice Princess. Her insides, her limbs, all of it was a wobbly mess again. She tried to invoke the cameras one more time, but it was useless. Another wave of laughter and conversation drifted up from downstairs and she forced herself to the sweeping staircase and grabbed the handrail.

It was time to give the shot. She could do this. Once she made it down she'd find a nice quiet corner to hide in. She was good at being invisible under the spotlight. And he probably wasn't even in the house. Nikhil hadn't mentioned him once. Uma hadn't mentioned him. Then again, they had stopped mentioning him around her ten years ago. Okay, time to stop this. She took a deep breath and took the last shaking step into the foyer.

And there he was.

Vikram.

Of course he was the first thing her eyes found in the crowd. The floor shifted beneath her feet. The entire polished mass of wood slid out from under her. There was no way she was making an entrance on her bum. It was the worst possible way she could think of to meet him after all these years. She dug her fingers into the handrail and regained her footing.

He stood there against the flaming red tapestry that had hung over the mantel for as long as Ria could remember. He was deep in conversation, completely focused on the person he was talking to. She realized with a start that there were people everywhere. Dark bobbing heads, a sea of them flooding the house, the buzz of voices loud and raucous despite the music. As always, he stood apart. A head taller than everyone else. And somehow more still, more rooted than anyone else. As if he had been standing there forever. She couldn't remember how many times she'd seen him in that room or what he had looked like back then. She couldn't remember anything at all. It was as if he'd stepped out of her thoughts, leaving them empty and here he was.

She forced herself not to close her eyes. But then he smiled. And that smile, that slight, almost economical movement of his lips, made the mad panic inside her still. The tight knot inside her eased. A weight she had carried for years lifted off her chest. It felt like someone wrapped her soft pink comforter around her and pulled her close.

Vikram was smiling. The last time she'd seen him he had looked like he would never smile again. She had looked into his eyes and watched him break, watched the gray-blue crystals shatter to bits.

He was smiling.

Breath whooshed out of her. A lifetime of crushed-up memories floated from her and settled on him and disappeared.

She had been afraid for nothing. It had been ten years. Of course he had moved on. Of course the world had continued to spin and had not stayed frozen in place the way she had left it. And she could ask for nothing more.

He turned his head, as if he sensed someone watching him.

Ria's limbs unlocked. She moved swiftly away from the steps. He hadn't seen her and she wasn't ready for that yet. She slipped out of the foyer. It had been ten years, but the house was part of her. She knew every corner, every door, every passageway. Crushing the chiffon of her scarf against her heart, she moved through the house, soaking up the warmth even as she fought falling back into the comfort of the memories.

That smile of his swirled inside her, pulsing sweet, warm pain through her veins.

Some men looked hard, their handsomeness rough and earthy. Some were more finely etched, almost angelic. Vikram had always been some sort of heartbreaking combination of both, rugged, but with something incredibly soft and yielding. He could conquer your every breath and get completely lost in you at the exact same time. His face was a perfect reflection of *him*—arrogant, demanding, and yet so steadfast, so very gentle that ten years weren't enough to erase his touch.

A touch that had healed her once, and, ironically enough, taught her how to go on even after she gave up the right to it.

She had to find Nikhil. Remind herself why she was here, find a way to pinch herself awake. She found Nikhil in the family room, adorable in his silk *kurta*, his arm wrapped around Jen, who wore her matching black *salwar kameez* with the ease of a born and bred *desi* girl. Jen had fallen madly in love with everything Indian two years ago when she had met Nikhil and then been embraced by Uma and Vijay with their usual unconditional fervor. Uma Atya kept wanting to include Chinese and American rituals in the wedding plans. But Jen hadn't been to China since she was three, when her American parents had adopted her from an orphanage, and she had steadily insisted on a traditional Indian-Marathi wedding. Ria for one understood the need to separate from one's history better than anyone.

Nikhil said something and Jen's eyes sparkled. They were surrounded by people, seemingly enjoying the company, but they kept stealing glances at each other as if everything else were just a distraction.

It was strange, almost funny to see Nikhil like this. He had always been so disdainful of all things romantic, mocking the gooey nonsense he thought couples wasted their time on. But watching him look at Jen was almost like watching someone pray. He became reverent and peaceful and lost in her. The first time Nikhil and Jen had visited Ria in Mumbai, Jen had seemed embarrassed, almost uncomfortable with the attention. Now she owned it, basked in it. Ria sent up silent thanks for the twist of fate that had thrown these two no-nonsense workaholics together.

Nikhil caught Ria watching them from the doorway and his face split into that familiar grin. He had the family dimples too. Their gift from Uma Atya and Baba, who had got them from their mother. It was about the only thing Ria remembered about her grandmother—those deep dimples in her chubby face and her constant worry. *What will happen of you after I'm gone, my sweet child?* All Aji's worst fears had been realized only weeks after she died. And in the aftermath of that disaster Ria had found her way here when her father had finally taken his mother's advice and let his sister have a go at fixing the daughter his wife broke.

On Nikhil the dimples came and went as they pleased. He hadn't leashed them into potent weapons the way Ria had. His career wasn't built on the angle at which he tilted his mouth or how the light balanced the shadows his face cast. His career was based on the pure grit it took to act on your beliefs, and on having the kind of heart you could expose to hurt every day by taking on only the most insurmountable of challenges.

Nikhil pulled Jen's hand briefly to his lips before letting it go and came to Ria. "You okay, starlet?"

She manufactured one of her best smiles for him. "Of course. I'm great."

He narrowed his eyes, not buying it, but he didn't press her for more. And when she wrapped her arms around him, he pulled her close and held her for a long moment.

"Why didn't you wake me?" she asked, looking up at him.

"I didn't think you'd be done with your beauty sleep so soon."

She pulled a face at him and he relaxed.

"Come on." Taking her hand he led her to the lively knot of people he'd just left.

"Do I have to?" But she followed him. The all-too-familiar dread of strangers made her heartbeat skitter, yet another reflex she'd worked hard to suppress slipping to the surface. She had to find a way to put it all away again, fast.

She must've squeezed Nikhil's hand, because he squeezed back. "It's all right, starlet, relax, you don't have to perform, just say hi and let your cousin show you off a little, okay?"

She gave an exaggerated sigh. "Okay. But I'm not signing autographs."

"Oh no! How will they bear the disappointment?" He pushed his palm dramatically into his chest and she punched his arm.

Jen gave Nikhil one of her tolerant smiles and threw her arms around Ria. "Everyone, this is Nikhil's cousin, Ria. I believe most of you know her," she said, one arm still tightly wrapped around Ria.

Jen was a good five inches shorter than Ria's five feet seven, but the gesture propped Ria up. She wanted to go on leaning into Jen, but she pulled away and faced the crowd.

Like everything else here, the faces that smiled at her were familiar. Uma and Vijay's friends' children, neighbors, Nikhil's school friends. People Ria needed no introduction to, even after all this time. People who, like this house, had been witness to her childhood. The air thickened with nostalgia as everyone started to reminisce about those long-ago days.

With each memory a cold trickle of sweat ran down Ria's back. One of the reasons this house had been her safest haven was that she had first come here at her most broken, with no hope and no ability to make words.

One of the neighbors had asked Nikhil if Ria was "dumb" once. "No, she's not. She's smarter than you'll ever be," Nikhil had told him. "And the word is *mute.*" And then he'd never spoken to the boy again.

It had been years since it had happened, but Ria's tongue grew heavy and glued itself to her palette at the memory, and panic gripped her. She focused on Nikhil and Jen, on the easy warmth glowing between them and forced her heartbeat to slow.

One of Nikhil's high school buddies winked at her. "Seriously? You of all people, an actress!" he said. "I mean, all those years I don't think you said a total of ten words! We thought you were shy, but you were just saving it for the cameras, ha?"

Everyone looked at her, waiting for a response. But her tongue wouldn't move. A sheen of sweat moistened her palms. This hadn't happened to her in years. The last thing she needed right now was to think about her first time in front of a camera, because the paralyzing helplessness of the memory flooded through her all too easily. She looked around desperately, searching the room for an escape, and found an empty platter on the coffee table.

"You must be starving," Nikhil said in his calmest voice, and handed her the platter. "Sorry we cleaned out the samosas. But I'm sure there's a ton more in the kitchen. You want me to get you some?"

Ria kept her eyes on Nikhil until her tongue eased. "No. Thanks," she said gratefully. "I'll get refills." It was all she could manage before leaving the room, affecting as much dignity as she could muster to hide the shame that flooded through her.

Coming here had once given her back her words. But she had never felt so close to that year of silence as she just had. If there was ever a place that held the power to snatch away all it had given her, she was in it.

# 4

One step into the kitchen, with its high white cabinets and black granite that looked like it had stars trapped inside it, and the painful knot in Ria's stomach eased. She came to a standstill under the arched entrance, the platter balanced on one upturned palm, and soaked up the warmth that suffused the room. A huge, perfectly round moon shone through a wall of windows across from her. She had forgotten how much bigger the moon was here in America and how for some reason it hung really low, like a paper lantern at the edge of the sky. You didn't have to lean your head back to look at it like you did in India.

Great, now the moon was making her nostalgic.

The moon, the house, the kitchen, it was all too much, all of it. It was muddling her brain. Filling her up. She was eight, ten, fifteen, eighteen. She was Ria Pendse again before she had let someone callously discard her name and turn her into someone else. She was uprooted, then cherished. Happier than she'd ever been. This was the only place on earth where she had ever been only one person. Just Ria. Not Ria Pendse. Not Ria Parkar. Just Ria. Nothing in the world had felt like that.

She entered the kitchen gingerly, as though any sudden movement might shake off what she was feeling. Every surface was crammed with signs of festivity. Candles sparkled in red glass mosaic holders everywhere. Brightly wrapped sweet boxes sat stacked up in colorful towers. Aluminum food trays and bottles of wine lay strewn across the granite. The clutter intensified the warmth, made the room part of the celebration. It looked ready to explode with excitement.

This kitchen, this house, it was the only normal Ria had ever known. Her childhood hid in every corner. Breakfasts with Nikhil, perched on the high bar stools, watching wide-eyed as her uncle flipped pancakes chef-style, one hand stretched out like a pirouetting ballerina. Her aunt coming down in her pajamas, her hair piled in a twisty knot on top of her head, her sleepy eyes taking in the scene with quiet pride as she grumbled about the mess they'd made. Sneaking into the kitchen with Nikhil and Vikram late at night after the adults were asleep, pulling out Sara Lee cheesecake from the freezer and polishing the entire thing off straight out of the box as they talked until dawn.

And then that summer, when everything had changed.

When the threads of friendship that had always tied her and Vikram together had stopped being invisible. When their connection had seared into something hot and hungry, sizzling through their eyes and burning between their fingertips, consuming them in a crazy kind of desperation that could only be quelled when parts of them were touching.

It had terrified Ria, made her feel like the shadow of craziness that never followed her into this house had finally chased her down. But Vikram, with his healthy wholeness, was never threatened by anything. When he threaded his fingers through her hair and tugged her lips to his, she had melted in his arms, crumbled into infinite pieces, and allowed every single one of them to merge into him.

Her gaze rested on the door across the room and her heart gave a painful squeeze. She pressed the platter she was carrying to her chest. It was the door to the basement, where they had snuck away so many times. She walked toward it. The leaded glass gleamed. She reached out and touched the doorknob. The slightest twist and the door swung open.

*There's no lock, Viky. What if someone finds us?*

*No one ever comes down here, Ria. It's just us. . . .*

*Just us.*

Her feet sank into the thickly carpeted steps. Her childhood artwork hung on both sides of the stairway. She couldn't believe her aunt had saved her pictures. The puppy with huge eyes. A family of five in front of a big red house. Vibrant splashes of color that had given her so much solace. Her fingers trailed the textured wallpaper as she went from picture to picture, memories piercing through her at every step.

The sounds of her childhood rang in her ears. Shrieks as she was thrown into the air, her stomach catapulting into her throat. Laughter. The silly tickling games they had played. Her little-girl giggles, and then the not-so-little-girl ones. Laughter he had liked to steal from her lips with his own.

Her hand tightened on the platter as she stepped onto the hardwood floor and turned the corner into the room. More laughter. Not in her head anymore, but a chilling blast slamming into her. Sharp. Real. Erupting from the two intertwined bodies pressed against the back of the sofa in front of her.

"Holy, crap! Vic. Shit!" A yelp from the girl, more laughter.

Vikram's hands froze on the girl's bare bottom, taut flesh squeezed and spilled from between his fingers. The platter slipped from Ria's hand and hit the wood floor. It shattered. Of course it shattered.

The girl's legs unwrapped from around his hips. The bunched-up red *ghaghra* freed itself from around her waist and slid down her legs, the heavy weight of sequins pulling it down. She climbed off him as if in slow motion, but her hands stayed locked around his neck. His hands stayed on her bottom, clutching, even as the *ghaghra* fell like a curtain over long fingers pressed into supple, intimate skin.

Ria looked up bewildered by the pain that tore through her, and her gaze met his.

His eyes were glazed over, unfocused. The crystal of his irises smoldering, aroused. Not broken. No, certainly not broken.

"Shit. We are so sorry," the girl said. She couldn't stop giggling. Or was that Ria's ears ringing? Ria wanted to look away from him. She should've looked away, but she couldn't.

Their gazes melded into each other, locked in place, stripping bare everything she had struggled ten years to forget. And then his eyes hardened. Remembrance slid like molten lava over the naked vulnerability she recognized like her own breath and turned it into such unadulterated hatred that Ria gasped and took a step back.

Hot angry color flooded his face. He pulled the girl closer, one hand still molded around the globe of her butt under her *ghaghra*. His other hand trailed up her spine and caressed the back of her neck, his thumb making deliberate strokes against her skin. He watched Ria follow the movement of his hand, savored it, then turned away and looked into the girl's eyes. His expression softened, the harshness turning so tender, so intimate, that parts of Ria's heart she'd thought were dead twisted to life in her chest.

"No. I'm sorry." The relief of finding words made her want to weep, made her voice too thin, too brittle. She forced herself to deepen it. "I had no idea—I didn't know anyone was here. I'm sorry. I—" She squatted and started to pick up the pieces of broken glass.

Locks of hair freed themselves from her bun and spilled around her face as she leaned over. Her scarf slid off her shoulders. Her legs started to tremble on the pencil thin tips of her heels. *Damn strappy sandals. Damn ghaghras. Damn weddings. Damn it all.*

The girl pushed away from Vikram and sashayed over to Ria. She squatted down next to her. "Here, let me help you. Vic, honey, could you grab that trash can, please?" Her voice was equal parts tinkling and husky and it sparkled with confidence. She beamed at Ria with the impishness of a child who'd been caught doing something naughty, but knew she wouldn't be punished for it, because she had never been punished for anything, ever.

Ria looked at her and forced out one of her dimpled smiles. Pushing with all her might to turn her lips up at the perfect angle. Anything to keep from looking back at him as he moved across the room. Anything to keep from falling apart in front of this girl who vibrated with so much life just looking at her made Ria weary.

"Hey, aren't you that actress cousin of Vic's?" the girl asked in her tinkling voice.

"She's not my cousin."

It was the first time Ria had heard his voice in ten years.

She pressed her hand into the floor and leaned into it. The deep, low tones washed over her like rain after a drought—so long-awaited every parched inch of her soaked it up.

Time had turned the bass in his voice up just the slightest bit, but the sound was so distinctly him, Ria's flesh prickled with recognition. A voice that had haunted her silences. A voice her ears had searched for in all other voices. She wanted to close her eyes and drown in it.

"But she's Nikhil's cousin and Nikhil is your cousin. So it's the same thing," the girl said, looking from Vikram to Ria. "Didn't you guys grow up together, weren't you friends?" She picked up a shard and dumped it in the bin Vikram handed her.

For a long moment nothing but the sound of glass on metal clattered against silence. Ria found her gaze locked with his again, although she didn't remember looking up at him.

"No," Vikram said finally, his spine impossibly straight as he backed into the dark paneled wall behind him. "We were nothing."

The words fell from his lips, raw and jagged. His face was cast in stone, expressionless, but he hadn't quite mastered the storm in his eyes. Pain twisted in Ria's gut.

A confused frown crinkled the girl's forehead. She waited for Vikram to say more. When he didn't, she turned to Ria and stuck out her hand. "I'm Mira," she said, as if they were standing in Uma Atya's living room, mingling, not squatting on the basement floor gathering remnants of broken things. As if Ria hadn't just caught her with her bare legs clutching Vikram in the most intimate embrace. "It's so nice to finally meet you. Nikhil talks about you all the time."

Ria forced herself to reach for Mira's offered hand. Mira's handshake was firm and warm and self-assured. It made Ria aware of the limp lifelessness of her own hand and she strengthened it. "I'm Ria," she said. "And I really am sorry."

"Don't be. We should be more careful." Mira threw an accusatory glance at Vikram, a look that left no doubt that this had been his idea. "But you know how it is." She gave Ria a conspiratorial smile. "We lost track of where we were. Vic said no one ever comes down here. That it would be just us. I'm just glad it was you and not one of the aunties who found us or we'd be married off tomorrow." She giggled.

"Maybe it should've been one of the aunties then," he said, his voice light now, his eyes indifferent. All signs of pain gone. The storm mastered.

He walked toward Mira and held out his hand. Everything inside Ria reached for his outstretched hand. She wanted to touch him so badly she had to clench every muscle to keep from moving. The shard of glass in her hand poked into her skin. She eased her grip. Mira reached out and grabbed his hand. As he pulled her up and she jumped into his arms, Ria knew this girl never did anything in half measures.

"Aw, Vic, is that a proposal? You hopeless romantic, you!" Mira made a face at him and smiled into his eyes.

"Is that a yes?" His answering smile was kind, amused.

"What, and make it that easy for you?"

He laughed. And his laugh sounded real.

Ria stared at her, this girl with her messy curls, her flat shoes, and that unencumbered smile that swallowed up her eyes and made no pretty dents in her cheeks. Everything about her spoke of ease. And it seemed to seep into Vikram and relax him. Ria knew his smiles as well as she knew herself, and she knew the one he was smiling at Mira came from deep within. In a moment of startling clarity Ria knew walking away from him had been the right thing to do. He could still smile like that—like happiness lived inside him. Ria hadn't taken that away from him.

The relief made her sick.

She tucked her hair behind her ear and looked at the gleaming shard in her palm. A physical, tangible wound would do nothing to distract from the pain in her heart. She let the piece drop into the trash can.

"You be careful with that." The impossible familiarity of his voice slid over Ria like a beloved, well-worn scarf.

She looked up at him, but he was looking at Mira. His eyes saw only Mira, the blue gray melting with concern. He cupped Mira's hand in his own and plucked the piece of glass out of her hand with the gentleness of someone catching a butterfly and let it drop into the trash.

Ria rose to her feet.

Vikram's eyes stayed fixed on Mira even as she looked away from him and gave Ria another apologetic grin. He was completely in control now. Ria felt the control stretched taut across his body and mirrored it.

Mira opened her mouth, but Ria couldn't take another apology. "It was nice meeting you, Mira." This time her voice didn't tremble. She blasted a Ria Parkar smile at her, the best one she could muster, pulled herself up to her full height, and with all the practiced grace of an Ice Princess she floated up the stairs without a backward glance.

Behind her Mira sucked in a breath. "Stop it, Vic! What's the matter with you? She can still hear us." Mira's breathless whisper turned into a throaty moan, painting pictures in Ria's head. The Ice Princess melted around her. She sped up, running the rest of the way up to the door.

"Why would I care?" His voice chased after her, hot and seductive and just loud enough to hit its mark before she made it out the door.

# 5

Ria pulled the door soundlessly in place and moved away from the gleaming glass before she gave in to the urge to slam it so hard it shattered. Vikram's voice lingered in her ears, burning graphic images into her brain. The heavy silk of her *ghaghra* swirled around her legs like tethers. Her ankles wobbled in her too-high heels. The beadwork on her halter clawed into her neck. She wanted to pull at it, but she couldn't. She'd spent too many years holding her fingers back. She'd had too much practice—with uncomfortable clothes, with unbearable feelings. She had too much control.

She pulled herself together, gathered up her *ghaghra,* barely lifting it a few inches off the floor, tugged her scarf around herself until it squeezed her shoulders together, and made her way across the kitchen. As long as no one spoke to her, she could handle this.

The entire house was exploding with people. Cozy groups gathered everywhere like tangled-up human knots. Laughter rang through the air. It was like one of her movies playing out in real life. Colorful clothes, beautiful people, the thumping beat of *shaadi* music. The sizzle of warm memories buzzed through the air like an electrical charge.

Her aunt and uncle had spent their entire lives collecting these people, building the right to gather so much happiness. At every path that converged they had made the right decision, made the right sacrifices, and held on to the right values. Nikhil was a culmination of all the good they had ever done and this day was a celebration of all they had earned.

Suddenly Ria couldn't breathe. This beautiful day, these beautiful people—she couldn't bear it. Her own ugly choices twisted into a noose that wrapped itself around her neck like the guilt she could never shake off.

Someone called her name from a distance. Her tongue bloated and filled her mouth. She couldn't make the words to respond. Turning away, she escaped into the mudroom and stumbled into the night. It was too cold for October. She let her scarf slide off her shoulders. The chill hit her skin like razor blades. With the first step she tripped over her heels. Reaching down, she yanked them off and kicked them across the grass. Then, pulling up her *ghaghra* all the way to her thighs, she broke into a run.

The freezing blades of grass stung her bare feet as she flew across the yard. Her legs knew where to take her. The gurgling of the river was as loud as ever, rising in pitch as she crested the hill and headed down to the bank. The sound of the water drowned out her thoughts. She ran toward it, unable to stop until she came to the water's edge, where an enormous oak rose out of the ground and brought her to a grinding halt. She looked up at it, panting. It loomed in the darkness, the shadows making it even larger than she remembered.

Their tree.

A low branch shot out across the water, reaching halfway across the river. A bridge its builder had abandoned before it could make it to the other bank.

Their bridge.

Their home. Their haven. Their memories. Them. Two strays Uma and Vijay had taken in. And loved.

This is where he had dragged her that first day, when he hadn't been able to stand by and watch her cry without doing anything about it. She'd been eight years old. And he'd been the most determined eleven-year-old she'd ever met.

*Can you teach me to climb like that?* he'd asked her.

And her words had come back.

*You want to be friends?* he'd asked her.

And her life had changed.

Ria tilted her head back and stared up at the thick canopy above her. Milky moonlight filtered through the black-on-black patterns that should've been eerie, but were comforting instead. They'd sat here a thousand times, Vikram and her. They'd scampered up these branches, torn their clothes against the scraggly wood, torn their skin and not cared.

They'd walked to the forked edge of the bridge like pirates on a plank and thrown themselves into the water. Pushed each other off with no warning. Leaned back into space until their world turned upside down.

Ria reached out and touched the trunk, every dip and bump on the bark familiar. The insanely loud gurgle of the river, the distant glow of the only home she'd ever known, everything far too familiar, far too precious to have lost. A reminder of how easily she could lose what was left of her if she wasn't careful.

She twisted around and leaned against the trunk. Sharp ridges scraped into her bare back as she slid to the ground. Her *ghaghra* pooled around her, the gold-and-copper thread trapping moonlight and sparkling against the silk.

When her father had sent her away to his sister's house all the way across the world, it had felt like the worst punishment for Ria's disobedience, for not being able to talk, for letting herself be hurt. It had felt like being shoved over a cliff into an abyss. On the flight here she had believed without a doubt that Baba had washed his hands of her and that she had lost the only family she knew forever.

Instead she had found this—home, family, a friend who somehow dug out joy from the deepest parts of her, dug out words, dug out all the things Ria never knew hid inside her.

He was her Uncle Vijay's nephew, his sister's son, but unlike Ria he had chosen to come here. His visit that first summer had been the result of a tantrum when he'd refused to spend another summer stuck at his home in San Francisco with a nanny while his entrepreneur parents took the world by storm.

After that summer, neither one of them had wanted to be anywhere else. Year after year Ria had counted the endless months at her boarding school waiting for the summer to come. She had learned to use her silence as armor and her memories as escape from the sniggers and name-calling. Being The Girl Who Came From Insanity for ten months had been easy to bear with this to look forward to. It had taught her how to remove herself from the present, save herself for the future, and hide herself in the past.

*I don't have to be near you to be with you, Ria,* he had told her once when it was time to say good-bye and she couldn't make herself. It's what she had used years later that first time the camera had turned on and her bones had melted and sweat had poured from her. *I don't have to be here to do this,* she had told herself, and then she'd let her body become whom it needed to be.

Unlike the great love stories Ria played out in her movies, there had been no moment when the heavens opened up to the frantic wail of violins. No lightning bolt had cracked through the sky when she had realized she was in love. There had been no declarations, no grand gestures. No transition from not knowing to knowing. It had just been there, just like that. Always.

This is where he had first kissed her. Pulled her out of the water, pressed her against the tree, and dipped into her. They had spilled and soaked into each other, growing into adults in each other's arms.

This was also where he had kissed her that last time.

They had sat under the oak, their arms, their legs, all of them entwined. She had pressed her face into his neck, the strength of her feelings making it impossible to meet his eyes. His fingers tangled in her hair, tipping her head back to face him. His teasing smile melted, turned hot and intense.

*I don't have to go,* he whispered against her lips. Her stomach did that thing it did only for him.

But he did have to go. For two years he'd been obsessed with getting into the research program, with exploring the Amazon rain forests of Brazil. He'd been selected from thousands of applicants, one of only forty to make it from all around the world. She had never doubted he would. He always made it. He thought it came easily to him—the scholarships, the perfect scores, the skipped grades. But she knew his focus, she knew how much he gave. How could she take this away from him?

*It's just eight weeks, Viky. And I'll still be here when you get back. Can you believe it? This time I'll be here forever!* After ten summers worth of good-byes, this was going to be their last one.

*Finally,* he said. His mouth, those lush lips that didn't quite fit together smiled against her lips. *It took long enough, but I rescued the princess from the dungeon.* His nickname for her boarding school in India couldn't be more perfect. And she was done with it.

She smiled, a dimple dipped into her cheek beneath his finger. He lifted it and kissed the sensitive dent. Sparks flew across her body. She pressed into his lips.

*But who will rescue me from you, Ria?*

She stroked his beloved face. *Don't say that, Viky.*

He covered her hands with his own and pulled them to his chest, his crystal eyes so vulnerable, so completely lost in her that panic gripped her. *It's true. Ria, do you remember what it was like before us?*

She couldn't answer. Truth was she didn't remember.

*Last year I tried to find out.*

*Viky.* She didn't want to know.

*I was at a party. My friends had been on my case, trying to get me to hook up with someone. And I tried. I'm twenty-one, what if we think this is more than it is? They kept introducing me to these girls. But I couldn't feel anything. Nothing. Except that I wanted to be with you so badly, I couldn't breathe. I'm me because I'm yours. Without you I don't know who I am. You've ruined me, Ria.*

She covered his lips with her own, dug her fingers into his hair, tried to crawl into his skin. She poured all of herself into her kiss, promising him everything, giving him everything.

His breath caught. He reached into her, returned the promise with every tug of his lips, every stroke of his tongue. Over and over, until every thought, every doubt was gone.

When he pulled away, his eyes closed, his beautiful mismatched lips wet and parted, his chest rising and falling in an uncontrolled rhythm, she felt as if someone had unplugged her. The loss of his touch, the space separating them, it made panic well up inside her again.

*Sweetheart, it's all right.* He stroked her back, her hair, her face, soothed her until she could breathe again. *It's just eight weeks. After that, we have a lifetime. . . . After that we'll never be apart again. . . . I promise.*

Ria lifted her face off the soaking silk draped across her knees. Everything was wet. Every part of her felt like a sodden mess. She swatted her cheeks with the back of her hand. *Bloody hell.* Not this.

She couldn't believe she'd let the tears start. Once the tears started she didn't know how to stop them. Words and tears—they were the twin gauges of her mental health that took over when she lost control, one drying up, the other oozing from her without consent.

She stood up, rubbing her arms, trying to wipe off the sensation of being touched by him. She had to get it off. She had to focus on how he had looked at her today. Not ten years ago. Not like she was precious, but with impotent rage and disgust, as though she were a festering, paralyzed limb and he wanted nothing more than to be rid of her.

And then there was the way he had looked at Mira. With tenderness, with ease.

*Vic will move on*, his mother had told Ria. *When you're young everything seems like the end of the world. But no one is unforgettable.*

Chitra had been right. She was forgettable.

Vikram had figured out who he was without her. He had found someone. Someone healthy and strong like himself. Someone who wouldn't ruin him.

She counted to ten, to fifty, to a hundred, then checked her cheeks again. Not completely dry, but not a monsoon either. She wiped off the remnants of moisture with the tip of her scarf. There. No tears were going to drown her.

* * *

"Seriously, Uma Atya, I'm fine." Ria tried again to stop her gaze from darting all over the place and focused on her aunt's concerned face. She hadn't seen Vikram and Mira since she'd come back inside, but every time someone moved her heart jumped. And from the expression on her aunt's face, she wasn't doing a very good job hiding it.

Fortunately, dinner was served and her aunt was a little distracted with bullying the guests into eating far more than they wanted to. One unsuspecting soul ventured too close to Uma and she heaped syrupy sweet *jalebis* onto his plate before he could escape. Three other guests promptly changed course and ran in the opposite direction. Being next to Uma right about now was probably the best spot in the house if you wanted to be left alone.

"There, that's so much better." Uma turned back to Ria and tucked a loose lock of hair behind her ear and Ria realized she was smiling.

"I told you. I'm fine. Just a little exhausted. I know I shouldn't be after sleeping all day."

"What, 'shouldn't be'?" Her aunt blasted her with her classic college-professor glare. "The way you kids work yourselves, I don't know how your bodies hold up. We are human, not machines, *beta.*" Ria would never get tired of hearing her aunt call her her baby. "I'll bet you haven't eaten a thing since you woke up. Am I right?"

Ria shrugged and gave her aunt her sweetest smile.

"Don't flash those dimples at me, I'm immune. I have my own, remember?" Uma smiled and two deep dimples dug into her cheeks. She thrust a plate into Ria's hands, but before she could spoon food onto it, a chorus of voices rang out behind them.

"Oh good God, it's Ria!" Four women surrounded her, coming at her like blasts from her past, their silk saris, bronze lipsticks, and smoky eyeliners warming her from the inside out, their Chanel and Estée Lauder scents enveloping her as tight as their hugs. She found herself smiling as they appraised her, tipping her chin back with diamond-studded fingers, making sure little Ria was all right.

For over thirty years these women had been her aunt's friends, her sisterhood. "The Auntie Brigade," Vikram had called them. Little shocks of recognition sparkled inside Ria. A mole on a cheek. A cleft on a chin. The way one of them raised only one brow when she laughed. The way all of them called her honey, as if she belonged to them.

Just the way she remembered it, they all started talking at once. "I can't believe it. It really is Ria. . . . Well of course, it's Ria. It's Nikhil's wedding, after all. . . . *Oh ho,* but she's a film star! . . . *Arrey,* so what? She's our Ria first. . . . Look how beautiful . . . Of course she's beautiful, she's Ria. . . . Look at that *ghaghra!* . . . Forget the *ghaghra,* look at that blouse. . . . Remember when we could hold a halter up with those tiny strings? . . . My memory isn't *that* good. . . . Look at those arms. . . . Why do you kids like muscles? Muscles are for men. . . . Not our men!"

As a little girl, Ria had loved listening to their banter. She would squeeze into Uma, close her eyes, and pick out their voices as they talked. Radha had come to America very young and she sounded as American as the grocery-store lady. Sita's South-Indian accent was thick and earthy but completely un-self-conscious. Anu had the clipped Queen's English of a fancy Delhi private school and she refused to Americanize it in any way. Priya had a soft-edged North-Indian lilt which she mixed freely with her acquired Americanness. She stretched out her words and rolled her *r*'s so that each sentence became a linguistic potpourri, a mix of all the things she'd been and all the things she'd become.

Each one of them had extended the band of their innate motherliness around Ria, tightening up her barrettes when they slid off her pigtails, dusting off her knees when she fell. Piling her plate at parties and picnics and bullying her into finishing her food.

Smiling, Ria leaned over and touched their feet, each one in turn, and the timeless sign of respect made every one of them tear up, even the no-nonsense Anu Auntie. They fretted self-consciously and kissed her forehead, mumbling blessings into her hair.

"May all your dreams come true, *beta.*"

"May you live a long and happy life."

Ria thanked them softly. For one long moment, everyone stopped talking. Emotion hung heavily in the silence, memories sparkled in everyone's eyes along with questions no one would voice, not on this auspicious day in the midst of this celebration.

Uma cleared her throat. "Can we let the child eat, please?"

"What, you haven't eaten yet?" they all exclaimed in unison, and Ria quickly picked up the plate she had put down and held it up.

"I was just about to eat. I swear," she said, and let Uma Atya pile obscene amounts of chicken *biryani* onto her plate.

"It's preposterous how skinny you actresses are these days," Radha said.

"It's the camera," Sita said. "It adds ten pounds they say, no?"

"Really? My pictures look like it adds forty," Priya said.

"Yes, that's definitely the camera," Anu said, and patted Ria's cheek. "Eat, eat. We'll leave you alone so your *atya* can hog you. But only for today. After that you're all ours."

They all mumbled in agreement, kissed and petted Ria some more, and went off in search of dessert.

Uma Atya pointed at the *biryani* on Ria's plate. "It took me six hours to make this, so you better eat up."

"Don't you want to go get dessert with them?" Ria asked hopefully.

"Oh, I'm not going anywhere until that's all gone."

Ria jabbed the rice with her fork, pulled a long face, and thrust some into her mouth. The most delicate blend of spices exploded on her tongue. "Oh God, Uma Atya, this is incredible."

Uma adjusted the scarf on Ria's shoulder, smiling away. "No wonder you're my favorite niece."

"Actually, I'm your only niece."

"And therefore even more special." Uma switched to her native Marathi, like she always did when she wanted to be especially affectionate.

"You do realize that makes no sense at all, right?" Ria switched to Marathi too. A giggle escaped her, the sound taking her completely by surprise.

Uma's eyes glowed, her smile one part pride, one part protectiveness, three parts pure joy at having Ria in her life. "I'm so glad you're home, *beta*." That smile had lit up the love-starved corners of Ria's childhood. Now its warmth melted the sharp edges of hopelessness inside her and despite the horrors that lay ahead, for one precious moment, she was glad to be home.

# 6

The house was dead silent when Ria awoke. When she had slipped upstairs last night it had still been buzzing with activity. It would be a while before anyone else woke up. She threw on a silk kimono over her white-eyelet pajamas and knotted the corded sash at her waist. The huge turquoise flowers on the kimono made her feel like she was in a commercial for bathroom fixtures.

Turquoise was her designer's color this season. He'd picked up an obsession for it on his Mediterranean vacation that summer. And he'd virtually drowned Ria in it ever since, insisting it was perfect for "that particular beer-bottle brown" of her eyes. *It makes that silent sensuous thing you do scream out, darling!* A few years ago red had done the same thing. That had been the year he'd visited China.

Ria slipped her feet into silk thong slippers, also turquoise, and padded down the stairs, determined that today would be different from yesterday. Was it really just a few hours since the last time she'd come down the stairs terrified about seeing Vikram again? After ten years of living a life that felt as much like suspended animation on the inside as how fast and eventful it appeared on the outside, in the past day she had traveled years through time. The lines between her memories and reality turned fuzzy, like the wind messing up the edges of a *rangoli* painting drawn with colored dust.

With or without jet lag, sleep had been impossible. Images of Vikram and Mira climbing all over each other had haunted Ria all night. She gave her head a violent shake. Some of the positions she'd imagined them in technically weren't even possible, unless you were a particularly skilled acrobat.

She tightened the cord around her waist and ran her fingers up and down the twisted silk in her hands, focusing on the texture, and consciously anchored herself in the present. Admittedly, yesterday's encounter with him had been a disaster. But then, how could it not have been? If she was anything she was a realist. She never lied to herself. It would have been nice to have handled it better and to not have let herself turn into such a colossal mess afterward. But it was over now. The drama and the shock of seeing him again—even though she would give anything to have changed the specifics of the meeting—was behind her.

Uma Atya, Vijay Kaka, Nikhil, and Jen needed her. She had so much she'd missed with the aunties that she needed to catch up on. Those were the things she needed to focus on, and with all that remained to be done for the wedding, two weeks would be gone in a heartbeat.

"It's two weeks. Just two measly weeks," she chanted it under her breath as she entered the kitchen. Starlight streamed through the windows and mingled with the fluorescence of the appliances to cast a fuzzy glow over the room. Not that she needed mood lighting to make it magical. One step in and it was like her fairy godmother had tapped her with a wand and sprinkled stardust all over her. She would have spun around, Disney-princess style, if she were given to doing that sort of thing.

She didn't bother to turn on a light. She knew exactly where everything was. Reaching into a cabinet, she pulled out a glass, and then turned on the faucet. A lullaby Uma had sung to her played in her head as she let the water turn warm before filling the glass, humming softly. Bubbles danced in the water and she watched them fizzle before downing the entire glass.

Her trainer insisted three glasses of warm water with lemon first thing in the morning washed away all the toxins in your body. She had already sent Ria a text last night reminding her to "stay on top of her program," and Ria couldn't bring herself to let her down. It was bad enough that she wasn't bothering to squeeze half a lemon in each glass.

Feeling quite the rebel, she sucked in her breath, pulling her stomach all the way back to her spine, and did a quick set of breathing exercises—a separate text had been sent for this. Quick in-and-out breaths pumping through her stomach, like someone was punching her. *Oof. Oof. Oof.* She chugged the second glass. Then another set of breaths. *Oof. Oof. Oof.* Then another glass and she was done.

She put the glass in the sink, which was piled high with dishes. The party must've ended really late last night if Uma and the aunties had left the dishes unwashed. She turned around to survey the rest of the kitchen.

"Hi."

She jumped and slammed into the counter behind her. Her hand flew to her mouth, muffling the yelp that escaped nonetheless.

Vikram sat at the dining table, leaning over a huge bowl of cereal, his face a mask of indifference. He popped a spoonful in his mouth and started chewing as if Ria routinely walked in on him eating cereal in the middle of the night and subjected him to absurd breathing routines.

Sparkles of pain danced across her back and her heart hammered as though she were having a heart attack. She dragged her hand from her mouth to her chest and waited for the beat to slow. "I—what—I didn't see you."

He lifted his shoulders in the slightest shrug. "Obviously," his eyes said.

"I was waiting for you to put the glass down before I said anything. Don't want to demolish all of Uma's glassware." He didn't smile, just disinterestedly pushed another spoonful in his mouth and looked away.

An awkward silence settled between them. All that terrifying anticipation and it had led to this?

At least his hands were holding a spoon, not squeezing someone's butt.

Great, that visual again. She felt like the reel of film she was on was jammed. Across from her, Vikram continued to eat as though she wasn't even in the room. His jaw moved in a strong, steady rhythm. The subtle ridges along his throat bobbed as he swallowed. Despite the rumpled hair, despite the shadowy stubble and that cold, hard set of his jaw, he looked like you could put him on a billboard and the public would buy whatever you were selling. He looked perfect. There was just no other word for it. Warm and vital and perfect.

She gripped the cold granite behind her.

Of course he chose that precise moment to look up and catch her staring.

"Your back okay?" he asked, his tone sharp. He might as well have snapped his fingers in her face to snap her out of her trance.

"I'm fine. Thank you."

Another shrug. Another long silence.

"It's a mess in here." Saying something inane and obvious was possibly the only way to make things more awkward. So, naturally that's what she did.

Before he could present her with another shrug she turned away and started to unload the dishwasher, pulling out a plate, and then completely blanking out on where it went. She hugged it to her chest and studied the cabinets, waiting for it to come back to her, willing her brain to start functioning again.

"The cabinet next to the microwave," he said.

She turned around to thank him, but no words came out, instead, she just stood there like a buffoon. He pointed to the cabinet with his spoon and started studying the cereal box, shifting it so it stood between them like a shield. He had loved to read cereal boxes aloud, cracking up at the silly jokes on them the way only he could.

*What do ghosts put in their cereal? Boo-berries.*

There wasn't a trace of humor in him now. The furrow between his brows was almost as deep as the wrinkles in his shirt. Her eyes traced the creases draped around the bulges on his arms and shoulders—which had widened to twice their size. Somewhere in the back of her mind she'd noticed yesterday that he had filled out.

But how had she missed this? He hadn't just filled out. He had expanded and burst out of all his youthful leanness into some sort of ridiculous athletic buffness. His arms looked like they lifted lumber for a living, not a scalpel.

A groan escaped her. She tried to turn it into a cough, but just ended up making it louder. Vikram's hand paused for a second on its way to his mouth. Other than that, he gave no indication of having noticed. Heat rose up her cheeks. She forced herself to move before she embarrassed herself even more, and put the dishes away, stacking them perfectly, adjusting them until they were just so. It wasn't easy with fingers that turned suddenly into rubber bands and eyes that wouldn't stop seeking him out, punishing her for starving them so long.

He was still wearing the same clothes from yesterday. A midnight-blue shirt, the cotton embossed with a bold paisley batik print. Something she could never have imagined him in. He had always been such a conventional dresser—T-shirts and jeans alternating with jeans and T-shirts. Come to think of it, there was nothing conventional about the way he looked anymore. His hair was long, curling at his neck and falling over his forehead, completely different from the closely cropped haircut he had sported with the neatly spiked front. It wasn't just his body that was different, it was everything. Every feature had weathered into manhood. His jaw was wider, his neck thicker, everything had a rougher, wilder edge to it, every evidence of the clean-cut boyishness of her Viky wiped away.

Except for his mouth. Time hadn't touched his mouth. It was as lush and wide as ever, with that pronounced gap right in the center—a tantalizing little notch where his lips didn't quite fit together. She had loved his mouth, loved tracing that vulnerable dip with her fingers, loved to watch it when he talked, sketched it over and over again in her sketchbook the way other girls wrote boy's names. But most of all she had loved how it felt against her lips.

He looked up and caught her watching him again. His eyebrows drew together over angry eyes. She looked away and stared at the empty dishwasher, her arms dangling uselessly at her sides, longing pooling in her belly like warm, thick honey.

His body was none of her business. His mouth was certainly none of her business, especially since it had been all over someone else not too long ago. And now he was apparently only just getting home. Which meant he and that mouth of his had been out all night. With Mira. All night. What time was it anyway?

"It's five o'clock," he said.

Her gaze flew up and met his. She hadn't said the words out loud. The moment stretched out, pulsing between them like a raw, exposed nerve.

They had never needed words.

Vikram came to the exact same conclusion at the exact same moment. Panic flashed in his eyes, throwing him wide open for one beat of a second. With a deliberate gulp he regained his composure and pushed away from the table, rising up to his full height. The oversized kitchen shrank around Ria.

He picked up the empty bowl and looked at the sink behind her. She was leaning so far back into it, she was halfway inside it. He set the bowl back on the table.

"See you around. It's been a long night." His voice came out even and in control and completely at odds with what had flashed in his eyes moments ago. He turned and started walking away from her. Good. He was leaving. Perfect.

"So, you're staying in the house?" She heard her own voice, but she couldn't possibly have been stupid enough to speak.

He stopped mid-step, veering forward as if she had yanked him back by his belt. He stood like that for a moment, suspended by his struggle to walk away without answering, but then he turned around. Impatience and anger darkened his eyes and colored the crests of his cheeks over all that thick stubble. He couldn't have made it more obvious how little he wanted to be here talking to her.

"You think Uma would let me stay anywhere else?" Despite his anger his tone softened on Uma's name.

He always called everyone by their first name. Uma, Vijay—no auntie, uncle, *atya*, or *kaka*. For anyone else it would've been unthinkably rude and disrespectful. For Vikram it was just plain natural.

Ria shook her head. No, Uma Atya would never let him stay anywhere else.

"Why? Where else did you want me to stay?" The faintest hint of a challenge simmered in his voice and she knew stopping him had been a huge mistake.

Why had she spoken? Why?

"No, that's not what I meant. I was just—Did you just get home?"

His eyebrows shot up. Ria wanted to tape her mouth shut. She had never had trouble speaking around Vikram. Words that hid from everyone else had bubbled up around him unbidden. It's what had set him apart, pulled her to him with such force. But she wasn't eight anymore and this was ridiculous.

His eyes hardened. "All right, I'll play," they said. "I drove Mira home. She lives in the city."

Mira.

The name dropped between them like a ton of rubble. Ria knew she shouldn't react, but she couldn't stop her arms from wrapping around herself.

He took a step closer. "You remember Mira—you met her yesterday." His eyes were so cold, a chill prickled up and down Ria's arms. "She's my—We're together."

He studied her, intense as a hawk in a hunt, registering every reaction, and zeroing in on the pain his words caused. The way he savored it grated against something deep inside her.

She stopped rubbing her arms and forced her voice to sound as cool as his. "Yes, I noticed. Congratulations. She seems really nice."

Anger sparkled in the arctic depths of his eyes. "Yes. She is. She's great."

Their gazes locked. "And pretty. She's really pretty too."

"And she's not just looks either." Ria flinched and a satisfied glimmer lit his eyes. "She's fun. Things are never boring when she's around."

"No. You didn't look bored last night."

He started. The anger he'd been controlling popped in his eyes and filled them, turning the crystal gray almost opaque. "You're right, I was far from bored. Although you did walk in before the best part."

The punch landed hard in the center of her chest and she almost gasped.

He smiled, ready to walk away. But those bloody words were out of her control now. "Good thing you had no trouble starting where you'd left off. You didn't even wait for me to leave."

His smile disappeared. "Oh, we had no trouble at all." His jaw clenched. "What can I say, it's a gift." He took another step closer. He was a few feet away now, and Ria felt like someone standing at the foot of a tidal wave as it rose and rose, waiting for it to fold over and take her down. "But you know how that goes. It didn't take me much to heat you up either, or don't you remember?"

Ria sucked in her breath and watched helplessly as the last of his control snapped. The wave crashed over and pulled them under. "No, wait," he said. "That wasn't just me. That was any man. Any man you needed something from." It wasn't just anger in his eyes anymore, but disgust, and it turned him into someone she didn't recognize. Shame fell like ice water on the adrenaline that had been pumping through her veins.

"How is he, by the way? Your—" He swallowed. "I'm sorry, if he's old enough to be your father, do you still call him your *boy*friend?"

A horrible ache filled Ria.

"Tell me, does he need his goons to do all his work for him? Or just beating the crap out of the poor fucks you're done with?"

Ria closed her eyes. She couldn't bear to look at him. Memories of his bleeding face, his battered, limping body, swam in her head. Ved's bodyguards had tried to send him away when he came to see her after he returned from Brazil and found her gone. But he'd refused to back down until they let him talk to her, attacking them, over and over, like a desperate bird flying into glass. Finally, she had feared for his life and agreed to see him. She had let Ved hold her, pretended to want Ved's arms around her even as her skin crawled and her stomach churned. Vikram had taken a beating without wincing, but the sight of her in Ved's arms had broken him, as she'd known it would. He had walked away without a backward glance.

Ria opened her eyes. He watched her, his eyes fixed on her face. For one fleeting second, she saw the pain tearing through her heart mirrored in his eyes.

He took a quick step back, his jaw working furiously. "Damn it." He squeezed his eyes shut and shoved his fingers through his hair, clutching the jet-black strands until his knuckles turned white. For the longest moment he stood utterly still.

When he opened his eyes a curtain had fallen over them again. "You're good." He looked at her as if he were seeing her for the first time. "You're really good. I didn't stand a chance, did I? Hell, your sugar-fuckin'-daddy didn't stand a chance, did he?" A short, mirthless laugh whooshed out of him. "But you know what? It doesn't matter. Not anymore. I can see right through you now. Right fucking through you."

Her knees buckled. She sagged against the unyielding granite digging into her back. Deep dark exhaustion closed around her. This time the silence in the room was impregnable. Vikram gave her one last look, challenging her to say more, then walked to the table and picked up his bowl and brought it to the sink. She was still in his way, but it didn't seem to bother him anymore. He leaned across her and dumped the bowl on the pile of dishes.

Through the deadening hurt, his fresh musky scent washed over her. Another achingly familiar piece broke from the tangle of memories and clicked into place. She felt the thick steel of armor he'd drawn around himself and moved to get away from it. But he moved too, rushing to get away from her, and his arm brushed hers. All on its own, her body leaned into his touch.

He jerked away.

Mortified, she withdrew into herself. Breath gushed from him—short, heavy bursts as he backed away. She couldn't bring herself to look up at him. But she heard the haste in his steps, heard him yank open the basement door and run down the stairs.

For a long while she slumped there like a rag doll, hair spilling around her face, his footsteps ringing in her ears, his scent filling her senses, his touch gouging out memories that were thorns lodged too deep.

She forced herself to turn to the sink and attacked the pile of pots and pans, seeking out each grimy patch of dried-up food and assaulting it as if it were the abomination. When the sink gleamed, each dish propped meticulously in the dishwasher, she turned to the countertops, spraying and scrubbing until her fingers wrinkled up like prunes. Everything gleamed, but nothing felt clean.

*I can see right through you.*

She stormed to the basement door and pulled it open. But she couldn't make herself take a step down.

What was the point? What could she say to him? *I threw up in Ved's toilet after you left. And I didn't stop until I had passed out from it. Letting Ved touch me where you had touched me hurt so much, I've never let anyone touch me after that.*

She rubbed her arm where the imprint of his skin still lingered. The impotence of her feelings rose and grew from that spot and spread through her.

He'd seen right through her—and he'd seen nothing.

Not the things Ved had made her do once he'd found out about Vikram. *Wow, you really broke that boy's heart! You're not just a cold greedy little thing, you're ruthless too.* He'd made her kneel in front of him and pay. He'd folded her over and made her pay. But she'd deserved it. For taking the offer: a role in the year's biggest production for her body. And for having nothing but that one thing to sell and so many things to pay for.

Not that she would survive it if Vikram ever found out about any of it.

She backed away from the door, hating herself for needing to wipe away his touch, hating the hopeless wanting that had no respite. Her feelings for Vikram weren't the only thing that hadn't changed. Nothing had changed. The dark sadness spreading too fast inside her proved it, the tears that lurked too close to the surface all the time proved it. In just one day she'd moved closer to breaking down than she'd been in a very long time, losing all the control it had taken her years to gain. She was a ticking time bomb and he was angry enough to be her fuse. And together they were a tragedy waiting to repeat itself.

She pulled the door shut and dragged herself up the stairs, craving the solace of her room, craving the solace of something. Knowing it would never be hers, but wanting it all the same. Wanting it so badly it made her feel like the stark raving lunatic who hid inside her. It had called to her once from the creaking attic above the timber ceiling of the house Baba had banished her from. Now it lived in the tiny particles that barely held her together.

# 7

Ria threw open the louvered white shutters of her closet. Earlier she had unpacked her suitcase and arranged her clothes in perfectly aligned stacks on the wood shelves. The sequined silk and chiffon looked out of place where ten years ago nothing but shirts and jeans had sat. Ria looked up at the closet ceiling. The small square door leading up to the attic seemed even smaller now. The colored fingerprints had faded, but she could still see them. She went up on her tiptoes and pushed at the thin, painted plywood. It resisted only for a bit, and then flipped back as it had always done.

Stepping on the lowermost shelf she reached up into the darkness. The last time she had done this, Vikram had lifted her up, his arms wrapped tight around her thighs, his chin digging into her belly between her shirt and her jeans. His stubble had scratched her skin and tugged at her most intimate parts, and awakened them.

The memory made those parts clench again as she reached into the attic and found the cardboard box. She tugged it down, kneeled next to it on the floor, and lifted the dusty lid off. Inside sat a box of acrylics, the misshapen tubes half-empty, a few still-sharp 4B pencils, and the dried-up stubs of oil pastel sticks. And two brushes. She picked one up and stroked the fine sable hairs.

In her year without words, a well-meaning art teacher had given her a brush and paints. And for one precious hour, it had set her free. When she'd dipped a brush into the thick silk of the paint, she'd slid into the paper, flown over it, bled into it. All the things she couldn't say, everything she was afraid of had come pouring out, turned into color and form, into torment, and anger, and pain.

*This is what she drew when we asked her to draw a coconut tree, Mr. Pendse.* The teacher later told her father as if Baba and not Ria had given the tree a face and limbs and then violently dismembered it with bleeding wounds so grotesque it had made the poor art teacher drop the wet paper as though it were dipped in poison. *This isn't the work of a normal seven-year-old. We strongly suggest a psychiatrist, Mr. Pendse.*

Baba had wordlessly removed Ria from that boarding school and found another, but he hadn't taken her back home. Ria had never painted again. At least not until Vikram had caught her sketching on the back of a magazine a few years later. *I can't let anyone see, please,* she'd begged him. The next day he'd bought her colors and a sketchpad hidden in brown paper packaging. *Don't let anyone see.* That's all he'd said.

By that time everything inside her was no longer quite so ugly. Especially not when she was here. Her pictures hadn't been exactly beautiful, and she was sure they continued to not be the work of a normal child. But Vikram had loved her drawings and refused to throw them away. Instead he had helped her hide them in the attic above the closet. Finally, a few years later, she had let the rest of the family see and Uma had gone on a framing spree. But Ria had only ever painted here during the summers, never in her other life at the dungeon.

A few years ago, she had found herself sketching on set on the back of a script, an image of a girl having her head torn off by her hair. The ugliness had been so stark it had been like Ria's mind had hemorrhaged and oozed out. She had burned the picture before anyone saw it and had become progressively more obsessed with holding her mind together for as long as she could.

She shut the box again, wishing she could shut all the things that were opening up inside her with the same ease, and pushed it back into the attic. Out the window, orange morning light tinged the sky. But the house was still disturbingly silent. The sting of Vikram's anger still wrapped around her like the too-tight clothes her designer insisted on making her wear.

There was only one thing to do. She pulled on her running tights, a sports bra, a hoodie, and sneakers, and ran down the stairs and out the kitchen door.

Ria wasn't a natural runner. In fact, she hated running. But other than solving puzzles and following a desperate vitamin regimen that the Internet promised kept the chemicals in the brain balanced, physical exercise was her only hope of postponing her fate. Of all the forms of exercise her trainer conjured up for her, only running numbed her mind. Aerobics was too much like her Bollywood dances. She had to analyze every move to get it right. Yoga made her mind race all over the place instead of centering it, which made all that breathing and stretching pointless. Running was real live work, every muscle, every breath had to be engaged, every ounce of will had to be dredged up.

Today Ria needed to run.

She took off along the DuPage River that snaked through the woods behind the house. Naperville was a lush quiet suburb and the crisp promise of a beautiful day surrounded her. Every mossy rock, every birdsong, kindled memories of long-ago summer days, just as perfect, but far too few.

Ria sped up, willing the pounding in her chest and the cramping in her calves to block everything else out. Sweat poured from her. Warm trickles slid over the barely visible scars on her shoulders, her chest. Memories of ancient wounds that just wouldn't stop bleeding flooded her mind—the rip of hair from her scalp, the crush of ribs against her lungs.

She sped up until the merciless pace took her breath and her thoughts. Finally, when the towering oak came into view, she knew she was almost home and she let herself slow. The sounds of children playing reached her before she caught sight of young boys playing soccer in the clearing next to the oak. Her heart squeezed at the sight. They must've been ten years old, scruffy, sweaty, and loud, and wearing matching football jerseys just like the one Nikhil had worn when he'd played soccer for the park district.

Ria was about to head past the boys when a familiar form shot across the rolling hill. When he saw the boys he stopped and bent over to catch his breath, hands resting on his hips. The movement was so distinctly him, she knew it was Vikram even before she took in the wide shoulders, the jet-black spikes falling across his forehead, and the determined profile silhouetted against the sky.

She slipped behind a thicket of trees.

He was a few hundred feet away, but she could see his bright white running shirt cling to his body, the rise and fall of his muscles making patterns on the wet fabric. Her breath fell into rhythm with his labored breathing.

"Wanna play, Vic?" one of the boys in the group called out, and threw the ball at him.

Vikram caught the ball with one hand, threw it up in the air, and kicked it back at them.

"Not today, guys." He lifted his shirt and wiped his face, exposing a lean, muscled midriff glistening with sweat.

"Come on, Vic. One game, Vic. Please, Vic." A chant rose from the mob. They ran up to him and surrounded him, bouncing up and down exactly like the ball they'd been dribbling.

"What, you afraid we'll kick your butt?" the biggest one said with impressive swagger, given that he was exactly half Vikram's size.

Vikram laughed, ruffled the boy's hair, and stole the ball from under his foot. "Only if you can catch my butt first, squirt." He ran the ball down the hill. "You men up for some five-on-one?"

"You're on!" All five boys raced after him. But they couldn't catch him or steal the ball away from him. He faked moves, skipped the ball backward, across, forward, controlling it with such deft grace it was as if the ball was connected to him by invisible string. Every now and again, he let one of the boys take it, then stole it back. They followed his moves, mimicked him. Before Ria realized what was going on, the game turned into a coaching session.

"Jack, back at Josh . . . There, keep passing it. . . . It's a team sport, Sahil, don't show off. . . . Awesome. Slow down. . . . Speed up. . . . Don't think about it, Sean, just run with it."

She pressed her cheek into the prickly bark she was hugging. Despite the deep shade that hid her, every inch of her warmed as though soaked in sunshine.

One of the boys finally managed to get the ball away from Vikram and dribbled it all the way to the goal. He whooped in delight and did a cartwheel. Vikram doubled over laughing, joy emanating from him like a live thing.

"You should put these moves on V-learn, Vic," one of the boys shouted, imitating Vikram's dribble and kick.

Vikram froze. He lost track of the ball and it struck him square on the head. The boys collapsed laughing. Vikram kicked the ball up, bounced it on one knee, and grabbed it in his hands. "You've been on V-learn?"

"Sahil's mom showed us." The boy pointed to the Indian boy. "I just aced my pre-algebra test from it. Thanks!"

"What unit?" Vikram's tone was suddenly serious. His body radiated so much eagerness he looked almost as young as them.

A car honked. "That's my mom," someone said, and the mob ran across the hill toward the street, signaling Vikram to throw them the ball.

"What unit?" he shouted after them.

"Simultaneous equations."

Vikram kicked the ball through the air at the boys just as they disappeared over the hill. He didn't really whoop for joy, but he might as well have.

Ria had no idea what they had been talking about. She didn't know if it was playing soccer with the kids or what they had said, but whatever it was, it lifted a veil and gave Ria a glimpse of *her* Viky—unencumbered, buoyant. The way he used to be.

It didn't last. Just as suddenly his shoulders stiffened again. Slowly he turned around and stared at the oak. For a long while he didn't move, then he broke into a run and headed full tilt toward the massive trunk, springing at the low-hanging branch and heaving himself onto it.

Their bridge.

He reached for the branch above him and pulled himself to standing. Then with the ease of a tightrope walker he strode across the branch to where it stopped over the gurgling water. His body leaned forward as if he were about to dive in, clothes and shoes and all. Ria bit her lip to keep from crying out. But he didn't jump. He just stood there, the morning sun setting him on fire, tension coiled in his body like an arrow slung into a bow and pulled tight.

It wasn't until a wisp of breeze caressed Ria's cheeks that she realized they were wet. Again. She pulled away from the tree, away from the heart-wrenching sight of him. She wanted to go back home. She wanted to stay right here and spy on him forever. She wanted to be on their bridge again, by his side, with her hands on his sweat-slick skin.

But more than anything else she wanted to see him smile like that again. She pushed away from the tree and ran toward the house.

He had always loved being around kids. Even when he had interned at their uncle's pediatric practice for two summers, he had been excited about every child who came into the clinic. He'd known every child's name. What a brilliant pediatrician he must be. Even better than Vijay Kaka, if that were possible, but only because he was Vikram and he was always the best at everything.

She, on the other hand, wanted nothing to do with kids.

Giving birth to her had triggered her mother's psychosis. A month after giving birth to her mother, her grandmother had thrown herself into a well and killed herself. Genetically the doctors had pinned Ria's chances at thirty-five percent. Never in a million years would she put a child through that numbers game. This was going to end with her.

She swiped at the tears with the cuffs of her hoodie. Letting herself cry yesterday had been a mistake. Now the bloody tap just wouldn't turn off and the worst part was how absurdly good it felt.

* * *

"Good God, *beta*, did you go running? You were as exhausted as a dead rat last night, have you no sense at all?" Despite the scolding tone, seeing Uma at the kitchen table with that look on her face made Ria go to her aunt and wrap her arms around her and hold on.

Uma pressed her cheek against Ria's. "Great, now how can I be mad at you?"

"How is it she gets away with anything with just one hug?" Nikhil looked up from the newspaper he was reading over his father's shoulder.

Her uncle, Vijay Kaka, smiled one of his twinkling smiles. That smile alone could heal a sick child merely by its presence. She let her aunt go and wrapped her arms around her uncle. He patted her cheek and pointed to the two familiar faces next to him. "You remember Matt and Mindy, Ria?"

"Of course." Matt was Vijay Kaka's roommate from his residency days. And Matt and Mindy's son, Drew, had been Vikram's roommate at Northwestern.

Mindy stood and pulled Ria into a hug. "How wonderful to see you, Ria," she said. "Uma, how lovely to have the entire brood under your roof again. I'm so glad we decided to stay the night." They had driven up from Indiana last night for the engagement ceremony just the way they had done a few weekends every summer.

"I'm so glad you stayed." Uma poured a cup of coffee and handed it to Ria. "It's a *lagna ghar,* a wedding home. It has to bustle, overflow with people. Otherwise what's the point?"

Ria took a sip and smiled at her aunt. "Speaking of *lagna ghar.* It's close to noon and all this looks a bit relaxed. Don't we have a wedding to plan? Where's the panic? The bustle?"

"Well, we were all set to panic this morning, but elves visited last night and cleaned up." Uma made her typical admonishing eyes at Ria. "Now we don't know what to do with ourselves."

Ria gave her a sheepish smile. "So you made *idlis* instead." She leaned against Vijay Kaka's chair and peered into the steamer stacked with fluffy white rice cakes and the most delicious smelling lentil *sambar.* Her stomach gave the most unladylike growl. Before

Uma could launch into a lecture, Ria picked up a plate and helped herself to an *idli*. Uma reached for the *sambar*.

"You need a dropper for that, Aie?" Nikhil grinned his most annoying grin.

Ria smacked his shoulder.

"What? We can't have fat starlets running around." He looked far too amused with himself. Ria glared at him, but everyone else laughed. The traitors.

"Oh, this is just like old times," Mindy said. "I wish Drew were here. You remember our son, Drew?"

Ria nodded. Drew had called her "Mrs. J" because Vikram's last name was Jathar and it had turned Ria all shades of red. Which had made Vikram adopt the name anytime he felt the need to make her blush. "How is Drew?" she asked.

"He's psychiatry faculty at U of M and he has his own private practice in Ann Arbor," Mindy said, and then proceeded to fill Ria in on every detail of Drew's illustrious career and wonderful family at length, which inspired Nikhil to make gagging faces behind her. Ria spooned rice cake into her mouth, her straight face a testament to her own illustrious career. But she was going to kill Nikhil if she choked.

"Of course he'll be at the wedding." Mindy was still talking about Drew. "He won't pass up an opportunity to see Vic, and they've been working on that project of theirs," she said to Uma with such pride that her eyes misted over.

"I know! Isn't it just wonderful what they're doing?" Uma said, her eyes just as proud, and Ria had a hard time swallowing.

Suddenly Uma turned to Nikhil, all the pride on her face turning into worry. "Where *is* that boy? I haven't seen him since yesterday."

"Your thirty-one-year-old 'boy' is fine, Aie. He just had his hands full last night," Nikhil said, grinning so suggestively that the graphic visuals of Vikram with Mira wrapped around each other sprang back to life inside Ria's head. "He'll show up. Don't worry, he hasn't disappeared into thin air again."

Blood drained from Uma's face. Her hands tightened around

her cup until her fingers turned white. The *idli* stuck in Ria's throat.

Nikhil went to Uma and folded his arms around her. "Come on, Aie, I'm kidding. Relax. He's fine. You worry too much." He rested his chin on Uma's head, carefully avoiding Ria's eyes. "We are all grown up now. And perfectly capable of taking care of ourselves."

Ria pushed away from the table, needing to move. What on earth were they talking about?

Uma turned and glared at Nikhil. "You kids really think that's possible, don't you? That we can actually stop worrying about you? Wait until you have kids of your own, then you'll know what it feels like. 'Relax,' he tells me!"

Mindy nodded fiercely from across the table. Vijay and Matt looked at Nikhil and shook their heads at his stupidity. Nikhil groaned and apologized again.

Ria carried her plate to the sink, clutching it hard. She waited for them to say more, but they moved on to something else, and she didn't know how to get them to turn back. All these years of biting back questions about Vikram and it still made her want to burst.

Uma could never find out how far things had gone with Vikram, or how things had ended. And she definitely could never find out about Vikram's mother's role in the whole sorry mess. Uma would never understand what had motivated Chitra to come after Ria, or why Ria had listened to her. Just like Uma had never understood why Ria couldn't let anyone help her with the asylum bills. But there were just some burdens Ria would never share with anyone. She just couldn't.

The spicy *sambar* that had tasted like heaven two minutes ago burned back up her throat like acid. She dumped the half-eaten *idli* in the trash, making sure no one saw her do it, then she shoved it under the other garbage with her spoon, covering it up.

*How convenient to have Vic to leech off,* Chitra had told her.

*Just like your crazy mother leeched off your father. She knew what she was doing when she married him. And you want to do the same thing to*

*Vic? You know what he'll do. He'll quit med school to take care of you and your crazy mother. How can you ruin his life like that? You call that love?*

She hadn't leeched off anyone and she hadn't ruined his life. And she never would.

Somewhere between showering and pulling on a pair of faded jeans and a turquoise sweater, Ria remembered that she hadn't called DJ since she'd arrived. Since the day really couldn't get any worse, she might as well get an update on the blackmailer.

"I got him to pipe down for now," DJ told her. "But I don't trust the bastard. I don't think we've seen the last of him."

It should have been unsettling, but Ria couldn't bring herself to care. She felt every one of the eight thousand miles that separated her from Mumbai. Another thing that hadn't changed. Her summers here had eradicated her life in India from her mind, wiped her clean. Two months of being one person. The ten months in India, on the other hand, had been all dissonance between the person everyone in school saw, The Girl Who Came From Insanity; the person Baba saw, The Girl He Wished They Hadn't Made; and the person who wished she weren't either one of those girls.

She tucked her phone between her ear and shoulder and started to straighten out the bed for the nth time. DJ couldn't stop complaining about the fact that she hadn't called him sooner.

"It's been one day, Big. I'm on holiday, remember?"

"Yes, but we have to make a call on the *StarGangster* script, remember? I have Shivshri breathing down my neck. They're threatening to sign someone else."

Shivshri was India's largest production house and Shivji, the patriarch of the family-owned business, would never sign anyone else. Ria had been in five of their biggest hits in the past ten years and he believed she was their lucky mascot. Even if they did sign someone else and Ria changed her mind, they would throw the other actress out and sign Ria on. And they'd do it with a big *pooja* service to thank the gods of fortune.

Ria stopped stroking the creases off the bed. As thankful as she was for Shivji and his superstitions, she hated violence. "I'm really not sure about this, Big. I'm not sure I can run around shooting people." She was the kind of star who sold happy dreams. She didn't want to sell darkness. Pain was best left in the real world where it belonged, where it burrowed so deep you needed a multimillion-dollar industry to escape from it.

"Babes, you've done the same thing for ten years. Don't you want change?"

No. What she wanted was for everything to go back to the way it was and stay that way. Although, really, how many more wedding movies could she possibly play the blushing bride in?

"Listen, babes. This is all there is." He took one of his long dramatic pauses. "Unless . . ." he trailed off.

Ria knew exactly what he was up to. "I've told you, DJ, I'm not doing art films."

"They're not *art films*." He spat the words out as if they tasted foul. "This isn't the eighties. It's parallel cinema. Sensible scripts, not your usual commercial formulas. Maybe it's time to give it a shot."

"Why? Because I'm almost thirty and all the commercial heroine roles are written for eighteen-year-olds?"

"You're not thirty," he said irritably, just like she knew he would. Her aging-star status bothered DJ more than he'd admit. "You're barely twenty-eight and this has nothing to do with age. I actually think you'd be very good."

She laughed.

"Listen, babes, there's some really kickass scripts out there, really gritty, emotionally honest stuff. Real opportunities to dig into yourself. What's the harm in trying it out?"

That was the precise reason she didn't want to try it out. The last thing she wanted to dig into was herself. She wanted to bury what was inside her deeper where it would stop haunting her. She patted down the last remaining crease in the comforter, but it still didn't feel smooth.

What DJ really meant—what he'd been trying to tell her for months—was that she didn't have a choice. The public wasn't interested in twenty-eight-year-old heroines dancing wedding numbers with smitten heroes. They had plenty of twenty-year-olds peddling the real thing. "Okay. Send me *StarGangster*. I'll look at it."

"Fantastic." As usual he didn't bother to mask his triumph. "It's on its way."

"Can't wait," she mumbled, and pulled the comforter and sheets off. She needed to make the bed all over again.

As soon as she got back from Jen's tonight, she was diving into that script. It was time to focus all her energies on work once more and to block everything else out.

# 8

Jen lived in a converted warehouse building in the city. The building felt like a fancy hotel, doorman and lobby and all. The apartment overlooked Lake Michigan, which felt like a bluer version of the Mumbai ocean, waves and beach and all. The apartment itself felt nothing like the hypermodern white space Ria lived in. This place breathed. Warmth engulfed Ria the moment she walked in.

"You like?" Jen asked as Ria stared, mesmerized, at the high ceiling, the exposed concrete walls, and the most stunning artwork she had ever seen.

"I love." Ria walked to one of the huge unframed mounted canvases hanging from one high wall and touched the textured surface. The vibrant exuberance of the strokes traveled up her fingers and touched her heart. Unlike her own art, the artist seemed to have danced on the canvas in joy, and it set off a ripple of something deep inside Ria that she was too afraid to name.

The paintings offset the earthy simplicity of the fabric sofa, the stone-topped tables, and the wide-planked wood floors, and gave the space such serenity Ria wanted to curl up with a book and listen to soft music. She exhaled. This was exactly what she needed, time away from the house.

She hadn't seen Vikram after her run and Nikhil hadn't mentioned him on the drive here. They had talked about everything but Vikram, carefully skirting his name the way they had done for the past ten years. She ran her fingers over the canvas one more time. This was perfect. An afternoon with just Nikhil and Jen.

When she turned around she found herself alone in the living room. They were both gone. The bedroom door was open, so she went looking for them. Nikhil had Jen plastered against a wall and was devouring her mouth as if he hadn't seen her in years.

"God, guys, at least lock the door or something," she said, spinning around.

They pulled her back into the room, identical goofy expressions on their faces. Jen slapped Nikhil's shoulder, but then ruined it by letting her hand linger too long. "Nikhil, behave," she said.

Ria laughed. "Yes, saying it like that is going to make him behave."

Nikhil planted another noisy kiss on Jen and she pushed him away and pointed toward the low Asian-style bed. "There they are."

The saris Ria has brought with her from Mumbai sat unwrapped and arranged across the bed. "You like?" Ria asked.

"I love!" Jen's eyes sparkled as she sifted through the yards of silk and chiffon, and it made the hours Ria had spent with her designer worth every moment. He had insisted on talking to Jen over a webcam and "getting to know her." He had made Jen walk, sit, stand. *I'm doing this long-distance thing only for you, darling. I'm Manish Jain and Manish Jain does couture, not off-the-rack.*

He had done great. The colors were perfect. A deep midnight blue chiffon with *aara* work for the henna ceremony, a more traditional *kanjivaram* jade silk for the wedding, and the most vivid crimson crepe edged with Swarovski crystals for the reception that was the perfect blend of red and copper and brown merging into one magnificent wine-colored gem.

"These are just beautiful, Ria. I don't know how to thank you." Jen ran tentative fingers over the shimmering fabric as if trying to skim the surface of water without causing ripples. "But I have no idea what to do with them." Suddenly Jen looked lost, and more bewildered than Ria had ever seen her look.

"I have a few ideas," Nikhil said, rubbing her shoulders, and planted a kiss on her neck.

She didn't react.

"Nikhil, let's focus on putting the clothes on right now, not taking them off, okay?" Ria said, smiling, and unfurled the midnight-blue silk across the bed.

Nikhil laughed, but his eyes stayed on Jen, who continued to stare at the saris nervously. "I've never worn a sari in my life. And the wedding is in twelve days." She gnawed at a cuticle.

Ria slung the jade silk over Jen's shoulder. "Really, Jen, it's not hard once you get the hang of it. Here, let's drape one on you and you'll see how easy it is. Don't worry, we're going to turn you into the perfect *desi* bride."

Given what a *desi*-phile Jen was and how naturally she took to everything Indian, her nervousness was adorable, and Ria gave her a quick hug. She had no doubt Jen was going to be dancing the bhangra in her sari before she knew it. "You already know more about Indian history and culture than both Nikhil and me put together, and by the end of today, you'll be better at wearing Indian clothes than us too."

"Ria's right," Nikhil said, "I can already see Aie rubbing it in my face. 'For shame, Nic, learn something from your fiancée!'" He waved his hands about and did a perfect imitation of Uma Atya.

Ria smiled and zipped up Jen's blouse. Then knotted the skirt-like petticoat at her waist and wrapped the sari around her, pleating and tucking the slippery fabric in place. Jen stood there stiffly, her arms held up at right angles like a traffic cop. "I feel like I'm being gift-wrapped."

Ria couldn't think of a better way to describe it herself, especially since Nikhil was watching her as though she were a midwife delivering their first child. She adjusted the fabric on Jen's shoulder, pinned it in place with a safety pin, and turned Jen around to face Nikhil. "Nikhil, your wedding present."

Nikhil looked smitten.

No surprise, because Jen was stunning. The jade silk brought out the golden glow of her skin and the deep black of her hair and eyes. "Jen, you look absolutely gorgeous. Manish is going to put you on a billboard, I swear."

"Thanks."

Jen speaking in monosyllables was not a good thing and Ria had never heard her mumble. She tucked a lock of hair behind Jen's ear. "Why don't you try to walk around a bit? It doesn't come off when you move, I promise."

Jen took two steps forward like a wind-up doll and stopped. "But how do you move in this thing? It's tied around me like a bandage. Shit, what am I going to do?" She stared at herself in the mirror not seeing what Ria and Nikhil saw. "I don't think I can do this. And the wedding is ten days away." She turned to Ria, her panic real and clear in her eyes. "You have to help me."

Ria had never been able to expose her own fears to anyone. She had never been able to ask for help. Something incredibly sweet warmed inside her and she gave Jen another hug.

"Jen, you're going to be fine. Millions of women wear saris. And most of them aren't brilliant surgeons who work miracles under the worst possible conditions. Trust me, you can do this."

Jen's shoulders sunk even lower. Nikhil took a few restless steps back and forth and wrung his hands. He tried to rub Jen's shoulders again, but she gave him such a fierce look he turned to Ria looking so helpless Ria wanted to photograph it for posterity.

"Okay, guys, time to relax. I know exactly what to do." Ria picked up the midnight-blue sari. "Nikhil, out." She pushed Nikhil out of the room. "Go get us some coffee."

Then she stripped off her jeans and pulled on the blouse and petticoat. The blouse was too short and too loose on her, but she couldn't care less. She wrapped the sari around herself with quick, sure movements. Jen gaped at her as though she were performing robotic surgery.

"Really, Jen, there's nothing to it. It's just a matter of getting used to it. Just follow along and do as I do." She pulled the flowing end of the sari across her hips and showed Jen how to hold herself in it. How to wrap it around her waist while standing, how to drape it across her shoulders while sitting, how to pinch the fan of pleats between her fingers and lift it just an inch while walking.

With a little bit of prodding, Jen started to move. Slowly at first, then more surely. Ria broke everything down into baby steps. Finally, Jen realized that moving didn't make the sari fall off. She relaxed and started to follow along, the sparkle returning to her eyes. Ria's relief had to be completely disproportional to the situation, but still she let it fill her up.

Soon they were both sashaying up and down the room, with Jen mirroring Ria's every move. They flicked their heads back and threw siren looks at the mirror and then burst into giggles. Jen had specifically asked for blouses that were more modest than the current style. Even so, most of her midriff and waist remained exposed between the blouse and the petticoat. "Why does it have to be so short?" She tugged at the blouse, crinkling her nose and trying to cover her exposed belly.

"The sari *pallu,*" Ria said, running her hand over the flowing end of the sari that draped across the front of her body and fell over her shoulder, "is supposed to cover your tummy, not the blouse. When you wear a sari, the *pallu* is your best friend. You can control how much you show or hide with it. Let it slide off your shoulder a fraction, and there you have some cleavage. Wrap it tight around yourself and there you have every curve outlined. It's really quite handy."

"It's ingenious!" Jen let the *pallu* drop over her shoulder the way Ria had done, her eyes shining with mischief, then lifted it up and twirled it around herself.

Jen's spirit was infectious. It made Ria want to draw aside the curtain she pulled between herself and the world. Before she knew it, she was playing the blushing bride for Jen and then the sexy siren. She wrapped the *pallu* around herself, stretching her neck long and graceful as a queen, then pleated it into a narrow strip between her breasts, suggestive as a nymphet. "You can be whatever you want in a sari, prim and dignified or a real femme fatale," she said, smiling away.

Jen loved that. She pulled the *pallu* up to her lips, caught it between her teeth, and batted her eyelids. She pulled it in a veil across her face, letting only her eyes show and arched her brows, giving Ria a smoking hot look so over the top, Ria doubled over. She couldn't remember the last time she had laughed so hard she had tears in her eyes.

The doorbell rang and Ria ran out to let Nikhil in. He had to see this.

"You're getting really good at this. The wedding guests are going to be sweating," she called over her shoulder, wiping the tears from her eyes, and reached for the door. "Can you imagine a hall full of people turned on by the br—"

Vikram stood across the doorway. Ria's smile slid off her face. Jen's too-loose blouse followed suit and slid off her shoulder. Vikram's gaze hitched on her exposed shoulder, lingered on the blouse that ended just below her breasts and traveled downward, tracing her bare midriff down the curve of her waist to the swell of her hips.

Mira walked up behind him.

"Hi!" she said chirpily.

Vikram blinked and released his breath.

Ria pulled the *pallu* around her shoulders, wrapping it around herself as tightly as she could. Under the sheer fabric, every inch of skin was on fire.

"Wow! I love your sari. It's beautiful." Mira beamed at her.

Ria stepped aside to let them in.

Mira sauntered into the apartment with the familiarity of a frequent visitor. She dumped her bag on the open kitchen bar and headed straight for the bedroom just as Jen stepped out of it.

"Don't look so surprised, girl," Mira said to Jen. "We were in the neighborhood, so we had to stop by." She pointed at Jen's sari. "Absolutely love it!" They gave each other a hug and kept on talking. Neither one noticed that Vikram hadn't moved.

"Isn't it beautiful?" Jen twirled around like an old pro. "Ria picked it out. She was just teaching me how to be a sexy siren in a sari." She winked at Ria.

Ria tried to smile, but wasn't sure if she managed. Vikram walked past her to the open kitchen.

"Hey, I want to be a sexy siren too! Teach me too." Mira laughed and turned to Vikram. "What d'you think, Vic?"

"I think you're perfect the way you are." He pulled a bottle of beer out of the fridge.

"Isn't he the best?" Mira asked no one in particular. She went up on her toes and gave him a peck on the cheek. It took him a moment too long, but he put his arm around her shoulder and Ria kicked herself for noticing the moment he'd taken to do it.

"He's the best suck-up, that's what he is," Jen said, laughing.

Vikram twisted the cap off the beer and took a deep swig.

Ria had never been more thankful that people never expected her to say anything. Being an Ice Princess had its advantages.

Jen looked from Ria to Mira across the polished concrete breakfast bar. "You guys haven't met, have you?" she asked. "Ria, this is Mira. Mira, this is Ria."

"Oh, we met yesterday," Mira said. "She found Vikram and me in the—"

"Where's Nikhil?" Vikram cut Mira off and glanced around the apartment. The pulse in his throat beat out a frantic rhythm. His eyes met Ria's for a split second. His hand reached for his neck and he pressed the pulse down with his thumb.

"He's getting coffee. Or growing it. He's been gone a while, I'd better call him." Jen headed back into the bedroom. "Oh, by the way, Mira, Ria loved your paintings." She pointed to the artwork on her walls and left the room.

Mira rounded on Ria. "You like them, really?"

Words stuck in Ria's throat. These paintings were Mira's? The flutter of envy that Ria had refused to recognize earlier flared inside her.

Mira stared at her, waiting for a response. For the first time since Ria had met her, Mira looked insecure about something.

"They're beautiful. I love them," Ria said, and meant it.

Joy blossomed on Mira's expressive face as though Ria had just handed her a medal. It made her look so young, so guileless, a ridiculous surge of protectiveness rose inside Ria. "Seriously. The strokes, the colors, the movement, it's impossible to look away from them."

Mira jogged around the wide bar and threw her arms around Ria. "Aw. I love you, thanks!"

Startled, Ria patted Mira's back and caught Vikram's eyes over Mira's shoulder. He was giving nothing away today. His eyes stayed flat and unfathomable. Which was just as well, given their last meeting.

"I hate displaying my work," Mira said, walking to a painting. "I can't handle it when someone doesn't like it. You're an artist too. You know what I mean, right?"

Blood drained from Ria's face. How did Mira know she had painted?

"She's talking about your movies." Vikram's voice broke through her panic. His gaze steadied her, then pulled away. He pushed away from the bar and paced out of the kitchen, restlessness pouring off him in waves.

"What else would I be talking about?" Mira asked, following him, but she didn't wait for an answer. "You put your soul into something and people think they can pass judgment on it just like that." She snapped her fingers. "I'll never get used to the critics."

Ria didn't know how to respond to that. What the critics said about her performances usually made her want to laugh, mostly because she agreed with their clever little reviews. But her art, there was only one person who'd ever been exposed to that part of her.

"It takes courage, Mira." Ria heard Vikram's voice from behind her. "You put yourself out there. Not everyone has the balls to do that. It's easier to hide things, to never let anyone see what you're capable of."

Ria refused to reach for the concrete and steady herself.

*Don't let anyone see.*

She turned around to face them and found Mira leaning against him, her back to his chest. His arms hung at his sides.

"What's the point of art if you hide it away?" Mira said, looking appalled, as though the very idea of hiding anything was inexplicable to her. "All artists dream of sharing their art with the world. Right, Ria? I mean, who wants to make a movie no one watches?"

Ria nodded, not sure how to respond to that either.

"So, Ria, how did you become an actress? Did you always want to be one? "

Vikram went completely and utterly still.

The very air around him went still. It strained and tightened. The tightness dug all the way into Ria's lungs.

Mira stroked Vikram's shoulder. He stepped away, letting her hand slide off. Mira didn't seem to notice, but Ria felt Mira's hand fall off his shoulder in slow motion. Suddenly everything moved in slow motion.

"I'm sure it's a great story. Tell us." Mira sank into the couch with an interested smile and waited. Vikram stood there motionless, and Ria knew his mind was miles away, years away.

Just like that Ria's tongue turned to lead in her mouth. She reached for words, but try as she might, she couldn't make them. She stared at her hands, clenching them together, the familiar paralyzing helplessness engulfing her.

"Maybe it's something she doesn't want to share, Mira," Vikram said softly, the echo of too many memories making his voice raw.

Ria looked up at him.

The kaleidoscope of his eyes was alive again, the cold flatness gone, crystals shifting to expose all the things she wished she didn't see.

For a long moment she couldn't look away.

"Maybe it's something she isn't proud of," Vikram said finally.

Ria wanted to wrap her arms around herself, but she didn't. She wanted to look away in shame, but she didn't. She forced all the emotion from her voice, from her face. One of them had to stop this, whatever this was. She relaxed her jaw, opened her mouth, and focused only on Vikram. As she'd known they would, her words came when she looked in his eyes. "It was just such a long time ago, I hardly remember it."

His jaw tightened. The pulse in his throat jumped to its beat again. He turned away and stalked to the wall of windows overlooking the lake and stared out at the waves that had turned dusty gray in the fading light. Water and sky meeting and melding into one.

"Was it one of those stories where a talent scout saw you at the mall and thought you'd be perfect for a role?" Mira asked, persistent and blind to the silence the moment begged for.

Ria looked back at her, disoriented. "Something like that," she said.

Only it hadn't been the mall. It had been her father's funeral.

# 9

Back in Jen's bedroom, Ria took her time stripping off her sari. It had been ten years since Baba's funeral. But it might as well have been yesterday. The heat of the cremation pyre was still fresh on her skin. The lungful of smoke still made it hard to breathe. The fire painted the white cotton sheet tied around him black before the orange licks of flame ate it up. Uma and Vijay flanked her on either side, but it was the most alone she had ever been.

The only other person present was Baba's photographer friend. He freelanced for film magazines and happened to know that India's largest production house was looking for a new girl—someone who combined innocence and sex appeal. Ved had told her later that was industry-speak for a young girl with big breasts and empty eyes. She had been a perfect fit.

Against all Uma's protests Ria had gone with the photographer to Ved's office.

"Ved Kapoor personally picks the girls he wants in his films," he'd explained solicitously. And by "the girl he wants" he had meant "the girl he wants to fuck for the duration of the film." But she hadn't found that out until it was too late, after she had signed the contract for both the film and the asylum.

With Baba gone, the house gone, and a year's cost of the asylum more than her entire college tuition, the promise she had made Baba had tightened like a noose around her neck. The only thing that had made sense was that Vikram was too far away to witness it.

He'd been spared having to see what she would become, or where he would end up if he stayed with her.

Vikram's camp in the Amazon basin was entirely disconnected from the outside world, but he had told his parents about being in love with Ria just before leaving. Baba's death had brought his terrified mother rushing over to Mumbai to see Ria. But she had wasted her time. By the time Chitra got to Mumbai, with her threats and her predictions of doom, Ria had already sent Uma and Vijay away and signed the film. She'd also already learned it would turn her into a whore.

Ved had felt her up and got instantly aroused when it made shameful tears spring in her eyes. *Such an Ice Princess!* he'd said, with that smile they said drove women crazy, but to this day made Ria physically ill. *You know, you're too fancy-schmancy for a* ghati *name like Pendse,* he'd said, using the slur people from other states used for people from Ria's home state. *We should call her something fancy and English,* he'd said to his secretary as he typed up papers for Ria to sign.

A Parker pen happened to be lying on his desk. Ved's spelling had been just as lax as his morals and Ria had become Ria Parkar.

She pulled her sweater over her jeans and folded the saris into perfectly edged rectangles. If she took long enough, maybe Vikram and Mira would be gone.

But Mira's animated voice was the first thing she heard when she came back into the living room. Jen and Mira were making dinner plans.

For all five of them.

If things had gone badly before, this put the day in a whole different class of disasters. Vikram was talking to Nikhil in the kitchen and looking perfectly calm—that loaded-spring-like calm that was such a part of him now.

How had Vikram allowed this to happen? Given the anger she'd seen in his eyes, he should have done everything he could to not be stuck with her all evening.

How had Nikhil allowed this to happen? The way he had looked at Jen when they were trying on the saris, he should've wanted nothing more than to get rid of everyone. Ria had loved every minute of her time with Jen and Nikhil today, but she had definitely been the third wheel. Now the crowd of three had turned to a crowd of five, and she was a third wheel twice over. How much worse was this day going to get?

As if in response to that question, the beginnings of a migraine nudged at the back of her head. With her medication back at the house, her only option was to convince Jen and Nikhil to let her take a cab home. She pulled them aside, but neither one of them would hear of it. Nikhil had already made reservations at Ria's favorite restaurant in the city. And that was that.

Their procession of five marched down Lake Shore Drive toward Millennium Park with Vikram and Mira heading up the front, Nikhil and Jen bringing up the rear, and Ria sandwiched somewhere in the middle. The sun was almost gone from the sky so at least she had the encroaching darkness on her side. She pulled on her sunglasses and buried her face in the high collar of her jacket. A few Indians stopped and did double takes, but Ria didn't wait long enough to let recognition dawn. She kept moving.

She couldn't remember the last time she had gone traipsing down a public street without a security detail. DJ was going to bite her head off if he found out. He had called a local security company and set up a bodyguard, but Ria couldn't imagine bringing her film world into this world. It seemed like a violation of something sacred. The truth was that with Nikhil and Vikram so close, she felt safer than she had in years. At least physically.

Nikhil and Jen looked so cozy walking hand in hand she smiled at them, dug her hands into her pockets, and tried to give them some space. But when Nikhil pulled her close, she unabashedly sidled up to him.

As for Vikram, his mood had completely altered. He seemed to have decided to compensate for whatever had happened earlier by giving his complete and undivided attention to Mira. He laced his fingers through hers and plastered himself as close to her as was humanly possible.

When they reached the restaurant, he squeezed in next to Mira on the curved couch, leaving the rest of the booth jarringly empty. Ria sank into a chair across from them and steeled herself for an excruciating evening. It was one of those Asian fusion places where you threw your own ingredients into a bowl and let a bunch of exuberant chefs cook them on an enormous smoking griddle.

Ria had loved the place as a child. It had given her the same freewheeling feeling she experienced at amusement parks, like she could do anything she wanted, like reality and rules were just far enough away to not matter. But today the crowd was too loud, the smells of soy and ginger and searing meat too overpowering, and her lemonade too sweet. That migraine was getting closer by the minute and try as she might Ria couldn't invoke a single happy association with the place.

To make things worse, Jen went over every moment of their day together in painful detail. The shimmies, the sashays, the sexy pouting, playing Ria up to be some sort of avenging angel for all wardrobe issues. Fortunately, Vikram was too preoccupied with plastering himself against Mira to notice. Between Nikhil and Jen making an obvious effort to keep their hands off each other and Vikram nuzzling various parts of Mira's anatomy, Ria almost prayed for the migraine to put her out of her misery.

If she had any sense at all she would get up and leave right now. But she felt like she had to stay and show Vikram that she was just as okay as he was and even more to show him that she was okay with how okay he was. Maybe this is what it was going to take for them to attain some modicum of normalcy. To fake it first. As they said in the industry, you have to act like a star if you want to be a star. So she squared her shoulders, pasted an expertly crafted smile on her face, and focused on the conversation.

Mira launched into the story of how she and Vikram had met a few months ago at a charity gala for Asian artists where Mira had shown her work. "Vikram told me his name and I said, 'Did you know that's an Indian name?' Because seriously, I would never have guessed he was Indian. With those eyes and that skin, who would know? And he says, 'You know, it might just be, since my Indian parents named me after my Indian grandfather.' After that it was just a matter of asking him out over and over again before he said—"

"I was traveling." Vikram cut her off. "I was out of the country. And then we found that Mira went to high school with Jen."

"It was meant to be," Mira said.

Ria smiled politely. But when Vikram caught her polite smile, his eyes grew harder. She then tried to act disinterested. But with every sign of indifference, the set of his jaw grew tighter. The changes were almost imperceptible, but they screamed at her. She wished she could block it out, this insane awareness of his every movement.

"You know how Vic does that silent brooding thing? It's very hard to resist." Mira smiled at Vikram as if he were some sort of enigma.

Why couldn't he be an enigma to her? Why did she have to see his every thought?

Vikram had the grace to look embarrassed. He shot Nikhil a warning look. Nikhil put down his beer and grinned like a five-year-old with a bowl of candy. Anyone calling Vikram an enigma was preposterous. Everything about Vikram had always been out in the open, all the time. He wore all his feelings on his sleeve. If he loved you, you knew it. If he wanted something from you, there was no keeping it from him.

"You should ask my mom about Mr. Enigma here," Nikhil said. "He got us in so much trouble when we were kids because he couldn't keep a damn thing off his face."

Vikram took a long drag of his beer. "That's only because Uma had some sort of witch's sixth sense when it came to me."

That was true. It was almost as though Uma had been able to sense Vikram's schemes even before he came up with them.

"Remember Nuts?" Nikhil said, and despite herself Ria smiled. They had tried to domesticate a chipmunk in the basement when she was ten. "Vic named the chipmunk Nuts because, to quote Vic, 'look at the size of his!' " Nic cupped his hand and pointed at his belly and he and Vikram both started laughing. "Poor guy was probably some sort of chipmunk alpha-stud and Vic decided to put him in the old doggie crate in the basement and tried to teach him tricks."

"Hey, we almost made history with him," Vikram said, still laughing. "And the only reason that experiment failed was you. If you hadn't bawled like a baby, Uma would never have known."

"He bit me! I had to get ten shots. Ten!"

"He nicked you. Didn't even break the skin." They were both laughing so hard Ria found her own shoulders shaking. "And he was responding to his name."

Nikhil shook his head, "No, he wasn't. Ask Ria."

"I don't remember," Ria said. Although she was sure Nuts had responded to Vikram calling his name.

"Of course you don't," Nikhil said as they got up to get their food.

Ria threw some vegetables into her bowl and sprinkled them with olive oil. The idea of eating with the headache pushing at her temples made her sick to her stomach. But if she didn't eat there would be a million questions and the atmosphere had just turned casual enough that she could hope for a quick dinner and an uneventful end to the evening.

Her food was cooked long before everyone else's, and she took it back to the table and watched as Nikhil and Vikram argued about the laws of physics that enabled them to fit as much food as they possibly could into their bowls until towers of vegetables and meat and noodles teetered in their hands. Ria found herself smiling again. For the umpteenth time she was struck by how little had changed under all the changes. Maybe things didn't have to be uncomfortable around Vikram. Maybe things could be normal.

"Uma was so calm about all the stuff we got up to. I have no idea how she put up with us," Vikram said as everyone gathered back at the table. His face, his entire body, was more relaxed than she'd seen it in the past few days. Maybe he'd also come to the same realization that they could come up with some version of peaceful coexistence. Vikram attacked the overflowing bowl in front of him. "I think Ma tried to sell me to Uma a few times."

Nikhil raised his hand, stuffing copious amounts of food into his mouth. "Correction: Chitra Atya tried to barter you for me. It's no wonder the woman is such a brilliant businesswoman."

"When do your parents get here, Vic?" Jen asked.

Great. Ria's two minutes of warmth evaporated in an instant.

"They're in Copenhagen for a conference. They'll be here in time for the wedding."

Fantastic. Here she was hoping for the weeks to race by, and Chitra was waiting for her at the other end.

"I can't wait to meet your mother," Jen said, "if Uma is anything to go by."

Nikhil raised his beer. "To moms."

Jen raised her glass. "To family."

Vikram raised his bottle. "To a house full of brats for Jen and Nic."

Mira raised hers. "To finding the love of your life."

Vikram's hand faltered on the way to his lips and Ria tried to look away before their eyes met.

"So, Vic, you were telling us how you and Mira met," Jen said with her best matchmaker smile.

Vikram watched Ria over his bottle and she knew that nothing good would follow. "At first it was Mira's art that drew me," he said. "But I had never met anyone so open. So uncomplicated. So loyal."

"Do go on." Mira laughed that exuberant laugh of hers. But her eyes glowed under her offhandedness. Vikram didn't notice. His gaze was fixed on his beer bottle.

And they were back where they had started. A sick sort of irritation rose inside Ria. She was stuck in a preposterous tragic farce, spinning around and around in all that they couldn't change, churning it like the legend where the gods and demons had churned up the ocean in search of the nectar of immortality, but poison had churned up instead and Lord Shiva had had to drink it before peace could prevail.

"Sounds nice," she said before she could stop herself. "I've never met anyone quite that special myself."

Vikram's eyes narrowed and the poison of their past bubbled up even higher around them.

"Come on, you're not saying you're single. I mean, look at you!" Mira threw an incredulous look around the table. Jen nodded in agreement. Nikhil shifted uncomfortably in his chair. Vikram's entire attention seemed focused on ripping off the beer-bottle label.

"Seriously, how do you keep them away? Guys must be climbing over themselves to get to you," Mira said, yet again missing the tight set of Vikram's shoulders, the hard clench of his jaw. "I can't imagine any man not wanting to go out with you." She looked from Nikhil to Vikram, and Ria had a sense of watching someone wander onto a minefield. She wanted to throw a blanket over her head and whisk her away to safety.

Vikram rubbed his fingers over his temples. When he finally looked at Mira his eyes gentled. "It takes more than just looks, Mira," he said, ruining any hope Ria had of peace, and she didn't know why she was surprised. He wasn't going to let a single opportunity to put her down pass by. It was the nature of churning up poison. Someone had to skim it off and drink it. That was the only way to get rid of it.

"What is that supposed to mean, Vic?" Jen jumped into the fray from across the table, turning it into a free-for-all. "That's the most awful thing I've ever heard you say. Any man in his right mind would want to be with Ria. And it has nothing to do with looks." She glared at him.

Nikhil placed a calming hand on hers. "I don't think that's what Vic meant, Jen."

"What did you mean, Vic?" Jen asked with exaggerated sweetness, and Ria wanted to hug her and ask her to leave it be all at the same time.

Vikram shrugged. "Just that. That looks aren't everything." He met Jen's glare, refusing to back down. The set of his jaw, the willful steadfastness of his gaze, it was so classically Vikram, Ria forgot what they were talking about. This was the Vikram who had believed so completely in them, in her, that ten years later his heartbreak still bled fresh.

Like an idiot, warmth prickled in her eyes. But she couldn't let the tears fall.

Jen jabbed at her noodles. She wasn't done glaring at Vikram. Ria pushed away the useless surge of feelings. She had to get off this roller coaster. She smiled gratefully at Jen and reminded herself that Vikram had done nothing but insult her and provoke her since they had met. It didn't matter that she deserved every word. He was hungering for the fight they had never had. The one she owed him, but could never give him. And she'd encouraged him enough.

"It's okay, Jen," she said. "He's right. It does take more than looks. It takes time and effort, which I can't give a relationship right now."

"It sounds like you just haven't found the right person then," Mira said, leaning into Vikram, who was getting more stiff and tight by the minute.

"Something like that." Ria's voice was so calm she surprised herself.

Instead of calming down, Mira brightened as though a few lightbulbs flashed on inside her head at once. "You know what?" she said, almost jumping out of her chair. "We should find you someone while you're here."

Both Vikram and Nikhil sat bolt upright. Ria gripped her chair.

Jen's eyes lit up. "That's a great idea, Mira!"

"You know who'd be perfect?" Mira spoke directly to Jen now, the usual enthusiasm on her face a full-blown riot. "Sanjay."

Jen clapped her hands and beamed. Both Mira and Jen turned to Ria. She cleared her throat and schooled her features with every bit of skill she possessed.

"Sanjay's my brother. He's a writer," Mira said. "He teaches creative writing at Northwestern. He's the nicest guy you'll ever meet."

"And he's *really* hot," Jen added, widening her eyes to prove exactly how hot Sanjay was.

Nikhil groaned.

"Come on, Nic, you have to admit that Sanjay is perfect for Ria. They're both so sincere and creative and contemplative. It's a perfect fit."

"No, really, it's not. The last thing Ria needs is someone contemplative. They'll both contemplate themselves into an early grave." Nikhil looked from Ria to Vikram like someone trying to diffuse a bomb.

The bomb ticked away in Vikram's neck. *Please, not again.* A horrible sense of foreboding came over Ria, but the idea of Vikram's girlfriend setting her up with her brother was so absurd, so completely unexpected, it left her speechless.

"Stop being so overprotective, Nic." Mira joined Jen in frowning at Nikhil. "Ria doesn't seem to have a problem with it."

"Like hell she doesn't have a problem with it!" Vikram's voice boomed across the restaurant.

All four of them turned to him, startled. Four pairs of eyebrows flew up in unison, four mouths gaped open like caricatures in a comic strip.

"What is wrong with you people? Can't you see the look on her face?" His chest pumped as he struggled to lower his voice. People at the neighboring tables shifted uncomfortably in their seats. "She just told you she didn't have time for a relationship. Didn't you guys hear her? She's a frickin' film star. She's not interested in giving it up for some guy."

Mira pouted at him. "Sanjay's not just some guy. I thought you liked him."

"Of course I like Sanjay," Vikram snapped, and Mira drew back. His eyes bored into Ria. "He's a great guy. Which is precisely why you need to stop this. He doesn't need this shit. Fuck, no one does!"

The sound of Ria's indrawn breath was magnified by the sudden stunned silence at the table. Vikram was shaking. Rage radiated from him in hot palpable waves and slammed into her. Little explosions of pain went off in her head and blasted through her control. She leaned forward and glared back at him. Everyone else at the table disappeared. Everything around them disappeared. Leaving just them, and this moment. And another moment ten years ago. Everything between those two moments went up in flames.

All the hurt and pain disappeared. All the loss. All the yearning. It all disappeared. The sheer rage that had piled up and blistered between the two moments drowned everything else out. It pounded through Ria and rang in her ears like clashing cymbals.

"Vic!" Mira's voice seemed to come from miles away. "What is wrong with you? I've never seen you like this. Vic!" She tugged at his sleeve, but he yanked his arm away.

"You know what?" Ria said, swallowing hard. "It would be great to meet a nice guy. I seem to have met only jerks so far." Her voice trembled and cracked, and it was more than she could bear. Pain flashed across her skull, grabbing her temples in a vise. The food she had eaten churned in her belly.

*Bloody hell.* She was going to throw up.

She pushed herself away from the table. The scrape of chair on tile ripped through her pounding head. She fled.

Voices buzzed behind her like swarming bees. Nikhil, Jen, Mira, beseeching, cajoling voices. *Sit down, man. Calm down.* The collective attention of the entire restaurant focused on her. Shit. Shit.

She heard footsteps behind her and broke into a jog. But it was no use, he was right behind her. His breath blew into her back. The waves of anger that had become too familiar rammed into her. They went down a narrow corridor. The red Exit sign blared and pierced through her blurring vision. She kept going, out the door and into the night. She heard his hand slam against the door and wanted to turn around and shove him back inside.

They were in an alley outside the restaurant. A spasm of pain so vicious screamed through her temples she doubled over. The smell of rotting food punched her belly and something horrible spurted up in her throat. She pressed into the wall, trying to control the spasms, trying to clamp her mouth shut and focused on not emptying her insides.

"Ria," he said behind her, his voice suddenly helpless. But he didn't make a move to touch her.

"Leave me alone. Please." She wrapped her arms around her stomach to stop the cramping waves of nausea and rested her head against the rough brick. Shame at her lack of control mixed with the burn of bile in her throat and the starbursts of pain in her head.

Before Vikram could respond Nikhil stepped out into the alley.

"Ria? You okay?" Nikhil asked, pushing past Vikram and pulling her away from the wall.

"No. I'm sorry. I just want to go home, Nikhil, please."

Nikhil lead her through the alley to the parking lot. Vikram didn't move. He didn't say anything. He just stood there. Ria didn't have to look at him to know exactly what his face looked like.

# 10

As if guilt and shame weren't enough, now Ria was overcome by embarrassment so acute she didn't think she could ever get past it. Even running wasn't blocking it out. With every pounding step along the snaking river the tangle of memories in her head tightened, and the only clear thing she could distinguish from the bloody mess was the rage on Vikram's face. And the rage that had exploded inside her in response.

She had thrown up after coming home last night, silently, so no one would know. And then tried to sleep. But ever since Nikhil's engagement party, there had been no sleep. Close to forty hours without a wink. Her eyelids had turned into screens that played her memories on a loop. Memories that kept reaching past the anger and homing in on the feelings that had spawned such rage.

Shafts of light pierced the foliage and fell in polka dots on the grass around her. A few of the trees had already changed color. Splotches of orange and yellow flamed against the thick green canopy that edged the water. She had never seen Chicago in the fall. She had never been here in the spring or winter either—she had seen only the summer. She was a one-season girl. Incomplete.

Numbness ran up and down her legs, but she picked up her pace and kept on running. That last summer she had almost stayed and watched the seasons turn with her acceptance into Purdue and the I-20 firmly stapled to her passport. After years torn up by endless separation, finally, Vikram and she would've had nothing but a two-hour train ride between them. They had worked out a schedule for weekend visits, leaning over a calendar at the kitchen table with sunlight streaming in through the mullioned windows, their fingers interlaced under the table, their dreams intertwined in their hearts.

A fallen tree trunk blocked her path. She leapt onto it and then onto the other side. A jolt of pain zinged down her leg to her ankle, but she didn't stop.

Montages from the past whizzed by her like the view from a moving train. The way Vikram had kissed her at the airport, grabbing her hand and pulling her into an alcove. The pain of letting his hand go that last time as he disappeared through the gate had felt like having her heart sliced out of her body. But then she'd gone home from the airport, and seeing the look on Uma's face had taught her what real pain felt like. The never-ending flight back to Mumbai. Back to Baba. *God, please let him be alive.* That had been her one prayer, her chant. *You can take whatever you want from me. Just let Baba be alive.*

Pain clamped around her legs, around her chest. She clung to it and kept on going. The smell of the burn ward—like drowning in waxy petroleum jelly with something rotten trapped inside your lungs. The screams. Mad with pain. As if they'd eat their limbs to escape it. Screams that would never fade from her memory no matter how many years went by.

Baba's burnt body with its skinless flesh. No screams, just mute agony and single-minded purpose in his eyes. The labored movement of his tattered lips. *No municipal hospitals, Ria. No authorities. No one but you. You have to care for your mother. You. Swear you'll find a way.*

She hadn't been allowed to touch him. His body mush under the gauze.

*Yes, Baba, I swear.*

So many words she wanted to say to him, but her last words to him had been the promise to protect his murderer. The wife he had spent a lifetime caring for before she had thrown an oil lamp at him and turned him into a wick to ignite the entire timber house. But he hadn't left without her, he had wrapped her in a blanket and carried her out, his own body in flames. The nurse never made it out.

Ria, the child of their accursed marriage, had been left with the ashes of the house that had never been her home, the ashes of a father she had wanted so badly to be her home, and two promises—one of which she had to break in order to honor the other.

Vikram and Baba. Two men who were everything to her, but always separately. She'd been so close to bringing them together. So close to closing the gap between her two lives. And then an entirely unexpected third life had taken her.

She flew across the path, desperate to push the putrid stink out of her lungs. She had seen Vikram's face that day, on her dead father's body, and she had known what she could do to him.

*Viky, Viky, Viky,* her feet beat into the ground. She had been running for hours and instead of her mind calming, her body felt seriously deranged. Pain screamed from every overstressed muscle. The familiar row of houses came into view just as it became impossible for her to run another step, and she finally allowed herself to stop, wondering how she was going to make the long limp home.

Each step threw her more and more off-balance until everything around her tilted off its axis. She needed to sit down. There was a wooden bench across from the oak tree just around the corner. She hobbled in its direction.

But it was occupied. Much like all the spaces she wanted to be in these days. She groaned—the melodrama of her thoughts would do the drama queens she played proud—and tried to change course, but her legs were no longer taking orders from her. They wobbled and jerked. The figure on the bench rose, emerging from the shadows with a self-possession she would have recognized even without the electric jolt that sparked down her belly.

She recognized the exact moment when he changed his mind about waiting for her. He pulled his hands out of his pockets and jogged to her. "What the hell, Ria? What happened? Did you fall? Are you hurt?" He searched her body with his eyes.

She shook her head. Fresh pain shot through her at the movement. "I'm fine." What kind of idiot ran until her body felt like it was broken?

An agonizing cramp twisted in her calf and she fought to keep the wince off her face. He reached out, but stopped before he touched her.

"How much did you run? Did you at least stretch first? What is wrong with you?"

She ground her teeth to block out the pain. *Please, Viky, not now.*

His face softened. "Let's get you to the bench. You need to sit down." He nudged his arm closer and waited for her to take it.

But she couldn't move. The cramp in her calf jammed her in place.

He squatted down beside her and slid one hand beneath her shoe. "Put your hand on my shoulder. I don't want you falling over." His voice was as rough as his fingers were gentle.

She touched him. Her fingers melted into the thick muscled warmth of his shoulder.

"Try to pull your toes up toward yourself." He nudged the pad of her foot up with steady pressure and massaged the cramping muscle.

A spasm of pain shot up and down her leg. Her fingers fisted the slippery material of his shirt.

"Shh. It's okay. Try to relax, let it stretch. You need to stretch out the muscle for the cramp to release."

Only a fool would melt at his kindness. He was a doctor. He was just doing his job. It had nothing to do with her.

Just like he asked, she tugged her toes toward herself. Sure enough, after a few moments of stretching the cramp eased.

He let her foot go, and not lingering for even a second, rose back up.

She let her hand slide off his shoulder. Wanting to linger. Oh, so badly wanting to linger.

Except for that pulse in his throat he stood as still as a statue. "Can you walk on it?" He offered his arm.

She didn't take it, and started toward the bench, focusing on putting one foot in front of the other.

He fell in step beside her. "What were you thinking going for a run after yesterday?"

Her cheeks warmed with embarrassment at the memory of their last encounter. "I told you, I'm fine."

They reached the bench. Again he offered her his arm. Again she didn't take it. She squeezed her eyes and bent her knees and landed gracelessly on the bench. The pain was definitely a good distraction.

"No, you're not. You were sick yesterday, you should be in bed."

"I'm not sick. It was just a migraine. I shouldn't have ordered that lemonade, it was too sweet."

"Migraine?" He looked livid. "You ran with a migraine? What the hell is wrong with you? How often do you get them?" He looked so large looming over her like that, and yet she had that old sense of safety as she looked up into his eyes. As though everything would be okay as long he was near.

"I told you I'm fine. But I really don't have the energy to fight right now." *Or to deal with that look in your eyes.*

He took a deep breath and sank down on the bench beside her. "I'm not here to fight." He squeezed his temples, his fingers working to ease what he was struggling with. When he looked back at her, there was an apology in his eyes. "I mean it. I really don't want to fight anymore."

Her heart gave another squeeze. She attempted a smile. "No?" she said, feigning surprise.

When he responded with a small smile, stupid unchecked warmth burst in her heart.

"I know. Shocker," he said. It was the first time he had smiled at her since she'd come back. For a moment she forgot the pain in her body. She forgot everything.

He ran his fingers through his hair. It was damp, freshly washed. "I'm actually here to apologize. I'm sorry about yesterday. I was a real ass."

It was probably just the heady soapy scent of him, but her own smile sank into her heart and made her loopy. "Well," she said, stretching out the word until his smile widened too.

"Hey, I was. I admit it." He raised his hands in surrender. "You know I can be an idiot when I'm mad."

She swallowed and he looked away.

She waited for the awkward moment to rekindle his anger as it had done before. But he didn't say anything more. Her Viky had made up his mind and she knew that it was done.

Still, her mind fought the calm that came over her as they sat there listening to the river gurgle over rocks. It had always been far too loud for such a small river. He traced the wet grass with his sneakers. The movement made muscles ripple against the black athletic jersey and sweatpants he wore with such careless ease. Another zing arced from her heart to her belly. Ten years of being frozen from the inside out and here she was, her body unable to remember the disgust it had felt at human touch. An Ice Princess without her armor of ice.

The men she worked with looked like this after teams of experts spent hours putting them together. He was the guy her heroes were trying to look like. And failing, if her body's reaction was anything to go by. Where she had felt nothing but cold disgust with her costars, with him the need to touch him, to feel the changes, to seek out the familiar, was so strong it made her belly clench. Her body just as much as her heart had always recognized him and would never stop punishing her for what she had done.

"He really isn't the right guy for you, you know."

She looked up. "Who?" she asked absently, breathing in the wet earth smell of fall mixed with the soapy scent of him—only, no soap in the world smelled quite like that. She wondered how long he had been waiting for her on the bench.

"Sanjay . . . Mira's brother," he said with a frown.

So that's what this was about. Mira and her stupid professor brother. Ria twisted toward him and welcomed the stab of pain. "You're right," she said, sounding every bit as disinterested as she felt.

"That's it. That's all you're going to say?"

"What do you want me to say?"

"I don't know, last night you were all for the setup. Don't you have anything to say now?"

She swallowed her groan. "Why don't you just tell me what you want to hear?"

"I want to hear how you can lose interest in someone so easily."

The sound of the river heightened the silence that followed his question. She shifted on the bench, but the pain didn't work this time. His eyes shone with the intensity of what he was asking. His entire body waited, but she had no answer to give him. Not to the question he had asked, and definitely not to the question he hadn't.

His damp hair fell in thick spikes across his forehead. His mouth puckered the way it always did when he frowned. His every expression was so familiar it was as if she had never left. He was second nature to her, like the scars that marked her—after avoiding them in the mirror year after year, there was no forgetting exactly where each dwelled on her body.

"I was never interested," she said finally. "That's what I was trying to tell Mira, but then you kept provoking me and I let you push me into a corner."

Something raw and unexpected darkened his eyes. He had loved to push her into corners when she least expected it. Loved surprising her shyness out of her. The way it had felt to touch him, with her entire body, skin to skin, cell to cell. The way they had fit together filled her mind.

The blue-gray kaleidoscope of his eyes opened up, sucking her in. Water closed above her head. If she didn't swim back up she would drown. She squeezed her eyes shut and caught her breath. "Is that why you were waiting here, to protect your precious professor from my clutches?"

His silence was his only answer.

How was it possible that he could look at her the way he just had and believe that she was some sort of callous man-eater? How could he have forgotten all the things he had known about her?

But he had. She had done unforgiveable things to make him forget. And she would do it again. It didn't matter that the thought of being near anyone but him made her want to vomit. She couldn't tell him that, no matter how badly she wanted to, so instead she said, "Listen, I was serious yesterday. I have no interest in a relationship. With anyone. I just don't have the time for it. And I'll be gone in ten days, so what's the point? Your friend's safe."

The tension stretched across his shoulders didn't ease.

She made herself smile. "Relax. I'll just have to find someone else to sink my talons into."

One side of his mouth quirked, but his smile was sad. "It won't be hard either," he said. "They must be lining up for one single poke."

Ria's hand flew to her mouth.

"Oh come on! You know that's not what I meant. That came out all wrong. Your talons. I meant your talons. A poke of your—" His smile turned genuine and crinkled his eyes. "I'll just stop talking now."

She nodded. "Please."

And just like that they were laughing. The kind of laughter that starts out in your belly and vibrates through your shoulders. Equal parts relief and embarrassment tied together by so much shared laughter from the past. Sweet pain jabbed at her muscles with every soft staccato burst.

"Shit, that was terrible. I'm sorry," he said, his shoulders still shaking. "I can't seem to say anything right anymore, can I?"

"Nope."

Their eyes met and held. An unguarded moment passed between them. No anger, no pain, just them. Ria and Viky.

She wrapped her arms around herself and let the flash of pain bring her back to reality.

"How's Mira?" she asked, trying to keep herself grounded in it.

He studied her face, searching for something, but he didn't shut down. "Pretty upset. I think I really scared her."

"I'm sorry." It was Ria's turn to apologize. She hadn't been able to get the bewildered hurt on Mira's face out of her head.

"I can't hurt Mira like that again. I can't believe I did that to her yesterday," he said sounding weary and disappointed with himself.

All his life he'd met every standard he'd set for himself and every standard those around him had set for him. It couldn't have been easy with two legends for parents. It was the first thing people ever asked him. "You're Chitra and Ravi Jathar's son?" His parents had started their company as students at Stanford and grown it into a Fortune 500 corporation within years. As if that weren't enough, Vikram's grandfather was the first Surgeon General of India and his grandmother had almost singlehandedly revolutionized fertility treatments in India. His other set of grandparents were decorated social activists who had pioneered community banking in villages to empower women. There were no black sheep in the Jathar family, only grand legacies. But Vikram had never shown any signs of pressure. He'd thrived on it, made it look easy.

Now he looked tired. For the first time since she'd seen him again, there wasn't an ounce of anger in him. And it broke her heart more than any of his insults had.

"I think we should both stop saying sorry," he said, his voice completely in control, and far too distant again. And the change in it stung far more than it should have. "I shouldn't have said any of those things. Ever since you came back, I've been acting like an asshole. The truth is I never expected you to come to the wedding. You took me by surprise."

He had thought she would miss Nikhil's wedding? How could he think that? He knew what Nikhil meant to her. All the pain in her body gathered in her heart.

But this was exactly what she needed—for him to think of her this way. Not that warmth that had just sparkled between them.

"Actually, I wasn't going to come back." The breeziness in her voice was all Ice Princess. "But I needed to get away for a bit. Paparazzi trouble, you know?" She gave a delicate, camera-worthy shrug. "This was the easiest way out."

Disappointment clouded his eyes. And the dance they'd been dancing between lies and truth continued on to the blaring background score of their past.

He straightened, widening his shoulders to their full glory. His disappointment seemed to ease him. Disappointment was easier than the alternative. "I'm sure Nikhil is glad to be of service."

She didn't react. It would've been too easy to start another argument.

"I'm sorry, I'm doing it again," he said quickly, shaking his head. "This should be about Nikhil. Not about us." His voice hitched slightly on the word *us,* but that might just be her mind playing games. "I thought Nikhil was going to kill one of us yesterday. We can't do this to Jen and him. It's not fair."

"True." Finally something they agreed on. No lies, no half-truths.

"We're going to have to live in the same house for another ten days. Are you going to be okay with that?"

She nodded. "You?"

"Of course. We were friends once. We can at least be civil to each other now."

She smiled. "I'd like civil."

He stood up and looked down at her. "You ready to head home?" His hands dug deep in his pockets.

Ria stood. Pain stiffened her legs. She had to force herself not to fall back down. *Oh please, just let me get home without completely humiliating myself. Just this one time. I swear I'll never ever run again. Ever.*

She took a few steps, but her legs had turned so heavy and rubbery she wasn't sure they were even connected to her body anymore. She forced one foot in front of the other, putting all her strength into it. Just when she thought she was going to pull off a graceless hobble back, her foot found a loose rock and twisted around it. Her entire body pitched at the most awkward angle and she landed with a painful thud on her hands and knees.

In a second Vikram was down on his knees next to her. "God, are you okay?" He looked so surprised Ria wanted to laugh. A jolt of pain shot through her knee and she cried out instead. Gently, very gently, he slipped his arm around her and helped her up, supporting her weight with his body.

His strength, his heat—her entire screaming body came alive beneath his touch and made every excruciating stab of pain worth it.

He dusted the gravel off her palms, revealing streaks of blood under scraped skin. The crease between his brows dug deeper. "Can you walk?"

Ria tried to take a step, but her knee couldn't take her weight and she buckled again. In a single, effortless move he leaned over and swept her up in his arms, pulling her against his chest.

"What are you doing? Put me down." But it felt too good, too right, and her words fizzled on her tongue. She fought to keep her body rigid, to not notice the irregular strum of his heartbeat against her breast, to not melt into the warmth of his chest, to not reach for that patch of skin at the base of his neck where she had burrowed so many times. The pain, focus on the pain.

"And do what, let you drag yourself home on your elbows?" He strode down the path to the house, carrying her as if she belonged in his arms.

"I can walk," she said, and his lips curled, tiny crinkles radiating from his eyes.

Her face was too close to his. She could see the hints of tan and pink in his cheeks disappearing into the freshly shaved bristles on his jaw. She could feel the warmth of his breath, the dampness of his hair.

She leaned away from him.

His jaw hardened. "We're almost home," he said. "Try to focus on the pain. That should make this more bearable."

"I thought we were being civil."

"I'm carrying you. That's civil enough, don't you think?"

She didn't answer. She took his advice and tried to focus on the pain. Her knee pounded, her palms smarted, but all she could think of was the strength of his arms around her and the insanely intoxicating smell of his skin.

As he stepped onto the deck and knocked on the kitchen door with his foot, Ria searched desperately for something, anything, to stop them from opening the door so she could stay in his arms for just a moment longer.

# 11

As soon as Nikhil opened the door and Vikram carried Ria into the house, a flurry of activity erupted around them. Uma and Vijay jumped out of their chairs and ran after them into the living room.

"There, it's over." Vikram's whisper was harsh in her ear, but he put her down on the couch with such gentleness, her stomach contracted in protest to the loss of his touch.

Before she could say anything, Uma went off into a tizzy. "Good God. Ria, *beta*, are you all right? What on earth happened?" She sat down next to Ria, took her hands, and stared at them in despair. "You're bleeding. Oh God, she's bleeding. Vijay, she's bleeding, do something."

Before Vijay Kaka could react, Vikram rubbed Uma's shoulders. "Relax, Uma. She tripped. They're just surface scratches." His voice was calm, but the crease between his brows was a deep slash across his forehead. "I think she hit her knee. Nic, can you take a look?"

Nikhil was already squatting next to Ria and rolling up her pant leg.

"It's the other one." Vikram pointed to her right leg.

"Look at you, my poor baby." Uma pushed Ria's hair off her face and tucked it behind her ear. She licked her thumb and wiped a streak of dirt off Ria's cheek and dusted her elbows, cluck-clucking the entire time. "You went running again? What's wrong with you, child? You're on vacation. Can't you just stay home and relax?"

"It's all that food you've been feeding her, Aie," Nikhil said, easing Ria's pant over her knee. "She's going to kill herself working it off."

"Shut up." Ria winced as he straightened her leg.

Nikhil made a tsking sound. "That doesn't look too good." Her knee was bruised, the skin an angry red with a few dots of blood.

Uma glared at Nikhil as if they were ten and he had pushed her and made her fall. Vikram walked back into the room with a bag of ice and handed it to Uma. Her face softened. She looked at Vikram as though he had just descended from heaven on angel wings. "Thanks, *beta*. Thank God you found her. Were you out running as well? What happened?"

"Ouch!" Ria shrieked. "Will you stop doing that, Nikhil?" Although poor Nikhil had been doing nothing more than examining her.

"I'm sorry." Nikhil pressed the ice into her knee. It was only a little swollen, but it throbbed as if it had a life of its own.

Nikhil removed the ice and inspected it again. "I don't think anything's broken, but we should get an X-ray to make sure. Dad, what do you think?"

"It's not broken, Nikhil. I really don't want to go the hospital. Please," Ria said. She knew broken bones and this wasn't how it felt.

Vijay squatted down next to her and examined her, nudging and moving her leg so gently she hardly noticed. When he was done, he patted her cheek. "I agree. I don't think it's broken either. We can wait until tomorrow. My guess is some analgesic, lots of ice, and lots of rest, and she'll be ready to dance at the wedding. That okay with you, Uma?"

Uma stopped in the middle of pacing the room. Instead of answering she turned to Ria. "I've been up for three hours now and you've been gone the entire time." The horror on Uma's face made Ria want to kick herself. "Please tell me you haven't been running that long."

Vikram's head snapped up and his eyes met Ria's. Her cheeks flared with embarrassment. It had been an incredibly stupid thing to do. But she hadn't meant to run that long. She just hadn't been able to stop. Vikram's jaw clenched, anger suffused his face again.

"Uma Atya, I'm fine. Seriously. You heard Nikhil and Vijay Kaka. It's just a scraped knee. It's feeling better already. Really."

Vikram took a step back, moving away from her, away from all of them. "I have to go." He tapped his watch. "You got this, Nic?"

Nikhil nodded. "We're going to knock her out and keep her in bed for the rest of her trip. She'll be fine."

Vikram smiled a distracted smile that didn't make it anywhere near his eyes. He looked so restless and eager to get away he might as well already be gone. "Go," she wanted to tell him before they lost whatever peace they had garnered by the river. Within minutes he was gone, his hands filled with long, rolled-up tubes of paper.

Ria watched his retreating back, and exhaustion and pain descended on her with such violence, it stole the air from her lungs and the strength from her limbs. She couldn't even pretend to keep up with Uma's worried inquisition and closed her eyes, unable to hold her lids open anymore.

Uma let up and shifted her energy to making her comfortable.

Before she knew it, Ria was fed, medicated, and led up to her room, where she changed and sank gratefully into bed. Uma tucked her in and the last thing Ria remembered was Uma's soft hand stroking her forehead before darkness closed around her and at long last sleep claimed her.

Ria had no idea how long she slept. It felt like days, like months. She slept like a hibernating animal who slept and slept until the world was ready for it again, until life seeped back into her limbs. Loving hands checked up on her in her dreams, touched her cheeks, her forehead, spoke caring words, propped her up, and gave her pills. Healed her.

When her mind started to form thoughts again, she tried desperately to quiet it, to burrow under her comforter and steal a little more peace. But once the thoughts found a crack there was no pushing them away. They seeped into her brain like molten lava and pushed out the numbness of sleep. She opened her eyes. Even lifting her heavy eyelids felt like an effort. At first only fuzzy images appeared around her. A tall form slumped in the chair next to her. Her heart stuttered and her eyes flew open.

He straightened. "Hey, starlet. You done with your beauty sleep?"

She smiled. She could never be disappointed to hear that voice.

"How long have I been out?" She sounded scratchy and parched.

Nikhil helped her up and handed her a glass of water. "Long enough. How are you feeling?"

She sat up and stretched her neck, twisted her body against the headboard. Nothing hurt. "Amazing," she said truthfully.

"How about your knee?"

She bent her leg, expecting pain, but felt no more than a pinch. "Nothing. It feels fine."

She let Nikhil look at it. He poked and prodded, and made her push into his hand with her toes just the way Vikram had done by the river. But she felt nothing more than a little soreness. Her heart mimicked her leg—calm and rested and only the slightest bit sore. "Seriously, I feel really good. What did you guys give me?"

Nikhil laughed. "Trade secret. If I told you I'd have to kill you."

"Yesterday I might have taken you up on that." Ria smiled. "Can you at least set me up with more?"

"Sure. I'll hook you up with my dealer. You think you can get out of bed now? Aie's ready to cancel the wedding."

Ria sprang upright. "Seriously?"

"She's pretty close. Honestly, I think she's a little scared of Jen, otherwise she'd have done it already."

"Jen is a bit scary," Ria said, smiling at Jen as she entered the room.

"Only a bit?" Jen asked, sounding offended. She handed Ria a tray of steaming peppery *rasam* soup. Something suspiciously close to hunger gnawed at Ria's insides. Ria didn't remember the last time she had felt hunger. Really, what had they given her? She gulped down the soup while Nikhil teased her about it. "Really, starlet, it's not that hard," he said. "You eat, you sleep, and you don't exhaust yourself until your body goes into shock. Can we try that please?"

Ria glared at him, but couldn't stop eating.

Jen punched Nikhil's shoulder and settled on the arm of his chair.

"You're right, she is a bit scary." Nikhil rubbed his shoulder where Jen had hit him and gave her one of his caressing glances, obviously done with his little reprimand.

Not that Ria didn't agree with him. She had behaved horribly irresponsibly and she should have known better.

"You look terrified," she said, and spooned the last bits of the red lentils into her mouth. "But damn, she makes a great soup! Where did you learn this, Jen? It's delicious."

Jen beamed. "Aie walked me through it. She has to be the most patient woman on the planet and definitely the best cook ever."

Jen had never met her birth mother. She'd lost her adopted mother at five, after which her adopted father hadn't done much more than drink himself to death and leave her to spend her adolescence in foster homes. Uma and Vijay had taken her into their hearts with the same unconditional love they showered on all the children who came into their sphere. Jen's connection with Uma gave Ria a special kinship with her. It was like they were sisters, lost ducklings taken under a common wing.

"How do you feel?" Jen took the empty bowl from Ria and touched Ria's cheek with the back of her hand. "No fever."

"I had a fever?"

"Low grade. It was basically exhaustion. Your body needed rest. Lots of it." Jen mirrored Uma's admonishing look perfectly, reminding Ria of how idiotically she had behaved. Instead of helping with the wedding, she had put the family through all this worry.

She swallowed. "I'm sorry." From now on this trip was going to be about the wedding.

*This should be about Nikhil. Not about us.*

*Us.* She refused to think about how Vikram's voice had melted around the word.

"I'm just glad you're feeling better." Jen smiled at Ria, but she threw Nikhil a worried glance.

"What was that look for? Bad diagnosis? Is it fatal?"

"No, drama queen, you're fine. And it's 'prognosis.' But Aie's gone nuts on us. She wants us to cancel the bachelor and bachelorette parties and those aren't until Friday. She's already cancelled the dinner at Anu Auntie's house tonight. The Auntie Brigade is hopping mad they haven't got to spend time with you yet."

Ria frowned fiercely at Nikhil. "I'm dying to see the aunties too. Uma Atya can't cancel. I'm perfectly fine." She pushed the sheets away and swung her legs off the bed.

"Well, Aie already bit Dad's head off for suggesting you were fine. So I'm not going to be the bearer of that piece of good news."

"I'm marrying a wimp." Jen pushed off the chair.

"Why don't you tell her, warrior princess?" Nikhil goaded.

Jen took a deep dramatic breath and went off to do it, dropping a kiss on Ria's head before leaving.

"I just love Jen," Ria said as soon as Jen left.

"Yeah, me too." Nikhil looked dreamily at the door.

Ria reached out and ruffled his hair. "You lucked out, baby. She's perfect for you."

Nikhil didn't respond. No smart-aleck comeback. He turned to her, his face suddenly serious. If he gave her one of those trite lines about there being someone out there for her, she was going to scream. She felt better than she had in days, but hearing Nikhil spew that rubbish would make her sick.

He didn't.

"Ria, what happened yesterday?" he asked instead, his tone so uncharacteristically accusatory her defenses shot right up.

"My family drugged me and knocked me out because I was an idiot and almost killed myself running."

His frown deepened. "What was Vic doing out there with you?"

Nikhil was bringing Vikram up? Ria couldn't believe it. It had been the unwritten rule between them for the past ten years to never mention Vikram. Nikhil was the only one in the family who had known about Vikram and her, and he had kept their secret well. He had never asked any questions and she had never shared the sordid details of the breakup. She certainly was in no mood to change that now. But he sat there, his eyes boring into her for a response.

"Nothing. We were just talking. Trying to make up for making fools of ourselves the day before."

Apparently it was not the answer he was looking for. He continued to stare at her as if he would explode if he didn't say what was on his mind.

"Spit it out, Nikhil. What's bothering you?"

He took a deep breath and did just that. "I think you should stay away from Vic."

"Excuse me?" Her fingers tightened around the comforter.

He had the gall to look sympathetic. "Listen, Ria, there's a lot you don't know. He just met Mira and he seems happy. I haven't seen him like this in a long time. But ever since you've come back . . . Just don't start anything, okay?"

Now Nikhil was protecting Vikram from her? Despair fisted around her heart. Anger rose inside her so fast and furious she wanted to shake Nikhil. Her first instinct was to suppress it and walk away. Instead she met his eyes and didn't bother to hide her disappointment or her rage. He flinched.

"Didn't you hear me the other night?" she said. "I'm not interested in a relationship. Not with anyone. Now, if you don't mind, I'd like to get up and get dressed. I'm sure I look far too bedraggled for a man-eating vamp." She threw off the covers and pushed herself off the bed. Her knee gave only the slightest tug. Right about now she would've welcomed a nice, mind-numbing jolt of pain.

"Ria, don't be like this. He's just—"

"I don't want to talk about him, Nikhil. It might make me start something you don't want." And with that she headed for the shower feeling dirtier than she had in a very long time.

# 12

"Absolutely not." Uma Atya looked immovable. It would be easier to let her have her way, but Ria needed a distraction. She couldn't stop fuming, or stop Nikhil's words from playing in her ears over and over.

"Please, Uma Atya, I'm dying to see the aunties, and look at me, I'm fine." She pointed at herself. She had changed into jeans and a turquoise striped button down hoping against hope that her designer's claim that the color made her glow held enough truth to convince her aunt.

"You are not leaving the house today. You were out like a light, moaning and groaning in your sleep for two days. It's out of the question."

Ria opened her mouth to argue. Uma raised a hand to stop her. "But the girls suggested moving the dinner here." Before Ria opened her mouth again, Uma raised a stern eyebrow. "*If* you promise to stay on the couch the entire evening, we can move the party here. Anu's been cooking for days, so it doesn't make sense to let all that food go to waste."

Ria hugged her aunt. "Anything you say, Uma Atya," she said into the sweet jasmine scent of her aunt's hair. "But you're not changing any other plans after this."

Uma kissed Ria's forehead and gave her another arch look Ria had no doubt kept her students on their toes. "The bachelor party is safe. That Nikhil needs to fight his own battles, don't you think?"

Oh, she did think. And he also needed to butt the hell out of everyone else's battles.

Of all people, how had Nikhil got everything so dismally wrong? She refused to think about the fact that he had no way of knowing any different. She had never given him an explanation. She'd let him believe what she had wanted Vikram to believe, that she was a betraying bitch who had sold herself for a shot at stardom. She pushed away the bitter thought that wouldn't stop niggling in her mind—that neither one of them had believed in her enough to push past her lies. She knew it wouldn't have changed her choices, knew it was unfair to blame them, but it still stuck in her heart like the thinnest, sharpest splinter.

The ever-present tangle of lies tightened around her like a hunter's net. The more she pushed it away, the more it clung to her like sticky, spindly spiderwebs. But the truth had to remain hidden inside that godforsaken asylum and inside the cone of silence that was Uma, Vijay, and her, and, tragically enough, Vikram's mother.

If Vikram ever found out that Ria's mother was alive, if he knew why she had really left him, if he saw any hope at all, she knew everything would change. Even now, despite all she'd done, he would flip everything over like a well-laid table without a thought for the priceless, irreplaceable china on it.

It had taken one look into his eyes for her to know that.

Just like it had taken only one look into his eyes to answer his question all those years ago.

*You want to be friends?*

And to know he meant it forever.

No, Vikram could never find out the truth, or she would have no means to protect him. But she wanted Nikhil to believe in her with or without the truth. He was Nikhil. He had always been in her corner. He was her corner. It was horribly unfair of her, but she wanted him to know without being told that she would never do anything to hurt Vikram again.

*Just don't start anything, okay?*

As if she needed Nikhil to tell her that. As if she needed anyone to remind her that starting anything with Vikram was like hanging an insane invalid around his neck and leaving him to drown. She knew only too well the devastation that was coming once her mind was gone. But while she had no choice but to follow in the footsteps of the woman who'd given birth to her in that one thing, unlike her, Ria would make sure she left as little wreckage behind as she could.

Vikram and Mira were holding hands when Ria came down the stairs. Or, more accurately, Mira was holding on to Vikram. Her hand clutched the crook of his arm while his hand was tucked into his pocket. It was a minor detail, but it jumped out at Ria like a zoomed in close-up shot. The memory of his arms around her as he carried her across the yard sprang to life on her skin and she rubbed it away.

Vikram caught her eye and gave her a polite nod, but Mira refused to meet her eyes or acknowledge her in any way. Ria wasn't sure if she returned his nod before slipping away into the kitchen.

"There's our Ria!" The chorus of voices she'd been waiting to hear greeted Ria as she entered the kitchen.

There was something so overwhelmingly familiar about seeing the Auntie Brigade packed around the kitchen island that for a wonderful instant Ria felt like a little girl again. They launched themselves at her, and she burrowed shamelessly into each of them as they pulled her into hugs. They were all draped in *kurtis* over jeans today, and Ria knew that an endless number of calls had been made to come up with the decision. For as long as Ria could remember, they had discussed what to wear for every occasion however big or small. "Are we doing Indian or regular?" or "I'm too tired to doll up, let's just do jeans today," or "We haven't worn saris in ages. Everyone's wearing a sari." Whether it was a party, a play, or a picnic, they always came up with a dress code.

Their husbands and kids teased them about it, but the dress code was as much a part of them as their friendship and the world of dependability they had created for each other as they turned a foreign land into home. Despite their moods and their personal preferences they always complied with the dress code. It was their thing.

"I love the *kurtis,*" Ria said and they collectively launched into detailed accounts of where each *kurti* had come from, including how much each one had cost.

Ria couldn't help but smile.

"See, now she's laughing at us," Radha said, one hand on her hip.

"You deserve to be laughed at. I mean, who ever tells a film star how much they paid for a *kurti* in Delhi Haat on their last trip home?" Priya said, although she had done exactly the same thing.

"I'm not laughing at you, Radha Auntie. I'm smiling because you all haven't changed even one bit."

"*Leh,* why would we change?" Radha said, pointing at herself with exaggerated incredulousness. "Why change something so perfect, ha?"

They laughed and Ria agreed heartily.

"*Vaise,* you haven't changed either, *beta*. Such a big star, but still as sweet as you always were," Anu said, patting Ria's cheek.

"So true." Sita smiled at her. "Not one spot of scandal. With all the dirty stories you hear about Bollywood, we were so worried when you joined films." She squeezed Uma's shoulder. "But Uma had one hundred percent faith in you and you've proved her right. We're so proud of you."

Their faces glowed with pride, but it was Uma's pride that stuck in Ria's throat like a lump she couldn't swallow around.

"*Arrey,* I raised her. How could she ever do any of those dirty things?" Uma said, and Ria found it hard to breathe.

She would not think about Ved. Not now, not here. The only remotely positive thing about her sordid liaison with Ved was that he had kept it out of the press. It had been his deal with his wife that he keep his filthy sluts private, and he was powerful enough that the press only printed what he okayed. Uma would die of shame if she or the aunties ever found out exactly how filthy Ria really was.

"Ria, are you tired, *beta?*" Uma searched Ria's face. "You know what, you promised to stay off your feet, let's go." She pushed Ria out of the kitchen. "Ria needs to rest and we need to get dinner ready," she said to the aunties.

"Go, go, before your bossy *atya* throws us out of the house." They waved Ria out of the kitchen and made her promise to fill them in on all the latest Bollywood gossip soon, every juicy detail of all the scandalous things they were so proud of her for not doing. Then they turned their attention to the endless foil trays filled with food.

Uma pulled Ria into the family room, pushed her on the couch, and tried to prop her foot up on an ottoman.

"Uma Atya, please. I really don't need to." Ria put her foot back on the floor.

Uma glared at her and put her foot back on the ottoman. "Keep your leg up there and don't make a promise if you can't keep it."

As if on cue Vikram entered the room. "She's right, you know." He picked up the platter of vegetables and dip from the coffee table. Then he took in her expression and looked at her leg. "I meant she's right about your knee. Keeping it raised will help it heal."

"See. Vic always was the smartest of you lot." Uma stood briskly, pulling Vikram's face down and kissing his head. She pointed to the plate in his hand. "Make sure Ria eats some before you take it away," she said to him in Marathi before hurrying off.

"*Ho*," he answered in that accented Marathi Ria had always found so endearing. Usually, Nikhil and Vikram always answered in English when anyone spoke to them in Marathi. But there were a few Marathi words they let slip every now and again, and Ria had loved when they did that.

"How's it feeling?" Vikram threw a quick glance at her leg and held the platter in front of her, waiting stubbornly until she picked up a cucumber spear.

"It's fine. All healed."

He narrowed his eyes and ran a disbelieving glance down her leg. "I doubt that. Your bruises stay forev—" Color drained from his face. His gaze caught on her bent little toe with its zipper-shaped scar.

Ria put her foot on the floor and slid it into her slippers, but his gaze followed her foot.

He had dropped a hammer on her little toe when she was seventeen and they had been building shelves for Uma in the garage. Ria's toe had always stayed a little crooked after that.

"Vic—Oh!" Mira stopped in her tracks. One glance at Vikram's guilt-ridden face and she looked like someone had slapped her.

Ria wanted to tell her that his guilt had nothing to do with what they'd been doing just now. In fact it had nothing to do with anything. It was completely unfounded. The fault had been all Ria's. But she could hardly tell Mira that she had been stupid enough to kiss someone with a hammer in his hand.

"Hi, Mira." Ria broke the silence. Mira gave her the barest nod, but still didn't make eye contact. She looked at the platter in Vikram's hand. "Everyone's waiting for the dip, Vic. You coming?"

"I'll be there in a minute." He stared at the spot where Ria's foot had rested on the ottoman.

"That venture capitalist friend of Vijay Uncle's is looking for you. I thought you wanted to talk to him. Come on."

"I'll be there in a minute," he repeated absently, still lost in his thoughts.

Mira glared at him for a few moments, waiting for him to look at her. When he didn't she grabbed the platter from his hands and left the room without another word.

Ria stood. If Uma Atya wanted her off her feet she could sit just fine in the kitchen. "You should go after her."

"I plan to." His gaze moved from her toe to her face. "And you should be more careful. Do you have any idea how irresponsible it is to run long distances without training?"

Ria opened her mouth then shut it again. She had no intention of getting into another fight.

"I'm not trying to start a fight," he said, meeting her eyes. "I'm serious, you can't do things without thinking about the consequences. You can't just wake up one day and run a marathon. The first guy to attempt it dropped dead." He turned to leave the room, then stopped and faced her again. "And don't worry, when I said I'd be civil, I meant it. You don't have to look so terrified every time I open my mouth. I keep my word." And with that left-handed jab, he jogged out of the room after Mira.

Ria tried to remember the last time she had done something without thinking about the consequences. It was probably that kiss that had ended with having her toe smashed with a hammer.

# 13

Ria had forgotten to shut the blinds last night. The sun filtered in through the sheer drapes. She released the pillow, a pathetic substitute for the body she'd been clutching in the stupid dream she'd enjoyed far too much.

Her phone buzzed next to the pillow. She picked it up.

It was a text from DJ.

*What's wrong, babes?*

Mindlessly she pressed the letters *Wrng?* and hit Send. What was he talking about?

*The script . . . ur never late responding . . . who died?*

Me. She was dying a slow death.

And becoming outrageously dramatic.

She jabbed at the keys.

*I'm on vacation. . . . Gime a bldy break. . . . BTW, I'll do the film.*

Before she could backtrack, she hit Send. Then instantly regretted it. She hadn't even opened the script yet.

Her phone rang. It was DJ. She didn't answer. It buzzed again.

*Gr8 . . . Call when ur ready to talk . . . complete silence frm blkmailer.*

She sat up.

*Great! Maybe he's dead.* But she deleted that and instead typed: *THX. Keep me posted.*

At least now she was awake enough to get out of bed.

She took the longest shower she had ever taken. Poured lotion on every inch of skin, rubbing more and more in until it formed a white layer and she had to wipe it off with tissue. She brushed her hair until the brush simply slid off it. She changed three times and still she felt all wrong. Finally, after Nikhil had hollered from downstairs for the third time, she settled on a black sweater with only the thinnest turquoise edging, thank God, and black jeans, and slunk down the stairs dragging lead with her feet.

"Wow, starlet, that was the longest shower in human history." Nikhil gave her a sheepish grin and tried to be his usual endearing self, but she was still too angry with him. She hadn't said a single word to him since he'd tried to protect Vikram from her notorious talons.

She focused on rolling her hair into a bun and ignored him.

Vikram nodded at her over a cup of coffee, all freshly bathed and looking as good as the coffee smelled.

She returned his nod and turned to Jen. "Hey, Jen. You look lovely."

"Thanks." Jen twirled around to display the white *kurta* she wore over jeans. "You're going to the temple with us to meet the priest about the vows, remember? Coffee?"

"Yes, please. Use the biggest cup in the house." She finally managed to twist her hair into a semblance of a knot and jabbed it with a chopstick.

Vikram took the cup from Jen and poured the coffee. The chopstick slid from Ria's hair, bounced off the floor, and rolled to his feet. Hair unraveled and spilled around her shoulders. His gaze grazed her tumbling hair, and hunger flashed in his eyes, hot and bright. He dropped to his knees and picked up the stick. Instead of handing it to her, he put it on the countertop between them.

"Thanks." She tried again to roll up her hair. She had done this a million times and never had trouble. Today, her hair refused to cooperate. Jen took the stick from her, rolled her hair into a bun for her, and wove the stick through it.

Vikram dropped a spoonful of sugar and a few drops of cream into the coffee and pushed the cup toward Ria.

She took a sip and almost moaned with pleasure. Perfect cream. Perfect sugar. Perfect.

And he knew it. She saw it in his eyes before he looked away.

"Where's everyone?" She wrapped her fingers around the hot cup and took another long perfect sip.

"Aie and Mindy went to the craft store. Something about the centerpieces for the cocktail dinner," Nikhil said. "Dad and Matt are going to try to squeeze in nine holes."

"Wow! Golf? Really? That was brave of Vijay Kaka," Ria said.

"Yah. Brave. Stupid. Whatever." Nikhil rolled his eyes. "He's going to be making up for it for a long time, the poor man."

"More like poor Uma Atya," Ria said, wondering what she had missed that morning. "This isn't exactly the time for golf, is it?" she said loyally.

"Why not?" Vikram met her eyes over his cup. His voice was nonchalant, but the way he held his shoulders and pressed his lips together wasn't.

"Yeah, why not?" Nikhil asked. "We have another week before the wedding, and everything is under control. I don't know why Aie is so stressed out."

Instead of answering him Ria pointed her cup to the to-do list tacked on the refrigerator door. Items written neatly in black marker stretched all the way down two legal-sized sheets of paper taped end to end, each line bulleted with a star. A few items were crossed out, but most of the list remained starkly undone.

"Oh please." Nikhil walked to the fridge and scowled at the list. "Pack coconuts? Seriously? That's a to-do item?"

Vikram and Jen smiled.

"Coconuts are an important part of the wedding ceremony," Ria said as calmly as she could. "You need them for every ritual."

"She's right, man," Vikram said. "You've got to respect the coconuts."

Nikhil and Vikram guffawed and Ria glared at them

"Shut up, guys," Jen said. "Ria's right. The details are important."

"Of course they are. The wedding's all about the rituals. God forbid you had to get married without coconuts." Vikram shuddered and took a sip of coffee.

She was getting really sick of all these insinuations. "That's not what I meant. It's a wedding. The rituals mean something."

"It is a wedding. The rituals don't mean squat. There's a bride and a groom and they make vows. Those mean something."

His look was pure danger. The response slamming in her heart was pure danger. She should have backed down. With anyone else, she would have. But his eyes did it every single time. Made the words burst out of her. She had spent a year not talking even as everyone tried to pry words out of her. Not being able to talk was about fear, about being terrified of what might come out, of what you might expose. But even now, with so much to be afraid of, one look in his eyes and her fear dissipated like stars in the dawning day.

And it made her even angrier. "How does making vows respectfully and traditionally diminish them?" she asked.

"You mean like in your movies?"

"No. I mean like in real life. Like Nikhil and Jen want to do and like everyone in our families has done for centuries."

"I thought vows were about the promises you made. I should have realized it was about how you made them." How did his eyes do that? Go from mocking to intense, from angry to hurt, in the span of one breath? How did they fill up like that? There was just too much there. Too much he didn't understand. Too much he wanted to stop feeling, but couldn't.

She couldn't take it anymore. Not another second of this crushed down feeling. "I know about vows," she wanted to shout. "I know what it means to make them!"

She couldn't remember one single reason why she shouldn't say the words. Why she couldn't tell him how she felt. He was here, right in front of her. If she reached out she could touch him, and her entire body hurt from the effort it took not to. Something inside her reared up and shook itself loose, something desperate and voracious. That look in his eyes agitated it into existence, and fanned it until it filled her up.

They stared at each other, no longer able to look away, no longer needing words.

Jen's phone rang and the trance broke.

"Oh no," Jen said into the phone, panic spilling from her voice.

Nikhil moved closer to her, all his attention shifting from Vikram and Ria to her.

"That was the altar guy," she said when she was done. "His warehouse caught fire. Our altar is gone! Burned to a crisp. He was able to salvage a few others, but we need to go pick another one out right now before they're all gone." She gnawed at her cuticle, looking distraught.

"But we have an appointment with the priest to go over the vow translations," Nikhil said, rubbing her shoulders. "We need to hand those out to the guests and the priest only had time today."

"Ria was going to help us with those anyway, right?" Jen looked hopefully at Ria. "You can do it by yourself, can't you, Ria? You don't need us. Vic can drive you."

All of Jen's panic jumped straight into Ria.

Nikhil gave her a pleading look. "Please?"

Really? Suddenly he was okay with her spending hours alone with Vikram? "What if I start something?" she almost said, throwing him a dirty look.

Vikram raised a questioning brow at Nikhil, then turned it on Ria.

She ignored them both and looked at Jen. "Vikram can go with Nikhil. I'll go with you."

Jen shook her head. "Vikram and Nikhil don't understand that stuff. Only you do. None of us can tell what is what. It has to be you. Please." Jen's voice cracked, and Ria put a quick hand on her shoulder.

"Of course I'll go," she said just as Vikram wrapped his arm around Jen.

"Relax, Jen," he said. "We'll take care of it. It's at the Lemont temple in half an hour, right? Easy enough."

Jen sniffed and smiled a wobbly smile. "I'm so sorry. I swear this wedding is turning me into a basket case."

Vikram dropped a kiss on top of Jen's head. "I think the word's *Bridezilla*," he stage-whispered, and she laughed and thanked them again and again, before Nikhil pulled her out of the room.

"Thanks, starlet," he said to Ria, pulling her into a hug before he left.

"Don't worry, I'll keep my claws to myself," she said into his ear. But she gave him a quick hug back. She might be angry with him, but she knew that the intensity of her anger far exceeded what he had done. None of this was his fault.

The garage door clicked shut, and Vikram and she were alone in the house.

Alone for the first time since that awful magical summer when they had made vows of their own. And then she'd torn them to shreds. The remnants of those shreds hung in the air now. They lingered in his eyes, and clung to her body. Impossibly stubborn.

Needing to move, Ria gathered all the cups that were lying around the kitchen, and took them to the sink.

Vikram stood rooted to the spot, as though no force on earth could move him, and watched her through lowered lids. The heat of his gaze warmed every inch of her body all the way to her aching heart. Silence stretched between them. She didn't want to know what was going through his mind. It was too much, all this knowing, all this feeling.

She rinsed out the cups, rubbing at each mud-colored stain until steam rose up to her face and her fingers reddened under the scalding water. Finally he moved. Stepping close behind her, he reached around her and turned off the faucet. His breath caressed the back of her neck. The downy hair at her nape prickled and stretched toward him, reaching for the familiar heat of his body. Just a whisper of a move and she'd be in his arms, her back pressed into his chest, his warmth wrapped around her. The cup slipped from her hands and landed in the sink with a clang. He backed away, moving quickly, not stopping until he was all the way across the kitchen. "We should go," he said, his voice barely a whisper. "Let's find out what makes these vows so special."

# 14

Ria followed Vikram to the big red truck parked on the street. This was his car? He held the door open for her. Even with her height she needed a ladder to get into this thing. With all the awkwardness of a newborn filly she pulled herself up into the seat. He slammed the door shut and jogged to the other side, leaping into the driver's seat with all the easy grace of a stallion.

The humongous monstrosity of a car purred to life beneath his fingers. He fit inside it as if it were built for him. Despite the preposterous amounts of space the car took up on the outside, the interior was tiny, with a single bench seat. Who made cars with bench seats anymore? She sucked everything in and squished herself into a sliver against the door.

It didn't work.

Vikram's presence beside her consumed her. She felt every breath entering and leaving his body. She felt his every move. Every time he changed gears or turned the steering wheel the muscles in his arms bunched and a zing shot through her. She would've given anything for a hand rest or a gearbox—something solid to provide separation. She placed her handbag between them and pulled her denim jacket tightly around herself, clutching it so hard her fingers turned numb from the pressure.

Vikram leaned over and turned up the heat. "Do you want me to turn on the seat warmer?"

She shook her head. The silence between them was heavy and

exhausting. By the time they drove into the temple parking lot, Ria found that her knees were locked from the tension. Vikram opened the door for her, and she hopped off the high platform. His fingers wrapped around her elbow and their eyes met, making that spark she was getting used to zing through her belly again. Even when he withdrew his hand the awareness of his touch lingered on her skin.

They walked side by side, the tug between them so strong, so palpable, it was a physical force. Silence followed them into the temple, trailing them as they went up the wide steps, hanging between them as they bent to remove their shoes in the shelf-lined room and walked barefoot across the cool ceramic tiles to the priest's office. They'd visited the temple with Uma and Vijay a few times every summer and it was as familiar as everything else. The only thing new was the silence between them.

And it was so disorienting that even when the priest launched into a lecture on the seriousness of marriage, neither one of them could find the words to correct him. Finally, when the priest asked how long they had known each other, Vikram cracked. "We're not the bride and groom." His voice was a low rumble in his chest. "We're the groom's cousins."

Not that his admission made a dent in the priest's ministrations. He went on with his sermon regardless, his head shaking benevolently as he dispensed wisdom at them across the metal desk. Two ornate rosewood statues of the goddesses Laxmi and Durga flanked the window behind him and sunshine danced on his generously oiled bald patch like a halo. He had his lecture to give and he was giving it no matter what.

"Temptations are ubiquitous," he said in an accent so thick it was like an entire different language. "Coming at us from all directions, feeding on our desires, on our hunger for momentary excitement. The true nature of marriage is not external pleasure, it is internal oneness." He paused, looking from Ria to Vikram as if they were part of a larger audience. Ria had the urge to turn around and make sure there weren't more people behind her. She caught Vikram's eye and almost smiled.

The priest's hands made sweeping motions. "The minds must

marry first." He clasped his hands together, then pulled them apart with drama befitting the finest character actor. "If we allow the external to transcend the internal we see only differences, and that can cause only separation, never harmony." Another pause. Another emphatic nod. "Our intellect skews reality. We have to be connected to what is real and ignore that which masquerades as reality. It is your insides that must fit together." He gave them a long meaningful look.

Vikram was holding himself completely still as only Vikram could. His stillness was its own language. This one wasn't an angry stillness. The effort it took him to keep his lips from quirking made his eyes shine. He gave her a warning look—*Don't you dare smile.*

The priest sighed contentedly, glad to have done his duty by them and curiously unconcerned by the minor detail that they weren't the bride and groom. He reached into the desk drawer, pulled out two booklets, and placed them in front of him. "You will need the Marathi-language vows, correct?" he asked.

Ria nodded.

"This one is more thorough. All the ceremonies are explained in detail." He patted the substantially thicker booklet covered in heavy stock paper. This one"—he lifted the second, thinner one—"is the shortened version, easier for the Western mind to grasp. Why don't you look through both and decide which one you want and I will make a Xerox copy for you. No hurry. I'll be back in few minutes." With that he left the room with surprisingly brisk strides.

Vikram pushed himself off the chair. For a moment Ria thought he was going to follow the priest out. But then he walked to the other side of the table, leaned his hip on it, and waited, totally somber again.

Ria pushed one of the booklets toward him. "Why don't you look at one and I'll look over the other."

He jumped back as if she had suggested something completely irrational. "No way." He slid the papers back at her. "This is all yours."

She frowned at him and flipped the thick booklet in front of her open. The bold, ornate lettering was all curves and swirls, each paragraph bulleted with a miniature Ganesha symbol.

- *The Hindu wedding ceremony comprises the seven steps of matrimony signifying the seven vows. The first step of the seven vows is taken to pledge that the marrying couple would provide a prospered living for the household, avoiding those that might hinder their healthy living.*

Ria blinked at the heavy-handed language. Two paragraphs explaining exactly how the marrying couple might do this followed. She skimmed over them and moved on to the next step.

- *During the second step, the bride and the groom promise that they would develop their physical, mental, and spiritual powers in order to lead a lifestyle that would be healthy.*

Another two paragraphs explained what "healthy living" meant. Impatience bristled inside Ria.

- *During the third step, the bride and the groom vow to expand their heredity by having children.*

Ria suppressed a groan.

- *For these children, the fruits of their union, the couple will be responsible. They also pray to be blessed with healthy, honest and brave children—*

Ria slammed the booklet shut and pushed it away. She knew she was being irrational, but she was so annoyed with the person who'd come up with this, she wanted to toss it across the room.

She opened the other one.

*We come together in our human forms—man and woman—but the divinity inside us joins today . . .*

*I will start where you end.*

*I will be your strength when you weaken.*
*I will be your health when you sicken.*
*I will be your wealth when you are wanting.*

A vision of Jen in her bridal sari formed in Ria's mind. Nikhil followed close behind her, his right hand clasped tightly in hers as they stepped around the fire, each step deliberate, mindful.

*I will forsake all that comes between us, and embrace all that enriches us.*
*I will be your spiritual guide, the embodiment of your values.*
*I will bring security and prosperity into your life and fill it with the joy of family.*
*. . . But above all else, I will be your friend.*

Suddenly the bride in Ria's mind wasn't Jen anymore, it was her. And she didn't have to see the groom's face to know who he was. She looked up, conscious of Vikram's gaze on her. He watched her, his eyes intense.

"Looks like you've decided which one you want," he said, and pulled away from the desk.

"You sure you don't want to take a look?" Her voice was breathless.

"Yes, I'm sure. Do you mind if I meet you outside? Need to make some calls." Before she could answer he was gone.

By the time the priest had copied the pages and lectured Ria some more about the Hindu vows, another twenty minutes had passed. Vikram wasn't on the patio when she came out of the ornately carved entrance. She looked around, squinting to find him in the sudden brightness. He stood at the bottom of the steps, leaning against the concrete balusters. He lifted his head and looked at her as she walked out into the sunshine. Light bounced off his hair and caught the crystals in his eyes. A soft, glowing fire started between her ribs, right at the center of her. Very gingerly, she took a step toward him, making sure she didn't trip. Although at this precise moment she wanted nothing more than to go flying into his arms.

He ran up the steps, coming to meet her halfway.

Something in his eyes made panic well up inside her. "What's wrong?"

"Nikhil just called. It's not a big deal, I don't want you to worry. . . ."

"Vikram, what's wrong?"

"Uma had some pain in her arm—her left arm. So Vijay's taken her to the hospital."

"No."

Vikram grasped her elbow and steadied her with his gaze. "Ria, she's fine. Vijay just wants to be sure. He doesn't think it's anything. Chances are she pulled a muscle or something."

"I want to go to the hospital. Right now."

"Of course. I already told Nikhil we're on our way."

As they ran to the car, his hand pressed into the small of her back. But instead of the usual burning impact, this time his touch calmed her, infused her with strength. This time when he helped her into the truck his hand lingered for a moment, making sure she was okay before letting go. The cab of the truck was still too small, and Vikram's presence next to her still overwhelming, but instead of sparking tension, a strange mix of emotions buzzed inside Ria—an unyielding cocoon of safety wrapped around her restlessness and anxiety, and kept her from breaking down.

But she couldn't hold herself still. She kept twisting around and asking him again and again what Nikhil had said. She tried calling Nikhil and Vijay Kaka, but they were probably inside the hospital and she couldn't get through to them. She pushed Vikram for details, asking him for the tenth time exactly what Nikhil had said.

"Nikhil didn't sound like there was anything to worry about. I don't know exactly what happened, but I'm sure Uma's fine. We're almost there. Just a few minutes more." He twisted his entire body around and faced her when he spoke, just the way he'd done when they were younger. Even back then he had always looked away from the road when he spoke to her, whether he was riding his bike next to her or driving. And it had always scared the living daylights out of her and made her scream at him.

"What are you doing? Keep your eyes on the road, Viky!" Her voice came out shrill, and scared, and sixteen.

His hands tightened on the steering wheel. The muscle in his jaw jumped to life. He turned back to the road and kept his eyes there for the rest of the drive, not saying another word.

Silence settled between them again, edgy and thick, making the echo of the name she hadn't called him in ten years that much louder.

# 15

The sprawling hospital buildings came into view and Ria's jitteriness turned to full-blown panic. Ria hated hospitals with a vengeance. The first time she'd been in a hospital, she'd been beaten within an inch of her life. The last time she'd been in one she had lost her father.

The memory of her broken body mingled with the memory of Baba's blistered face. Maroon-tinged gauze on his cheeks. White wads of cotton stuffed up his nose. More than anything else she had wanted to wrench that cotton out of his nose. *He can't breathe. It's suffocating him. Take it out, he can't breathe.* But she hadn't been able to say the words. They had laid him on the pyre just like that: white sheet, white gauze, white cotton. It had taken the orange flames seconds to paint all that white black before consuming it.

She wished that wasn't the last memory she had of him. She should've been with him, doing something to help the pain. Just like she should've been with Uma today. Instead, she had been with Vikram both times, dreaming impossible dreams instead of accepting her destiny.

She couldn't think of Uma lying in a hospital bed.

Vikram pulled into a parking spot and jumped out of the car. He ran to her side and opened the door. "Ria." He took both her hands in his, she was shaking. "Hey, listen, we're here. And I promise you, Uma's okay. Can you look at me? Please."

She looked at him.

"We're here. Let's go see her, okay?" His voice, his eyes, all of him was calm and sure.

She nodded, and followed him out of the car.

The redbrick building loomed in front of them and nervousness bloated in Ria's belly again, filling it up like a balloon. But she didn't stop until they reached the lobby. Awful antiseptic hospital smells assaulted more memories out of her, dragging her back through time. Vikram's hand cupped her elbow and pulled her back to the present.

They found Jen and Nikhil in the waiting room. Nikhil took one look at her and wrapped his arms around her. "It's just a muscle pull, drama queen. Relax."

"You're sure?" Ria asked, studying his face.

"No, it's a random guess. Of course I'm sure. Ten years of med school, remember?"

Relief washed through her, and she pressed her face into Nikhil's shoulder and refused to cry. "Where is she?"

"They're getting some final vitals on her. Dad, Matt, and Mindy are in there with her. We were waiting out here for you. Seriously, stop looking like that. They didn't even do an EKG. Dad just brought her in because it was the left arm—and because she's been so stressed out. I shouldn't even have called you."

"Are you crazy, Nikhil? I'll kill you if you ever hide something like this from me." She glared at him.

"Okay, then I promise to call you every time anyone we know pulls a muscle."

Nikhil was right, Uma Atya was fine. So fine in fact that she couldn't stop biting Vijay Kaka's head off about having forced her to come to the hospital.

"What kind of doctor are you," she kept saying, "if you can't even tell the difference between a pulled muscle and a heart attack?"

"No one can tell the difference, Aie. That's why it's so dangerous," Nikhil said in his best physician voice.

Uma slapped his arm. "There is no need to defend your father.

He just wasted an entire day on golf and the hospital—six days before the wedding!"

"It's Vijay, Uma," Vikram said. "Sounds like his dream day."

And, because it was Vikram who said it, Uma smiled.

Nikhil and Jen had a few more errands left to run before they all met up for dinner at one of the auntie's homes. Matt and Mindy left to drive to the city to meet Mindy's sister.

As Vijay and Uma went through the long, drawn-out checkout procedure, Vikram and Ria waited for them in the waiting area. It was huge, but it made Ria claustrophobic. The restless worried faces closed around her. Now that she knew Uma was fine, all she wanted was to get out of the hospital.

Vikram stood. "Let's go wait outside, get some fresh air."

Wordlessly, she followed him through the revolving doors. The early evening chill hit her face like a splash of cool water, and she soaked it in.

Vikram pointed to a bench in the small garden across from the patient drop-off area and they walked toward it. "You sure you're okay?" he asked for what seemed like the hundredth time that day. She reminded herself that he was just being civil, just like he had promised. Nothing more.

"I'm fine. It's just that I hate hospitals. They make me so bloody uncomfortable," she said without thinking. If she wasn't careful all the memories crowding her head would come spilling out.

"Yeah, me too."

She stumbled and looked up at him. It was the oddest thing for him to say. "What are you talking about? How can you not like hospitals?"

"Oh, I hate them. They completely freak me out. I can't believe I ever wanted to be a doctor."

The entire behemoth hospital complex spun behind him and kept on spinning. Blood drained from her face, her limbs, her feet.

It took Vikram a moment to notice she'd stopped. He turned around, his eyebrows drawn together as he took in the expression on her face. One muscle at a time, understanding dawned on him.

"You didn't know?" His lips moved, but the din in Ria's ears was so loud it made the words soundless.

She watched the pieces click in his head. Her own head had gone completely blank, like the buzzing white light on a malfunctioning screen. Blank.

Blank.

Blank.

"You didn't know," he said again. The words formed this time. He pressed his fingers into his forehead, hiding eyes that had turned stone cold. "Of course, you didn't know."

She brought her hands to her cheeks. They were on fire. Her throat was on fire. "But you—Oh God, Vikram, that can't be. How could you—"

"How could I what?" His voice was still so soft she could barely hear him. But it sliced through her like a scream. "How could I what, Ria? How could I not go on like nothing happened? Like everything was normal?"

All the gentleness, all the warmth from before drained from his body. "Did you really believe that? That everything just went on as before? Back to life. Back to business as usual?" A mirthless laugh burst from him. "Is that how it worked for you? New day, new dream?" Patterns of pain, raw and immutable, swirled in the blue gray of his eyes.

*I'll never have a chance like this again, Viky. It's like a dream come true. How can you get in my way?* That's what she had said to him after Ved's bodyguards had tossed him on the pavement. This was exactly how his eyes had looked then.

It had been the only way she knew to make him go away. To force him to leave her so he could live the life he was supposed to live.

*Vic is destined for greatness.* In that one thing she had agreed with Chitra Jathar. And she thought she had given that to him no matter the price.

Only he hadn't gone back to that life.

She pressed her hands into her cheeks. It couldn't be true. He had worked so hard to make it to med school, it had been all he'd ever talked about doing.

"You loved medicine. How could you have—"

"Quit? Oh, it was easy. I just couldn't go back. It wasn't what I wanted anymore."

How could he say that? How could a dream just have disappeared like that?

And yet she had expected him to let the dreams he'd shared with her disappear, without giving him a choice.

Not that she herself had had a choice. Not that she had one now.

"Why?" But she already knew the answer.

The streetlamp glowed behind him like a halo, casting his face in shadows. "Because I wasn't that guy anymore. The one who thought he knew everything. The one who had his entire life planned out. He—he died when you left him. I couldn't go back to his life."

Her tears blurred his beautiful face. "Where did you go?" she whispered. This was what Uma had been talking about that day at breakfast. This is what Nikhil had meant about him disappearing into thin air. And she had blocked it out.

He looked at her tears and his face softened. He dug his hands into his pockets. "Everywhere. Anywhere. Where no one knew me. I had just been to Brazil, so I went back there first. But I had to keep moving. Brazil, Peru, Columbia, all the way up to Costa Rica. Anywhere I could get by, get high. Anywhere I could find work that stopped my brain from working. Construction sites mostly, but oil rigs, fields, factories. You name it."

Horrible, distorted images formed in Ria's mind. Vikram, who cherished family, who basked in their love more than anyone she knew, all alone. Vikram, who had known nothing but privilege, punishing his body with labor. She thought of all the awful things she herself had done. Things that made her skin crawl. And it had all been worthless. Tears choked her. She couldn't swallow, couldn't breathe.

He watched her cry, his body inches from hers. All of him absorbing her pain. A heart-wrenching moment of complete understanding passed between them. *Oneness.*

Finally he moved, wiping the tears off her cheek. "You know what finally brought me back? I was in Lima at a restaurant getting hammered after work. There was an Indian family there on vacation. They had a magazine with you on the cover. It was the first time I had seen you in five years.

"You were dressed like a bride, draped in these shimmering clothes, decked out in jewels, your eyes lowered, your cheeks blushing. 'Bollywood's Favorite Bride,' they called you. There was something about your face, the way you were looking away from the camera, something about that picture, it made me so mad I wanted to kill someone. I got in a fight. I got beaten so bad that day that the guy I worked for freaked out and called Nikhil. He was in Africa. He flew all the way from the other side of the world to get me. He brought me home and knocked some sense into my head."

"He never told me." Her words were sandpaper in her throat, his fingers silk on her cheek. "How could he not have told me?"

"He's never told anyone. Not Uma, not Vijay, not my parents. I don't think Jen knows either. I never gave him any details. He never asked. That was our deal. It was the only way I agreed to come back home and stay. Like everyone else, he probably thinks I was in Brazil living with a woman I met there. They thought I was having my rich brat identity crisis, trying to find myself. Which I was, come to think of it." A sardonic smile touched his lips and pain twisted Ria's heart. She wanted to grab his fingers and hold them to her cheek. Instead, she pressed her fist into her chest to keep from doing it.

"I'm sorry." It was the most insufficient thing to say. But she was sorry, so very sorry.

For a long while he didn't respond. Emotions sparked in his eyes like stars in a cloudless sky, too many to separate and identify. She didn't know when she closed her own eyes, or when his lips moved close enough for his breath to caress hers. Every inch of her body recognized the intimacy and reached for him, waiting for him to close the distance, to take her lips. It had to be the only way to ease the pain, to make sense of the madness. She reached up. It was a whisper of a movement, but he backed away from it as though she had shoved him with all her might.

She stumbled forward into nothingness. Cool air slapped her cheeks where his fingers had been.

He didn't stop until he had put several feet between them. "I don't want your apology, Ria. I don't want your guilt." His chest rose and fell as if he had sprinted a distance. "It wasn't you who ran away. I did that. I hurt the people I love. I put my family through hell. It was me, not you. I had never lost anything, never not got what I wanted. I had no idea how to handle failure."

She wrapped her arms around herself and squeezed her eyes against the pain in his voice. *You didn't fail, Viky. I did. I broke my promise.* All these years her guilt had been a constant burden, but she had carried it knowing it was punishment she deserved. But the punishment he'd taken was so unjust, so wrong, she couldn't bear it.

"Say something, damn it. Don't just stand there and look at me like that."

The raw pain in his voice reached into her and demanded words she could never say. "I'm sorr—"

"No. I said I don't want your guilt and I don't want your pity either."

"Then what do you want, Vikram?"

"I don't know." He raked his fingers through his hair. But he took a step closer and his eyes couldn't follow through on the lie.

She wanted to go to him, wrap him in her arms, disappear into him. But she stepped back, because how could she take any more from him?

He looked like she had slapped him.

He dug his hands into his pockets again, his jaw working, and let out a breath. "All I know is that we have to get through this. Nothing else matters until the wedding. Jen and Nic need us and they deserve to enjoy their wedding without having to worry about us."

"I know that," she said softly. "That's what I want too. I just want to be here for Jen and Nikhil and then I'll leave."

"Good," he said gently. "Because Nikhil can't seem to do anything without you anymore." A small lopsided smile quirked his mismatched lips. "He asked you to stay away from me, didn't he?"

She wiped her cheeks with her sleeve and smiled back. "My talons seem to be making everyone nervous these days."

His eyes got serious again and so intense they engulfed her. "Can you blame us? Any man would be a fool not to be nervous around you, Ria."

# 16

"It's completely preposterous, Uma Atya!" Ria couldn't believe that her aunt wanted to drive straight to a dinner party from the hospital. They had been doing the rounds of pre-wedding dinners with the Auntie Brigade for the past few nights, as was tradition. Every evening Uma told them where to go and they got in the car and went, much like they had done when they were kids. After Ria started to spend her summers here, Uma had taken summers off from her job as mathematics professor at the College of DuPage. And she had driven them to every obscure museum, park, and theater in the greater Chicago area, always a tornado of energy.

Now she looked so exhausted Ria wanted to bodily push her into a bed. "You were just in the hospital, for heaven's sake. Why can't we cancel and just go home?"

Uma patted her cheek. "Says the girl who gave me such a hard time for not letting her gallivant around town after she knocked herself out cold for two days."

"But I listened to you and stayed off my feet. I didn't even go to Jen's bachelorette party." Actually she had used Uma as an excuse to not go because Mira had organized the whole thing and she'd become extremely uncomfortable around Ria. "Why can't you listen? Please. What if your arm starts hurting again?"

"Do you know how many doctors will be in that house? Nothing can possibly happen to me that won't immediately be pounced upon," Uma said firmly, and that was that.

After seeing Uma in a hospital, learning that she was fine should have been a huge relief, but Ria felt too unhinged by everything that had happened that day to feel anything but worry. Her mind wouldn't stop latching on to darkness, unable to trust any glimmer of brightness.

It was paranoia and it was part of her special gift of depression, along with sadness and fear. Vikram was right to be nervous. And he didn't even know how right he was. Her own nervousness was an inferno in her gut.

"Which auntieji is it going to be today, Uma?" Vikram said, and Ria caught the cheeky grin he gave Uma in the rearview mirror. How could he be so undisturbed after what he'd told her? But his life hadn't just flown off the rails. It was just that she had only now found out about it.

"Today's Friday, right?" Uma slapped her head. "I'm having a senior moment. Oh, of course, it's at Priya's house. And I told her we're coming straight there." She leaned back in her seat laughing at herself and Vikram, and Vijay laughed too.

Their levity fanned Ria's nervousness. There was too much she didn't know, even more she couldn't control.

She met Vikram's eyes in the mirror. His calm gaze was like ice and warmth, the two best remedies for pain, and it kicked dirt on the disasters of the past against all good sense. *Relax. Everything's going to be okay*, it said. *I'm fine*, it said.

She shook her head at him, negating his silent claims. *No. Nothing's going to be okay.*

Priya Auntie lived in the same wooded neighborhood in Naperville as Uma and Vijay. Vikram pulled into the driveway and jogged over to open the door for Uma, who winced while undoing her seatbelt. "Ria's right, Uma. Maybe we should have gone home," he said, frowning at her.

"You two need to stop mothering me. Now get out of my way, child, and let me get out of the car. We're already late." She patted his face.

He caught Ria's worried frown and suddenly his eyes sparkled.

"Well then, the least you can do is stay off your feet." He reached over to lift Uma out of the seat. "I think we can arrange a ride."

Uma yelped and smacked Vikram's hand away. "This aunt of yours isn't that old yet, and we don't need to go back to the ER when you break your back."

Vikram groaned. "Great. That sounded too much like a challenge. Now I'm going to have to do it."

"Vikram Jathar, don't you dare!" But he had already scooped her up in his arms. She squealed and grabbed his ear as he lifted her out of the car and carried her down the path. "Put me down, right now!" She twisted his ear with one hand and started slapping his arm with the other.

"Don't make me drop you," he said, laughing.

Vijay jogged past them and held the door open and gave Uma a gallant bow when she screamed for help.

"Someone order a stubborn aunt?" Vikram strode through the house. Nikhil, Jen, and the entire Auntie Brigade and their broods rushed in to see what the commotion was about.

As soon as Vikram put Uma on the couch he ran for it, grabbing a little boy from the laughing crowd and holding him up like a shield when she came after him.

"Vikram, you brat, just you wait until I get my hands on you!" Uma tried to catch her breath, glower at him, and reach around the child he was holding up, but she was laughing so hard she fell back on the couch.

Vikram turned the boy around and kissed him on the forehead. "Thanks, Rahul. I think you saved my life." He was about to put the boy down when the boy grabbed Vikram around the neck.

"Rahul stay on Vic Bhaiya lap."

Vikram groaned. "Rahul break Vic Bhaiya back." But he tucked the boy to his side and smiled when Uma rolled her eyes at him.

"Rahul want Vic Bhaiya to steal Gulab Jamuns like last time. I know where Naani hid them."

Vikram pushed one finger to his mouth. "Shh. Vic Bhaiya get in big trouble if Rahul's *naani* finds out." He threw one surreptitious glance around the room and took a giggling Rahul into the kitchen.

Ria laughed, but her heart ached so much it made an awful mess inside her. She sank down on the couch next to Uma, who was definitely laughing. The aunties, who were all dressed in black today—some in saris, some in *salwar kameezes*—goaded Uma to go up and change into something of Priya's so she was wearing black too.

Uma followed Priya up the stairs and Ria went with them.

"You're not off your feet, Uma Atya," Ria scolded. Although she had to admit that Uma Atya definitely had her usual glow back, and Ria couldn't quite conjure up the level of panic she had felt before.

"Neither are you, *beta*," Uma scolded back. "Mine was a false alarm, you really did hurt yourself."

Ria had completely forgotten about her knee. But she shamelessly milked it when it was time to dance. The aunties claimed that the party was technically part of the wedding celebrations, so of course there had to be dancing. Not that they needed an excuse to dance. "Dancing is the real plastic surgery," Uma loved to say. "It's what keeps you young."

One of the uncles had compiled a playlist of the latest Bollywood party music. After another outrageously elaborate dinner, the rug in the living room was rolled up and propped against a wall and the floor pulsed with hip shaking *thumkas*, shoulder-bobbing bhangras, and shouts of *Oye! Oye!*

"Oh, look, our Vic is without his cute girlfriend today," Sita said as the aunties watched Vikram enter the room.

"She's hardly his girlfriend," Uma snapped. "They've barely known each other for a month." Ria took a page out of Vikram's book and picked at the label on her bottle of water.

"*Arrey,* so what? Every relationship starts somewhere," Radha said in a placating tone. The aunties exchanged glances.

"Please don't call it a relationship," Uma said. "Vijay had to chase me for a good two years before he got to call me his anything." How had Ria never noticed how Uma Atya felt about Mira?

"And what about Nic? He knew Jen for just a month before you were ready to print out wedding cards." Trust Anu Auntie not to mince her words.

Uma cut Anu a sharp glance. "It was more than a month, but look at Jen and Nic. Who can't see the match there?"

Sita patted Uma's arm. "We all agree on that. Jen and Nic are perfect together. But come on, Uma, calm down and let the kids have some fun."

"And us too," Anu said as Vikram walked up and they surrounded him, leaving Ria sitting cross-legged on the couch.

"Look at you! Getting more and more handsome every day!" Priya pinched his cheeks and winked.

Anu pulled him to the dance floor just as a new song started. "*Chalo*, today you get to dance with your old aunties!"

He spun around, scanning the room. "What old aunties?" he said, and they all giggled like little girls.

"That boy!" Uma shook her head at Ria. "How did a witch like Chitra ever produce a child like that?"

Ria had asked herself that question only about a million times. She mirrored Uma's eye roll before Uma went off to join them.

On the dance floor, Vikram grinned his most disarming grin and picked up the beat as the aunties made a circle around him and started dancing.

"Look at the boy move," one of them said, not that Ria could stop looking. His body moved in perfect rhythm to the music and he easily matched it to the auntie he turned to. He danced with all of them at once and then with each one of them in turn, twirling them and dipping them. He even lifted Anu up in his arms and spun her around as the music reached a crescendo.

"Just for that," she said, blushing in the most un-Anu-like fashion, "all my working out has been worth it."

He was gallant and generous and so irresistibly charming that each one of them preened and glowed, and Ria found her heart so full it hurt beneath her hand. No matter how hard she tried she couldn't keep her eyes off him. Her heart did a skip every time she stole a glance at him and then skipped a beat every time he caught her doing it. Finally, she peeled herself off the couch and left the room to keep from making a complete fool of herself. But then Vikram and Nikhil broke into one of their break-dance routines and Uma pulled her back into the room.

"Come, come," she said, "the boys are doing that walking on the moon thing."

They had done this at every party when they were kids. They always did the worst moonwalks, but today they were so bad Ria laughed until her stomach hurt, and even when Vikram caught her laughing, she couldn't stop. And instead of turning away he hammed it up and made her laugh even more.

Much later, when the entire crowded dance floor was jumping up and down to the latest Bollywood hit, Nikhil hopped over to her, doing some sort of one-legged step that looked like he was being electrocuted, and dropped down on his knees in front of her. "I'm sorry," he shouted over the music, "I was an insensitive ass." He joined his hands together. "Please forgive me."

"How much has he had to drink?" Ria asked Jen in a stage whisper.

"Enough to make a perfect fool of himself and not care at all," Jen stage-whispered back.

Nikhil scooped Ria up in his arms and carried her to the middle of the dance floor, jumping up and down with such gusto, fresh laughter spilled from her.

"The best sister in the world," Nikhil shouted over the thumping music, and she threw out her arms as he spun her around.

Someone up there must time the joy she was allowed because Ria's phone buzzed in her pocket like an alarm signaling her to come back to earth. She gave Nikhil a hug and ran into the relative quiet of the kitchen. Vikram was already there, holding his own phone to his ear.

"Hi, Mira," she heard him say just as she said, "Hi, Big," and they turned away from each other and moved to opposite ends of the room.

"I thought you promised to be careful?" DJ fumed without so much as a hi, and Ria slipped into the backyard, pulling the French doors shut behind her.

Somehow the fact that Ria was in Chicago had leaked to the media and speculation about what she was doing here ran rampant across the Internet, ranging from a new secret foreign film project to a hush-hush elopement and everything in between. It wasn't anything they hadn't seen before.

Ria leaned against the deck railing and watched Vikram pace inside the kitchen with the phone pressed to his ear.

"Calm down, DJ. What happened to 'there's no such thing as bad publicity?' "

"Don't be purposefully dense, Ria. I'm thrilled you're all over the Internet. But why do I have this awful feeling you're going to be your usual stubborn self about security?"

"It's out of the question, Big." There was no way she was letting him use this to get some stranger to tag along with her. She had just six days left to be someone who didn't need a bodyguard to leave the house, and she wasn't letting this ruin it. "I swear there's no chance of me going to any public place in the next week. There's just too much to be done at home. I don't have the time to go gallivanting around town."

Inside, Vikram stopped pacing and rubbed his forehead.

On the phone, DJ's voice deepened. "Ria, we have a blackmailer holding pictures of an attempted suicide over our heads. We don't need any nasty incidents in America to add to this and increase the selling price of his pictures. You know the media. If one story takes up the public's imagination they'll go all out to dig up more stories."

Vikram looked at her, and what he saw on her face made his eyebrows draw together in concern. She turned away and faced the backyard and gripped the deck railing. "I thought you took care of the blackmailer."

DJ hesitated. DJ never hesitated. "Don't panic, but someone's been asking questions, trying to dig up information about your past."

"And when were you planning to tell me this?"

"Babes, I'm handling it." He took an uncharacteristically hesitant pause. "There's another little problem. But I don't want you to worry."

Ria dropped into a deck chair. When Big DJ told you not to worry, it was time to worry.

"Ved Kapoor—you know how publicity hungry he's been since he stopped getting roles. Seems like he's enjoying reminiscing about his past conquests with the press these days."

Ria thought she was going to throw up. And not because the mention of Ved's name always did that to her, but because of how proud of her Uma had looked the other day.

"Please tell me he hasn't mentioned me." Ved was the one who had referred Ria to DJ when DJ had been a young upstart, so he knew about Ved and her.

"Not yet. But if anything else puts you in the papers, you'll become irresistible as a publicity vehicle for him. So please listen to me about the damn bodyguard. There's too many whackos out there."

She got up and paced the deck. Inside Vikram shoved the phone in his pocket and stormed out of the kitchen without looking at her.

"Nothing's going to happen to me, DJ. I'm really safe here. My uncle and aunt literally know every Indian within a two-hundred-kilometer radius. The Indians here don't even notice me. I am not getting a bodyguard, but you need to make sure the blackmailer stays down."

"I'm already doing that," DJ said. "Can you at least promise me you'll be careful?"

"Of course I will. I'm always careful," she said, watching the big red truck speed down the street and vanish into the night.

# 17

When she'd spoken to DJ last night, Ria had fully intended not to leave the house except to go to one of the auntie's homes. But that was before the shipment of Nikhil's wedding clothes that she'd ordered before leaving Mumbai was lost and Uma and Jen or the "Stressed-Out Twins," as Nikhil and Vikram had taken to calling them, had twin coronaries.

Fortunately, Anu Auntie in all her resourcefulness recommended an Indian men's boutique on Devon Avenue and just like that Ria found herself in the back of Uma's sixteen-year-old Town and Country watching Nikhil and Vikram on the driveway argue about who would be "caught dead" driving the mommy mobile.

Jen wasn't going with them. After the altar burned down, and the shipment got lost, Uma, who wasn't usually superstitious, didn't want to take any chances with any more bad omens. She had suggested, in a gentle tone she reserved only for Jen these days, that the bride choosing the groom's wedding clothes could be considered bad luck.

Vikram was going with them because his plan to wear a suit to the wedding was shot down by the Stressed-Out Twins so vehemently that even he knew better than to try and talk his way out of it. Mira was going to meet them at the store and Ria tried to think of a way to put the girl at ease and convince her that Ria was not a threat to her.

Nikhil was back to being his old self again. Anything on the mile-long to-do list made him instantly serious, but the rest of the time he seemed to be walking on clouds, dizzy with happiness. Ria kept expecting him to break into a skip over everything. A spotlight followed him everywhere he went, and it helped Ria focus on what mattered and not on the frown slashed across Vikram's forehead.

Finally, Nikhil bowed to the bad mood Vikram was sporting and took the wheel.

"It's good practice for when you and Jen make babies," Vikram said, still talking about the car and sliding his seat all the way to the back to fit his long legs.

"Oh, we both know who is going to need a minivan to stuff all their kids into. The way you suck up to all the neighborhood kids, I don't think I'm the one going for Daddy of the Year."

Vikram grinned from ear to ear, his bad mood melting away. "They're a great bunch of kids. Did you know they're on V-learn? Josh said he aced a test on simultaneous equations with it. Isn't that something?"

Nikhil high-fived him and backed the car onto the street.

*V-learn.* The word had stuck in Ria's head from the day she had spied on Vikram playing soccer with the kids. It had put the same buoyant look on his face that day that he wore now.

"What's V-learn?" she asked.

Vikram turned to her. "It's just this thing I'm working on."

"This 'thing he's working on' might revolutionize education across the world," Nikhil said.

Vikram shrugged, but his eyes did that thing they did when something was taking up all his attention. "I used to tutor some kids in Brazil and I promised to keep doing it after I left. So I started creating these videos and putting them online for them to watch. And they loved it so much they started sharing the videos with other kids." He scratched the back of his head sheepishly, but his eyes shone like bright lights.

"And then Vic went all Vic on it and kept adding and adding videos. And now he's got all these venture capitalists clamoring for it. And he won't get off his high horse and take help."

Vikram crossed his arms across his chest. "It's still not where I want it to be. And I don't want investors messing with it yet."

"Vic, you get a million hits a day. You have over ten thousand videos on there. It's being used on every continent. Dude, VCs will give you all the control you want. Plus Chitra Atya is begging to fund it. Especially with the piece you're working on with Drew."

"So, I'm working with Ma on it. I'd much rather do it with her anyway. Plus, I have other stuff going on right now."

"What kind of other stuff?" Ria was at the edge of her seat. Since when had Vikram become so laid-back about things? The Vikram she knew went hurtling at things with no brakes, no caution.

For a moment he looked like he was going to ask her to mind her own business, but then he shrugged. "Shopping trips with my wimpy cousin who can't tell his fiancée that he wants to wear a suit to his own wedding."

Nikhil made an obscene gesture at him.

Vikram steered the conversation toward the weather, the stock market, the price of plane tickets, whatever he could think of. Ria stayed at the edge of her seat, angry at herself for how badly she wanted to know more about the thing that could put that light in his eyes. Even angrier at him for all that loose-limbed indifference, sitting on him like a stolen coat.

By the time the slightly wretched neighborhoods around Devon Avenue came into view, Ria was happier than she had ever been to see the colorful storefronts. She needed to get out of the car. This part of Devon Avenue was Chicago's biggest Indian shopping district. It was not one of Ria's fonder memories of Chicago. Uma had dragged her there to buy the more obscure Indian groceries that weren't available at the local Indian store, but Ria hadn't liked going. She hadn't liked the sights or the smells or the oily, disconnected shopkeepers. She had found everything about it disconcertingly foreign. It was neither American like the rest of the city nor Indian like the bazaars back home, but some sort of mismatched mash of the two.

From the polythene-wrapped grain to the candy boxes stacked

on metal racks, everything had seemed somehow out of place. The plastic Indianness of Devon had accomplished what nothing else ever did. It had made Ria miss India. Made her miss the noisy market streets, where lentils and grain sat in jute gunny sacks on worn wooden shelves, where grocers scooped the grain with brass measures and folded it into newspaper packages with the deftness of origami artists.

Today the multi-aisled grocery stores on Devon didn't look that different from the supermarkets that had sprung up all over Mumbai, except that the ones here were less glitzy and busy. Here the world seemed to have frozen in time, suspended in the exact same state she had left it ten years ago. Even the movie posters sharing space with the pictures of ornament-laden gods and goddesses on stark white walls seemed outdated by at least a decade.

Ria pushed her giant sunglasses in place, wrapped the turquoise scarf around her head, and followed Nikhil and Vikram past the grimy display windows. Fluorescent Sale signs festooned everything from mannequins in beaded saris to bushels of potatoes. A mix of techno beats and bhangra music spilled out of open doors, and the smell of frying dough hung heavy in the air.

A few people stopped and stared, and panic prickled up and down Ria's spine. She kicked herself for not having remembered to ask Nikhil to drop her off before parking. She stepped closer to Nikhil and sped up. Vikram took one look at her and flanked her on the other side, his big body making a better shield than Nikhil's lean and lanky frame, and relaxing her in ways she didn't want to acknowledge.

A woman pushing a baby carriage reached into her pocket and pulled out a cell phone. Ria pulled the scarf lower on her head and dug her face into her denim jacket, and ran straight into Vikram, who had stopped in his tracks next to Nikhil. Neither one of them noticed the gathering crowd, too busy gaping at a neon store sign looming over the storefront.

*KOMAL . . . INDIAN STYLE FOR THE MACHO INDIAN MAN.*

Nikhil turned to Ria. "I swear if you say one word I'll kill you." A tone of such cold warning colored his voice that despite the panic that had flooded through her a second ago, Ria almost burst out laughing.

She grabbed his sleeve and dragged him into the store. "Time to get you dolled up, macho man."

The store was lit like a spa. Gentle sitar music floated out of discreetly hidden speakers. The lounge-y boutique atmosphere contrasted so starkly with the rest of the neighborhood that the three of them actually blinked in unison to adjust to it. Wooden elephants in every size stood on pedestals, brushed chrome shelves stacked with neatly folded *kurtas*, silk shirts and *churidar* pants lined the walls. *Sherwanis* of heavy brocade hung from rods suspended by metal wires from the high ceiling, creating meticulously coordinated rainbows of color sprinkled with flecks of gold, silver, and copper.

One of the shelves was lined with pre-tied turbans in shades of red and gold. If Nikhil had looked horrified before, the sight of the turbans made him look like he was going to have a stroke right there in the store. Vikram put a hand on his shoulder either to give him strength or to draw some for himself.

Ria smiled. They gave her looks of such loathing she should have wilted.

"Oh, come on! You fix dying children for a living, for God's sake, Nikhil. Stop acting like you've entered a war zone."

Both Nikhil and Vikram opened their mouths like goldfish and then closed them again. She walked up to a rack of *sherwanis,* filed through the ornate suits, and pulled out a maroon one with gold threadwork. "They're clothes, they won't bite." She held up the garment against Nikhil. Both he and Vikram stepped back horrified.

"You're not serious," Nikhil said.

"You are here to buy yourself a *sherwani* for the wedding, aren't you?"

"But that's red."

"It's maroon. Actually, more burgundy."

Both men looked at her as if she had sprouted a trunk and two tusks like the elephant next to her. She rolled her eyes, went back to the rack, and found a cream one with muted bronze embroidery.

"That's golden," Nikhil said, his voice straight out of his whiny brat phase at age ten.

She wanted to smack him. "No, it's cream with bronze work."

"That makes it golden."

She looked at Vikram for help, but it was clear where his sympathies lay.

"You're not shopping for a tuxedo, Nikhil. You're shopping for a *sherwani*. There's going to be color."

He didn't respond, and she started to lose her patience. She took a deep breath. No point her acting like a child too. "If you are more comfortable in a tux, why don't you just tell Jen that?" She threw a pleading look to stop Vikram, but he went right ahead and mumbled the word *whipped* under his breath.

Nikhil gave an incoherent growl and turned on Vikram. "Why don't we do Vic first," he said, as though what they were doing involved jumping in front of speeding trains.

Vikram scampered back and almost toppled over the rack of silver *kurtas* behind him. Nikhil strode to the brightest rack, pulled out a blue *sherwani* with a profusion of maroon embroidery, and held it up against Vikram. "Perfect. The *aqua* goes so well with your eyes." He did his best imitation of Ria.

Vikram's eyes narrowed to angry slits. His gaze darted desperately around the store and perked right up when it landed on the turbans. He lifted a bright red turban edged in gold and thrust it on Nikhil's head. "You need one of these too, don't you?"

Nikhil was about to yank it off when a small birdlike man dressed in an over-starched silk shirt rushed up to them. "Welcome to Komal," he said, struggling to conceal his irritation behind the stiffest salesperson smile. "Can I help you find something?" He took the *sherwani* out of Nikhil's hands with exaggerated care and threw a pointed look at the turban sitting askew atop his head.

Nikhil handed the turban over and tried to look dignified. Vikram looked very pleased with himself. Ria suppressed the urge to slam their heads together.

The man walked over to the shelves and put the turban and the *sherwani* away, making a point of demonstrating how these precious garments deserved to be handled. He turned around and addressed them in his best authoritative voice. "Is there a special occasion you are—" His mouth fell open mid-sentence and his eyes went round and dopey.

Vikram and Nikhil followed his gaze and found him staring at Ria as though she were some sort of celestial being who had sauntered into his store and was blinding him with her brightness.

Ria threw a warning glance at the two of them and gave the man one of her perfectly dimpled smiles. Automatically her stance changed. Her back got straighter, her chin higher. She slipped into celebrity mode.

"Oh God! Are you—? You look just like—are you—" His body went slack with something akin to servitude, and he smiled like one dumbfounded by his own incredible luck.

Vikram groaned. "You've got to be kidding me."

Ria forced herself not to look at him.

"I'm your biggest fan," the salesman said, taking a step closer to her. "I've seen every one of your movies. Right from *Oh Honey*!"

"Thank you. That's very sweet," Ria said, her smile firmly in place.

"It is such an honor to have you in our store. We are the best Indian clothing store in North America. We can get you absolutely anything you want. One hundred percent *hot cootoor*. It's such an honor. Such a great honor."

"Oh for God's sake." Vikram glowered at the man, who looked at him, confused.

"My cousin is getting married," Ria said gently. "We need some *sherwanis* and *kurtas*. Off the shelf should be fine."

"Congratulations! What wonderful news!" He turned to Vikram. "Congratulations, sir. You have any color preference?"

Vikram looked at him like he was going to wring his neck. "He's the one getting married." He jabbed a thumb in Nikhil's direction. Nikhil raised his hand like a schoolboy.

"So sorry. My apologies. Do you have any color preference, sir?" The man asked Nikhil.

"He likes burgundy," Vikram mumbled.

The man turned back to him, even more confused.

Ria flashed Vikram a glare. "Actually, they both need something. We are looking for something understated. Cream or beige with *zardozi* work, preferably antique, would be perfect."

The salesman's eyes widened with awe. He looked like he was going to fall at Ria's feet and kiss her shoes. She ran her fingers over some ornate cream *sherwanis*. "Something like this."

His eyes bulged with reverence and Ria withdrew her fingers self-consciously.

Vikram stepped between them and cleared his throat.

The man started and scampered away from Vikram. "No, no." He waved away the shelf Ria was looking at. "Forget about these. I have the perfect thing for you. A new shipment just came in. We haven't even put it out on the floor yet. Let me get it out for you." He started to rush off, then turned back. "Feel free to look at anything. Think of this as your own store. Can I get you something to drink? Anything. Some cold drink? Chai? Coffee?"

"A glass of water would be nice," Ria said quickly before Vikram or Nikhil could respond.

"Only water? We have Vitamin Water also. And Smart Water. I can order mango *lassi*." He took a step closer to Ria. "Anything you want."

"We want the *sherwanis*." Vikram cut him off with a scowl that made him take several hurried steps away from Ria.

"Yes, yes, of course, sir. Let me get that for you, sir." He rushed off.

Before Ria could say anything, Vikram turned away and started glaring at the shelves again. His bad mood was back in full force, and Ria tried to temper her own irritation, and turned to Nikhil. He looked a little pale. "You're going to look great, baby. You wear *kurtas*, don't you? *Sherwanis* are just fancy *kurtas*." She hadn't used that tone on him since his whiny brat phase.

"You're right." Nikhil squared his shoulders. "But no maroon." And then quickly added, "No burgundy either."

"Got it. Nothing remotely red. Let's see, Jen's wearing jade—I mean green—so we need something that complements that. "

"Uh. Okay."

"Since reds are out, creams are our best option. This steel gray is really nice. But it won't go with green. Plus, it doesn't have enough work on it."

Vikram turned to her as though she had said magic words. He took the gray *sherwani* from her hand. "You're right, this one isn't half bad."

Nikhil stared at it longingly. "Why can't I have that one?"

"Because you're the groom and you need to look like a peacock to attract your mate." Vikram held up the *sherwani* and studied it through narrowed eyes, chewing his lower lip in concentration. The silver-flecked gray silk was the exact color of his eyes when they got intense.

Ria's hand tightened on the silk-draped hanger she was holding. The thought of him in a *sherwani*, the silk hugging his shoulders and falling down his body, made her lightheaded. Even that black golf shirt and the faded jeans he was sporting today looked like they had been tailored for him. The shoulders exactly wide, the waist exactly narrow. The muscles of his thighs pushing into the well-worn denim of his jeans. She swallowed.

"Why don't you try it on?" She tried to keep her voice light.

Apparently not light enough. His eyes darkened to a deep hungry gray and everything she was feeling stared right back at her.

The hanger she was clutching slipped off the rod and collapsed in a heap on the floor. By the time she retrieved it Vikram was gone.

She helped Nikhil pick out a couple pieces and sent him off to try them on just as the salesman hurried in with a clothes cart filled with such garishly embellished *sherwanis* she was glad Nikhil and Vikram weren't around to see them. The salesperson unhooked two and held them up. One was covered in golden netting and the other one was studded with crystals and pearls. "This is completely exclusive stuff, Ms. Parkar. All the grooms in Mumbai and Delhi are wearing these. Only at the most upscale . . ."

Vikram emerged from the fitting room behind him. The raw silk stretched taut across his shoulders and hugged every plane in his chest. The soft gloss of the fabric picked up the light like the ocean on a moonlit night. His entire body glowed.

The deep gray intensified the gray of his eyes, the way she'd known it would. His disheveled hair fell in spikes across his forehead. She wanted to brush it back, to feel the thick dark locks. He ran slightly unsteady fingers through his hair without taking his eyes off her. A deep, self-conscious breath shuddered out of her. He took a step closer.

The embellished high collar was twisted around his neck. She reached out and unfolded it. His muscles clenched and hardened beneath her fingers. Sparks shot from her fingers to the very center of her belly.

"Ma'am?" The salesman looked at her, his eyes wide with anticipation. He seemed to be waiting for an answer. Ria stared at him blankly. "So, what do you think?" he asked.

She withdrew her hand and pressed it into her stomach. Evidently, she wasn't thinking at all. "I . . . well."

"Isn't it a good idea?"

"Sure." She had no idea what she had just agreed to.

Vikram's eyes stayed glued on her. His gaze burned her skin, moisture gathered at the backs of her knees, in the dents at the base of her spine. She took a step back.

"Oh my God! Aren't you Ritu, from *Ritu and Raj*?" A girl ran up to her. She must've been about thirteen. Her mother followed behind her. They looked at once elated and embarrassed. "Can we have a picture, please? We love you."

Ria brought out the smile, thanked them, and posed mechanically, all the while aware of Vikram's eyes on her. By the time they were gone, he had slipped back behind a mask. He was angry again and she didn't know why. Or maybe she did, but there was nothing she could do about it.

The salesman pointed to Vikram. "So, Ms. Parkar, very nice, no? It fits Sir like it was made for him. Even around shoulders and hips. No need to alter, even. I told you we have the best fits in North America. What do you think?"

Vikram's eyes bored into her.

"Ma'am?"

"She likes it." Vikram's voice was a growl.

The man beamed. "She's right, it's per—"

"Unfortunately, I don't," he said so sharply, she drew back.

"I am sorry about that, sir. Why don't we try one of these?" The man raised the hangers he was holding, looking hopefully at Vikram.

Vikram's voice gentled a notch. "No, I'm sorry. I've changed my mind. I don't think these clothes are for me. I think I'll stick to a suit."

"Like hell you will." Nikhil stepped out of the fitting room in the cream-and-bronze *sherwani*.

Vikram pressed his fingers to his temples. "Come on, dude, look at me. Don't make me do this."

Nikhil picked up a turban and placed it on his own head. Then he pointed at himself with both hands. "Don't make you do this? Look at me."

Vikram looked unmoved. Nikhil glared at him. "Listen, Vic, Jen wants the family to dress Indian and that's what she's getting. You're family, remember?"

"Come on! Don't pull that shit on me," Vikram said.

The salesman looked from one to the other, utter confusion on his face.

Enough was enough. Ria stepped between Vikram and Nikhil. "Are you guys for real?" she snapped, one hand on her hip. "What the hell is wrong with you, Nikhil? This is your wedding. Your *wedding!* And this is your heritage. Jen's not even Indian and she gets it. And here you are. Standing there looking like veritable princes and acting like clowns. Acting like this is some sort of awful punishment. You know what—you should wear suits. Hell, wear jeans, for all I care. I am not standing here and doing this with you for one more minute."

She turned to the salesman. His mouth was hanging open again. Every other customer in the store was staring. When had the store become so crowded? A man in a yellow shirt held up a cell phone. He had probably recorded her entire meltdown. *Bloody hell!*

The man quickly lowered the phone and ran toward the exit, but Vikram pounced on him and snatched the phone out of his hand.

"Give that back." The man scrambled to his feet and lunged for Vikram. This time Nikhil pounced on him and held him back while the salesman danced around making squealing sounds.

Vikram furiously jabbed buttons on the phone. "What is wrong with you, man? Can't you respect a person's privacy?" Once he'd deleted the video, he threw the phone at the guy, who grabbed it and pried himself out of Nikhil's hold.

"If your fucking girlfriend is so precious, bastard, why don't you keep her at home instead of letting her shake her booty at us like a whore?"

Vikram lunged at him again, but he ran to the door, picking up one of the small elephants from a pedestal and flinging it at Vikram as he went. Screams rose from the crowd; people ran helter-skelter. The wooden elephant hit Vikram's temple and thudded to the floor, leaving a gash that started to bleed. The man pushed past the crowd and ran full tilt out the door.

Ria flew at Vikram, pulled off her scarf, and pressed it against his temple. Her hands shook, all of her shook, he was shaking too.

He recovered first. "Shh, Ria, it's okay." He wrapped an arm around her waist and steadied her hand against his forehead. "Sweetheart, I'm fine. Breathe. It's fine." He wiped the tears from her cheeks.

She took a breath, but the shaking only got worse.

"Let me take a look," Nikhil said, but Vikram tightened his grip around Ria.

"Nic, seriously, I'm fine. Bring the car to the service entrance in the back. I'll bring her out in five minutes." His voice was calm. So calm. The steady thud of his heartbeat wrapped itself around her. She focused on it and increased the pressure on his wound. Warm wetness tinged the scarf in her hand, and panic tore through her.

The salesman brought her a first-aid kit. "I'm so sorry, Ms. Parkar, nothing like this has ever happened at Komal. Never," he said sincerely, but Ria couldn't respond.

"We're buying these." Vikram pointed to the *sherwani* he was still wearing and extracted a credit card from his wallet with one hand. His other hand was an unbreakable circle around Ria's waist.

"Yes. Yes. Of course, sir." The salesman took the credit card from Vikram and scampered away.

"But you didn't like it," Ria whispered into Vikram's shoulder, inhaling the scent of him as if it would set the world straight.

For a second he looked like he had no idea what she was talking about, and then he smiled down at her. "It's fine. If you reacted like that, I can only imagine what Uma would do to us if we went home empty-handed. And you can stop pressing that thing into my head now. I think it's stopped bleeding."

Very gingerly Ria lifted the scarf away from his head. "It's called a scarf," she said, and studied the gash. The bleeding had slowed, but it looked angry and swollen and painful.

His fingers touched her chin. The gentlest, softest touch. "Please don't cry. I can't even feel it."

She closed her eyes.

"Why is there a crowd outside?" Ria's eyes flew open at the sound of Mira's voice. She lurched away from Vikram.

Mira stood there gaping at them.

Vikram let Ria pull away from him, but he kept a hand under her elbow. "Someone tried to take a video of Ria and run out of here with it."

Mira pushed a hand into her mouth. "Oh no."

Ria pulled her arm away. "Vikram caught him. But he hurt himself." She pointed at his wound. Mira's eyes widened to saucers.

Ria opened the first-aid kit and held out gauze and tape. Mira pushed it back at her. "No. You do it." Her voice was so sad, Ria's heart twisted.

She pushed it back at Mira. "No. You do it."

Vikram snatched the gauze from Ria's hand and pressed it into his temple. "I can do it myself." It must have hurt, but he was so angry he didn't even wince.

Ria tore a piece of tape and pressed it over the gauze. Vikram refused to look at her. Which was a good thing, because she didn't want him to see the shame she was feeling. Her fingers trembled against the warmth of his skin. He steadied her hand with his.

She pulled her hand away again, but this time he didn't let go as easily.

"Mira, can you take him to the hospital?"

"I don't need a hospital. I need to get you home." By the set of his jaw, Ria knew he would be immovable.

She tried anyway. "I'm fine. I'll wait for Nikhil, you go with Mira."

"Nikhil should already be in the back. And you're not fine, you haven't stopped shaking." He grabbed her hand and led her to the back of the store. "I'll be back in a minute, don't leave," he told Mira.

The service parking lot was empty except for Uma's van. Vikram's hand was a vise around hers as they walked to it, and it made her feel too safe to struggle out of his hold. His palm splayed against the small of her back as she climbed into the car and lingered on her waist before he withdrew it. The contact between them tore like a Band-Aid ripping off sore skin, one cell, one pore, at a time. She sagged against the seat, Vikram looming over her.

"Go, Vikram, please. I'm fine." But she couldn't meet his eyes.

He didn't move. Neither one of them was fine. Neither had been fine for a long time. She was a bloody liar.

"There she is!" Someone shouted from a distance. A mob turned the corner and rushed into the isolated parking lot.

Vikram stepped back and slammed the car door shut. "You got her?" he asked Nikhil.

"Aren't you coming?" Nikhil said.

"Mira's in there. There's something I need to talk to her about." Vikram touched Ria's hand as it clutched the door. She wanted to draw it away, but she couldn't make herself.

And she couldn't look away from the mirror, where his form grew more and more distant as he stood there watching them drive away. Vikram, hurt and bleeding. Her worst fear come true.

# 18

Ria heard another car and rushed to her bedroom window. She pulled back a slit in the curtain and peeked out at the street. It was two in the morning. Light spilled from a solitary lamp at the end of the driveway and painted everything a surreal gray. She had run to the window so many times since coming home from Devon, she was amazed the carpet didn't have a permanent path carved into it. Absently, she rubbed the depressed fibers with her big toe, and watched the car drive by without stopping.

Her laptop sat open on the bed, providing the only light in the room. She had tried to read the blasted script, but she couldn't get the cut slashed into Vikram's skin out of her head. Instead of taking her mind off the metallic stench of blood that clung to her nostrils like rotten molasses, the script had only intensified it. One gruesome death followed another against the backdrop of exploding vehicles and burning buildings. Fire and blood interspersed with more fire and blood.

Another car purred down the street, and Ria inched back the drapes to take another peek. This time the car turned up the driveway and bounced to a halt. The lighted AMERICAN TAXI sign on top flickered. Vikram staggered out of the backseat, his big body almost flying facedown on the concrete.

"You need help, man?" the driver asked from inside the cab.

"Nah, thanks, man. I got it." Was he slurring?

He righted himself and gave the driver a salute before he drove off. He had changed back into his golf shirt and jeans. Light reflected off the tape she had pressed against his temple. Slung over his shoulder was her bloodstained scarf.

He weaved slowly up the path to the house. Suddenly, he stopped and looked up at her window. She jumped back, ducking away from the drapes, and plastered herself against the wall. Oh please, let him not have seen her.

For long seconds she heard nothing more. The only sound was her heart pounding in her ears. She tiptoed to her bedroom door and pressed her ear to the cool wood, straining to listen. Finally the key turned in the front door. It opened with one click, then shut with another. Another long moment of silence followed. Then she heard his footfalls going down the stairs.

Only instead of fading away, the footsteps grew louder.

She pulled away from the door. He wasn't going down the stairs, he was coming up the stairs. *Shit.* She ran to the bed, slammed the laptop shut, and dived under the sheets. In the dead silence, she heard the precise moment when he reached the top of the stairs. She heard every slow deliberate step he took toward her door. She heard the precise moment when his hand touched her doorknob. The softest thud sounded against the door.

Her heart raced in her chest. She tried to relax her grip on the comforter, to even out her breathing. He twisted the doorknob. The tension in the springs coiled inside her belly. She held her breath and waited for the door to open. Every passing second stretched and pulsed in the stillness.

The door didn't move.

Very slowly she heard him release the doorknob. With a whisper of a sound it clicked back in place. Just as softly, she heard him take his hand off the knob and make his way back down the stairs.

She was shaking. But it wasn't relief she felt. It was something else entirely. She tried not to acknowledge it, tried to push it away before her mind articulated the thought. But she couldn't. She had been waiting, praying for the door to open. For a long time, she lay there motionless, the deadening pain in her heart weighing her down into the suddenly cold bed.

She hadn't thought about going crazy in close to a week. The constant noise inside her head asking to count, to check, to stay in control had gone completely silent, and she hadn't even noticed—but now the warm slickness of his blood came alive on her fingers and brought it back. She rolled over and rubbed her fingers into the sheets, but she couldn't wipe it off. The slickness spread up her arm and covered her body and she fell back in time, her body shrinking into tiny breakable arms, into tiny curious feet.

Tiny seven-year-old feet she had used to follow the moans up the creaking stairs all those years ago. It was the moans that had called to Ria. They had been her earliest memory, those animal cries that had echoed through the house and woken her in the middle of the night.

But she'd never gone up those stairs before. She'd known they were forbidden even before Aji had cupped her face in her hands and issued the soft command. *You don't ever go up there, you hear me?*

But a few days before her seventh birthday Aji had died, and Aji's cousin had come to stay the day of her funeral. Ria didn't like Aji's cousin. The moment Baba left the house, the gnarled old lady pushed Ria out of the kitchen. *Stay away from me, you cursed child,* she hissed. *That woman should never have married your father. Never brought her curse into the family. He should have made her spill you before you were born. Now he's stuck with you and your devil's possession.*

*You come from insanity. It's your destiny. As if hiding it in an attic will make it go away.*

Then she lit an oil lamp in the altar and walked it around the kitchen to get rid of Ria's cursed presence as Ria watched her through the slit in the door.

Suddenly the strangeness of her life made sense to Ria—why Baba never sent her to school or let her play with the kids down the lane, why the neighbors disappeared like raindrops on gravel when Baba and she walked past them to the market. Why her gentle father turned dark and menacing if anyone so much as approached their wooden gate.

She stared up at the green painted attic door with its huge brass latch and threw one last look over her shoulder.

*You don't ever go up there, you hear me?*

Did you have to keep your promises to dead people?

She reached up and grabbed the massive latch with both hands. She could just about reach it, and it took all her strength to drag it back and forth until the door swung open. And she staggered into the room.

The animal grunts hit her first. Matted hair and tattered cloth flew at her and knocked her flat and straddled her body. Spittle sprayed Ria's face. Wild eyes darted all over the room. Ria shoved at the creature, trying to get away, and it sprang off her, struggling with its bound wrists, moaning and grunting. Ria scooted back on her elbows, tried to scream, but it lunged at her again before the sound made it out.

Teeth sank into flesh. Razors pierced Ria's skin, crunched against bone. Wetness slithered down her body. The grunting moans grew to a fevered pitch. Something hard and heavy crashed into Ria's head. Pain exploded in her ribs, something tore inside her belly. Hands lifted her, threw her against a wall. Blood filled her mouth and pooled under her on the cold cement floor. Fingers grabbed her throat, shaking her and squeezing and squeezing. She struggled to keep her eyes open, but warm liquid dripped onto her lids.

Baba rose from the red haze. He lifted the creature off her. He was sobbing. His eyes ablaze with anger, but his hands gentle on the thrashing creature in his arms. "Shh, please, it's just Ria. It's our daughter."

Blood dripped in rivulets from the creature's teeth. Her eyes bulged with confusion, pleading with Ria, wanting something.

Darkness wrapped around Ria, fading the face from view. But not before she'd seen the widow's peak on the wide forehead, seen the bottle-brown eyes, and felt the shock of knowing that looking at the creature was exactly like looking in a mirror.

Ria sat up in bed, the pain in her seven-year-old body swelling to fill her adult form, the insanity inside her clawing like a beast. She rubbed her skin. All the near-invisible scars carved into her body throbbed to life. Tattoos commemorating her one and only encounter with the monster who had brought her into this world. Indelible brands of what she was destined to become.

She stepped off the bed and slipped into her kimono and slippers. She had to get out of her room.

*It's your destiny.* She would never let herself forget again.

*You come from Insanity.* Vikram's mother had repeated those words a decade later, the terror of what Ria could do to her son making each word a trembling whisper. *You. Come. From. Insanity.* As if Insanity were a planet from where ticking time bombs were launched onto Earth, where they ultimately detonated into madness.

*It's genetic. All the women in your family have had it. Why would it stop at you? Why?*

It wouldn't. Ria had been stupid enough to forget once. The mistake had destroyed her life and almost destroyed Vikram's. Almost.

There was only one place to go. Only one place that could drag her back into the present. She slipped out of the kitchen onto the deck and let her feet take her to the oak. The canopy was tinged with yellow. The early-morning light caught each yellowing leaf and turned it into gold. An intense urge to capture it with brushstrokes, to wrap it in paint, overwhelmed her. But the last thing she needed was another way to draw out the crazies.

She wrapped her arms around herself and leaned her back into the trunk. Her body still hurt from her dream. That was the thing about being beaten—you never forgot the pain or the shock of how much it hurt. Or the shame of having deserved it.

So much shame that it had taken her words. All of them. She'd woken up in the hospital with Baba stroking her face.

"There's my *rani*, my baby princess. How are you?" he'd asked, tears streaming from his sad eyes.

And she'd had no answer. Not to that question, not to all the questions that came after that, from doctors, from teachers, from Baba. Questions that had turned to pleading and goading and threats.

She'd had no answers.

Until those pale gray-blue eyes, the kind she had never before seen, had finally asked a question she could answer. *You want to be friends?*

She was about to close her eyes when the branch above her moved. She looked up and found those eyes staring down at her again.

Not him. Not here. *Please.*

His eyes were more weary than she'd ever seen them, tinged with red and ringed with shadows. They widened with panic when they caught what she was so desperately trying to hide. He hopped off his perch and landed on the wet grass next to her. "My God, Ria, what happened?" He grabbed her by her arms.

She closed her eyes and let her chin drop to her chest, letting hair cascade around her face and hide her from his searching gaze. If the tears started again she would never forgive herself.

"Hey." He tried to pull her close.

She shoved him away. "Why can't you leave me alone, Vikram? What's wrong with you? Can't you just go away and leave me alone?"

He didn't budge, so she pulled her arms from his grasp and moved away herself.

"I would love to, Ria. But first I need to know what the hell is going on with you." The pulse in his throat set off its familiar beat.

"I don't know what you're talking about."

He touched his bandage with two fingers. His forehead was tinged purple under the gauze. The jeans he'd worn all day still hung low on his hips, but he had changed into a white T-shirt that caught the dawn's light. "You keep telling me you don't want me. But I would have to be blind to believe you. I would have to be a fool to buy any of this bullshit." He waved his hands around. Her scarf was rolled around his fist. "What's going on, Ria? Why do you even do it?"

"Do what?" She didn't bother to conceal her weariness and leaned back into the gnarly bark.

His chest rose under the snug cotton. "For starters, why do you deal with this shit—the fans, the attention? It's obvious how much you hate it."

"I don't hate it." At least not as much as she used to.

"Come on, Ria, things didn't turn out like you expected, why is it so damn hard to admit it?" He reached out and tipped her chin up, forcing her to look into his eyes. "We were so young. So we made mistakes, so what?" Understanding softened his eyes, tinted them with insidious hope. For a few seconds his hope seeped into her heart. Then it gave way to panic.

She pushed his hand away. "It turned out exactly as I had expected." She thrust her chin up. "I was given an opportunity and I took it. And it turned out great. Why is that so hard for you to accept?"

That earned her a disbelieving frown.

She matched it with a determined one. "At least I took the opportunities I was given. At least I didn't run from them."

His eyes narrowed. He took an unconscious step back, and that pushed her over the edge. "What about V-learn? It puts that stupid ecstatic look on your face. How can you not do anything with it?"

"You don't know anything about V-learn. You don't know anything about me anymore. Stop acting like you do."

"Fine. Then tell me. Tell me what you do." *Tell me I didn't ruin your life.*

"Okay. I teach a class at the University of Chicago. A special workshop on sustainable construction techniques. You have to qualify for my class, you can't just take it. Because when I was running around the world after my girlfriend dumped me, I spent so much time on construction sites I figured out that indigenous populations use some amazing technologies that won't fucking kill our planet. And because I couldn't sleep for years I figured out how to apply them to modern construction. And now they think I'm some sort of fucking expert. But you know what else I figured out? That there's more to life than chasing shit. That I didn't have to achieve things to be someone everyone wants me to be.

"Oh, and those videos on V-learn—they didn't make themselves. I put them there and I put more on every day. But V-learn is mine. I can give it to whoever wants it, whoever needs it. I don't want someone to take it and turn it into another moneymaking machine. I don't want it to turn into another screw-the-little-guy tool. Does that answer your question?" He was breathing hard. And he had put several feet between them.

"So what you're telling me is that success still chases you the way it has chased you all your life and that you've learned to run away. When did you turn into a coward, Vikram?"

He had the gall to laugh. "Really, you're calling me a coward?" He stared her down until heat suffused her cheeks and his eyes softened. "Fine, so I'll stop being a coward first. I'll come out and say it. It's time for us to stop lying to each other."

"I'm not lying. I'm trying to tell you the truth, but you won't listen. I don't regret becoming an actress." She couldn't regret it. But he deserved at least a piece of the truth. "But I do wish I hadn't put you through what you went through."

Again he laughed. Was he crazy? Her heart was breaking into pieces—what was there to laugh about?

"That's the first honest thing that's come out of your mouth since you came back. But it doesn't matter. What I went through doesn't matter. It was a long time ago. What matters is what's happening to us now." Hope surged in his eyes again.

She had to find a way to snuff it out. She forced her mind to count all the damage done. Baba's body burned to the ground. The nurse, an innocent bystander, burned to the ground. Her ancestral home burned to the ground. Vikram's career burned to the ground. A murder she had covered up, allowed to go unpunished. Generations of insanity coiled up inside her, waiting to spring lose.

The only kind of future they had together was more horrific than what they had already endured. Ria knew she would make the same choices again.

"Vikram, I would do the same thing again."

He flinched, but instead of stepping away he stepped closer. "That's not a lie either. But why?"

"Because I love what I do, that's why. I love the fame and the fortune. It's the greatest high there is."

He threw back his head and laughed as if she'd given him exactly what he was waiting for. Then he leaned into her, bringing his face so close their breath mingled. "Bullshit." She smelled the barest sting of alcohol. But she knew he was as sober as she was. "I'm calling bullshit on that one too. I bought your lies once, Ria. Not this time."

*This time?* There was no "this time." She searched desperately for something to turn things around. "What about Mira?" How could she have forgotten Mira? Now she clung to her like a drowning woman.

Vikram took a step back. "None of this has anything to do with Mira." Guilt dulled the intensity in his eyes.

"How can you say that? It has everything to do with Mira. She's your girlfriend."

"Actually, she's not anymore." The guilt in his eyes grew so heavy he squeezed them shut. Thick dark lashes spiked from his lids.

"Oh God, Vikram, what did you do?"

He opened and closed his mouth, but he couldn't bring himself to say what he was trying to say. Instead he said simply, "We broke up. Actually, she broke up with me. Two days ago."

"That can't be. She came to the store today."

"Only because she wanted to talk, and I wanted to make sure she was okay and to let her know she should stay for the wedding if she wanted to. But she didn't. She's going to Michigan to spend some time at home. I'm not proud of what I did, but it's over, Ria."

She wanted to ask him what had happened, but something in his face told her she didn't have the strength to hear it. Not right now. Not with his eyes on fire like that.

"And really, it was coming from the day you stepped into that basement." He watched her face, the full strength of his focus back on her. "Actually, long before that. I had no business being with Mira. With anyone."

She wanted to clamp her ears shut with her palms, but her arms had turned to lead. "No. That's not true. She's perfect for you. You said so yourself."

"No, Ria, she's not the one who's perfect for me."

A massive airless space formed inside Ria, tugging everything into it. This wasn't happening. She turned away and headed back to the house, needing to get away from him.

He fell into step next to her and she sped up. "You can't outrun this, Ria. Mira didn't deserve to be caught in the middle of it. There's no place in this for anyone but us."

She climbed up the deck steps and stopped. She made herself

turn around and look at him. He stood one step below her, eye to eye with her, the decision in those gray blue cystals a physical thing. "Vikram, listen to me." She wanted to shake him. "Don't do this. Don't do this to yourself again."

His eyes bored into her, his laser-like focus trapping her in place. It was a look she knew only too well. A look that was so *him* it made her light-headed with wanting. It was the kind of look most people got before they flew into a skydive, but one Vikram got every time he decided he wanted something.

"Too late," he said just as Uma slid open the kitchen door and stuck her head out.

# 19

"Are you kids trying to kill me?" One look at Vikram and Uma slapped both hands around her cheeks. "I'm not thirty anymore, you know?"

"It's a little scratch, Umu." Ria hadn't heard Vikram call Uma that since she'd come back, and it made Uma grin like a little girl. "Oh, and we aren't ten anymore, so please stop acting like we hurt ourselves just to get your attention." He dropped a kiss on Uma's head and pushed her into a chair. "Coffee, anyone?" The look he threw Ria zinged straight down to her belly.

He was talking about coffee, for heaven's sake. But it made her entire world careen on its edge as if they had taken a sharp turn in his monstrous truck and spun off a cliff. Her worst nightmare and all the dreams she'd been too afraid to dream tumbled on top of each other.

Uma had loved to tell them stories from Indian mythology when they were young. Tales from the *Ramayana* and the *Mahabharata*, stories Ria had heard many years ago from Aji, but were often new to Nikhil and Vikram. Vikram had especially loved the Pandava prince, Arjun, the most heroic of heroes and the most legendary archer of all time.

"The royal guru was giving the princes a lesson on archery," Uma had said as the three of them huddled around her on the bed. "He placed a wooden bird on a tree and asked each prince to load the bow and aim. Then he stopped them and asked them what they saw."

Uma had waited for them to guess the answers.

"Why would an archer see anything but the bird's eye he's supposed to shoot?" Vikram had asked incredulously, ruining Uma's punch line and making her laugh.

The other princes had seen the leaves on the trees, the clouds in the sky, the flowers in the meadow, but Arjun had seen only the bird's eye. And so had Vikram.

Vikram moved to the coffeemaker, a new lightness in his step. All that sullenness that had clung to him like a disease, gone. All his defenses laid down, all of him laid so temptingly bare it made her as helpless as the leaves swirling in the wind outside the window. She had to find a way to wrap him back up, to protect him from the disaster he was hurtling toward.

She fidgeted with the carton of eggs sitting on the island.

"Will you make your spicy scrambled eggs, *beta?*" Vijay asked, bringing the newspaper to the table and sitting down next to Uma.

"Wow, the starlet's making her spicy scrambled eggs?" Nikhil strolled into the kitchen in his pajamas and tugged Ria's hair.

Ria hadn't cooked in ten years, but she desperately needed something to do. She searched the kitchen for a frying pan.

Vikram came up behind her and placed the pan on the stove in front of her. His heat wrapped around her. His closeness mussed up her brain. But she was cooking for her family after ten years and somehow that made the world exactly as it should be. She tightened the cord of her kimono around her waist and took the coffee he handed her.

She started chopping onions, he started cracking eggs. She sautéed the onions, he whisked the eggs. She plucked toast out of the toaster, he buttered it. He poured the eggs into the pan and she stirred them into the onions, sprinkling in cumin and red chili powder. They moved together, they moved apart, synchronized as dancers, two halves of a whole. Warmth danced behind her lids. A smile bloomed in her heart.

Nikhil set the table, balancing the forks and knives in the center of the table like a tent, just like he had always done. The world clicked into place one more notch as the five of them took their places around the table. Everyone oohed and aahed about the eggs, and it led to reminiscing about their summers together, and Ria found herself soaking up every timeless detail, even the heat of Vikram's thigh, inches from hers. He didn't close the distance as he had always done, and need built in her belly like a monstrous thing.

She had to tell him how wrong he was, how his hope was hopeless. But Uma's to-do list had taken on a desperate note in terms of priority with just three days to go, and so, they all got to work. Vikram was sent out with a grocery list that ironically enough included coconuts, Vijay and Nikhil went off to have their clothes altered, and Uma and Ria sat cross-legged on the family room floor and got busy wrapping gifts for the wedding guests, who were flying in from all over the world starting tomorrow.

Ria slipped the gifts Uma handed her into gift bags—saris for women, jewelry for girls, shirts for boys and men, and tablecloths for seniors—as Uma made notes in her notebook and stuck labels on the bags. All the while Ria searched for the resolve to tell Vikram once and for all that they had no chance in hell.

But two minutes after he came back home the doorbell rang, and the aunties streamed in, all four of them. Their husbands trailed behind them, their hands laden with platters of food, bottles of wine, and boxes overflowing with decorating supplies.

Vikram took a box from someone's hand and caught Ria's eye over a tangle of Christmas lights, and she knew he knew where her mind had been all afternoon. On him.

The aunties settled in, laying food out on the kitchen island and setting a pot of chai to boil. Soon they were all eating and talking and starting projects in groups around the kitchen—peeling and chopping vegetables, cutting and hemming fabric for table runners for the cocktail dinner, rolling out the sweet milk fudge *pedhas* that Uma had labored over for hours yesterday and wrapping them like candies in squares of cellophane to distribute after the wedding.

Anu looked at the tray of samosas and poked Vikram in the shoulder. "Remember those samosa-eating contests Nikhil and you used to have?"

"I'm still up for it," Nikhil said. "But pretty boy here is probably too worried about his girlish figure."

Vikram picked up a samosa and saluted Nikhil with it. "Pretty boy here can still kick your ass at pretty much any contest." He popped the samosa whole into his mouth.

Nikhil did the exact same thing, perching on a bar stool next to Vikram. They proceeded to stuff obscene quantities of the savory pastries into their mouths, trash talking each other between grotesquely ill-mannered bites. Everyone stopped what they were doing and gathered around, clapping and cheering and whining about how unfair it was that these two could get away with eating like that without showing it around their waistlines.

Vijay pulled out the camera. Uma popped another tray of samosas into the oven. Nikhil and Vikram had had food contests involving everything from pizza to rotis to chocolate cake. Once, Uma had stood in front of the stove frying puffy dough puris for two hours before one of them had given up. How was it that so much had changed and yet nothing had?

Vikram saluted Nikhil with another cone-shaped pastry and took a giant bite. Nikhil tried to look like he was just getting started. Someone started taking bets. If she were the betting kind, Ria knew exactly whom to put her money on. Sure enough, a distinctly green pallor was starting to spread across Nikhil's face.

As the samosas on the second tray dwindled, Jen looked like she was going to throw up, and called a stop to the madness. "Don't worry, Jen. Those two have had years of practice being stupid. They'll be fine," Ria said.

Vikram grinned at her like a little boy, and her own years of training at pushing her feelings away disappeared faster than the tray of samosas had.

Her fingers itched to wipe off the flaky crumb that clung to the corner of Vikram's mouth. He pushed it into his mouth with an unsteady thumb. She backed away from his gaze and joined the group at the dining table putting finishing touches on the centerpieces.

As the aunties went back to their projects a sense of old-world femininity settled over the kitchen. The men started to stick out like sore thumbs, growing uncomfortable with the sewing baskets, the fabric cascading from the table, and the platters of candy twisted into pretty bows. Conversations started to shift to hormones and relationships, and the men fled.

They escaped into the yard, carrying their boxfuls of festive lights, and started their own project of decorating the house. For the next few hours the women huddled over their projects in the kitchen while the men decked the house with lights, laboring to transform it into a traditional wedding home, a *lagna ghar*, just like they would have done back in India. Some of the neighbors joined them, throwing their own Christmas lights in for good measure.

When they were done Vijay knocked on the kitchen window and beckoned the women to come outside and inspect their handiwork. Ria followed the aunties as they crowded onto the front lawn. The house looked like a bejeweled bride dripping from head to toe with twinkling gems. The aunties went into raptures and clutched their hearts. Their husbands beamed shamelessly.

The beauty of the house swirled around Ria like magic. She squeezed into Uma, hiding behind her. Her eyes swept the crowd, but she couldn't see Vikram anywhere. She knew he had been helping with the lights because she had heard his voice and his laughter from the kitchen. Her eyes searched the yard, the driveway, the street. Finally, something tugged at her heart and she looked up. He was perched on the roof above the garage, his elbows resting on his knees, the twilit sky wrapped around him.

He watched her, waited for her to find him, to meet his eyes. Something so possessive, so tender, so incredibly magnetic flickered across his face, she couldn't look away. He rubbed his chest, completely unconscious of the action, so heartbreakingly vulnerable that in that moment Ria would have done anything to protect that look on his face, to keep him safe. Absolutely anything.

The crowd around them cheered and Ria pulled her gaze away. Vijay popped open a bottle of champagne and everyone started passing around glasses as he poured it out. Vikram walked to the edge of the roof, jumped off, and landed on his feet. Everyone clapped and cheered again and he bowed, taking a glass from Vijay Kaka. They toasted the house, the couple, family, friendship. Someone asked Vijay how long he had been waiting for the sun to go down to bring out the booze, and they toasted the short days of the Chicago fall.

Somewhere along the way Nikhil and Jen had disappeared. They had been around until the samosa contest, but that was the last she had seen of them. She searched the crowd.

"Don't worry, they're somewhere in the house," Vikram said, his mouth so close to her ear she swayed on her feet. His steadying hand burned a hole through her sweater and singed the small of her back. She turned around to tell him off, but the look in his eyes made her swallow her retort. She managed to blink, not quite breaking the spell, but knowing she had to break it, fast.

"I thought you were looking for Nikhil. I was just trying to help."

"I don't need your help," she hissed. "I was just wondering where they were. I don't need to find them."

"I'm sure Nikhil will be relieved to hear that. I don't think they want to be found right now." He smirked, and the mismatched center of his lips parted.

"You don't know that," she said, because she had to say something and not just stare at his mouth.

"Some things you just know." The look in his eyes turned so openly seductive she took a step back.

"You need to stop this, Vikram. You don't know anything." But she couldn't stay and watch him try to prove her wrong. Because he was wrong. She went back to the house, made an excuse about work, and escaped to her room.

Desperate for something to jerk her back to reality, she opened the script on her laptop. DJ had exercised an immense amount of control and texted her only ten times a day to remind her to finish reading it. She called him.

"Have you seen Indiastars.com?" he asked in that awful admonishing tone she had heard him use only with other clients, never with her. She'd never needed admonishing before.

She opened the Web site and found a picture of herself in Vikram's arms. His face wasn't visible. Thank God. But his arm was wrapped around her with such protectiveness, she reached out and touched the picture. She was pressing her scarf against his forehead. It was a badly taken picture, someone had obviously captured it on their less-than-stellar cell phone from a distance. Her face was too blurred to tell what seeing Vikram like that had done to her. But the memory wasn't nearly as blurred.

"You didn't tell me your cousin got hurt."

"He's not my cousin." She closed her eyes.

"It doesn't matter who he is, but you're in the media, babes, and you know how they get when the public laps up a story, they just want more and more."

She shouldn't have called DJ. "Anything new on the blackmailer or Ved?"

"No," he said, but he didn't lecture her about getting a bodyguard again.

"Anything new on *StarGangster*?" she asked, because she knew it would cheer him up.

And it did. He spent the next hour telling her how thrilled the producers were that she had said yes and that she was diversifying into a new space under their banner. They had done a big *pooja* to thank the gods of fortune that she was on board.

DJ reminded her that since it was an action role, one of the requirements was a lean and toned body.

"You mean it's the only requirement," she said.

He ignored her. "The producers have a fitness boot camp planned for six weeks before they start shooting. I hope you're not getting too used to wedding food, and keeping up with your workouts."

It was the best piece of news he could have given her. She was going to need that boot camp to kick her back to reality when this was over.

# 20

Finally, it was here—the henna ceremony, and the wedding celebrations were officially in full swing. Uma was going to play the mother of the bride for the day and host the ceremony that was traditionally held at the bride's home. It was an all-female affair—mothers and daughters and sisters. The men had been banished until dinner. Left to their own devices, they had picked golf. Uma looked relaxed and excited for the first time in days, and Ria couldn't help the relief that washed over her.

She looked at the five women gathered around the kitchen table. The aunties had arrived early to get the last of the to-do list taken care of.

Today the dress code was red saris, and each one was decked out in five different shades and five different fabrics. From Anu's simple chiffon to Radha's ornate georgette and everything in between, there was no way to keep their unique styles and unique personalities from shining through. As they worked around the kitchen with busy hands and purposeful eyes, a sense of belonging so intense wrapped around Ria that she never wanted to let it go.

Anu, who had been keeping track of the dreaded to-do list, scratched forcefully at one of the few remaining items and they all cheered. By now almost all the items on the list had been crossed off with emphatic lines. Including packing coconuts, which Vikram had crossed off with a pointedly sheepish nod at Ria. All the supplies for the various ceremonies were packed into laundry baskets and plastic hampers and stacked in the garage to be taken to the hotel for the wedding. The table runners for tomorrow's dinner were finished and folded into neat stacks. The milk fudge candies were wrapped and put into silver baskets lined with tie-dyed silk. Even the ginger for the evening's chai had been grated and packed away in a Tupperware container in the fridge.

Appetizers for the day's ceremony sat stacked on the island in foil containers, ready to be popped into the oven. The rest of the dinner had been catered, and Uma had reminded Vikram and Nikhil several times before they left that they were supposed to pick it up at five. "We're doing it, really?" Vikram had asked lazily when Uma had repeated herself for the tenth time. "Let me write that down."

Uma would have glared at Nikhil for saying it, but with Vikram she laughed like she had never heard anything funnier.

Ria thought it was pretty funny too. But she shouldn't have smiled, because he looked at her as soon as the words left his mouth and caught her grinning like a fool. The smuggest, most self-satisfied grin spread across his face. She tried to look annoyed, but his smile didn't fade and he gave her a private little wave before walking out the door.

That unshakable look in Vikram's eyes as he waved good-bye stayed plastered inside Ria's head for the rest of the day. As Jen sat on a thick pillow on the floor surrounded by a circle of women. As the henna artists piped swirling patterns onto their palms. As Radha beat her *dholki* drum and Priya sang folk songs in her earthy voice. As all the women joined in for the choruses, clapping and dancing in circles. As they played word games and talked about what they were going to wear for each ceremony. As they munched on fresh fried *bhajjias* and sipped spicy chai, Ria found it impossible to get the unflinching faith in his eyes out of her head.

And he seemed to know exactly how her day had been when he returned. The moment he walked in his eyes searched the room, the silver depths brightening with relief and darkening with yearning when they found her.

"Can I see?" He strode up to her, not stopping until he was too close.

His scent filled her brain, his body filled her vision. She stared up at him with no idea what he was talking about, her brain refusing to process anything but her body's reaction to him.

"The henna." He pointed to her hands. They hung by her side, carefully suspended away from her body to keep the dried paste from staining her *salwar kameez*. She lifted them up and cupped her palms in front of him.

He studied the intricate patterns swirling across her palms, his brows drawn together in concentration. "Wow," he breathed. "This is amazing." Automatically, his hands came up and cupped hers, a featherlight caress because he didn't want to damage the henna. The warmth of his touch seeped into her skin and traveled up her arms. It reached inside her and spread through her. She soaked him up, branded the feel of his skin into her consciousness. She didn't realize she had closed her eyes until she opened them and found him watching her. Familiar and painful panic flooded through her, and she pulled her hands away, taking them from his open palms.

"Ria?" He said it as if he wasn't sure she could hear him.

She turned and hurried away. For the rest of the evening she kept her eyes under control and kept as far away from him as she could, not staying in the same room if she could help it. He didn't make an effort to seek her out. Every now and again she felt his eyes on her, but she ignored him, ignored what it did to her. The evening spun by in a blur of activity.

After dinner Vikram disappeared. The guests had started to leave, so he might have gone to drop someone off at a hotel. She refused to acknowledge the force with which she wanted to know where he was, and tried to focus on the aunties as they settled into dining chairs looking exhausted. They had all scraped off the dried black henna paste before dinner, leaving behind the red-stained designs on their palms. The patterns would continue to darken overnight. Every woman's hands would take on a different shade as deep and dark, or light and bright, as her man's love, or so it was believed.

Ria's henna was already darker than anyone else's.

"Aha! You have an intense love," Radha said, studying Ria's palms.

"No, no. It means she has a steadfast love," Sita chimed in, looking over Radha's shoulder at the maroon patterns on Ria's hands.

"Wouldn't it be wonderful if they both went together?" Anu said wistfully, and they all sighed.

They took turns examining and analyzing the color of their own henna and what it said about their husbands. They had stayed back to clean up and finish the centerpieces for tomorrow's cocktail dinner, which was going to take place in a tent in the backyard.

The finished centerpieces, twelve silver plates with hand-painted earthen lamps, lay spread across the dining table and the island. A set of red and gold glass bangles tied with gold string, a packet of *bindis*, and plastic-wrapped cashew brittle sat in a circle around the lamps on each plate. Every round table was going to be dressed with cream silk tablecloths, gold runners, and the silver-platter centerpieces. It had taken the aunties hours to come up with the entire arrangement.

Everything but the tablecloths was ready to go for tomorrow, and Ria went down to the basement to find them so everything would be in one place. She found the twelve unopened packets on a shelf and tried to stack them up in her arms. It was impossible to carry them up in one trip, so she searched through the overflowing shelves lining the unfinished concrete for something to carry them in. There were no empty bags or boxes in sight. She wandered over to the guest room, thinking maybe she could find something there.

The moment she stepped into the guest room Ria knew she had made a mistake. A scent so intoxicatingly familiar hit her that all her senses buzzed to life and started to hum to a slow thumping beat. This was Vikram's room.

His imprint was everywhere. The clothes he had worn over the past few days lay in a careless heap in a laundry basket in a corner. Each balled-up piece of fabric sent a shiver of recognition through her. She rubbed her palms on her *kurta*. A blue-and-green checkered comforter was pulled across the bed, not overly neatly, but not sloppily either. He had made the bed but he hadn't brushed the rumples out like she would have done, like she itched to do now.

A stack of oversized books lay by the bed. *Sir Banister Fletcher's History of Architecture, The Postmodern Town Project, Chicago Modern.* Ria walked over and picked up one of the books. Vivid pictures of buildings, ancient and modern, stretched across the pages. An electronic drawing tablet with mathematical formulae scrawled across the screen lay on the bed. Her turquoise scarf was slung over the back of a chair. A pinewood drafting board sat on a desk pushed up against the back wall. Just the kind that Baba used to have in his office.

Why was all this stuff here? The room didn't look like it belonged to a wedding guest. It looked like someone lived here. There was so much she didn't know, so much she hadn't considered. She ran her fingers over the unfinished pine. With magical ease a picture of Vikram sitting at the drafting table formed in her mind. His body leaning over the board, intense concentration making his face meditative.

"What are you looking for this time?" His voice wrapped around her from behind.

The fine hairs on her nape prickled to life. She should've been used to it by now, this all-consuming awareness when he was near. Yet, it still engulfed her. Her breath sped up. Heat suffused her belly and tugged between her legs. She didn't turn around to face him. He couldn't see her like this. She was wide open, completely exposed.

She heard him walk toward her, his steps slow and deliberate, not stopping until the warmth of his body radiated through the filmy silk of her *kurta* and stoked each of her heightened senses.

"When are you going to stop searching and accept what you find?" His breath fanned the sensitive skin behind her ear, running feathers of sensation across her skin.

She spun around and backed away from him. "I don't know what you're talking about." She hated the tremor in her voice.

"Why is that every second line that comes out of your mouth these days?"

"Because I really don't. Why are you being so weird?"

"I'm being weird? You're the one jumping every time I get anywhere near you."

"That's ridiculous. I was just looking for a tablecloth for some bags—some cloth for tabl—" She took a breath. "I was looking for a bag. For tablecloths." Could her bloody heart stop pounding for just one second?

"So you came here looking for it?"

"Yes."

"To my room?"

"I didn't know it was your room."

"I've been staying here the entire time you've been here."

"I forgot."

"Bullshit. Bullshit again. How can you close your eyes to everything you don't want to see? Is that going to make it go away?"

"I don't know what you're talking about." Even to her own ears her repetitive mumble sounded pathetic and unconvincing.

He leaned closer, locked her in place with his blazing gaze. "I'm talking about the big, searing holes we're burning into each other. This insane, crazy thing between us. I'm talking about how badly we want each other. It's time to finish this, Ria."

"How romantic. Do you get far with these lines?" She scampered back, but everything inside her grew as molten as his eyes.

"You tell me. How far am I getting with you?" He knew exactly how far he was getting.

"Not far enough," she said, staring at the door behind him. "All the way out of the room would be better."

"Great, so we're going to go on pretending then? Aren't you tired?"

*Tired?* She had left tired behind a thousand miles ago. "I'm not pretending, Vikram. You need to stop this. You have no idea what you're doing."

"Then tell me. Tell me what's got you so scared."

"Don't you understand? I have just four more days here. After that I have to leave." Her voice was a whimper.

"I don't care. I don't care what happens after four days, about the future, about the past. I don't care. I just want you, more badly than I've ever wanted anything." And his eyes backed up his words, every single one of them.

She swallowed a sob. "You can have anyone. Mira will take you back." *And she'll keep you safe.*

"I don't want her to take me back! Don't you get it?" If he took another step closer, if he said another word, she was going to burst into flames. And yet if he didn't say what he was going to say, she didn't think she could survive it.

"When I look at Mira, when I look at any woman—all I see, all I do—is search for you. Your eyes. Your lips. No one is you, Ria. Nothing is *this*. When I look at you—what I see when I look at you—" He closed his eyes, the crease between his brows digging a gash into his forehead. Ria squeezed her hands into fists to keep from smoothing it out.

"God, looking at you—how you look at me. It—it puts me together. It's like being able to breathe again." He ran his fingers through his hair, raising it into spikes. "I hadn't breathed for ten years, Ria." His jaw clenched and his lips parted, opening up that vulnerable O. An intense urge to cover his lips with hers grabbed her.

"I know exactly what you're thinking right now, you know. How much longer are you going to wait?" He looked so tormented it hurt to look at him.

She crushed her *kurta* with her fists. "I'm not waiting for anything. Nothing is ever going to happen between us."

"Nothing is going to *happen?* What about what's happening now?"

"Nothing is happening, Vikram." She nodded vehemently, refusing to tear her gaze away from the stubborn hope-filled depths of his eyes.

He leaned into her. "So, when I do this . . ." His warm breath caressed her lips. "Nothing?"

Every cell in Ria's body kicked into consciousness.

She managed only the barest nod, pulling on everything inside her not to close her eyes, not to complete the kiss.

"And when I do this . . ." He cupped her cheek. The electricity of the touch jolted through her, her dimples dancing beneath his touch, sensation buzzing through her like madness. "Nothing?"

She didn't move. She couldn't.

"I can feel your body screaming, Ria. I feel what you're feeling." His eyes found hers again, his fingers found her hair. The gentlest tug and her face turned up to his, a breath away from a kiss. "Still nothing?" He blew the word into her lips.

Ria arched up on her toes and pressed into his mouth, finding that maddening gap with her lips. It was the merest whisper of a touch, but his taste soaked through her. Memories sparkled to life in every cell and threatened to explode out of her skin. Sensations sucked her in and she nudged at them with her tongue. The shock of the contact jolted like twin currents through their bodies. Hunger gathered like an inferno where their lips barely touched. Sparks burst behind her closed lids. He moaned deep in his throat and pulled her to him, and she was lost.

She wrapped her arms around his head and sank into the kiss, crushing his mouth, stroking every inch of it with her tongue, reaching into every part of him, letting soft wet skin slide against soft wet skin and drench her entire parched being.

He took her in, opened up every part of himself, let her invade places she knew he would let no one else touch. He let her find what his words could not show her.

The kiss slowed and lingered, then became fevered again. It wrapped her up in lushness, meshed her body into his, and sank into her soul. It was the kind of kiss that was going to cling to her lips forever, haunt every living moment. It was everything that was happening between them. Everything that had ever happened between them. Everything that could happen if she let it.

"Absolutely nothing," she said against his lips before pulling away, untangling her fingers from his hair, dragging her breasts, her thighs, her hips away from his full-bodied embrace, tearing her mouth from his drugging heat, dizzy and disoriented, and more alive than she ever remembered feeling.

"Liar," he said as she stepped farther and farther away from him, but he didn't follow. He stood there, his hands fisted at his sides, his mouth wet, his dilated eyes stripped bare of any defense. "I came after you once, Ria. I won't do it again. I can't. If you want me you have to come to me."

His eyes burned into her. Her brain was so flooded, so filled with him she had to touch herself to know she still existed. She heard a sob, but she didn't know if it stayed inside or if it escaped from her. She pulled every part of herself in, away from him, from a magnetic force field so strong it ripped her away from herself.

Then she ran out the door and up the stairs and all the way up to her room, not stopping until there was nowhere left to run.

# 21

Ria pulled her room door shut and fell back on her bed. The pink canopy did nothing for her this time. The warm walls, the cozy bed, all of it gnawed at her, made her burn. His lips, his skin, his smell flooded her, sucked the breath from her. The look in his eyes, seeing all the way to the deepest part of her, pulled out desire she could not push back inside.

She tossed and turned and then sprang off the bed and paced. Hours passed before she became conscious of distant sounds of people leaving, but she kept on pacing until she heard Uma and Vijay coming up to bed. She climbed back into bed then and pretended to be asleep.

When Uma knocked on her door and peeped in to check up on her she lay motionless while her mind continued to spin. She prayed that Uma wouldn't come into her room like she usually did to place a good-night kiss on her forehead. Any kind of physical contact would drive her insane right now. Uma must have sensed something, because she shut the door and left with a softly whispered "Good night."

Even after every sound had stopped and the house had gone absolutely silent, Ria's mind continued to spin. Every part of her hummed with wanting so intense she couldn't breathe. She tried to tell herself it was only desire, but she knew it was more than that.

Vikram was right. She was a liar. The thing between them was not nothing. It was more than anything. More than everything. And it filled every part of her up until there was nothing left except the longing for his touch. Just one time. That's all she wanted, just one time. All she needed was to be with him one time, that's all. After that this craziness would be over. After that she would find the strength to control it, to end it. But just one time she had to feel him, feel herself against him, feel who she was in his arms.

She got out of bed. She had no idea what time it was or how her feet moved over the carpet. She was in her pajamas, but she didn't remember changing. A chill prickled against her skin when she stepped out of her room, but inside she felt warm and strong and right. Her feet fell in mute thumps on the stairs, down and down until her hand clicked the basement door open. She flew down the stairs, then slowed when she reached his door. She didn't knock, just pushed open the door.

He was sitting at his desk, leaning over some drawings, looking exactly the way she had pictured him before. The sight of him made the warm fullness inside her turn hot and ravenous. When she opened the door he turned and looked at her. Right inside her, like he could see nothing else. Like there was nothing else in the world besides her. He stood and walked to her, each step conscious and decisive. She lifted her hand and touched his mouth.

The second her fingers met his lips, everything outside them froze. The moment stopped and wound itself around them. Years of longing, years of need exploded at the point where the tips of her fingers touched the curve of his lips. In one fluid motion he pulled her against him, replacing her fingers with her lips, crushing her body against his, devouring her mouth, sucking, nipping, consuming. Her lips, her cheeks, her eyelids. His fingers molded around her skull, pulling her lips closer, leaving no spaces between them. Wiping out all distance.

Her fingers grabbed his hair, grabbed his shirt, whatever she could hold on to. Her heart hammered, crashing against the beating in his chest. Their mouths opened. Every part of them opened, they twisted and curled around each other, meshing and molding into one hungry, desperate beast.

His hands slipped out of her hair, flying down her body, claiming every curve, every muscle, every melting bone. The cotton of her shirt stuck in his fingers and with an impatient grunt he grabbed at the front of it and yanked it apart, splitting it in two. Buttons flew from them and skittered across the floor. His arms reached around her under the torn flaps. His hands splayed across her skin, searching her with his fingers, his palms, the entire burning length of his arms. Every inch of skin he touched turned to fire. She reached deeper into him, wanting more, digging into him with her fingers, her lips, her tongue.

Her mouth left his and dragged sucking, consuming kisses across his jaw, down the taut tendons of his neck. Biting at skin, tasting salt, musk, heat. His stubble dug ridges into her tongue, her mouth found every sharp edge on the bones of his throat as he worked furiously to gulp air. He pulled her mouth back to his on a moan, as if he couldn't bear not kissing her. She dived into his hunger, her tongue darting into him, wanting him to engulf her. It wasn't enough, none of this was enough. She reached up on her toes and pushed harder.

Finally, he let his hands move lower, burning down her waist and lifting her against him. She wrapped her legs around his hips, wrapped her arms around his neck, clinging to him with her entire body. His hands slid around her bottom, cradling her, pressing her closer. Through the soft flannel of their pajamas, their burning centers joined and molded into each other.

Each part of them fit exactly into place, and for one second they were perfectly aligned, synchronized into one complete being. His head tilted back, hers tipped forward, every part of their mouths touched and stroked, her breasts flattened against his chest. Their shoulders, their abdomens, each one of their ribs, interlocked and fit together as if they had found their perfect other half.

For a few seconds neither one of them moved. The beating of their hearts and the pounding in their bodies pumped through them and then exploded in such a frenzy of wanting that no force on earth could have stopped what had to happen between them.

His arms unwrapped from around her, first pulling off her pants, then his own, in one fluid motion, her mouth still stroking his, her fingers still twisting in his hair, unable to let him go. He lifted her and brought her back to him. Skin against skin.

The shock of their bare bodies touching jolted through her. She gasped against his mouth and wrapped her legs back around him as he carried her to the bed. They fell across the bed, side by side, their mouths melting into each other, nipping and stroking and marking. Their fingers digging and holding, their hips grinding. Frantically, he rolled her over on her back and slid on top of her, spreading her thighs and wedging his hips between them, where he belonged.

Her hands reached around him, flattening and curving around the firm rise of his butt, pulling him closer. His hips quivered and jerked, trying to push into her fingers and into her at the same time, and she reared up to meet him.

Suddenly he stopped, rose up on his arms. There was such mad wanting in his eyes she wanted to flip him over and thrust herself onto him. He started to pull away and she grabbed at him, confused. "My wallet—we need a condom—" Panting, he reached for it.

They fumbled with his wallet, fumbled with the condom. Their fingers fighting, frantic, until it was done.

He took her lips again, grabbed the backs of her knees, yanked them up and spread her wide. Then he entered her, sliding into her soaking wetness in one strong unrelenting move.

His engorged width stretched her tight. He hadn't touched her with his fingers, hadn't opened her up. He just entered her, direct and thick and deep. The shock of it exploded inside her like blazing skewers of unbearable pleasure. The heart-wrenching familiarity of their fit stole her breath, liquid heat spilling inside her just as tears spilled from her eyes.

He thrust deeper and deeper, his jaw tight, his eyes squeezed shut, his relentless rhythm so intense, so long awaited, that every tightly coiled, deeply buried piece of her burst to life around him.

"Viky!" Finally. Finally, his name—the piece of him that was hers and hers alone spilled from her lips into his mouth. Hot, drenched satisfaction exploded inside her just as he exploded too, dousing her insides and gathering every one of her scattering pieces into himself, until they were one being, one life. Complete. Unfractured.

Slowly, so slowly, the crazy shaking inside Ria stilled. Remnants of pleasure peaked through her in waves. She came back to herself one breath, one fragment at a time. Only, the pieces fit differently, turning her into someone else. Someone whole and quiet. Vikram's warm breath collected in her ear, chanting her name. "*Ria. Ria. Ria.*" Her fingers relaxed their grip on his shoulders. His fingers released the softness behind her knees. The slickness on their skin glued their bodies together. Deeper still the slickness inside her cradled him. The beating of their hearts fell into a congruous rhythm. And the world was a different place.

In her entire life, Ria had never experienced sleep this deep. As she came awake, becoming conscious of Vikram's body next to her, she felt like she had been in a coma, been somewhere else. She felt utterly new. Reborn. No memories. No tiredness. Nothing carried over but a soul-deep quiet. With her eyes still closed she let herself feel him. The rough hair on his legs scratching her skin, his sharp kneecaps digging into her thigh, the smooth stretch of skin over muscle warm beneath her fingers.

She felt him lean over her and brush his lips against hers so softly she wasn't sure it had happened. She didn't move, and he smiled against her lips. He knew she was awake. If you could call this dreamlike buoyancy being awake.

She was utterly weightless, lighter than a ray of sunshine and yet too heavy and languid to move a muscle. Not even her eyelids. His lips left her mouth and rested gentle as feathers on her eyelids. First one, then the next. He trailed kisses along her brows, the crests of her cheeks, stopping to nip the tip of her nose. He trailed kisses along her jaw, down her throat, tracing her collarbone, her arms, the insides of her elbow. Dragging the softness of his mouth over every inch of her body, stopping to savor and play, to open and learn her. She experienced every touch as if it were his first, not knowing where he would go next.

But she didn't want to know, she didn't want anything. Not one thing more. Not one thing different than what she had in this precise moment.

Vikram continued to caress her body, every satisfied inch of it, strumming her senses until her stillness turned frantic again. He calmed her with more caresses, then made her frantic again, then calmed her again. She ebbed and flowed—she was the music he was making, the colors he was painting. He took his time, labored over her, made love to her slowly, so very slowly, she was sure it was never, ever going to end. He seeped through her skin like sunshine, blossomed in her heart like faith. And he didn't stop until the fullness inside her reached every corner of her, until the peace sank so deep it became part of her, until the joy became so real she believed it.

# 22

The second time Ria awoke, her eyes flew open. She could hear sounds of movement in the kitchen. Uma's frantic voice overlaid with Vijay's soothing tones wafted down through the ceiling. Ria's cheek was plastered against Vikram's chest, nestled in the depression below his shoulder. She rubbed her cheek against him and inhaled the heady scent of him. Mingled with his delicious scent, she smelled herself.

A pot clanged in the sink upstairs and she forced herself to lift her head off him.

Vikram was passed out, completely dead to the world. For some reason that made her blush. All the things he had done to her lingered on her body, not like a memory, but like sensation—real and tangible. She reached over and brushed his hair off his forehead. Her fingers tingled with the memory of the sweet slide of his thick locks between her fingers, grounding her even as his thrusts turned her ethereal.

Upstairs, Uma called out to Vijay. Her voice sounded high-pitched and tense, on the edge of full-blown panic. Ria tried to sit up, but her hair was trapped under Vikram's comatose body. She lifted his shoulder and tugged at it.

"Where d'you think you're going?" His gravelly sleep-drenched mumble did funny things to her insides. He tangled his fingers in her hair as it slipped from under him and pressed it against his heart. His eyes were still closed. Thick lashes fanned out against his cheeks. A stubborn, faintly arrogant smile kissed his lips, making him look like an overindulged child. He rubbed her hair against his face. "So soft," he murmured. "Liquid silk."

"Thanks. I had no idea you were such a poet." She smiled and tried to pry her hair out of his fingers.

"I'm a po-et, and she doesn't even know-it," he said wistfully, his eyes still closed. "Stay in bed and I promise to write poetry about more than just your hair."

"Very tempting . . . like what?" she asked, entranced by the mischief in his smile.

"Hmm. I'm so impressed . . . by the beauty of your breasts," he said it in a singsong tone, his smile coloring his voice.

She laughed. "No thanks. I think I'll pass."

More utensils clanged upstairs and Ria sat up. "What time is it? It sounds like a war zone up there. We have to get upstairs before Uma Atya breaks something."

Vikram opened his eyes, but didn't let her hair go. "It's Uma, the wedding's tomorrow, she's going to be nuts today. Nothing we can do about it. It might be safer to stay down here." He pulled her back down, rolled over her, and started nibbling her neck.

Tiny jolts of pleasure licked up and down her spine.

"Viky, I have to get up there right now. Uma Atya needs me." She forced herself to push him away.

"I need you too." He went up on one elbow and threw a leg over her hips.

"I think you've had enough for now, don't you?"

"Are you kidding me?" He looked so appalled it was funny. "I'm only just getting started."

"Seriously, Viky, she's going to come looking for us. I have to go."

"Then go," he said sulkily, but he didn't move his leg off her.

She slid out from under it and sat up again, clutching the sheets to her breast. She looked around aware of him watching her. A furious blush warmed her face. "Viky . . . My clothes, they're—" She looked longingly at her pajamas lying on the floor all the way across the room. "Close your eyes."

That made him laugh.

"Viky, please."

He closed his eyes and pulled the sheets off her, opening one eye as the sheet slid down. She yelped, ran to her pajamas, and started pulling them on. Vikram rolled onto his stomach, rested his chin on his hands, and watched her dress, his expression so intent, so absorbed, it made Ria want to undress and go right back to him.

"You have to help me." She tried to button her shirt, but all the buttons were gone. She pulled the flaps together and held them there with her hands.

"Anything," he murmured. "Sweetheart, right now I would do just about anything for you." He was smiling, but everything in his heart glistened in his eyes. How could she not go down on her knees next to him and kiss him? He sat up and lifted her into his lap, kissing her until her brains scrambled. When she came up for air, she felt invincible. She couldn't think of one single thing she could not do.

"You have to distract everyone while I go upstairs and get showered," she said against his bristly cheek, stopping his hand as it made its way down her shirt, and tugged him out of bed.

"Only if I can come up and join you afterward."

"You wish." She gave him another peck at the exact spot where his lips didn't quite fit together. "I'm a film star, remember?" She watched him pull on his shirt, those beautiful muscles bunching and stretching beneath taut skin. "No one gets between me and my shower."

"Is that a challenge?" His eyes said, but he let her drag him up the stairs, where he distracted Uma while Ria sneaked up to her room, unable to stop grinning like a fool.

"What's wrong with you?" Nikhil peered at Ria as if she had suddenly and inexplicably gone half-witted. "That's the third time today I've heard you giggle."

"I'm practicing for a part."

"Ice Princess plays schoolgirl?"

"Something like that."

They were dressing the tables for tonight's dinner under the huge white tent, which fortunately had gone up without a hitch, vastly improving Uma's mood. Out of one window-shaped opening, Ria could see Vikram perched on a ladder. He tugged at a rope mounted on a pulley at the top of the tent. About fifty strings of lights hung down from the other end of the rope. He had spent all morning securing the lights together and creating a mechanism to hold them so he could heave them over the tent with a single cord, and then have them cascade down the sides of the tent like maypole ropes.

Ria had sat cross-legged next to him on the deck as he worked. It was a perfect day, bright and sunny with the slightest nip in the air. Sunlight had filtered through the trees and caught the glowing white of their T-shirts and the shimmering black of their hair. Vikram had explained to her how all the parts fit together, handing her hooks and clamps to look at, putting things together and pulling them apart with his long, solid fingers. He had made detailed drawings of the assembly earlier, on a thick-papered sketch pad. He used them to show Ria what the result was going to look like.

Ria held the drawings in her hands, running her fingers over the bold, minimal lines. He had detailed out each part with meticulous care. Something about the strength of the lines, the decisive way in which they were hatched and shaded mesmerized her, making her want to wrap her arms around him.

He'd handed her a pencil, and flipped the page on the pad. "Why don't you draw something?"

She flipped the page back without responding. "This is brilliant, Viky," she whispered instead.

His eyes had warmed with a deep dizzying satisfaction. "It makes much more sense to do it this way. Otherwise we'd have to hang each string separately and find a way to hold it up at the top. Already this is taking up far too much time. I'd much rather be doing something else right now," he'd said, his knowing grin painting all sorts of pictures in her mind.

But watching him as he worked, so focused and wholly absorbed in it, Ria knew she wouldn't exchange it for anything. Another piece of her wove itself into him as she helped him string the hooks and clamps together, and he told her about his green-energy construction company. He had three patents pending, and one already approved for an eco-efficient construction technique he had developed to make buildings inherently energy efficient in design, so they restricted energy loss and required less artificial heating and cooling. He'd been working with one of the world's largest construction conglomerates to develop building material that suited high-rise construction, but replicated qualities of traditional materials used in indigenous construction.

He'd moved to Chicago late that summer to teach a seminar at UC for the fall, and to buy some time before signing the deal that would tie him down for a long time. Uma had insisted he stay at home and he had let her bully him into it. That explained his lived-in room.

Ria readjusted one of the centerpieces Nikhil had laid out as she watched Viky lean forward on the ladder and tug at the rope. His muscles rippled against the cotton of his tee, and the memory of how they had felt warmed her fingertips. Vikram's hair was still pushed off his forehead. She had brushed it back before he climbed on the ladder. He had been up there for close to an hour now, the look on his face so purposeful Ria couldn't take her eyes off him. Fortunately, Nikhil was horrible at what they were doing and he had to focus really hard, plus he was doing enough talking for both of them.

Vikram gave one last tug and the heavy bundle of lights thudded against the tightly stretched canvas of the tent. He jumped off the ladder and secured the rope to a peg he had hammered into the ground earlier. Then he threw his arms up and whooped.

Ria dropped the platter she was holding and ran to him. For a moment he looked like he was going to brush a kiss against her lips, but Nikhil yelled something from inside the tent and he frowned, pointing at his handiwork instead.

"Amazing!" She looked up at the light strings cascading from the top of the tent like a fountain.

"All we need now is to spread the strings around the tent and, voilà!"

"Just any string goes anywhere?" She held out her hand.

"Yup." He separated the strings into bunches and handed her a few strands. She placed one string tentatively in place. He reached around her to straighten it, showing her how to hook it against the clamps he had fastened to the tent. His shoulders, his arms, his entire body melted around her. When he left her and moved on to the next one, his eyes still on her, a part of her went with him.

They worked together in silence, separating and placing the strings until the tent looked like it was encased in an armor of lights, radiating down from the top like a crown. When they were done, Vikram walked over to the deck and flipped the switch. The entire thing lit up. The sun was still bright, but it was easy to imagine what it would look like in the moonlight.

"Viky, it's beautiful," she said.

"It's done," he said, reaching for her hand. "Let's get out of here."

Just as he said it Uma came out of the house, her hand pressed into her mouth, her eyes round with joy. "Oh, Vikram, honey, this is wonderful. Absolutely perfect! Oh my God, I can't believe you did this." She practically skipped around the tent in glee.

Vikram looked so frustrated Ria giggled.

"More giggling?" Nikhil strode out of the tent and turned to look at it. "Wow, man, this does look good."

Uma threw her arms around Vikram. "It's perfect, did I tell you that already? You're my best *beta*. This is going to look so beautiful at night."

"I did the tables all by myself," Nikhil grumbled. "Even the starlet abandoned me for the more glamorous project."

"Face it, man, Uma just loves me more than she loves you." Vikram hugged Uma so tight he lifted her off the ground.

"Aw. That's because you are just so damn adorable." Nikhil pretended to gag. "Seriously, though, Vic. This is really good. You should add it to your list of patents."

"Patent the pulley? Great idea," Vikram deadpanned, and Ria burst out laughing.

Both Nikhil and Uma stared at her like she had grown horns. She scratched her head and pretended to adjust the lights, but she couldn't stop smiling.

"If she starts humming, I swear I'm calling a doctor," Nikhil said.

"Because it would be too damn serious for a quack like you?" Vikram said, giving Ria a ridiculously possessive smile.

Uma looked from Vikram to Ria. "I love weddings," she said. "Something about them just makes you happy, doesn't it? Look at you two—I haven't seen you look this happy for far too long. Touch wood." She touched the wooden tent pole and her eyes misted over. Ria wrapped her arms around her. Vikram leaned over and pulled both of them close.

"Yay! Group hug!" Nikhil threw his arms around all of them and squeezed.

# 23

If Ria had to identify one day as the happiest day of her life, this would be it. From the spotless sunshine to the buzz of happiness in the air to the presence of every person who meant anything to her, it was flawless.

After working all morning with Vikram and Nikhil on decorating the tent and the backyard, they laid out a leisurely lunch of sandwiches on the deck. For the first time ever, Vijay regaled them with his version of how he and Uma had met and fallen in love. How she had pulled the ground from beneath his feet and then turned up her nose at him, and how he had manipulated his way into her heart. Ria had no doubt Uma had had no chance at all once Vijay Kaka set his sights on her.

They had heard the same story from Uma several times, but to hear Vijay tell it was completely different, so much more vivid and logical, even Nikhil and Vikram listened with rapt attention and without interrupting with their wisecracks. Then Vijay did something he didn't do too often—he offered his son advice. "The way the joke goes is that the secret to a happy marriage is for a man to wake up every morning and tell his wife he's sorry," he said, and gave Uma a look that made her cheeks color. "But the real secret is to wake up every morning and thank her. Because the happiness a good woman brings to your life is incomparable. No one else can make you happy the way she can. Not your job, not your friends, not even your children can give you what a good marriage gives you. A good marriage is all you need to make it all worthwhile. And *she* gives you that. The day you realize this is the day you no longer have to worry about a thing."

"Vijay, what's wrong with you today? Embarrassing me this way. That's too much in front of the children. You're incorrigible." Uma tried to look reproachful, but her eyes welled up and leaked onto her cheeks and ruined the effect.

Ria couldn't stop the tears either. They spilled from her eyes even as she smiled. Vikram threaded his fingers through hers under the table, making circles across her knuckles with his thumb. "This means you're never growing out of the blushing and the tears either, doesn't it?" he whispered close to her ear.

Later she cried some more. Cleansing, freeing tears of uncontainable pleasure as Vikram rose to the challenge and joined her in the shower. His soap-slick fingers both kneading tension away and stroking tension into her body with equal skill as she struggled to keep from crying out. Being in his arms again and doing something so incredibly erotic while hiding from a house full of people drove everything but him from her mind.

When she was eighteen their lovemaking had been all need and enthusiasm, urgent and self-conscious, safe in the knowledge that they had all the time in the world to get it right. Now, it was intense and consuming, a desperate giving and gathering and committing to memory.

When she came down the stairs for the dinner party, dressed in a soft beige empire-waist *kurta* that cascaded and swirled down to her ankles over turquoise tights, dark kohl outlining her eyes, her hair rolled loosely over her shoulder, she felt somehow naked, exposed, and vulnerable.

The entire evening pulsed with an intimate, simmering aura—a heady mix of afterburn and foreplay rolled into one drugging, intoxicating mix. Vikram's eyes never left her. No matter whom he was dancing with, no matter whom he was talking to, no matter what he was doing, all of him stayed focused on her, and she felt it with every inch of her being. She felt his eyes on her even as every one of the hundred-odd guests came up to her, wanting to dance with her, take pictures, and strike up conversations.

For the first time in ten years Ria couldn't get herself to slip into star mode. It had always come to her with such ease. But today she just couldn't get the split to happen. The transition jarred too much. Her film-star smile wouldn't form, because she was already smiling. The cool icy grace wouldn't wrap around her, because the warmth of her joy wouldn't let it stick. And no matter how much she reached for her distant politeness, laughter kept bubbling from her and spilling out.

When she wasn't shaking her hips with a bunch of teenagers who insisted on pulling her to the dance floor every time a song from one of her films played, she was showing the aunties how to do a crazy step she had done in some film. When she wasn't posing for a picture, she was answering questions about the latest industry gossip. Everyone wanted to know what was really going on in Bollywood, and she was their periscope.

Are Ranjit and Dolly really dating? Do the Kochar brothers really arrive drunk at parties? Are Vishal and Neha really married and hiding it? Is everyone really having plastic surgery? Whose boobs are real? Whose nose is fake? Has she had any work done? Ria gave them all her best canned answers, enjoying it more than she ever had, especially her favorite one, "Oh, all of me is fake!" Only this time it didn't feel like the truth, especially not when Vikram looked at her like it made him angry to hear her say it. There was nothing fake about the fierce jolt of pride that pierced though her in that moment.

There was also nothing remotely fake about what his hands did to her when he caught her in the hallway, and rubbed her shoulders because he thought she might be tired. Or when he brought her a plate of food, because she had been surrounded by a mob all evening and hadn't had a chance to eat. Or what he was doing now. He leaned into her, took the dessert tray she was carrying, and whispered words into her ear that made gooseflesh dot a trail all the way from her neck to the dents at the base of her spine. "I'll race you to the top." His smile flashed every shade of knowing. And then he was gone.

Ria crested the hill. On one side of her was the brightly lit house with its brightly lit people, on the other side the gurgling river, dark as pitch except for the moonlight floating over it like a silver veil. No one had seen her leave, but she turned around and checked once more just to be sure. Her heart beat with excitement so intense, she had to keep one hand pressed against it as she half walked, half ran to the dark shadow of the oak.

"Viky?" It was barely a whisper.

The leaves rustled above her in response.

Her gaze searched the darkness. A breeze whispered behind her ear. She turned only the slightest bit. Still nothing. And then one tiny twinkling light at a time, the tree glimmered to life—a galaxy exploding into the heavens before her eyes. Wonder drizzled over her like the first monsoon shower. She stepped closer to the tree and stared up into the disappearing darkness.

He had lit up their tree.

Thank God she hadn't worn a sari or a *ghaghra*. Gathering the flaring *kurta* that swirled around her, she wrapped and tucked it around her waist. The tights stretching snugly around her legs were perfect for this. She kicked off her heels, rolled her scarf around her neck a few times, and grabbed the lowest branch. It came to her with the ease of a trusted pet. She pulled herself up and planted her feet on the solidity of their bridge. It bounced with more than just her own weight.

"Can you teach me to climb like that?" he said from behind her ear, circling her waist and pulling her against him. She twisted in his arms, bracketed his smiling face in her hands, and kissed him. Stars twinkled inside and around her.

"It's beautiful, Viky," she said, then kissed him again, and again, unable to stop. "How on earth did you get power so far from the house?"

Another knowing smile. He pulled away from her, jumped effortlessly to the ground, and held out his arms. She jumped into them and slid down his body. He gave her another hurried kiss and dragged her around the tree to a clearing ten feet away. Sitting on the grass was a metal box, suspended between pivoting frames mounted on a stand. It looked like something out of a science fiction film. A grid of silver flaps floated like tiny levers on every surface. He flicked one flap with his finger and it rotated around itself.

She squatted next to him and touched the cable that ran from the box to the light strings wrapped around the tree. "It's a battery cell," she said in wonder, making his eyes brighten.

"A light-seeking high efficiency solar cell." He flicked the flap again, making it rotate in a different direction.

She looked up at the glowing oak, still mesmerized by what he had done. "How long did it take to gather enough power for that?"

He smiled a huge proud smile and kissed her nose. "Just hours. I set it out this morning when you and Uma were bullying the tent guys." He stood, taking her with him. "I've been tinkering with this prototype for years." His arms tightened around her. "But I wasn't ready to try it out yet. I kept avoiding it and I didn't know why."

Ria pressed her face into his neck, her heart suddenly too heavy to withstand his gaze. He twisted his fingers in her hair and tugged her head back, forcing her to look at him. "Now I know why. This is huge for me, Ria. I needed it to mean something." His eyes sparkled brighter than the tree, brighter than the starlit sky, and how could she not kiss him again?

He smiled against her mouth, a sensation that was etched into her soul, and ground his hips against her. "My battery pack's been waiting for you."

Laughter bubbled from her heart. "Oh my, Viky," she said, pressing into him. "You're right, your battery pack *is* huge."

They were both laughing when he reached for the elastic of her tights.

"I think there's another patent in the stars for our Vic," the aunties declared, sitting in a circle of chairs under the lit-up tent. The tree twinkled obligingly in the distance. It was the subject of much gushing. Uma pointed it out to every guest for the rest of the evening along with the tent lights, and she made Vikram explain the battery pack and the pulley to anyone who'd listen.

"I should have made a video," he said to Ria, but every time Uma showed him off he obligingly explained it all again.

Most of the guests had left now, and only the family and the closest friends remained. Vikram, Nikhil, and a few of the other "kids" carried the fire pit from the deck into the tent and started a fire. The loud thumping music was exchanged for some soft old melodies, and everyone sang along whenever a popular number came on.

Nikhil pulled Jen into his lap to some loud and lewd heckling and he wrapped his arms around her. A sweet old dance number started playing. Vikram pulled Anu Auntie up from the chair next to Ria and danced with her. She giggled and blushed and everyone cheered. When the music ended, Vikram casually deposited Anu in his own chair and sauntered over to the seat next to Ria.

"So sneaky," Ria whispered to him, her heart bursting in her chest.

"Why, thank you!" He raised his glass to her and gave her the most private of smiles, letting his arm fall close to hers so the backs of their hands touched. Anyone watching them would have thought they were just two people sitting next to each other. But Ria's entire existence converged at the point where they touched.

Priya Auntie's grandson, Rahul, the little boy who had saved Vikram from Uma the day he had carried her, climbed on Vikram's lap. Vikram pulled him against his chest, and within minutes his tiny body went limp with sleep.

Ria's fingers tangled in her lap. Vikram looked at her over the boy's head, so at home with a child on his lap, so happy. She shifted away from him in her chair and he raised his brows. "What's the matter?"

She smiled, shook her head, and looked away. How could she ever tell him she couldn't have children, wouldn't have them? Especially when he looked like that with a child in his arms. He shifted closer and pressed his leg into hers, and she forgot everything but the joy of his touch and this infinitesimal, stolen, precious dream she was allowing herself. This glimpse into *them*. Into Ria and Viky and what might've been. If she thought about anything else, it would be over. And she wanted it for just a bit longer.

A little past midnight, Uma stood and called an end to the night. "Time to wrap things up. Tomorrow's the big day. We have to be up by six and at the hotel by nine."

Ria was going to be staying at Jen's apartment tonight so she could help her get dressed in the morning. One of Nikhil's friends was going to drive them there. For the tenth time that evening Nikhil asked why they couldn't just stay in the house. Jen and Uma looked at him like they were too tired to argue. Jen leaned over and gave him a kiss before getting off his lap and starting her round of good-byes. Only Ria noticed the look on Vikram's face.

"There are at least twenty people staying in the house tonight, Viky. It's not like we can even see each other." But she felt as distraught as he looked.

He had come up to her room to help her with her bags, and he was following her around the room as she collected a few last minute things.

"Plus, haven't you—"

"No, I haven't had enough." He pushed her against the wall. "I haven't even begun." He tipped her chin up with his fingers and kissed her as if he was never going to see her again.

"It's not like I want to go," she said when he released her lips.

"Then don't." He rested his forehead against hers.

"But I want to stay with Jen tonight, and Nikhil will need you tomorrow morning. Oh God, Viky, Nikhil's getting married! Can you believe that?"

That made him smile. He brushed her cheek with his thumb and gave her a look so filled with all the things he thought she was, it was a miracle her already-overflowing heart didn't explode.

This time his kiss was a gentle nudge at the edge of her mouth. "Just promise me something," he said. "Promise you won't think about anything else tonight. Just us and how good this feels. Nothing more, okay?"

She pressed her cheek into his lips. There was no space in her mind for thoughts right now. Later there would be too much to think about, but right now, for once in her life, she had no desire to think about anything except this man, who was the love of her life in ways she could never explain to anyone, and that look in his eyes that made her feel like the person she wanted so badly to be.

"I promise," she said.

And at least for tonight, she meant it.

# 24

The fluorescent lobby lights made the shiny black of Vikram's hair glow like a halo. He was the first person Ria saw when Jen and she walked into the hotel the next morning. Her heart leapt with such pure, unadulterated joy that she had to make a conscious effort to keep her feet on the ground. He wore the steel-gray *sherwani* they had bought together. The thick, layered silk fell from his broad shoulders down to his knees, narrowing at his hips and skimming the heavy muscles of his chest and arms, making him look even taller and more imposing than usual. The *churidar* pants hugged the hard, thick curve of his calves. The last time they had made love, Ria had traced those calves with her fingers and marveled at how his body had grown and changed.

"I've done a lot of running, sweetheart," he had told her. "Marathons, the Iron Man, anything to keep my body moving and my heart pumping." It had made her own heart squeeze painfully, but he hadn't let her become sad. He had known exactly what to do to drive all sadness from her mind.

"I like what you're thinking," he whispered next to her ear as he leaned over to take her bag before turning his attention to Jen, who looked utterly lost in all her bridal finery.

It had been the most wonderful morning, and dressing up together like old girlfriends had been the most fun Ria had ever had with another woman. She had draped Jen's sari for her, piled her hair on top of her head and flat-ironed a few flicks in the front so they fell in tendrils over her incredible cheekbones. She had even helped Jen with her makeup. Jen had refused to let a professional makeup artist touch her, but Ria she trusted. "Make me beautiful, girl!" she had said.

"You are beautiful, Jen," Ria had replied, draping and pinning the sari around Jen's perfectly proportioned body. "Have you seen the way Nikhil looks at you? And he doesn't think anyone is beautiful. The man actually slept through *Pretty Woman*. He thinks Jessica Alba is a brand of athletic shoes!"

"Well, he's had to hang around you all his life," Jen said, looking at Ria without a speck of jealousy. "That would make anyone immune to beauty."

For the first time in her life Ria had actually snorted out loud, making a pig sound and not even caring. And Jen had found it so funny she had collapsed laughing, ruining the effect of the elegant makeup job Ria had just done on her. She had defined the beautiful upward sweep of Jen's eyes with kohl and shimmering smoky green shadow. Jen looked sparkly and doe-eyed and absolutely stunning—if only she would stop pulling and prodding at her sari.

"Wow, Jen!" Vikram clutched his heart. "Look at you. I don't think I can breathe." He gave her a big bear hug, and dropped a careful kiss on top of her head.

"Shut up!" Jen said, but she looked a little less unsure.

"Are you kidding me? Ditch that loser and marry me. It's still not too late. Did I tell you he used to be a snotty-nosed kid? He used to get all crusty around the lip." He pointed at his upper lip and pulled a face. "Ria had to carry tissues for him wherever we went." He smiled so irresistibly Ria wanted to clutch her own heart.

Jen just laughed. Vikram offered her his arm and led her to the elevators through the overly lit lobby with its gigantic chandeliers.

"Seriously, though." Vikram leaned close to Jen's ear. "You're the most beautiful bride I've ever seen. Now let's get you out of here. We have to hide you from the groom. Apparently, the sky's going to fall on our heads if you guys meet before the stars are perfectly aligned."

He took them up to the bridal suite, where the three of them waited for the stars to align. Vikram tried to convince Jen to take a swig of vodka from the minibar to make the incredibly long ceremony bearable. Jen stared longingly at the bottle, but she refused to be tempted. So he opened up a packet of M&Ms instead. Then Jen and Vikram proceeded to work their way through all the candy in the minibar as Ria watched.

"Seriously?" Jen asked, popping the last piece of Ferrero Rocher into her mouth. "You're not even tempted?"

Ria nodded. "I'm not tempted by much." She stole a quick glance at Vikram, knowing exactly what she would find there.

"So are you guys going to make it official, or is this like some big secret?" Jen raised an eyebrow and looked from Vikram to Ria.

Vikram choked on the piece of chocolate in his mouth, coughing so hard his eyes watered. Ria started thumping his back, waiting for his coughing to subside, and for her own heartbeat to slow. She avoided Jen's gaze, and handed Vikram a bottle of water when he finally stopped coughing. Just as he took a long deep gulp his phone rang.

He gave Jen the smuggest of smiles. "Hey, Uma! You have the best timing in the world," he said into the phone, winking at Jen and holding the door open for them. "Come on, Jen. It's showtime."

Jen had no family of her own, so she had asked Vikram to walk her to the altar. As they stood outside the arched doorway of the banquet hall, Vikram wrapped his arm around Jen's shoulders. "Ready?" he asked, rubbing his hand up and down her arm. Jen nodded and took an unsteady step into the hall filled end-to-end with wedding guests.

Nikhil stood under the ornately carved altar, flanked on either side by Uma and Vijay, his eyes searching, intently waiting for Jen to enter. One look at Nikhil and Jen's entire body relaxed. Tension slid off her shoulders like a discarded robe. Her limbs loosened and her feet steadied. All the fidgeting stopped. She transformed into someone who had been born to be a bride in a jade-green sari.

Ria slipped past Jen and walked up to Nikhil. She gave him a quick squeeze and adjusted the *mundavalya*, the ceremonial strands of pearls tied around his head, before slipping behind the high-backed chair on which he would sit through most of the ceremony. Vikram led Jen to the seat next to Nikhil and the ceremony began with the first ritual seeking blessings of Ganesha, the god of auspicious beginnings.

The priest sat on a low stool in front of Nikhil, Jen, Uma, and Vijay and started chanting.

Vikram walked around the throne-like chairs and sidled up next to Ria. Together they watched the ceremony in silence. The priest kept pausing his Sanskrit chants to explain each ritual's significance in his singsong English.

"He's going to do this for the next four hours?" Vikram whispered incredulously. "While the guests just sit there like that?" He looked at the guests watching the rituals being performed under the altar. Apparently Vikram had never been to a traditional Indian wedding.

"Don't look so horrified. They're not expected to just sit and watch. They'll socialize, they'll eat. There's appetizers in the next room. You hungry?"

His gaze heated. "Not for appetizers. Did I tell you how beautiful you look?" The look in his eyes made the words unnecessary. "No blue today."

"Turquoise," she said, and he rolled his eyes and toyed with the gold tassels edging her sari.

Of course Manish had designed a turquoise sari for her for the wedding, a chiffon with *zardozi* work. But yesterday Uma had pulled out one of her own wedding saris and asked Ria if she wanted to wear it. Ria didn't have to think twice. Even if she hadn't developed a strong dislike for turquoise, she would have preferred wearing Uma's wedding sari over anything else. It was a Paithani, a traditional fuchsia and gold silk hand-woven by artisans, an art form that traced their Marathi heritage back millennia. "I wanted you to wear it for your own wedding," Uma had said. "But I have another one hidden away for that."

"It's Uma's," she told Vikram, trying not to choke up.

He moved closer and stroked her exposed waist, the touch soothing at first, but turning seductive before long. Ria smiled, amazed at how long he had lasted. Waves of heat had been radiating from his body from the moment he came to stand beside her. He had held himself still, but so much latent restlessness jumped off him that Ria knew exactly what was going through his mind even before he let his hand snake around her waist behind the high backs of the chairs hiding them from the rest of the guests.

"If you don't stop that everyone else is also going to know." She wrapped her fingers around his wrist, meaning to remove his hand, but then she made the mistake of looking into his eyes and forgot what she had meant to do. Her fingers found the pulse in his wrist, its frantic beat suffusing her body with a dizzying sense of power.

"Going to know what?" Amusement pulled at his mouth.

"I don't know. I forgot what I was saying." She pulled her gaze away from his. Her cheeks burned and her heart pounded like it was going to rip at the seams. She wrapped her fingers tighter around his wrist, no longer trying to remove his hand, but holding on instead.

The priest started a fire in the *havan* fire pit and the heady scent of burning sandalwood and smoky ghee filled the air, turning everything ethereal and untainted. The fire, with its all-consuming purity, sat at the center of the ceremony, a timeless witness to the vows. Plump earthen urns rimmed in gold and vermillion stood stacked in vertical columns like sentries at each corner of the altar with scarlet silk drapes cascading down behind them.

Ria hoped the filmy fabric and the high ornate backs of Nikhil and Jen's chairs was enough to obscure Vikram and her from the guests' view. She threw a quick glance at the opulently dressed people either absorbed in conversation or in watching the ceremony. Vikram continued to watch her, his insistent gaze melting her insides.

She knew she shouldn't be standing here next to him in front of all these people. There were a million things to take care of. The caterers needed to be checked up on, the guests needed to be mingled with. But Ria couldn't move. Just having Vikram look at her this way made her feel things she had never thought she'd feel again. Feelings she had fallen back into with such ease, she couldn't remember the time when an unrelenting emptiness held their place. A dark thought niggled somewhere at the back of her mind. But she didn't let it take form.

Soon she would have to think. Soon she would have to find the strength to do the right thing, but not yet. Right now she wasn't even strong enough to drag her hand away from his. There was no way she could think about what was right or wrong. Right now she wanted more of this, just a little bit more to steal away before she found a way to give it all back.

"I'm not going to let you do that, you know," Vikram said, stroking her waist in a caress so tender, she wanted to weep.

"Do what?"

"Find a way to be sad right now."

"I'm not sad. I'm happier than I've ever been in my life."

Something primal pulsed in his eyes. "Happier than yesterday in the shower or happier than yesterday under the tree?" His voice turned husky. His hand burned fire into her skin.

"Something happened yesterday? I don't seem to remember," she said, knowing full well how he would react.

Sure enough, his hand moved to her butt, his touch so possessive heat gathered between her legs. "Does that refresh your memory?"

She leaned into the chair she was hiding behind. "Viky," she breathed without turning to him.

His warm breath behind her ear did nothing to help her stay standing. "Hmm?"

"There are at least two hundred people looking straight at us."

"Then let's go somewhere there aren't."

He gave her one long look and turned to leave. Two steps and he was back. He grabbed her shoulders and pushed her in front of him. "You're going to have to lead the way, sweetheart, or the guests are going to get more of a show than they came to see."

He took a step closer, and the evidence of exactly why they

needed to get out of here right now poked into her back. She jumped and let out a yelp. Nikhil and Jen turned to look at them. The priest raised one eyebrow without pausing in his chanting. Ria slapped her hand over her mouth and tried to turn the yelp into something between a cough and a sneeze. "Sorry," she said, and rushed out of the room with Vikram flattened against her back, his laughter rich in her ear.

"You're crazy." But she couldn't stop laughing either. Fortunately, there were no guests in the corridor and they didn't have to stop to greet anyone.

Vikram grabbed her hand and ran down the long passageway toward the elevators. He punched the button, and the elevator opened with a ding. He pulled her in and wrapped his arms around her. She went up on her toes just as he dipped his head down and captured her lips, his mouth frantic with urgency one moment, slow and thorough the next, driving her out of her mind. When the elevator bounced to a halt Ria pulled away, but no one entered and it closed again.

"Where are we going?" she asked.

He reached into his pocket and pulled out a key card emblazoned with a golden orchid. "Nothing but the honeymoon suite for you, my love." He pulled her close again.

"Is that the key to Nikhil's honeymoon suite?"

He nodded absently, and started nuzzling her neck.

"There is no way I am using Nikhil's honeymoon suite, Viky," she said as he nibbled his way down her throat, melting her spine. She had to fight to focus on what she was saying. "You're not listening to me . . . Viky?"

"I love the way you say my name." He trailed kisses along her collarbone. His breath collected in the hollow at the base of her throat and she leaned back, lacing her fingers through his hair and holding him there.

"Viky . . ."

"I've dreamed of hearing you call me that for ten years." He touched the sensitive hollow with his tongue. She moaned and fought to keep her train of thought.

"Viky, listen to me. I'm not going to use Nikhil's honeymoon suite. So if you don't think of something else all you're going to do is dream some more."

He straightened up and looked at her. "You're serious, aren't you?"

She nodded, and he looked so put out a giggle escaped her just as the elevator door opened again. He scooped her up in his arms. "In that case we're going to have to make alternate arrangements. Because, sweetheart, my dreaming days are over."

He hurried out of the elevator and looked up and down the long, red-and-gold-striped corridor. She snaked her arms around his neck and watched the determined expression on his face. Her Viky on a mission. He broke into a jog, turning the corner and going from door to door until he found a door marked EMPLOYEES ONLY. He turned the knob and the door swung open. He whooped in victory.

It was a storeroom of some sort with shelves on two sides lined with stacks of spotless white towels and the overpowering smell of detergent. He kicked the door shut behind them, put her down on the narrow table pushed against a wall, and shoved a utility cart against the door, his eyes never leaving hers. A heady combination of heat and laughter bubbled and spilled from her. He stole it from her lips. His fingers molded her scalp and pulled her impossibly close, held her impossibly tight, and stole whatever was left of her. Suddenly, all she could smell was him. All she could feel was him.

"Ria." He placed a kiss behind her ear. She pushed into his lips. She loved the way he said her name too and he knew it.

A string of kisses trailed her jaw. "Ria. Ria. Ria."

A nibble at the edge of her mouth. "Ria."

How did he do that? Take her name and turn it into everything in his heart. She grabbed his face and found his lips. But he allowed her only a peck, savored it, then pulled away. His hungry gaze branded her, lingered on her parted mouth, mirrored the ache in her body. In one smooth motion he grabbed her ankles and shoved them up, his hands hot manacles pinning her feet to the table, pushing her knees out, and spreading her wide. Body and soul he cleaved her open. "No more dreaming, Ria. This. Is. Real."

The kaleidoscope of his eyes sparkled brilliant with challenge. Brutally insistent. Unbending.

A jagged bud of terror sprouted inside Ria and fought for footing in the all-consuming inferno. Vikram wedged his hips between her legs, thrusting himself into her silk-covered center, and the darkness fled. All thought fled. She scooted forward and clamped her knees around him.

"Viky, please," she moaned into his mouth. "Please."

"Please what?" He found the dent of her dimple and burrowed into it with the tip of his tongue, teasing it, making it dance in her cheek until she grabbed handfuls of his hair and jabbed her tongue into his mouth.

He sucked her in. His fingers tightened around her ankles, pressed them into her thighs, and stroked the sensitive apex of her legs. She gasped for air, twisted her fingers in his hair, and pushed into his hands.

Instead of increasing the pressure, his hands gentled. Every part of her clenched and throbbed. Slowly, deliberately, he rubbed the layers of silk into her burning flesh, dragging the cascading folds of her sari like a million feathers along the sensitive insides of her thighs. Her legs kicked out, muscles spasming in response to his touch, feet arching in an erotic stretch. "Please, Viky." She wrapped her legs around him and locked her ankles at his waist.

"Please what?" His lips hot on hers, he reached behind him and grabbed her feet again, unlocking her legs from around him. "Tell me what you want, Ria." His voice raw with hunger, he pushed her feet back on the table and pulled away.

She heard a sob break from her own throat. "Please, Viky. Don't—" She pressed her face into his neck unable to finish.

His fingers stilled in the act of dragging the gilded hem of her sari up her legs. "You want me to stop?"

She bit his neck, hard. "Don't you dare stop."

He pushed his neck into her teeth and shoved the heavy fabric all the way up her thighs. She sucked on his skin, drawing in his heat, drawing a ragged moan from his lips. He increased the pressure of his fingers, caressing and kneading, moving up, then down her thighs until finally he found the lacey scrap of her panties on an indrawn breath.

He flitted over the swirling patterns, his touch tracing fire along the lacy petals and blooms, that barest caress creating enough friction to drive her into a frenzy.

"Viky," she begged, pushing her hands into the table and lifting her hips, thrusting herself into him.

He groaned into her mouth, but he didn't increase the pressure. His other hand moved to her breast, pulling the strapless blouse down and covering her aching flesh with his palm. Her nipple puckered into his touch, every nerve screamed. She might have screamed too. She didn't care. She pressed into him, begging for more. Begging with her lips, begging with her hips, begging with every part of her being. "Viky, please."

"Viky, please what? Say the words, Ria. Say them."

"More, Viky. Harder, Viky. *Now, Viky.*" She ground her pelvis into his hand.

He took her lips again and increased the pressure between her legs, strummed and stroked, used the textured lace to drag sensation from every nerve, inside her, around her, over her. She danced on the edge of explosion, liquid molten pleasure flowing from her like lava. He kept her there, his tongue in her mouth, his hands relentless in their demand, pulling back and pushing forward over and over again until she thought she would die from it.

"Like this?" he asked, and she screamed for release, her legs trembling, her body stiffening and arching.

"Yes," she sobbed. "Please."

He dragged off the soaking piece of cloth and replaced it with his mouth. Pleasure stabbed through her. She convulsed and fisted the thick silk covering his muscled shoulders, unable to discern one peak from another. And still he didn't stop. He kept going until she could take no more, go no further, and she sagged limp and consumed against the table. He pulled away, coming up to face her, his mouth glistening, his eyes drugged and ravenous and reached for his pants. This time she stopped him.

She slid off the table, her mind lost, her body unsteady with the cramping strength of her release. She fell against him, pushing him into the wall behind him. Fire radiated down her legs. She buckled. He held her up, his hands brands against her butt, his hard unspent length a raging throb against her.

She brushed his lips with her own and let her hands unknot the band of his pants. Then she left his mouth and the taste of her own pleasure, wrenching a raw sound from him as she slid down his body. Her trembling fingers rolled the silk down his legs, her mouth trailing in their wake. The contrasting feel of soft silk and hard muscle burned fire into her lips, her cheeks, her tongue. She devoured him, tasting every inch until she reached the taut stretch of him and tasted not just salt and skin, but him.

A breath hissed from his lips. "Oh fuck, Ria." Unsteady fingers entwined in her hair, shoving deeper, holding closer. But he couldn't last. Pulling her away, he dropped to his knees in front of her and brought his mouth to hers, mingling their need, their hunger. Without letting her mouth go, he tugged at a pile of still-warm towels, scattered them on the floor.

Suddenly he stopped, his gaze hitching on her face. His fingers traced the rivulet of tears streaming from the edges of her eyes. The raging heat in his gaze darkened and solidified to something so intense it stole every last thing left inside her. She was gone. All of her dissolved in him. Gone. He laid her down as though she were made of spun sugar and dragged her sari up to her waist, his gentleness reverence, his gaze worship, his entrance total and utter surrender.

She felt every instant of the joining. Inch by alive inch, she filled up and fit around him. Sheathed deep within her, he stopped. He stopped moving, stopped time. Her senses jolted as if he had thrust into her with wild force. An animal sound rose in her throat. She wrapped her legs around him, tugging at him, driving into him, desperate for friction. Desperate for him.

"Shh, love. Not yet," he whispered into her mouth. "Feel this." He took her lips, his tongue touching places buried so deep, it was as though he'd stripped her down to her soul. Her senses ripped between the insane stillness stretching her and the frenzied plunder of his mouth. Pleasure built and mounted inside her again and then exploded with such unbearable force, pain wrenched her womb from her spine. She screamed into his mouth and consumed his stillness with crazed, noisy thrusts.

He let her feel her own hunger, her own power, goaded her until she drowned in it. Then he joined her, giving her everything she begged for and then soothing her and soothing her, with his mouth, his hands, his body as she sobbed and shuddered and clung to him with her every breath.

# 25

"For an Ice Princess you can be really loud, you know that?" Vikram's chest rose and fell beneath Ria's cheek as if he had sprinted a mile. She lay draped across him, her hair spilling in rivulets around his body. The room no longer smelled of detergent, but of them, their smells indiscernible from one another. She no longer smelled like herself, no longer felt like herself.

A hot blush burned her cheeks. "Oh no! You think someone heard us?"

"Sweetheart, I think they heard us in the wedding hall twenty floors below." He ran his fingertips over the warmth of her flaming face. "Your blush is the exact color of your sari, you know that?" His eyes trailed his fingers as they traced her blush all the way down her neck to the swell of her breast.

"*Bloody Hell*, Viky, the wedding!" She sprang up, snapping out of her trance. How could she have forgotten about the wedding?

He didn't seem to care. His hand kept moving lower. She clutched it in place. "We have to go. Now." She tried to stand up, but couldn't. Her sari had come undone and twisted itself into knots around her. They were both still clothed, but she had never felt so naked in her life.

"Shit. Shit. *Shit*. Uma Atya must have sent out a search party by now. What time is it? How am I ever going to get this thing draped again?" She pulled her blouse back in place. Vikram pulled it down again and dropped a kiss on her breast.

"Viky!"

"Mmm?" He started drawing swirls around her nipple with his thumb. He looked so blissful her heart squeezed. For a moment she lost her train of thought. But then the thought of Uma's search party brought her back. She pulled his hand away and tried to look stern.

"Viky, focus!"

"I am focusing." He stared at her breast with an absorbed, reverent sort of look and tried to put his hand back on it.

"We have to get back to the wedding. Oh shit, I hope Uma Atya hasn't called nine-one-one." Ria quickly pulled her blouse back on and stood up before he could peel it off again. "Are you crazy? Is it even possible to do it again so soon? After that?"

He stood up and gave her a slow, lingering kiss. "Why don't we try to find out?"

"Viky. Please."

"Okay. But stop saying my name like that, otherwise we're not going anywhere."

"Like what?"

"Like it makes you breathless to say it."

That made her blush some more. "See, don't do that either," he said, leaning into her again.

"Viky—Vikram. Please. We *have* to get dressed."

"Okay, great. You can say *Vikram*. You sound exactly like Uma when you say it. And that's kind of scary." He grinned as though he hadn't a care in the world, and her heart gave another painful squeeze.

She unraveled what was left of her sari, chanting, "Vikram. Vikram. Vikram," in her most Uma-like voice, and tried to smooth out the yards and yards of fabric. Thank God silk this heavy didn't wrinkle easily.

He glanced lazily at his watch. "Relax, sweetheart, the endless ceremony isn't even halfway done yet. Everyone's probably zoned out and dreaming about lunch."

She smiled, but her hands shook. The sari was a mess. The tassels were and tangled in the sequins on her blouse. She tried to untangle it, picked at it with her nails, but it wouldn't come apart. Panic prickled in the pit of her stomach.

He reached over and unhooked each snarled sequin. His long fingers worked deftly to straighten and separate the tassels. Then he took the sari from her and shook it out and folded it as he watched her adjust her jewelry, her hair, her blouse.

When she took the sari from him and started to drape it around herself he stepped closer. "Here, let me help," he said, and followed her lead, taking a neatly folded section from her and holding it out of her way as she evened out the pleats, then handing it back and forth, helping her twist, wrap and tuck. His hands lingered on her skin, his eyes followed her every movement as though the notes of a breathtaking melody were unfurling around him and moving him in ways he couldn't comprehend.

He was lost. Lost in her.

The wisps of discomfort that had been edging at her insides curled into knots and twisted into a ball.

He dropped a kiss behind her ear. "Don't freak out. But I just realized we forgot to use a condom."

The free-flowing *pallu* she was trying to place on her shoulder slipped from her hands. He caught it, took the safety pin she was holding, and threaded it deftly through the sari and the blouse, pinning them together.

"You're amazingly good at this," she said before letting the words she really wanted to say out, because she couldn't not say them anymore. "I have an IUD."

"I worked in a sweatshop in the Honduras for a while folding clothes." He snapped the pin in place. "Why didn't you tell me before? Although Drew's wife Kayla actually got pregnant with an IUD. You remember Drew, right? My roommate in med school?"

The knotted-up ball of discomfort moved up to her heart, gathering terror as it went.

"They had to remove it surgically, but they saved McKenzie. And she's the sweetest baby in the world too." He stroked her neck. "I want one just like her. Actually, I want as many just like her as I can have." His smile was pure pleasure.

The bubble exploded. Guilt burned through her veins like acid.

He patted down her *pallu*. "I can handle fabric with my eyes closed," he said easily, as if he hadn't noticed her stiffen. "You should see me make towel animals. This old Chinese guy at the factory in Guatemala, he was an origami master, he used to teach us at break time over drags of some good *ganj*." He said the words easily, smiling as if it was of no consequence.

The guilt in her veins ruptured and flooded through her, destroying everything in its way.

He had been in a sweatshop, folding clothes. Because of her.

And he wanted babies. Lots of babies. That she couldn't have.

Her stomach lurched. She felt dizzy and disoriented, as though she'd been thrown off a merry-go-round and she couldn't stop spinning. These past two days with Vikram had been a dream. She had shut out every murmur of the fear and self-loathing that had congealed and calcified inside her all these years. Now it spun violently back to life inside her, growing so fast and so thick it choked her. In the space of one second, the dark niggling feelings she'd been ignoring swallowed her whole.

Vikram circled her waist, pulled her close, and rested his cheek against her head. "Ria, I didn't say that to make you feel bad. I didn't say any of that to make you do anything you don't want to," he whispered into her hair.

"I know." Her chest rose and fell, but no air collected in her lungs.

"It wasn't your fault, sweetheart. It was me. All me."

*It isn't your fault, beta, none of this is your fault.* Baba had repeated those words over and over before he sent her away to boarding school straight from the hospital. He had never let her return to the house again. Even then Ria had known that you couldn't feel this guilty about something if it wasn't your fault.

"Ria, everything turned out right. I don't regret any of it."

"I know you don't." But it was her fault. She did that to him. Sent him to hell, took everything from him. And she was going to do it again. No matter what she did now, it was going to happen again.

She rubbed the barely visible scar on her shoulder—shaped like the ring of the creature's teeth. The insanity lurking inside her took a step closer and wrapped its icy hands around her throat. Oh God, how was he going to survive it? How was she going to survive it? How could she have let this happen again? Suddenly, she didn't have the strength to be standing here with his arms around her, holding her as if she were something precious.

The smell of sex and the smell of his skin melded into a searing mass inside her head. She took a deep breath, trying to brand it all into memory. All the places he had touched were still warm, still sore from pleasure. She sucked on the sensations like a leech, shamelessly hoarded them, clutching the sand tight in her fist, even as it slipped from between her fingers.

She pulled his hands from around her. Pain paralyzed her heart, tears burned behind her eyelids, but she would not break down. Her crying days were over. It was over. All of it.

He stiffened behind her. She knew she would see panic in his eyes if she dared to look into them. "We have to go," she said, swallowing to keep it even. "By now the cops are probably looking for us." Even to her own ears her voice sounded contrived and cold. She pushed the door open and stepped into the corridor. Before he could pull her back in, she started walking toward the elevators.

He was by her side in an instant. "Ria, what's wrong?" She heard him fight to keep the panic out of his voice. "Did I do something?" He was trying to make eye contact, but she wouldn't let him. "Listen, I shouldn't have pushed you so hard back there. I'm sorry. Please don't panic."

They turned into the elevator lobby and Ria walked up to the mirror on the wall. She stared at herself, pretending to be absorbed in setting herself straight. She patted down her hair, rubbed at her smudged kohl, wiped at her swollen lips. She refused to look into her own eyes. She couldn't bear to see the remnants of what they had shared. Not with him standing so close and watching her every move.

"God, I'm a mess," she said, not giving a damn what she looked like.

"You're beautiful," he said, taking a step toward her. But she took a quick step away.

"The elevator. I think the elevator is here." She tried not to think about their last trip in the elevator. She prayed there would be other people in there.

For once her prayers were answered. An old couple all spiffily dressed for dinner smiled widely at them when the elevator doors opened. The smell of her flowery perfume and his expensive aftershave filled the space. It flooded through Ria and washed away the other smell from her brain. The old lady was leaning on a walker, one of those four-legged devices. It took up most of the elevator. Ria quickly moved to the far corner, squeezing past the walker, pretending to get out of the way.

Vikram followed her and stood all the way across from her, too polite to ask the lady to move and let him pass. Ria refused to look at him. She would never look him in the eye again.

The lady said something nice about Ria's sari and Ria thanked her profusely, clutching at straws to keep from drowning. The lady chattered away about her visit to Chicago. They were out to celebrate their fiftieth anniversary. They were from Ann Arbor. They had been here for four days. The children had paid for everything.

When they stepped out of the elevator, she gave Ria a hug. "Good luck to you both, darling, you make such a lovely couple," she said.

"You too." A raw sob constricted Ria's throat and she swallowed it and waved good-bye as they walked away side by side, the old man's gnarled hand resting on the small of his wife's back.

"Okay, Ria, what's going on?" Vikram reached out and held her arm, stopping her before she could make her escape.

"Where on earth have you been?" A loud authoritative voice said from behind them. "We've been looking all over for you."

Both Vikram and Ria turned around at the sound of the voice.

"Ma? When did you get here?" Vikram let go of Ria and hugged his mother.

Chitra Jathar reached around her son and squeezed him, her flawless angel's face glowing as she beamed up at him. She hadn't changed one bit. Not a line, not a gray hair. She was exactly as she had been ten years ago.

They had identical eyes, Vikram and his mother. At least the color and shape were an exact match. But on Chitra they were sharp and calculating instead of warm and vulnerable. Her skin was also the exact same color as his. Only, hers was pale and anemic from staying militantly out of the sun to preserve the lightness, where Vikram's was toasted bronze from never being indoors for too long. But unlike her son, Chitra was a small person. All of five feet tall and possibly ninety pounds. When Vikram hugged her she disappeared into his hug like a cloth doll.

A look of such possessive affection suffused her face when she kissed his cheek that for a moment Ria saw her as a loving mother and not the heartless monster she was.

"Where is Ravi?" Vikram asked, looking around.

Chitra gave him a reprimanding look and slapped him fondly on his arm. "Your *father*," she said, "is with Nikhil and that girl he's marrying. The garland exchange is about to start. Where were you?"

Suddenly she seemed to remember that Ria was standing next to them. She turned to her with the warmest smile Ria had ever received from her. Ria shifted uncomfortably and cursed herself for not making her escape when she'd had the chance. Vikram seemed to sense her thoughts and moved so that she was trapped between them and the elevators.

"So, this is Mira then?" Chitra said. "Hello, *beta*. It's lovely to meet you." Her smile was so openly fond and welcoming that Ria was tempted to pretend to be Mira, just for one moment. The pretending was starting to feel good again.

"No, Ma, it's Ria. You remember Ria?" Her name was a caress on Vikram's lips.

Chitra's eyes iced over, one liquid crystal at a time.

Ria had seen Vikram's eyes do that exact same thing so many times when she had first arrived that it was like going back in time. Only it didn't feel like twelve days, it felt like twelve lifetimes. Twelve of the happiest, most heartbreaking lifetimes anyone could ever live.

"Hi, Chitra Atya." Ria struggled to keep her voice even, her eyes dry. She could not get herself to lean over and touch the woman's feet like she should have. Chitra's eyes hardened even more.

Ria could see the flood of questions flicker across Chitra's face as she looked from Vikram to her, taking in every detail of their appearance. Ria watched her note every wrinkle on Vikram's *sherwani,* every hair out of place on Ria's head.

*What kind of whore opens her legs at such a young age?*

Ria's hands turned clammy and she itched to wipe them on her sari. She had to get away. Get out of this corridor, this hotel, this godforsaken country. Get as far away from everything as she could.

It was over. The wedding would be over in a few hours. Nikhil and Jen would be gone in a few days. There was no reason for her to stay another two days as planned. She would convince Uma and Vijay to come and spend time with her in Mumbai, the way they had done in the past. Nikhil and Jen would have to come there to see her too. She was never, ever coming back here again.

"Hello, Ria," Chitra said, noticing her son's expression and finding her voice. "I didn't know you were coming to the wedding."

"How could Ria not come to Nikhil's wedding, Ma?" Vikram said.

*Because she thinks she got rid of me forever.*

"All I was saying is that Uma always whines about how the girl never visits anymore. I thought she was too busy with her . . . um . . . career." Chitra said the word as if it sullied her mouth to say it.

"You were supposed to be here yesterday, Ma. Talk about pot calling the kettle black," he said, his voice fond but distant the way it always was when he spoke to his parents. If he sensed the tidal undercurrents rising between Chitra and her he chose to ignore them and turned his focus on Ria instead, hiding nothing of his feelings. "Of course Ria's busy. She's a *film star.*" He said the word the way Ria said it, and tried to smile his teasing smile.

If she stood here for another moment she knew she would pass out from the pain in her heart. "I have to go. I don't want to miss the garland exchange." She sounded desperately close to tears. Vikram took a step closer to her. She could sense the worried frown on his face. He was about to take her hand, but she jumped away from him, stumbling backward and almost tipping over the flower arrangement behind her. "Seriously, I have to go. Right now." Her voice came out high-pitched and out of control.

Chitra's eyes went round with shock. She stared at Ria as if she were already a raging lunatic and the dislike in her eyes turned to pure, unadulterated fear.

That was it. Ria couldn't take it anymore. She shoved Vikram aside and squeezed past Chitra and darted away, not looking back when Vikram called out her name. The panic in his voice tore into her heart and she sped up.

# 26

Ria didn't stop until she reached the banquet hall where the wedding was taking place. It wasn't time for the garland exchange yet. The Giving Away the Bride ceremony had just begun, where Uma and Vijay would welcome Jen into the family in the presence of everyone they held dear. Matt was going to give Jen away. He wore a *kurta* and loose *salwar* pants. Mindy stood nearby in a sari. And next to her stood her son, Drew. Even with his thinning hair and traditional Indian clothes, Ria recognized him instantly. Fortunately he was busy taking pictures with a humungous camera slung around his neck, and she didn't have to talk to him.

"This is Kayla, Ria, Drew's wife." Mindy introduced her daughter-in-law. "And this is McKenzie, our granddaughter." Mindy turned to the baby perched on Kayla's hip and her voice turned gooey.

McKenzie drooled onto a frilly bib that protected her frothy pink dress. Her chubby baby thighs squeezed around her mother. She gave Ria a wide, two-toothed smile and gripped her mother tighter. Ria tried to lift her hand and touch McKenzie, ruffle her hair, squeeze her cheeks, do something people did when they saw babies. But she couldn't. Her arms wouldn't move.

*I want as many just like her as I can have.*

She tried to pull a smile across her face like she had done a million times before, but all she could manage was a nod.

The priest asked Vijay and Uma to join hands and directed Matt to place Jen's hand in theirs, and everyone's attention shifted to the altar. Jen's hand trembled with emotion and Uma gave it the slightest squeeze and Vijay smiled at her in his reassuring way. A promise passed between the three of them, wrapping itself around them. Uma and Vijay led Jen to their side of the altar, repeating their vows after the priest in chaste, unaccented Sanskrit, promising to give their new daughter-in-law a place of love and respect in the family. A promise Ria knew they would never break.

Ria squeezed next to Uma as she sat cross-legged in front of the fire for the next set of rites, getting as close to Uma as she could, in desperate need of her warmth. Uma unconsciously put her arm around Ria and pulled her close and continued to follow the priest's directions without pausing.

Vikram sat down next to her. His heat, his smell, punched her in the gut and laid her flat even before his warm hand pressed into her back. Her stomach clenched and pain cramped through her like a disease. She couldn't bear it. She pushed into Uma, wishing she could disappear into her softness. Vikram's hand caressed her back, trying to get her attention, trying to get her to look at him. But she just couldn't do it.

His mother stood a few feet away, talking to his father. Two faces in a sea of faces. Ravi Jathar was even taller than his son, but lean as a beanpole with thick gray hair and the air of a man completely in command of himself and his world. It was like looking at a future version of Vikram. Ria's already aching heart crumpled in her chest.

Ravi had to bend almost in half to let his wife speak into his ear. Every few minutes Chitra threw a glance at her and Ria knew they were discussing her.

Had he been part of Chitra's ambush all those years ago? Was that what they were discussing now? *You remember Uma's crazy sister-in-law? . . . The one who burned their house down and killed her husband? . . . That's their daughter. . . . Uma's charity case . . . The pathetic kid who used to hang around Vikram all the time. . . . The one who tried to trap him when he was young and stupid and too generous for his own good.*

*The one who took him away from us. The one who almost ruined his life.*

Vikram cupped her elbow and the room spun.

"Ria, we need to talk, please," he whispered into her ear. She heard the pleading tremor in his voice and closed her eyes against a fresh wave of shame. She pulled her arm away and withdrew farther into herself. "No," she whispered, shaking her head, not looking at him. "I want to be here for the garland ceremony. It's about to start."

"Okay," he said stiffly. "But I need to know what's going on." He should have sounded angry, furious, but instead he sounded confused and helpless. As if they were having a lover's tiff. As if she were just some normal girl having a normal meltdown that he needed to get past.

God, what had she done? Somehow it was worse this time. This time she had no excuse. This time she had known exactly what she was doing. This time they had gone too far.

Her cell phone was in Uma's bag. She pulled it out and texted DJ.

Before the garland ceremony had begun she was booked on that night's flight out of Chicago.

Ria had been looking forward to the garland ceremony more than any other ritual. It was when Jen and Nikhil would finally become husband and wife. But when the time came for them to actually exchange the heavy rosebud garlands, Ria was beyond all feeling. Everything around her had started to pass by in a numb haze. She obsessively shadowed Uma, who instinctively kept her close, not asking any questions. Why hadn't this woman given birth to her? Why hadn't she been the one to give her life?

Ria remembered asking Uma that question as a child. *Uma Atya, why can't you be my aie? Why does Nikhil get you? Why not me?*

*I'll tell you a secret,* Uma had said, kissing her forehead and touching her heart. *Inside my heart, right here, I am your aie. You* are *mine.*

And she was. Uma's smell, her feel, it was the only thing that could keep Ria sane right now. One thought about anything else, any of the things Viky and she had done to each other, any of the things she had felt would drive her over the edge. She followed Uma as they went from ritual to ritual until finally, Ria found herself standing behind Nikhil as he stepped up to the final act that would make him a husband.

Nikhil stood across from Jen, separated from her by an intricately woven shawl. Vikram held one end of the shawl up and Vijay held the other, stretching it taut into a curtain. Nikhil and Jen stood on two sides of it, unable to see each other, separated and single for the last time, clasping the thick garlands in their hands, waiting. All their friends and family stood around them in waves of exuberant color radiating across the hall, saffron-stained rice grains cupped in their palms.

The *shehnai* flutes started wailing and the priest started singing the wedding song. Verse by verse. Every time he came to the chorus his voice crescendoed on the words.

*"It's here, the most auspicious of moments. Be aware! Be alert! Be prepared!"*

As he sang out the warning, the guests showered rice on the couple, the rice taking the form of their blessings and falling like raindrops on their hair, their shoulders, their feet, blessing them with fertility and prosperity and all the joys that joining together would bring.

Finally after the last verse, after the last call to "Be aware! Be alert! Be prepared!" Vikram and Vijay Kaka lowered the curtain and Nikhil and Jen exchanged garlands. Ria was shaking, the moment so powerful, its force so indelible, that it filled the room. Uma, all the aunties, Mindy, even Vijay Kaka, everyone had tears in their eyes. And just like that it was done.

The newlyweds moved around the room bending over to touch the elders' feet and seek blessings for the first time as a married couple, seeking blessings as one. When the blessings were done, the guests descended on the couple, hugging and kissing and congratulating. By the time Ria reached them, Nikhil and Jen looked love-worn and drunk on happiness. Nikhil lifted Ria off her feet as she hugged him and twirled her around. Jen pulled her close and whispered something that sounded like concern in her ear. But Ria didn't hear her.

Ria heard nothing. She felt nothing but the huge choking lump in her throat. But she couldn't cry. One single tear would drown her. She knew it would. She kissed Nikhil's forehead and he beamed at her with glistening eyes as though all his dreams had finally come true. How so much pain and such happiness could fit in the tiny space inside her, Ria didn't know. But everything receded behind a fog and sped by in a blur. Through it all Vikram watched her, tried to get close to her. She felt his eyes on her like his touch, hot and demanding. She didn't look at him once. She couldn't.

When the guests headed out to the patio for lunch, Vikram tried again to draw her aside, grabbing her arm when she tried to get away, weaving his arm around her waist, trying to lead her away from the crowd. But the crowd had grown too thick and Ria easily found someone to interrupt them, to shield her from him. His eyes pierced her, sought answers. His soft, slowly eroding voice called her, but he couldn't reach her. She was too far gone. Too dead to feel anything when he touched her. Too dead to feel anything ever again.

As soon as he got busy helping Vijay with something, she slipped away from the hall, crossing the sprawling hotel in search of an exit, desperately in need of air. She pushed through the heavy door and out into the open. Redbrick terraces led down to the swimming pool. She made her way down the disjointed steps to the edge of the pool. The smell of chlorine filled the air, acrid and pungent. The pool water gleamed an unnatural placid blue, undisturbed by swimmers. There wasn't a single person in sight. It was too cold for a swim. Relief flooded through Ria and she sucked in a breath, welcoming the burn of chlorine into her lungs, welcoming the sting of the cold on her bare shoulders.

"Can I have a word with you?" Chitra came up behind her. What was it with mother and son sneaking up on her like that? Ria closed her eyes and begged for mercy. She couldn't think of anyone she wanted to see less right now. She couldn't think of one single person she wanted to see less of for the rest of her life.

Dredging up every ounce of strength she had left, Ria opened her eyes and turned around to face Chitra. The yellow silk of Chitra's sari blazed against the blue of the pool. "I've had all the words I can handle from you. I can't do this right now." She started walking back toward the door.

"How are you feeling these days?" Chitra asked as if Ria hadn't spoken.

Ria kept walking, Chitra hot on her heels. "You showed up two hours before the wedding—shouldn't you be more concerned with how Nikhil and 'that girl he's marrying' are doing?" Ria said over her shoulder. "Her name is Jen, by the way. And she's a doctor, so we have the intelligence in her genes covered. Unfortunately, we have no way of knowing if there's any insanity in her gene pool—she was adopted." Ria finally stopped, because getting away from Chitra was proving impossible. Chitra showed every intention of chasing her down. Ria knew only too well how that would turn out.

"Who Nikhil marries is Uma and Vijay's problem, not ours," Chitra said in her smug, perfectly polished voice. "Vic, on the other hand, is our only son. What were you doing with him when I caught you?"

How could those eyes, those very same eyes, be this cruel, this hateful?

"Didn't you tell me once that you came from a line of intellectuals fifteen generations deep? You figure it out."

"Wow, quite a tongue you've sprouted. Who would've thought." The woman actually had the gall to look impressed.

Ria clasped her hands tightly together, trying to keep from running her fingers through her hair, trying to keep from pulling her hair out, trying to keep from letting Chitra see the uncontrollable shaking in her fingers. "It's been ten years," she said. "Did you expect me to be the same easy target?"

Chitra laughed. There wasn't even the slightest hint of doubt in her voice when she spoke. "You're the exact same person you were back then. Don't think just because you've garnered some cheap fame and money that anything has changed. Nothing has changed. I just wanted to make sure you knew that."

Ria's heart started to hammer. Her breath turned hot. She welcomed the rage that collected in her belly like lava and rose up inside her. This woman had pounded her into the ground on the saddest day of her life, and now here she was to finish the job. And Ria wanted to laugh at the timing of it.

"You're right. Nothing's changed," Ria said. "You're still the heartless witch you were back then. Are you going to threaten me again? Threaten to disown your own son if you can't control him?"

The words didn't make even a dent in Chitra's smugness. "It isn't about control. It's about protecting my child. I'm his mother. But how would you know? How would you know anything about how a mother feels?"

Ria's knees buckled, but she'd die before she let Chitra see it. "I might have had a mother who feels nothing for me, but at least my mother didn't crush my dreams and then act like she was doing me a favor."

"I crushed Vic's dreams? Was I the one who lured him in? Used my body to trap him? Was I the one who ruined his career? Almost ruined his life?" How could the woman's voice be this calm, this controlled, when she was spewing such venom?

"You threatened to cut off all ties with your son if I stayed with him. You threatened to disown him, to never see his face again. As if he were a sick pet you could put down and forget about. You threatened to take everything away from him when he needed you the most."

"He needed us? Or you needed us? And it worked, didn't it? Without our support, you didn't want him either. Where did your love go then? Who wants a penniless boy when you can have fame and fortune, right?"

Ria was shaking too hard now and she didn't care if Chitra saw it. "Fame and fortune?" she asked, her voice trembling. "Fame and fortune?" she repeated the words, spitting them out and throwing them up in the air as if they were hot coals she was trying to juggle. Her voice turned more and more high-pitched with each rendition. Chitra took a step back.

"If fame was what I wanted, you think I needed to leave Vikram for it? If fortune was my dream, you think Vikram would have stood in my way? He wouldn't have left me no matter what I wanted to be. He would've stood by me no matter what."

"And yet you chose to dump him like so much garbage. You took the easy way out. You could've ignored me. You didn't have to do as I asked. You could have struggled to build a life with him. But it was easier to open your legs and get what you wanted instantly, wasn't it? God knows you had enough practice."

Everything turned hot and black and singed. Chitra's blue-gray eyes sparkled with triumph and an intense urge to smash her angel head into the wall behind her overcame Ria. She pictured blood running down her hands as she kept slamming, unable to stop. She backed away from Chitra, putting distance between them as fast as she could, her fists clenched so tight her fingers numbed, her jaw clenched so hard her teeth ground out dust in her mouth.

"You have no answer for that, do you?" Chitra goaded, her sari billowing in the wind, her petite form turning gigantic and distorted in Ria's vision.

"Are you really that stupid?" Ria hissed through the physical, tangible heat of her breath. "Can you really not figure it out on your own? Didn't you ever wonder why I never told Vikram about your threats? Don't you wonder why he still doesn't know? Why I still haven't told him, all these years later, when I have nothing left to lose?"

Chitra took a quick step back, wobbling slightly on her heels. The triumph in her eyes popped like a bubble. No, Chitra wasn't stupid. Fear flooded her eyes as understanding dawned on her. Ria wanted to get away from her, but she couldn't stop now. This too had to end today.

"It was never about you. Never about your threats. Never about keeping you from disowning Vikram and throwing him out. It was about keeping him from throwing you out of his life. Even today, I can take your son away from you with one word." She snapped her fingers in Chitra's face. "If he ever finds out what you did, you'll never see him again. You'll lose him forever." She watched terror spread across Chitra's face and drew strength from it. "Fortunately for you, I would never do that to him. I am the only reason you still have your son."

Chitra had gone as white as the clouds streaking the blue sky behind her—all the fight squeezed out of her silk-wrapped body like a deflated balloon. A wisp of tinder that Ria could ignite with just one spark. And it made Ria sick to her stomach. Evil as Chitra was, she had to be better than the mother-shaped hole that had defined her own life. Hard as it was to imagine right now, even someone like Chitra for a mother had to be better than the indelible scars Ria carried on her body and the desperate craving and shame she had lived with all her life.

Chitra was Vikram's mother and the thought of losing him made all her arrogance, all her brutal machinations go up in smoke. Vikram had that. Ria would never have that. How could she take that away from him after everything else she had already taken?

Suddenly all her anger, every ounce of her strength dissipated, leaving her drained. Chitra stared at her—her Vikram-shaped mouth hanging open.

"Are you going to tell him?" she asked, her voice paper thin with fear.

Disgust rose in Ria's chest. She wanted the same thing Chitra wanted—to protect Vikram from the unforgiving secrets of her past, from the inevitable violence of her future. But she'd be damned if she gave Chitra the satisfaction of knowing that. "If you ever threaten me again, or if you ever try to control Vikram in any way, I'll make sure you lose him forever." She turned around and walked away.

This time Chitra didn't follow her. "Are you going to tell him?" She called from behind Ria, as persistent as her son.

"No. But I'm going to rip his heart to bits," Ria mumbled to herself. "Good luck picking up the pieces."

Ria pushed the heavy metal door with all her strength and it swung open. She stepped into the lobby and slammed it shut behind her, needing a physical barrier to separate her from the woman she hated almost as much as she loved her son. She never wanted to be faced with either of them ever again.

Across the lobby she saw an elevator open and rushed to it, reaching it just as it started to slide shut. She slipped in through the closing doors and started pounding on the Door-Close button as if this entire mess was its fault and not hers. But it didn't respond, didn't recognize her desperation. The mirrored doors took their time to make their way across the wide opening with lazy grace. A far too familiar hand wedged itself into the closing gap and the doors slid open again.

Vikram stepped in. Ria tried to rush back out, but his arms wrapped around her and held her in place. The doors closed, this time too fast. The elevator started to move. He tried to turn her in his arms, but she lurched away from him.

"Okay, that's it. Game over, Ria. What's going on?" Patience laced his voice, and strength, so much strength.

The shaking started again. Maybe it hadn't stopped at all. She had to do this right now. If she wanted to get away from him she had to get the words out. He wasn't going to let her go until she got the words out.

"You're right, game's over." She tried to imagine the heat of the set lights on her skin, but the ice wrapped around her was too thick. She willed it to harden in her veins and hold her up.

"What is that supposed to mean? Will you at least look at me?" The muscles in his forearms flexed as he controlled the reflex to reach for her again. "Sweetheart, at least look at me. Please. Tell me what's wrong. We can fix this."

*No, we can't. God, if only we could.*

The elevator stopped. Ria rushed out and kept walking, Vikram hot on her heels.

"There's nothing to fix. I should never have let this happen. I should never have let you suck me in again. I have to get back to Mumbai. I have a movie starting next week. I'm leaving tonight."

"Like hell you are." He stopped mid-step, his voice no longer gentle. "You're not going anywhere." His words slashed like a whip against her back.

She had to stop. She had to do this. "Don't, Vikram," she said, turning around. "Don't do this. You can't stop me. You knew I wouldn't stay. You knew I had to go back to my life in the end. The wedding's over. It's done. I was always supposed to leave after that. That was always the plan. You complicated everything by starting this up again and now it's going to turn into a huge mess."

"Like hell I started it," he said. "And don't call me Vikram. I hate it." She could see his control slipping, see the age-old anger and hurt kindle back to life inside him.

She stoked it. It was her only hope. "Believe whatever you want. But you did start it. You came after me. You were the first man in my life, my first relationship, and those are always easy to fall back into. But I have a movie to shoot and—"

"Ria, cut the crap. What's going on? The truth, plain and simple. Something's scared the shit out of you, what is it, sweathear—?"

"Of course I'm scared. Nikhil, Uma Atya, Vijay Kaka, they're going to kill me. If you run off and do something stupid again, they're going to blame me for it and I'll never be able to face them again." The words flowed fast, spurting from her, fuelled by the force of her mounting fear.

His breath sped up, came in spurts. He didn't want to believe her, but they had those ten years between them, and they overpowered him. She watched him turn twenty again, watched him fight it.

"Are you crazy?" he asked. "Weren't you there yesterday? Weren't you back there in the linen room just now? Where's that person I made love with? Where are you, Ria?" He tried to look into her eyes again. But she couldn't bring herself to let him. His voice rose. "How can you do this? Haven't you learned anything? You'll never find this again." He waved his hand between them, tracing that invisible arc, that bloody invisible arc that was her noose, her lifeline. "There's no more of it out there, Ria. Can't you fight for it? Can't you fight for us? Whatever it is you're so damn terrified of. Whatever the fuck it is. Isn't this bigger?"

His chest pumped, his *sherwani* caught the fluorescent light in silken flashes. His hair stood in spikes after umpteen assaults from his fingers.

"Ria?" He searched her face, lost, in shock, desperate for answers.

But her words were gone. She was wrung dry, empty. Words that were afraid of everyone else had never been afraid of him. Now he was their greatest fear.

His hands balled into fists, pushing against defeat, refusing to back down. Remnants of hope mingled with such pain in his eyes, shame burned through what was left of her.

"Just tell me what it is. Just open your mouth and tell me what the hell it is." His eyes beseeched her, opening up until each glistening crystal exposed his soul. He could take anything. He would pay any price, walk away from his family, his work, give up everything that mattered to him, give up being a father without so much as a thought. He wouldn't leave her, not when she turned into an animal, not when she turned his home into a mausoleum, not even when she set him on fire. This she knew with as much certainty as she knew she was alive. And she would never let that happen.

Every cell in her body hardened with purpose. With every fiber of her being she shut him out, and she knew the precise moment when he saw it. If his eyes had bled thick, black liquid pain, his hurt couldn't have been more visible to her.

"Fine," he said when the silence between them had stretched out long enough that he knew it was impregnable, knew she was immovable.

When he spoke again, his voice had a deadly finality to it. "So again, you've made up your mind. You get to decide. I don't get a say." Anger suffused some of the pain in his eyes. "If you can still hear me. If any of this is still reaching you, I want you to listen very carefully. I told you this once before—I won't chase you again. I can't. If you can throw this away, if you can live without it, then go. But if you leave me now, if you run from us again, it's over. Finished. Don't bother coming back. Ever. You hear me? Never again. If you walk away from me now, you will never see me again."

He waited for her to respond, his body locked in place, his chest stock still. No breath entered or left him, every part of him focused on her answer as if all he had to do was want it badly enough and it would be his.

"Ria?"

Nothing.

Finally he lifted her chin, unsteady fingers forcing her to meet his eyes. She lifted her eyelids and let him look. He searched the charred emptiness left inside her. She wasn't afraid to let him look anymore, because there was nothing left there to hide except the leftover scraps of her. He pulled his hand back, letting her go, unable to bear what he saw. And it finally pushed him away.

When she walked away from him, he didn't try to stop her.

Where Vikram went after that, she didn't know. She was barely conscious of her own actions. Somehow she got herself through the rest of the day. Nikhil and Jen tried to talk to her before they left, but she had this down to an art. No one stood a chance. No one would get through to her and they wouldn't even know it. She didn't say good-bye. She couldn't. They would find her gone tomorrow at the reception. She would make up for it later. Later, when she knew how.

The only person she spoke to was Uma. The only person who would understand that she had to go, without forcing her to come up with reasons neither one of them believed. "I have to go, Uma Atya, it can't wait." She dug the words out with all the strength she had left.

"You know you can talk to me about anything, right?" It was all Uma said when Ria allowed herself one last pleasure of letting Uma hold her close when she said good-bye.

Ria would have given anything to be able to talk to Uma, to put her mind at ease. But the words were all gone. Lost forever. There was only silence inside her. She could find only one word to whisper into Uma's hair before letting her go. It rose up inside her and slipped from her lips. "Aie," she said, and then she wrapped it up in the feel of Uma's softness and took it away with her.

# 27

*Mumbai*

DJ threw the drapes open, and Ria blinked and pulled the white cotton quilt up to her chin. Bright light rushed in through the windows and pierced daggers into her head. She crossed her arms over her eyes. Pain shot from her elbows.

Why was DJ in her bedroom? "How are you feeling?" he asked, and Ria had to clear the fuzz in her brain to know what he was talking about.

He put a cup of tea on the nightstand and leaned over to help her up. She pushed him away and sat up by herself, picking up the cup. The tea tasted like dishwater. Ria wanted coffee, with the perfect balance of cream and sugar and mellow bitterness. And a strong, steady hand to slide the cup toward her. She pressed her hand against the pain in her heart and straightened against the headboard. A more bearable pain spasmed in her back and smarted in her elbows, her knees, the side of her face, and the memory of that night came back to her. How long ago had that been?

"Do you need a painkiller?" DJ asked, frowning at her.

She shook her head. The pain felt good.

"Are you going to tell me what you were thinking, doing something so stupid?" He gave her the famous DJ glower. She had forgotten it.

The journey back to Mumbai had gone by in a blur. It had felt in part like the blink of an eye and in part like an eternity. Coming out of Mumbai airport Ria had been so numb, so disconnected from herself, she had forgotten that she should wait inside the terminal for DJ to come and get her. She had walked straight out of the airport, meaning to hail a cab. It had taken less than a minute for the mob to collect, and another minute for them to start pulling and tugging at her. Touching her hair, her clothes, groping parts of her she did not want anyone to touch ever again.

By the time she realized what she had done, it was too late to get herself to safety. Fortunately, DJ had been nearby looking for her. It had taken the combined strength of him, his driver, and two security guards to pull the mob off Ria and pick her up off the sidewalk, where she sat on her knees, her face pressed into the concrete with her hands over her head, her clothes ripped, her skin gouged off, mauled and bleeding.

DJ had asked over and over again how she could do something as stupid as that. She had no idea how to tell him that she had forgotten who she was. That she had forgotten everything she had been before she left. That she would never be any of those things again. She had no idea how to tell him how being torn on the outside was nothing compared to how she felt on the inside.

DJ stared at her, waiting for an answer. The impatience in his eyes pushed at the deadening sadness inside her. She knew she should answer him, but forming words was taking too much effort these days.

"Sorry," she said, forcing the word out and then coughing from the effort it took.

He waited for more, but she looked away and took another sip of the dishwater.

"'Sorry,' that's all I get?"

He wanted more? Maybe "I'm really sorry" would help. Again, she tried to say the words, but nothing came out.

"Ria, it's been four days since you came back and I've got a total of five words out of you. What's wrong, babes? What happened in Chicago?"

Ria wanted to laugh. Now *there* was a question worth sinking her teeth into, a question words had been invented for. He was a busy man. "How much time do you have?" she wanted to ask him.

"What the hell is funny?" Concern flooded his face. He waited for an answer, then gave up.

"Ria, it's past noon. You were supposed to be at a meeting with the director at ten this morning. I've called you a hundred times. Don't you answer your phone anymore? Where is it?"

She had no idea where her phone was.

He started to walk around her room looking for it. "Listen, babes, you have to snap out of it, whatever it is. You've never missed an appointment, what is—" He picked up the pillow next to her and found the phone under it. "It's completely out of power." He glared at the phone and started hunting for something else. "He's rescheduled it. But only because it's you. And because I spent all morning pacifying him." He found a charger and plugged the phone in. "We need to get there in an hour. Shit! Look at you! Ria? Get out of bed, please!"

He started to yank the sheets off her and she grabbed them in horror. She felt the sheet slide off her. Felt her bare body beneath it. Saw one of Viky's eyes open as he laughed at her absurd bashfulness. Frantically, she pulled the sheet to her chin, reached under the sheets, and ran a hand over herself, touching her clothes to make sure they were there. Her cotton shirt bunched beneath her fingers. Relief and embarrassment flooded through her, crashing against the pain wedged so tight inside her she was amazed she could feel anything else.

DJ looked at her funny again—a scared, pitying look you saved for rabid strays on their way to the pound. Ria forced herself to swing her legs off the bed and stood. Behind her DJ picked up the sheets that fell to the floor as she dragged herself to the bathroom. She hadn't showered in days, didn't remember the last time she had left the bed. She could smell herself, sticky and sour.

It took every ounce of strength she possessed to climb into the tub and turn on the shower. With every sharp, spraying droplet Vikram's fingers dragged across her body, gentle, then insistent.

His lips, his tongue, his smooth sliding skin caressed every inch of her. She squeezed her eyes shut and turned up the heat until her skin scalded and all feeling disappeared except the stinging burn of the water hitting her.

When she stepped into the living room, weaving on her feet from the heat, she saw takeout food boxes sitting on the dining table. DJ had even laid out a couple of plates. A tremor of gratefulness quivered through her hard, frozen insides. She sat down next to him. He muted the TV and forked some food on her plate. They ate in silence, watching the stiffly dressed news anchor on TV move her lips to stories that flashed in vignettes behind her. Suddenly, Ria's face splashed across the screen and DJ punched up the volume.

". . . Film star Ria Parkar was mobbed outside Mumbai airport on Sunday," the anchor said in formal, literary Hindi. "Sources have confirmed that the fiercely private star was returning to Mumbai after a closely guarded vacation overseas. Ms. Parkar was taken to the hospital where she is said to be recuperating from her reportedly severe injuries."

They both stared at the TV.

The newswoman picked up the sheaf of papers in front of her and tapped them on her desk, straightening the already neat stack in a practiced, professional-looking move. "The star is scheduled to appear in Shivshri's next magnum opus *Piya Ke Ghar Jaana—PKGJ*, which is slated to release next month. She will also be starring in their next film, *StarGangster*, which commences shooting soon."

As she signed off, asking the audience to stay tuned for news on the earthquake in Bangladesh, the promo for *PKGJ* came on.

"You've got to love this business." DJ stabbed his noodles with disposable wooden chopsticks. "Bastards. Not bad for hospital food, ha?" He lifted a clump of noodles at Ria in a salute and shoved them into his mouth.

Ria continued to chew, the oily spiciness jabbing at her taste buds. She swallowed to clamp down on the food, but it edged back up her throat. It had nothing to do with the news, her body just wasn't ready for food. Sometime soon she would work her way up to being upset. Right now she was just glad to find the strength to go on chewing.

As it turned out, it would have been a better idea not to eat. The meeting with the director was a disaster. Ria ended up spending the entire afternoon trying to keep the food down. She had never finished reading the script and her churning stomach made it impossible to keep her mind on anything anyone was saying. She had never worked with Samir Rathod, the director, before. Until now they'd always done completely different kinds of films. But he had been the media's darling for years, with a special talent for staying in the papers for all the wrong reasons.

"He's not the same Samir Rathod you're used to seeing in the papers," DJ kept telling her. "Trust me, you're going to love working with him."

But Samir was far too full of enthusiasm, far too intense. Far too tall, broad-shouldered, and buff. He made Ria's skin crawl with discomfort. He peppered every line that came out of his mouth with her name as if they were old friends. "The script is pure gold, Ria." "I'm sure you can't wait to get started, Ria."

Each time he said her name it sickened and violated her. All she wanted to do was get away from him.

"Sweetheart, are you okay?" he asked, placing his large gentle hand on her shoulder, and Ria jumped and backed out of the room, rushing out of the building, leaving DJ mumbling apologies in her wake.

"He was just trying to be nice, Ria. Just give him a chance," DJ told her in the car, carefully ignoring her bizarre exit.

But Ria was certain she never wanted to see the man again, never wanted to see the inside of a studio. She didn't know how to tell DJ that she wouldn't be there when shooting started to give him a chance. She just didn't have the strength to stand in front of a camera. She was fresh out of it. Whatever it was you needed to keep going.

The only time Ria felt remotely alive was when she talked to Uma. With Uma she was able to get the words out. Not too many, but just the few she needed to keep Uma from getting on a plane. She needed to hear Uma's voice. Even if she talked about the most inane of things. Even if everything Uma said was only to keep from saying the words she really wanted to say. Questions teetered and danced on Uma's tongue, but she held them in. Ria couldn't fathom how Uma understood exactly what she needed, but it gave her the strength she needed to go on.

Uma told Ria that the reception had gone well. Jen and Nikhil had both looked great. She never said anything about how upset the two of them must have been that Ria had left without saying good-bye. She never said anything about whether or not Vikram had stayed for the reception. She told her only about the food and the gifts and what each one of the aunties had worn.

Nikhil and Jen were all packed and ready to fly out to Malawi next week. They planned to stop in Scotland for a quick honeymoon before they started work. Uma did ask Ria again to call Nikhil. He had called Ria every day, but she hadn't been able to answer. She hated to put him through this, but the idea of speaking with Nikhil or Jen right now was unfathomable. Again, Uma seemed to know exactly how much Ria could take. She didn't push her.

When the story about Ria's mobbing and hospitalization broke, Uma had packed her bags, ready to fly to Mumbai. It hadn't been easy to convince her that the media had made up the thing about the hospital. Thankfully, DJ was able to convince her that Ria was not in the hospital and they had gone back to their calls once every few days. There was no way Ria could handle meeting Uma right now—and yet there was nothing she wanted more.

It was only two more days before the fitness boot camp for *Star-Gangster* started. But Ria still hadn't told DJ that she wasn't doing the film. He had scheduled a one-on-one for her with her trainer, and Ria sat in her living room listening to Mina chatter excitedly about the film. She was going to be one of the lead trainers on the film, a huge step for her career. At the meeting, the director had repeated over and over again how physical fitness was a crucial component of the story. "Think of fitness as one of the characters in the film, Ria," he had said, and his sharply outlined biceps had made Ria hate the very sight of him. Mina, on the other hand, seemed to be nursing a giant crush.

"Such a visionary," she said in a voice throaty from too much shouting and goading and steroids. "And totally hot too, no?" She winked at Ria. "He really understands the human body. It's rare to see this kind of knowledge in filmmakers."

Even though Ria couldn't begin to understand her fervor, she was glad for the opportunity this film would give her after all these years of working so hard. Mina measured and pinched Ria's body with tapes and calipers and furiously typed every detail into her laptop.

"Wow!" she said in the hyper-energetic way that always reminded Ria of a spinning top. "Looks like you've been following your routine diligently."

A million crushing memories rushed into Ria's mind. Ever since she had left Chicago it had been impossible for her to get any food down her throat, and her bones had started to stick out at sharp angles, making her trainer giddy with happiness.

"I wish all my clients were this disciplined." Vivid images of Uma wringing Mina's muscled neck flashed in Ria's head.

Ria hadn't said a single word thus far, but the conversation hadn't ceased even for a second. Mina pulled a measuring tape across Ria's breasts. "Oh no, your bust size has reduced. That's not going to make the producers happy." She sucked on her lower lip as if a minor tragedy had befallen them and stared at Ria's breasts like a doctor studies an X-ray. "You had such beautiful breasts."

The floor swam beneath Ria's feet. Vikram's basement room closed around her. His voice rumbled in his chest. *I'm so impressed, by the beauty of your breasts.* His smile soaked his voice. Love and laughter danced in the blue-gray depths of his eyes. He stretched across his bed, propped up on his elbows. All his beautiful surfaces glistened. She backed away from the trainer and tried to clear the images from her head. But the memories came at her so fast she lost her balance and fell back onto the sofa.

"Ria, babes, are you okay?" the trainer asked, unable to mask her panic.

*Stop asking me that. Oh God, will everyone just stop asking me that?*

Ria wanted the trainer out, wanted her gone. But she couldn't find the words to ask her to leave, to tell her that she was wasting her time.

"Do you want to sit down? Can I get you some water?"

Ria forced herself to relax, tried to smile. But she had lost her ability to manufacture smiles.

Just as Mina gave up all pretense of being in control of the situation, the doorbell rang. She ran to the door and didn't even try to hide her relief at seeing DJ. The two of them exchanged a secret glance that wasn't secret at all. Ria tried to work up some outrage at being treated like she wasn't right there, but nothing budged inside her. Nothing.

When DJ turned to Ria his face was thunderous. He looked enraged enough for both of them. He helped the trainer pack up her equipment and walked her out of the apartment. He was really great at that, at getting rid of people without letting them know he was doing it. When she left, DJ turned to Ria. "Good thing you're sitting down," he said without preamble. No "Hi," no "Are you okay?"

Relieved, she was so relieved. She sank deeper into the sofa.

He paced around for a few minutes without saying anything, his fingers tightly wrapped around a rolled-up newspaper. Tension rose from the newspaper and traveled up his arm, tying his muscles in knots.

What now?

Ria extended her arm, silently asking him to hand the newspaper over. He hesitated, moving the paper from hand to hand.

"This is bad," he said. "This is worse than anything you expected."

Wasn't everything?

# 28

Ria sat slumped on her sofa, her hand extended, while DJ paced the room, and waited for him to hand the newspaper over. For all his quick temper, she had never seen him this upset over anything. Right now, he didn't seem so much angry as defeated. He looked like a man in a crisis with no means to handle it. And that was someone Ria had never seen Big DJ be before.

He paced restlessly up and down the room one more time and came back to stand in front of her, looking at her with that same pitying look he had taken to throwing at her at regular intervals. She lost her patience and snatched the paper out of his hands.

She didn't even have to turn to the Celebrity pages—right there on the front page was a picture of her. Not the picture of her surrounded by the hungry mob that had been splattered across papers for the past week. But a picture of her with a crazy gleam in her eye, balanced on the ledge of her balcony with her toes clutching the concrete edge, ready to jump. A picture from another lifetime.

MENTALLY UNSTABLE STAR FLIRTS WITH DEATH

The headline screamed across the page, and Ria's sluggish heart kicked itself alive with an excruciating jolt. She sat up. Her eyes flew over the article wrapped around the picture in snaking narrow columns.

In overdramatic, pseudoscientific prose it explained the relationship between suicidal tendencies and fame. Apparently, she was ailing from an exhibitionist syndrome that ailed the pathologically narcissistic. She had shown all the signs over the past decade, but a very forgiving public had ignored it all and bought her Ice Princess cover. The truth was she was sick and the power trip of taking the public for a ride had probably worn off. A public suicide would be the ultimate swan song for someone who fancied themselves the ultimate artist. Or at least an attempted public suicide. Most pathological attention-seekers only went so far, never really intending to kill themselves.

Ria skimmed the bizarre, badly written piece with a mix of irritation and distaste. It was so full of holes it was a wonder the nation's leading newspaper had printed it, as a front page story, no less. She couldn't even get herself to read the words. Her eyes swept over them until out of nowhere the words *mental asylum in Bristol* jumped out at her and the room quite literally imploded into a vacuum.

She gasped, struggling for air to force down her constricting windpipe. The paper blurred in front of her. She focused on the page and fought to make sense of the words as they came back into view. This time every tiny etched letter jumped up and grabbed her attention, she absorbed every black newsprint word as it burrowed into her head and twisted inside her brain.

> Ria Parkar has spent ten years denying the existence of her schizophrenic mother. She has kept her locked away in a mental asylum in Bristol, England, under a false name and claimed to be an orphan. Unnamed sources have stated that Ms. Parkar has never visited her mother in all the time that she has been at the facility, a period estimated to be close to twenty years. Even as far back as school, Ms. Parkar never admitted to having a mentally ill mother.
>
> One classmate, who spoke under condition of anonymity, said that Ria Parkar (who changed her name from Ria Pendse when she joined films) was

> always self-absorbed and never interested in making friends. She went to great lengths to keep herself away from the other students and never shared anything about her family life with anyone. Even the teachers awarded her preferential treatment and Ms. Parkar took full advantage of this fact. The classmate believes that Ms. Parkar showed obvious signs of mental illness even back in school. She is impressed by how well Ms. Parkar has managed to hide her problem from the public.
>
> Ms. Parkar's costar in her next film, Mr. Shabaz Khan, is quoted as admitting that Ms. Parkar's mental instability might have led to difficulties during filming. However he urges the public to be kind in their judgment and remember that a mental illness is still an illness.
>
> It is hard to judge someone who has struggled with mental illness herself, but does that justify forsaking one's parent? Do these public suicidal tendencies mean that her condition has deteriorated? Is this a cry for help? Will her own mental illness be her ironic comeuppance for mistreating an ill parent in this shameful fashion?

That was it? One question mark and it was done? She wanted to go on reading until it made sense. But there was nothing more.

The numbing fog that had enveloped Ria in Chicago and followed her to Mumbai dissolved and crumbled to the floor around her. Everything inside her came alive in stark, sharp bursts. Dead feelings reared back up, buried memories roared to life. Her convent school with its carved steeples and rafters, Mother Superior's pitying eyes. All the faces of her past, schoolgirls whispering behind their hands, Ved's lust fuelled by his ability to hurt her, her father's hollow eyes, the creature's tears running down porcelain cheeks. Chitra's finger wagging in her face.

*Mental illness is not something we can allow into our family. Into the pure untainted bloodline we can trace all the way back to the Peshwa rulers. Ten generations of health, breeding, intellect. I will not stand by while my only son—the scion of our dynasty—lets you destroy his life. You will have to find someone else to watch you go crazy. Someone else to have sick children with. It will not be my Vikram.*

*It will not be my Vikram.*

"Ria?"

She looked up at the sound of DJ's voice. She had forgotten that he was in the room. Questions shot from his dark eyes like torpedoes.

A storm raged in the deepest part of Ria's chest and shuddered across her body. She wanted to shake DJ. How had he let the blackmailer pull this off? How? DJ reached out and tried to touch her. She sprang off the couch and ran to the front door. She wanted him out. She held the door open. "Please leave." It was amazing how quiet her voice sounded.

Inside she was screaming.

Gut-wrenching screams. They filled her ears, her lungs. Even in their silence they tore through her with such violence they gouged out her throat, stretched her vocal cords to breaking point. But she couldn't stop. They went on and on, and drowned everything else out.

When finally the screaming stopped, Ria found herself sitting on the floor with her back against the front door, her arms wrapped around her knees, her fingers digging into her calves, curled up like a fetus. Only there was no mother to shelter her with her body. Just her and her soul-deep aloneness.

And it made her sick with anger, filled her with so much rage she didn't know what to do with it. A lifetime of work, gone in an instant. A lifetime of running, and it had taken her nowhere. She was back to being The Girl Who Came From Insanity. *You. Come. From. Insanity.* Even worse, she was the insane girl who came from insanity. What could be funnier?

All the faces in her head burst into laughter. All that pity for the pathetic girl from insanity exploded into a cloud of hysterical laughter.

Her phone rang. It had been ringing for a while, but the screaming and the laughter had drowned out everything. Now the ringing finally cut through it all. Everyone fell silent. All the faces in her head quieted and waited to see what she would do. One of those faces had stolen her secret and sold it. Kicked her because she'd been rolled up in a ball.

She straightened herself out and pulled herself to her full height, unrolling from around a secret that was no longer there to hold, breaking through pain so old, it was like breaking bones and reforming them. But it was time.

The newspaper lay on the floor. She picked it up and carried it to the kitchen. Then she turned on the stove and set it on fire.

# 29

Everywhere Ria looked she saw her own face—the TV, newspapers, magazines. So much for a decade of reclusiveness. The police questioned her about the "suicide attempt" and closed the case with nothing more than a knowing chuckle about stars and their publicity stunts. No reporter bothered to report this vital piece of information. No one cared that she had been investigated and that she had come out clean.

All anyone cared about was the insanity—an almost poetic tribute to the rest of her life. No one cared about her father's murder. All of this digging and no one asked how he had died. Nobody cared that the poor nurse who had taken care of her mother for seventeen years had also died. All these healthy, vital lives lost and all they cared about was the darkness that had destroyed it all.

But the media was indolent as a satiated beast, drunk on the drama. The public had a new cause. Every mental health organization in the country squeezed as much mileage from the story as they could. Every obscure psychiatrist had an opinion. *Why the UK? Are our own mental health facilities not good enough? Isn't mental health as important as physical health? Shouldn't the government be doing more to raise awareness? Isn't it time to erase the stigma? How shameful is shame for a sick relative?* There were bleeding hearts everywhere.

One TV psychiatrist even issued a grandstanding public challenge to Ria over the airwaves, urging her to come to him and accept the help she so badly needed.

"The first step is acceptance," he goaded from the TV studio dressed in his best three-piece suit with his rimless glasses. "Get past the denial phase. Seeking help is the only path to recovery. You are a role model, take action, show the public how it's done. I can help you."

*Like hell you can*, Viky would have said.

But the opportunistic bastard was right about one thing. She did need to take action. A horrible weight had sat on her shoulders for ten years and she wanted it off. She had lost control over everything in her life, but there was one thing she did have the ability to do, and now she was finally free to do it.

The woman sitting across from Ria in her living room had exceptionally large eyes that made her look perpetually surprised. It was the one thing Ria remembered about the nurse who had cared for her mother. Her daughter had the exact same eyes and an alacrity that spoke of someone entirely at home in her own skin. The last time she had seen the nurse Ria was seven years old. At least that was the last time she'd seen her alive. Dead, there had been nothing left except a charred, swollen mess.

"I'm sorry." Ria had carried those words for so long, saying them was almost like giving away a piece of herself. But she had been sick with guilt for ten years and saying the words was like taking a step out of thick, heavy sludge.

Tears pooled in the woman's huge eyes. "Ms. Parkar, please. Please don't say that. Don't humiliate me like that. By saying sorry." She got off the chair she was sitting on and sat down next to Ria on the sofa. "You have nothing to worry about. I will never talk to the media about anything. I swear."

Shame sliced through Ria. "No. That's not why I'm saying sorry. Whatever you want to tell the media, it's your prerogative. If you want people to know what happened to your mother, I completely understand. I . . . I just wanted you to know how sorry I am for what happened." It had taken her ten years to say it, but she had been sorry every single day.

She stared at her hands clasped together in her lap. Suddenly, reaching out to the woman seemed like a horrible idea. What did her apology even mean? It's not like she was offering justice. She'd had the chance to tell the police what had happened, and she had lied. Or at least she had supported Baba's lie and told them the fire had been an accident.

"Ms. Parkar, did you know that my mother was illiterate? She used to clean your parents' house before your father hired her to care for your mother. I grew up in a slum. My mother's only dream was that I learn to read and write, that I don't spend my life washing other people's toilets. And ten years ago, just before she died, she had to pull me out of school, because she could no longer afford to pay the slumlord to keep a roof over our heads and send me to school instead of have me work."

She reached out and took Ria's hands. Her hands were soft, not labor-worn. "Last year I made tenure as Assistant Lecturer in the Chemistry department at Mithibai College." Her hands shook in Ria's and without meaning to, Ria squeezed them. "For ten years I have waited to meet you and thank you. For ten years my every prayer has been for your well-being. If you hadn't paid for my education, for everything, after my mother died, I can't even imagine where a homeless orphan like me would have ended up."

Ria pulled her hands away. "I didn't—"

"Of course I knew it was you. I had seen you at the cremation. When Mr. Veluri came to me, took care of admissions, and sent me checks every month, I knew it wasn't him. I knew the charity story wasn't true." She smiled. "Stupid people don't become Assistant Lecturer, you know."

Despite herself, Ria smiled back.

"I recognized you when your first movie poster came out, and I've followed your career ever since. You're only two years older than me, you know. You worked and I went to college."

Ria's first paycheck, all the money from selling the land, had been just enough to cover the asylum and the nurse's daughter's boarding school fees.

"But you lost your mother."

"And you lost your father. Life and death aren't in our hands, are they?"

Ria swallowed. Her throat burned, but she could no longer cry.

"But what you did for me. That was in your hands. You saved my life. All these things people are saying about you. They don't know anything. They don't know how much you took on at such a young age. How is putting your mother in the best care facility in the world a bad thing? And the only sick person in all this is the man who took those pictures of you in your home." She wiped her eyes with her *dupatta* and smiled through her tears, a pure luminous smile so peaceful it didn't belong to a motherless child yearning for justice.

"My mother never stopped talking about what a kind and generous person your mother was before she got sick. What a wonderful couple your parents were. She talked so much about them, in fact, that I've idolized their marriage all my life. I won't marry until I have a love like that." She smiled another luminous smile and touched Ria's hand again. "Someday when I can afford it, I want to go to Bristol and see your mother."

Ria stood, jerking her hand away, her relief turning suddenly cold in her gut. She backed away, putting as much distance as she could between them. Ria was glad she had met her and had a chance to apologize, but the woman didn't know what she was talking about, didn't know what her mother's murderer was capable of. "I'm sorry, I have another appointment. It was nice meeting you."

"Of course." The woman looked a little baffled at the sudden change in Ria, but her only reaction was to reach into her purse and pull out a thick envelope. "I don't need you to send me money anymore. These are all the checks you sent me after I got a job. I wanted to give them back to you in person." She put the envelope down on the polished slab of marble that served as a coffee table and joined her palms in a *namaste*. "You are my guardian angel, Ms. Parkar. I fast every Tuesday so Lord Ganesha will fulfill your every desire. And he has never disappointed me."

With that she was gone, easing guilt off Ria's shoulders even as she shoved unwanted thoughts into Ria's mind. *My mother never stopped talking about what a kind and generous person your mother was before she got sick.*

Ria slid the French doors open and let herself onto the balcony for the first time since that disastrous night on the ledge. Had it really been just a month? It didn't even seem like this lifetime. She leaned over the sandstone railing. Press vans and reporters clogged the street outside the building gates. How long were they going to lay siege? What more did they hope to find out? Everything she had ever hidden was out in the open.

Everything except what she had done with Ved. But it was just a matter of time. The pride in Uma's voice, even now when failure and shame were all Ria had left, felt like just another thing waiting to slip away. Over the past few days Ved had tried several times to call her. She hadn't spoken to him in years. That first film was all she'd ever done with him and after that he had moved on to newer girls and left her alone. The e-mail he had sent her yesterday still sat unopened in her mailbox. She had almost deleted it a few times. But it was time to stop running. She tapped her phone and his e-mail popped open.

> Dear Ria,
>
> I understand you not wanting to talk to me. But I can only hope that you will read this and absolve me of some of my guilt. Believe me when I say that I have not been able to sleep since I found out about your mother.
>
> I wish you had told me about her when we first met. I know I did nothing to support my claim, but I would have helped you had I known. My own mother suffered from schizophrenia for twenty years before she died, and my brothers and me barely knew her. Last year my youngest daughter was diagnosed with the disease. She is twenty years old. Obviously, no one outside of my family knows any of this, but I wanted to share it with you. If for no other reason at least to assure you that I will never speak to the media about us.
>
> The secrets destiny has burdened us with are cruel and inescapable. We can hide them, but never hide from them. The shame our society thrusts upon us for crimes that are not ours is too heavy, but such is the world we

live in. I wanted you to know that I understand and that I'm here in case you need anything.

May the Mother Goddess give you strength. *Jai Mata Di.*

Ved Kapoor

Ria blinked and had the strangest urge to burst out laughing. But if she laughed now, she wouldn't be able to stop until her laughter turned to tears. Maybe Ved meant it, maybe he would never tell, but she couldn't bring herself to care. Maybe she'd tell Uma herself and then it wouldn't matter.

She sucked in a long breath. Who could have imagined that Ved would get anything so right? But he had hit at the heart of it all. Her secret was inescapable. She could hide it, but never hide from it.

The secret was out and she no longer had to worry about anyone finding out. But that meant nothing. Hiding her mother had just distracted from what she really wanted to hide from. It was just concealer on her scars. The concealer had been scraped off and the scars were still there. They would always be there. She could hide from the woman in the asylum thousands of miles away, but the woman couldn't hurt her anymore. What could hurt her, destroy her, what she was really hiding from, was what she carried inside her, where it ripened day after day waiting to emerge full-blown.

*It's the child's destiny. . . . You should have made her spill the child before she was born.*

The insanity in her genes was her destiny. That was what was inescapable. The only comfort was that the one person whom she needed to protect from it was out of her life.

And that helped her make up her mind.

Ria watched the drama of her own life unfold like someone sitting in an audience. She finally told the producers that she couldn't do the film. She could've sworn they were relieved. They issued a statement saying they were dropping her because they were committed to wholesome Indian family values and a star who could so coldly forsake her own mother clearly did not share the vision of the production house.

The publicity was fantastic. *PKGJ* was assured a great opening even before it released. The film she had been dumped from was also assured a great opening even before they had started shooting. All the producers had to do was bring up the story in the media every now and again until release and keep it fresh in the public's mind. The new girl they signed to replace Ria was DJ's newest client, so it wasn't a total loss.

DJ stood by Ria like a rock. He didn't ask a single question and guarded her privacy like a pit bull. Even after she found her words again, there were no words to fit her gratitude.

When he told her about the new girl, Ria asked him to make sure there were no crazy mothers buried in her closet. DJ assured Ria that she was one of a kind and that scripts like hers weren't written every day. Ria smiled to herself. He didn't know the half of it.

# 30

*Bristol*

Ria stood outside the imposing iron gates of the historic manor house. A bronze plaque announcing the heritage of the building and a dedication to the family who had donated it for use as a sanitarium was inlaid into one of the two high brick columns housing the gates. It was a shaded residential street, and she could have been standing outside a wealthy friend's house waiting to be let in for breakfast.

A short buzzing sound indicated that the gate had been unlocked. Ria made no move to go inside. She had been inside the building only once before, ten years ago, when she had signed the admission papers. Even then, she had only gone as far as the administrator's office, waiting there while Vijay Kaka and Uma Atya made sure all the arrangements were acceptable.

Over the years, Vijay and Uma had visited regularly. At first Uma had filled Ria in after each visit, but it had made Ria almost catatonically withdrawn and Uma had stopped telling her about it. They had never asked Ria to join them on their visits and Ria had never considered doing it by herself. Maybe if she'd had the courage to face up to what she was going to become, she might have had the sense to keep away from Vikram.

She gripped the cold iron gate with one hand and stared at the stone façade. The one lone connection she had with this godforsaken place was the checks she wrote twice a year. It was the one thing she steadfastly took care of herself, refusing to let anyone help in any way.

*I won't let you leech off my son.*

Who would sign the checks for Ria? Who would make sure the arrangements were suitable? Would the money she had collected be enough? What if she outlived it? The buzzer went off again, breaking through her morbid thoughts. She tried to get herself to push the gate open, but she couldn't. Withdrawing her hand, she stared at the beautiful building that housed all her grotesquely ugly fears, unable to go in.

She had done this every morning for the past week. It had taken her a few days before that just to leave the flat she had rented half a mile away and make her way to the sanitarium gates.

When DJ had asked her what her plans were, Ria had surprised herself by asking him to find her a flat in Bristol. It had just popped out, but she hadn't taken it back. Like everything else, DJ had taken care of it quickly and efficiently. All Ria had to do after that was pack up all her possessions and leave.

Her maid had helped her put everything into boxes. Every time Tai liked something they were packing, Ria asked her to take it. She gave her everything in the kitchen, utensils Ria had never used, electronics she had never needed. Tai was the one who had used the stuff anyway; it belonged to her. Finally, the poor thing had stopped exclaiming over things, afraid that Ria would give her more.

"Babyji, God is there, just keep the faith. He is there," she kept saying, pointing at the ceiling as if her God sat on the ceiling fan. As she sat there sorting through the mess of Ria's life in her simple sari, with hair that had turned silver without ever seeing a stylist, and sun-worn skin that had never seen a moisturizer in its long hard life, she was overwhelmed with guilt to be taking things from Ria. Things Ria had no use for.

By the time they were ready to tackle Ria's wardrobe with the obscene amount of clothes and shoes and belts and scarves piled in unending stacks, Ria felt buried, tied down, and ashamed. She had worn most of those things only once. But the maid's eyes lit up.

Before Ria could ask her to take it all, she cut Ria off. "Babyji, I just had a fantastic idea! Why don't you give all these clothes away to those crazy people who are so angry with you?"

Although the "crazy people" themselves had no use for the clothes, the charities that took care of them could make a lot of money from all this stuff. Most of it had made appearances in Ria's films and had to be worth something. For the first time since she had left Chicago, Ria had voluntarily touched someone. She had given Tai a quick hug, making her tear up. Then Ria had done exactly as she suggested and given all of it to the mental health charities.

For the rest of their time together, as they wrapped and packed and taped boxes shut, tears had leaked down Tai's cheeks. When she left for the last time, all her new possessions crammed into the Tempo van her son had borrowed from his friend, she had sobbed like a baby.

"*Achha,* Babyji. I'll be coming now." It was what she always said when she left Ria's house, not wanting to tempt the evil spirits by saying she was going away. "You'll keep me in your memory, no?"

As if Ria could ever forget her.

Ria turned away from the iron gates and started walking away. Going in would have to wait another day. The past week in Bristol had gone by like a slow, suspended dream. Ria took turns hurtling between feeling like a clean slate and a ten-ton truck loaded with baggage, both ancient and newborn, sullied and pure as freshly tilled earth. Through it all, Vikram stayed with her, inside her. She clung to him. To the warm, soothing memories of him. It was all she had, it was all she would ever need. It hurt. Sometimes the pain was slow and aching, sometimes stark and maddening. She savored every bit of it like a gift. She would not give it up for anything. He was finally safe from her. She would never see him again, but she had this.

"Excuse me, miss," someone called from behind her.

She sped up, lengthening her stride across the cobbled sidewalk that edged the high sanitarium wall. The sun was just about making an appearance. Mottled sunrays sifted through the flaming red leaves that clung to branches one last time before they let go. A thick carpet of brown leaves crunched beneath her feet.

"Miss Parkar!" The voice came closer. Ria had no desire to engage in conversation with anyone. After the first wave of scandal had passed, the reporters had targeted her with renewed fervor. They were everywhere, clamoring for a sound bite. Apparently, now that the furor of all the other voices had died down, it was Ria's turn to be heard.

She had made it a point to leave the flat before dawn and return before the town woke up in earnest, and she never went anywhere for the rest of the day. No one should have known where she was. But somehow someone had figured it out. She hadn't heard him follow her, but then she hadn't been listening for it. Her mind had been too preoccupied with dredging up courage. He had to have been waiting for her, watching her as she stood at the gates too afraid to go inside.

"Ms. Parkar, why didn't you go inside?" The footsteps behind her sprinted toward her, gaining on her.

She tried not to let the sick violated feeling slow her down.

He was just behind her now, almost at her shoulder. His voice had that overfamiliar reporter quality that grated against her nerves. She broke into a jog.

He ran past her, stopping in front of her on the narrow sidewalk, blocking her way, and shoved a recorder into her face. There was no apology, no hesitation in his actions. He believed he had the right to do this to her. She stepped onto the grass and tried to keep walking.

"Come on, Ria, just one question." He moved to block her path as she tried to get around him.

"Please leave me alone," she said, without looking at him. Stopping and saying words made her feel like a victim, cornered and helpless. She had to keep moving. She considered turning around and walking back to the manor house, but she couldn't bring herself to do that. She rocked back and forth on her heels. Every time she tried to take a step he moved, dodging her footsteps, not letting her pass. He wasn't going to let her go.

"I've been waiting here all night. Just one question. Come on, Ria." Every time he said her name she wanted to gag, the need to slap him so violent it made her shake.

"I said no!" She shoved at his shoulder with all her strength. He stumbled back and she tried to run for it. But he grabbed her arm. She tried to snatch her arm away, but his fingers dug into her skin, and held her too tight. Trying to stay calm, she reached for the phone in her coat pocket with her free hand.

"When was the last time you visited your mother?" His tone was no longer pleading, but angry and demanding.

"Let me go." Her panic slipped into her voice. Forget staying calm, she had to get away. She started to struggle and pulled frantically at her arm.

His arm flew off her. She fell forward, but found her balance. He screamed and she swung around to see him flattened against the wall, whimpering. A figure in a long wool coat pinned him in place with one massive arm and loomed menacingly over him. Her body reacted instantly, recognizing the achingly familiar form even before her mind made the connection. Her entire being lurched into alertness.

"Viky? Viky, get off him! You'll kill him, let him go."

Vikram turned around and looked at her. Such raw emotion softened his eyes it was a miracle her legs held her up.

"She asked you to leave her alone! Didn't you hear her?" he said, his deep, honey voice harsh with anger, but his eyes never left Ria.

The man let out a whimper and thrashed about. Vikram's arm, a crowbar against his chest, rippled with so much power he couldn't have moved if his life depended on it.

"Viky! Seriously, let him go. Please. He's only doing his job."

Vikram turned to the man and lifted him up by his collar, his feet shuffled and kicked air. "If you ever look at her again, let alone touch her, you won't be able to so much as jerk off with those hands. You hear me?"

The man moaned and tried to nod and the camera around his neck swayed.

"Did you take pictures?" Vikram asked, reaching for his camera, and the man started struggling with renewed fervor.

Anger ripped through Ria like an explosion. He had been standing there taking pictures while she struggled with her obscene struggle. Her violation was so fierce she ran at him and grabbed the camera, trying to yank it off his head, surprising Vikram so much the man slipped from his grip. The bastard took the opportunity to knee Vikram in the belly and took off.

"Stop!" Ria shouted and raced after him. He would not get away, not with her pictures, not while she lived. She leapt across the distance between them and jumped on top of him, taking him down.

He slammed into the ground beneath her, screaming like a madman. Ria struggled with the camera, pulling it off his neck, anger slamming in her chest like a fever. Hands lifted her off, pulled her back. Vikram reached for the man again and pulled him up by his collar.

Ria was about to smash the camera to the ground when the man started sobbing. "Don't. Please don't break it. It's not even paid for yet. My wife's pregnant. Please. I needed the money."

"Shut up." Vikram twisted his arms behind his back, but the man was sobbing so hard Ria couldn't do it.

"Get the SD card," Vikram said to her.

She popped the card out. "You're a bastard," she said to the man, and dropped the camera on the grass. The man had stopped struggling and Vikram let him go.

"I'm sorry," he said, tears and snot leaking from him. He picked up the camera with both hands, as though it was a precious pet, and walked away.

Ria threw the card on the concrete path and stomped it with her boot heel and kept on twisting and crushing until it was nothing but black powder.

"Sweetheart, it's gone. It's done." Vikram said to her.

For a moment neither one of them moved.

"You okay?"

"I'm fine."

They spoke almost simultaneously, and then Vikram took a step closer.

"He didn't hurt you, did he?" He glanced at her arm, but he didn't reach for her.

She shook her head. "You?"

He shook his head too. They stood there like that for a moment. Their gazes meeting and retreating, their bodies paralyzed with feeling. Then his shoulders started to shake. "I don't think the bastard will ever be okay again. What the hell was that, Ria?" he asked, and she started to laugh too.

For a long time they stood there like that, laughing, unable to believe that she had actually jumped on top of someone and taken him down. An indescribable alchemy of emotions stirred inside her—disbelief, anger, embarrassment, shock, but also pride and an entirely unexpected heady sense of power. And of course that tingle, that joy that blossomed whenever he was near.

"You want to try and go inside?" he said finally, nodding in the direction of the high gates. Ria's heart sank to the pit of her stomach. She looked at her toes.

He took a step closer and tipped her chin up. Her eyes flickered up to meet his, the comforting gray so steady, so strong, her insides grew calm. All the weight she'd been carrying shifted to his outstretched hand. That barest touch of his bolstered her. For the first time since they had been apart she felt safe.

She reached for that sense of power that had nudged at her moments ago and took his hand when he held it out. Together they walked back to the gates. She pressed the bell and told the receptionist who she was.

"Good morning again, Ms. Pendse." The receptionist didn't even attempt to hide the sigh in her voice and unlocked the gates.

This time when the buzzer rang, Ria let her hand push against the cold weight of the iron bars until the gates swung open. Her legs faltered, but Vikram's hand tightened around hers and she kept walking.

She didn't let herself falter again after that. Not when the warden unlocked a smaller iron gate leading to a long corridor, not when they followed him into the back wing of the manor house.

They walked past more locked gates that led into more long sweeping corridors with high ceilings and polished terrazzo floors wrapped in silence. The tapping of their footsteps echoed against bright white walls. Ria had to force herself not to read the names hanging on the closed doors as she floated past them, her arms, her legs, all of her weightless, formless. She had no mass, no shape. All she had was Vikram's palm pressed against her own, his fingers tight against her own. Not so much support as proof that she existed in this moment. She had fought the moment so hard but it had arrived all the same.

Finally, they came to the end of a corridor, and the warden pointed to a window. Vikram thanked him and signaled for him to leave them alone. Ria let Vikram's hand go and walked up to the window. For the first time since she was seven years old, Ria's eyes rested on the surprisingly small, impossibly frail creature who had cast such a large, intractable shadow over every part of Ria's life.

The window was fitted with iron bars like a prison cell. Thick soft vinyl pads covered the bars. In fact, thick sheets of padding covered everything—the walls, the doors, the bed frame, even the chair. The creature sitting in the chair at the center of all that cushioned padding, rocking herself, was so delicate, so fragile that Ria couldn't imagine how all this softness could protect her if she went hurtling into something.

A red puckered burn scar covered half her clean-shaven head. A purple bruise stretched from the scar across her cheek to her soft pink mouth. Other fading, yellowing bruises patterned her arms and her neck and disappeared into her gray gown. Two of her fingers were bound together with tape the exact color of her pale beige skin.

Ria fixed her eyes on the delicate, long-fingered hands that rested in her lap. The fingers were moving, tapping out some sort of rhythm. Ria couldn't tell for sure over the ringing in her ears, but she thought she heard humming. For a long time all Ria could do was look at the drumming fingers and let the trembling inside her synchronize itself with the rhythm they were beating out.

"Hey!" the voice suddenly called out, and Ria looked up, surprised that it could speak. She had never imagined it with a voice.

It's voice was exactly Ria's voice. It looked at Vikram with eyes that were exactly her eyes. "Hey!" it said again.

"Hey there." Vikram smiled gently—that smile he saved for the little kids who adored him so much. He did a small wave with his hand. She smiled back. A big beaming grin split lips exactly identical to Ria's lips. Two of her front teeth were missing.

"How're you doing?" he asked.

"Hey!" she said again as if he hadn't spoken. The smile on her face stayed bright and blank.

Tears started to stream down Ria's cheeks.

Vikram pulled her close and pressed his lips against her hair. The woman in the room didn't notice.

"Hey!" she said one more time, before she went back to humming.

Ria stood there watching her, leaning into Vikram, her head resting on his chest, listening to the steady beat of his heart. His arms wrapped around her, collecting her into himself. They stood there like that watching her hum, watching her drum, watching her until she fell asleep, smiling to herself, and her fingers stilled in her lap.

# 31

The sanitarium sat on twenty acres of grounds with thick wooded areas alternating with clipped lawns and pruned shrubbery. Although what good these magnificent grounds were to someone locked in a padded cell, Ria couldn't imagine. Vikram walked next to her as she meandered along the path that wound around a retention pond and led to the back of the property, away from the road and the sound of passing cars. Away from the gates.

There was something safe about the place. It was cocooned in the silence she needed. The raw, torn-open feeling inside her was still too fresh. She hadn't armored it shut yet. She couldn't handle anyone seeing her like this, asking her questions. She had too many questions of her own, too many things she herself had hidden away from for too long. She wasn't ready for the world's obscene curiosity and she most certainly never wanted to take anyone down ever again, even though the memory made her smile.

They stopped at the edge of the pond and lowered themselves onto the sloping bank, sitting cross-legged on the thick carpet of grass that rolled down the hill and into the water. Their denim-clad knees touched. She felt Vikram's eyes on her as she watched the water.

She had no idea how he had shown up that morning out of the clear blue sky or what he was doing here. But having him next to her outside that padded room, it was so precious, so impossible to quantify, she held on to it, refusing to taint it with questions.

"It was Uma," he said, speaking for the first time since they'd entered the grounds. "Uma told me where you were."

Uma had promised Ria she wouldn't tell anyone. What had he done to make her tell him? Why had he even asked? He had made it clear enough he was done with her.

He touched her hair, tucked it behind her ear. "The article about the suicide scared me half to death. What the hell were you thinking getting on that ledge like that?" He was reprimanding her and instead of making her angry she held on to it. The strangest things in life were precious. Someone to tell you when you were wrong was one of them.

"I wasn't trying to kill myself." She wanted to explain about the phone, but she was too tired. And it sounded completely crazy when she thought about it now.

"I know that." The complete absence of doubt in his voice made her want to sidle up to him. "I know how much you love heights. But it was still a really stupid thing to do. What if you had slipped?"

Ria shrugged. It wasn't something she should have done. She wasn't proud of it.

"I couldn't believe the crap in that article. At first it made me so angry I couldn't see straight. But then a lot of shit started falling into place in my head." He went up on his knees and faced her. "How could you have lied to me about your mother's death?"

"Viky—"

"And I was such a fool, I walked away. I should've seen through it. I thought it was the shock of losing both your parents, I thought you wanted to leave everything about your old life behind. Including us. But the movies? I should have known better."

He scooted closer and wiped her tears. "And then I did it again at Nikhil's wedding. Ria, I'm—"

"Please, Viky. Please don't apologize." Anything but that.

"But I am sorry. I can't even tell you how sorry I am. I was an idiot ten years ago. But now? Instead of licking my wounds, I should've been with you when the story broke. I tried. I went to Mumbai to make sure you were okay. But you were gone. And no one knew where you were. Except that agent of yours, who's Fort

Knox. And Uma, who almost killed me for letting you go after I told her about us."

He had told Uma about them? And gone to Mumbai looking for her? "I thought you never wanted to see me again." She laid her chin on her knees, pulling them tight against the pain in her chest, and watched his face.

"God, Ria. How could you believe that? What I wanted was for you to not leave me again. I was desperate. I would have said anything. Done anything to stop you. And of course I said the one thing I shouldn't have." The regret in his eyes was so raw, she wanted to wrap her arms around him. She couldn't believe how good it felt just to look at him. To know his face so well.

"That's not true," she said, lifting her head off her knees. "You were right. If anything would have stopped me that would have been it. But you couldn't have stopped me. I just couldn't stay, Viky. I still can't."

He didn't react. Not even a frown. He just sat there on his knees looking at her like he never wanted to look away. "The first week after you left, I couldn't think, I couldn't do anything but work. I think I created a hundred videos for V-learn. The host site almost told me to take my business elsewhere because they couldn't keep up." He smiled. "But you were right. I was dragging my feet on the eco deal. I was being a coward and not putting my money where my mouth was with V-learn. I was afraid of believing in anything again."

He lifted her chin so she was looking in his eyes. "I'm done running now. I signed a contract with Clive and Hadley. They get to use my patents for the next ten years and work with me exclusively until we go into production. And Ma's foundation is funding V-learn and I get to run it, to hire people globally, to translate, to work with schools. We can do whatever we want with it."

She cupped his cheek. "That's fantastic, Viky." It felt so good to touch him.

"You don't have to worry about this on your own anymore." He pointed to the stately manor behind them. "We'll take care of it together now. Even if you don't want to act anymore, we can take care of it. You can do whatever you want. You can paint again. In fact—" He reached into his coat pocket and pulled out a brown paper bag. Inside it were three tubes of acrylic and a brush.

She pushed it away.

"Look at the colors," he said, extracting the tubes and handing them to her.

Burgundy, jade, and turquoise. She smiled and gave them back to him.

"I bought these in Chicago the day before the wedding. I was waiting for the right moment to give them to you." He put the tubes back in the bag and held it out to her.

She scooted back, away from him, away from the paints and twisted her fingers in her lap. "I don't want to paint, Viky. I've already told you what I want."

He put the bag back in his pocket. "It's what your lips tell me. But it's never been about the words for us." He stroked the fingers she was twisting together, easing them apart. "It doesn't make sense, sweetheart. Why won't you stop running from us?"

Was he blind? Hadn't he just been in there with her? Hadn't he seen what she was going to turn into? Suddenly, she was too exhausted to fight, too tired to lie, to give him explanations he refused to accept. He had seen it, the truth had stared him in the face. It was more powerful than anything she could make up.

"Viky, you just saw the person who gave birth to me. How can you possibly want to be with that?"

He blinked, his face blank. "Your mom? What does this have to do with—"

His brows drew together. Understanding suffused his eyes. "Shit! How could I have been so stupid? This is about your mother?" It sounded like a question, but he didn't wait for an answer. He sprang to his feet and started pacing. "How could I have missed it? This is exactly how you would think." He dropped back down on his knees, glaring at her. "You think you're protecting me, don't you? Just like you thought you were protecting me ten years ago. You think you're going to get sick like your mom."

She wanted to shake him. "She's not sick, Viky, she's mad. She's crazy. Terminally insane. Psychotic. Paranoid. Severely demented."

Her voice broke around the words. "She hurtles between violence and being catatonic." She threw out all the words they had thrown at her over the years. "She rips her own clothes and throws herself at walls. She doesn't know her own name. She sets things on fire. She—she—" *She almost beat me to death when I was seven.* But she couldn't say it. Even after all these years she couldn't say those words.

The tears that pooled in her eyes were hot, the cheeks they spilled onto even hotter. She swiped at them furiously. Her entire body started to shake again and it made her so angry she wanted to scream.

Vikram tried to reach for her tears.

She pushed away his hand and stood up and rubbed her eyes against her shoulder. The wool of her coat scratched her eyelids. "Don't, Viky, please don't. I can't have this conversation again. What you did for me today. It was—I can never—I just want you to leave. Please. Please don't put me through this again. I'm begging you."

He stood up and followed her. "I'm sorry, Ria," he said in that soothing, intoxicating, unwavering voice of his. It fell on her like cooling rain. "I can't do that. I've tried. I swear, I've tried and I just fucking can't." Very gently he circled his arms around her and pulled her close. She tried to stay rigid, to hold herself away from him, but she couldn't. Her treacherous body melted into his. Her face sought that patch of skin on his neck that was her corner, her peace. There was no expectation in his embrace, no urgency in his caress. He just held her, solid and strong and sane.

And she fell to pieces in his arms. Tears soaked his coat, his shirt, his skin. Finally when the tears slowed, leaving her lids raw and swollen, her lips moved and the words started to flow. He lifted her against him and sank back into the grass, settling her in his lap. Like her tears her words spilled from her in an uncontrollable stream. She couldn't stop them, she couldn't slow them, she couldn't make them anything they weren't.

She told him about the seven-year-old girl who had disobeyed her dead grandmother and gone in search of her destiny in the forbidden attic and had her bones broken for it. She told him how much it had hurt, not just her wounds as she lay in the hospital for months, but to see Baba by her sickbed every day, crying his shame, and losing her words. About being sent away for it, being banished from her home forever until she was left with its ashes and an impossible promise. About the deal she had made with the body she had vowed to him alone. About the sniggering schoolgirls, the need to be normal, the absolute certainty with which she knew that it was the one thing she would never be. She told him about the nurse's black, bloated body. She told him about Baba's eyes, his despair, his charred lifelessness.

"She burned the house down, killed him, killed the nurse, but he made me promise not to report it. I lied to the police, told them she was dead. Then I brought her here under the nurse's name, so no one would know she was alive. I promised him I would take care of her, Viky. I protected a killer.

"Did you know she was normal until I was born? Giving birth to me did this to her. It was me. I took her away from him and then I became the weight around his neck. If I had never been born, his life would have been completely different." She was the reason he was dead. And today, she had stood by and watched his killer hum herself to sleep.

Vikram's arms tightened around her, cradling her in so much safety, so much strength she couldn't exhaust it. She kept pushing at it, but it wouldn't give. He wouldn't let her go. He held her until the words dried up, until the tears stopped. He wiped the wetness from her cheeks and waited for the moisture in her eyes to dry. He looked into her eyes, his gaze as clear, as honest as a mirror. The same spotless invitation it had been all those years ago when he'd asked her to be his friend.

"I don't think your father banished you, Ria, I think he sent you away because he wanted to protect you. I think all he wanted was to give you the normal you so badly craved."

Baba had given her Chicago for the summers. But through the year he had visited her every chance he got, making the three-hour drive from Pune to Panchgani, bringing her bags of the buttery Shrewsbury cookies she loved, as though everything were perfectly normal.

She had never told him there was nothing normal about a father who visited alone or who let tears leak down his stubbly cheeks. Other fathers came only with the mothers and watched their wives play the role of caretaker. They didn't go down on their knees and feed pieces of cookies into their daughters' mouths and wipe around their lips with shaking hands while the other parents turned their children's faces away, as if witnessing this train wreck of a man with his unkempt hair and clothes and his desperately sad eyes could somehow damage their daughters beyond repair.

*Why does she let him come to see her?* She had overheard one of the girls whisper. *If I had such a weirdo for a father I would hide if he ever came to see me.*

But Ria had lived for the times when the school peon pulled her out of the classroom and she found Baba waiting beneath the high-arched ceiling of the receiving room, his eyes shining, his dimples digging deep crevices into his bony cheeks.

"All he wanted was to give you a chance at happiness," Vikram said, caressing her tears not so much as wiping them. "Ria, when was the last time you were happy?"

Her cheeks warmed. He knew exactly where her mind would go.

"Can you be happy without me?"

He already knew the answer to that one too.

"All that guilt you've been lugging around, what would that do to your Baba if he were alive?"

Ria swallowed. The entire weight of her fear, her hopelessness, descended upon her. She was broken and it would have broken Baba's heart to see her like this.

"I think you've had enough for today, sweetheart. Why don't we talk about this another time?" Vikram pressed his freshly shaved cheek into hers, pushed his lips into her swollen lids.

Then he took her hand and stood.

For all the terror she had felt about coming here, the idea of leaving the asylum grounds felt wrong. She just wasn't ready for it. She hesitated only for a moment before following him blindly through the neatly trimmed landscape, trying not to think about how comforting it was to hold his hand, trying not to think about how weightless and free it made her feel, like a kite that could fly free because its string was in safe hands. He led her through the grounds and away from the gate, knowing she needed more time before going back into the world. Despite her woolen coat, her shoulders felt bare, kissed by the wind and the sunlight for the first time in her life.

# 32

It had been four days since they had picked up Vikram's stuff from his hotel and moved it to the flat Ria had rented in a quiet, tree-lined neighborhood overlooking a park. They knew it was only temporary. Ria didn't have anywhere else to go and no idea what she was going to do when her two-month lease expired, and Vikram hadn't told her how many days he had before he went back to Chicago to start work with the construction company. But living in that charmingly furnished flat with its colonial furniture and floral trim was so much like a real life together, so much like every dream she'd ever dreamed of a future with him, she couldn't get herself to ask. It would be over soon enough.

She knew this because every morning they went to the asylum and visited. And every visit reinforced Ria's vision of her future and her decision that she would not do to Viky what the woman had done to her father. That first day they had watched her hum to that beat that seemed to beat inside her continuously. The next day she slammed her head to it, slamming and slamming against the padded wall for the entire hour that they watched. Yesterday she had reached for the bars and Ria had backed away in such terror she didn't know if she would ever be able to go back.

Actually, she'd felt that way after each visit. Every day when they came back to the flat Ria believed she wouldn't go back the next day, but coming home with Vikram erased the terror, infused her with strength, surged hope in her heart until she was ready for it again the next morning. And then the cycle repeated itself.

Living with Vikram held no surprises. She knew his every mood, his every action. She felt perpetually wrapped up, mussed, messed with, and alive. On their way back from the sanitarium they picked up groceries at the corner grocery store, usually meat and cheese and bread to make sandwiches, and readymade soups. A few times they bought eggs and vegetables and cooked something up. He had always eaten more than anyone she knew. No matter how much food they bought, there was never a morsel left over. And he had a way of filling up every inch of their space by leaving cups and books and pencils all over the place. Every time she made their bed, he found a way to muss it up. And he worked around the clock, his mind engaged all the time.

When he showed her V-learn it was like being able to walk through his mind, so inventive, so infinite, it saw with clarity the most intricate of concepts as though they were the simplest things. "Everything is simple at its core," he told her. And if V-learn wasn't enough for her to want to spend the rest of her days immersed in that brilliant, generous mind of his, she finally found out about that project he'd been working on with Drew that had put that proud smile on Mindy and Uma's faces that day.

On their visit to the asylum yesterday they had run into a teenage girl in a wheelchair. They had been strolling along the narrow concrete path that snaked through the grounds and had stepped off to make way for the wheelchair. Vikram had waved at the skinny, long-haired girl, twisting about in the chair, and she'd become so excited her jerking limbs had dropped the pink bunny she was carrying.

Vikram had squatted next to the wheelchair. "Hello there, beautiful," he'd said, dusting off the toy and holding it out to her until her flailing arms were able to take the toy from him. "I'm Vic. What's your name?"

"Rayna doesn't talk. But she loves making friends," the lady pushing the wheelchair had said, smiling at the girl in that way people smiled at very young children, even though this child was at least in her early teens.

Vikram's smile had been just his usual smile, open, playful, always the same for everyone. He'd chatted with the girl for a long while and she'd chatted back without saying a single word, just her sounds and eyes and expressive hands.

Before they said good-bye and continued on their walk, Rayna had wrapped her arms around Vikram's face and given him a noisy kiss on his cheek, and he'd given her mother a card and told her about the project.

Drew and he had developed software to help children like Rayna communicate using a keyboard. He'd explained it to Ria as they walked through the grounds. Drew worked with autistic children who wouldn't talk, but who could communicate through a computer. But the children tended to struggle with fine motor skills and often got frustrated with how long it took to type what they wanted to say. So Vikram had come up with a way to use word recognition based on context and customize it to each child so it wasn't as frustrating, and minimized the use of motor skills.

"We still have a ways to go, but the results are pretty spectacular," he'd told Ria proudly.

She'd held him and cried as though he'd broken her heart. He had found a way to help children who couldn't talk, children who were trapped inside their own world, whose words didn't cooperate with them. She had wanted to shake him for doing this to her. How much harder was he going to make this? How much harder was he going to make her fall for him?

She knew her war with words wasn't the same as Rayna's, but she knew what it felt like not being able to reach the world around you as a child with no control and no power. And she knew how hard he must've worked. For her. Because he'd known her struggle. Even after what she had done to him, even before she came back, he had fought her fight for her.

Their lovemaking had been crazed that night. She'd been frantic, wanting to crawl inside his body and become one with him, her hunger so elemental it had stolen every thought and doubt. He'd kissed and caressed every inch of her and loved her until she couldn't breathe, couldn't think, healing her cell by cell, forcing her to feel every shattering, life-affirming moment of it. "Choose this, Ria," his every touch said. "Don't leave me," his every breath said.

They hadn't talked about her fears or about their future since that first day when she'd broken down on the sanitarium grounds, but she knew what he was doing. He was chipping away at her defenses bit by bit. Problem was, no matter how strong and invincible she felt in their little haven, the moment she stepped through those wrought iron gates all her fears returned. She knew this had to end. But he seemed in no hurry.

It was impossible to keep his insidious confidence from seeping into her own treacherous heart. Without meaning to, she reached for the pencil and sketchpad he kept leaving all over the place, the need to capture the hope in his body, the faith in his eyes so strong she could no longer curb her fingers.

"I feel like Rose from *Titanic*," he said without looking up from his tablet. "Want me to take off my clothes? I'll even sling that pendant of yours around my neck."

"Maybe later," she said, unable to stop her laughter from making her strokes go all haywire.

But she couldn't stop and he didn't move. He stayed sprawled across the couch and turned his focus back on his work as if she wasn't trying to capture with her fingers what she couldn't seem to wrap her heart around.

When she was done he didn't ask to see the sketch, and let her hide it away. And he wouldn't ask until she was ready to show it to him by herself.

The rest of the day fell into its usual rhythm. They talked to Uma and Vijay as they had done every day. Yesterday Ria had finally spoken to Nikhil and Jen, and apologized for leaving the wedding before the reception. As expected, Nikhil and Jen had been nothing but relieved to talk to her again. "I was as wrong as can be, Ria," Nikhil had told her. "You and Vic belong together."

When Vikram called his parents, his father seemed completely at ease with knowing Vikram was there with her. Chitra tried to invoke her rights as his boss on V-learn to get him to go back home, and Ria had to smile at how Vikram reacted.

"I need to be here with Ria right now, Ma," he told her. "And I can work just fine from here. Once we know where Ria and I plan to go next I'll let you know. If that's a problem, let's revisit the contract. It's still in the grace period for rescission."

"I don't want you to break your V-learn contract with your mother," Ria told Vikram as they walked through the town hand in hand, heading to the sanitarium for their daily visit.

"Ma has to get used to us whether she likes it or not," he said as though them being together was immutable, and all Ria's fears come crashing back.

They approached the tree-lined street and she looked around to make sure no paparazzi were lurking in wait before they crossed the street. They were a little late today, and the sun was full and bright in the sky. Walkers and bikers dotted the sidewalk. The street looked nothing like the lonesome, deserted place it was when they got here a few hours earlier.

"Looking to jump someone again?" Vikram asked, laughing at the memory.

She punched his arm and stared at the stately building across the street. It looked calm and serene, not bad at all for a place where you could throw yourself at walls and hurt no one but yourself. If she was going to do it somewhere, this was as good a place as any.

Vikram turned her toward him and cupped her face in his hands. "You are the most frustratingly stubborn person I've ever met, you know that?" Then he leaned over and kissed her, softly, possessively, tugging at her lips so gently she felt it all the way down to her toes, and she forgot about all the craziness in all the sanitariums across the world.

"What am I going to do with you?" He leaned his forehead against hers. She voted for exactly what he had just done. But she didn't need to tell him that, because his eyes told her exactly what it was he wanted to do with her. The bigger question was, what was she going to do with herself? How was she going to end this once and for all?

He took both her hands in his and hopped off the sidewalk onto the street and tugged her along, making her heart dance and her body sing. His intent crystal gaze smiled secrets into her eyes, his irresistible mismatched mouth blew promises at her. For all her resolve to protect him from herself, he made her dizzy with hope, heady with recklessness.

His eyes froze in a moment of shock. The screeching of tires tore through the air. He tried to shove her away, but she grabbed his arm and pulled him out of the way as a car sped by, missing him by inches. A man stuck his head out of the car and screamed at them. "Watch where you're fucking going!"

"Sorry!" he shouted back, grinning at the car as though this was somehow funny. This time there was nothing gentle about the way she punched him.

"Viky! Are you crazy, are you trying to kill me? What is wrong with you? Why can you never keep your eyes on the damn road?"

"Hey." He tried to pull her close, but she pushed him away, her heart hammering as she imagined him bouncing off the bonnet of that car. "I'm fine. All in one piece. That guy just came out of nowhere."

"No, he didn't. Look right, then left. How hard is that? Keep your eyes on the road. How hard is that?"

"I'm sorry. I'll be more careful." He grabbed her hand and dragged her across the street. She knew he was trying not to smile.

"You think this is funny?" As soon as they reached the other side, she pulled her hand away and glared at him.

"No, not funny. But you should see your face. Here you are still trying to justify walking away from me, and the thought of losing me does this to you. What do you think it does to me, every time I watch you contemplate leaving me?"

"So you were trying to make some sort of sick point by trying to walk in front of a bloody speeding car?"

"Is that what it will take, Ria?"

She refused to dignify that with an answer, and stormed toward the gates.

"What happens if I get in an accident and end up in a wheelchair?" he asked, as usual having no trouble keeping up with her no matter how much she sped up.

She pressed the buzzer and shoved the gates open. "Please don't do this. Not right now." She took the now familiar path into the building. He followed in silence, pressing his hand into her back as they approached the padded room.

Her mother was sleeping today. Using that word for her made Ria's stomach tip and turn, but in that state she looked so peaceful, so harmless, so delicate, Ria's mind settled around it. She didn't quite feel like a mother, but she did feel innately human, and sadness squeezed in Ria's heart for all the times she had thought of her as anything else.

They stood there watching her the way they had every day, and then headed for the retention pond. Amazing how fast things became habit.

"You didn't answer my question," Vikram said when they had walked in silence for a while.

"That's never going to happen. What you're asking me is hypothetical. This . . ." she looked at the building. "This isn't hypothetical, Viky."

"What if I told you it isn't hypothetical, that it did happen. I was in a wheelchair for six months after an accident five years ago. I got hit in the back by a crane. The doctors didn't think I'd walk again."

She turned around meaning to glare at him for lying, but when she looked in his eyes she reached for him instead. But he stepped away and this time he walked away from her.

"God, Viky, why didn't you tell me?" She followed him.

He kept walking. "Tell you when? When you were missing from my life for ten years?"

That age-old shame for the pain she had caused him squeezed her heart. "I'm sorry."

He stopped and turned to her. "What are you sorry about exactly? That somehow this, like every bad thing that's ever happened to me, is your fault?"

She looked up at the sky, a flock of birds was flocking home. How did he not see how much she had hurt him? Could still hurt him.

"You were trying to protect me, Ria. But bad things still happened. And you know what made them worse? That you weren't there. I would've given anything for you to be there."

She cupped his jaw. She would've given anything to be there too.

"You won't say it, but I know that if you'd known you would have come to me. If I ever got sick you would never leave me."

She nodded. If he ever needed her she'd be there in a minute. For all her confusion, that much she knew without a doubt.

All the fight went out of him. He took both her hands and kissed the tips of her fingers. "Isn't that exactly what your Baba did? He chose to stay with your mom even though she got sick."

Ria tried to tug her hands out of his. He didn't let go.

"It's not the same thing," she hissed, struggling to pull away.

"How is it not the same thing?"

"You had an accident. It wasn't your fault."

"What happened to your mother wasn't anyone's fault either."

"It was. It was her fault—*her* fault. She knew this would happen to her. It had happened to her mother too. She could have spared him if she had left him alone. She had no right. No right to ruin his life."

*She knew what she was doing when she married my father.*

"Ruin his life or yours?" He whispered the words, but a scream might have been less violent.

She couldn't believe he could be this cruel. She yanked her hands out of his with all her force. This time he let her go. She tried walking away again, but the asylum building loomed in front of her and she turned and headed away from it.

"So you're doing the right thing?" he said, following her. "You're doing what she didn't do?"

"I don't want to talk about it." She was headed straight for the lake and she changed course again, heading for a thicket of woods. Suddenly there was nowhere to go.

"Why? Because you can make the decision to stay with me, but I'm not allowed to make the same decision, and your parents couldn't either?" he said, chasing her every footstep. "Have you considered that maybe, just maybe she didn't know she was sick when she met your father? Or maybe they both knew what was going to happen, and they both still wanted it, wanted you, wanted whatever time they could have together? "

She came to a tree and pressed her hand into it. She was panting, restless energy trapped inside her chest like a caged animal.

"But I don't. I don't want just a little bit of time and then a lifetime of pain for you."

He spun her around. "Are you for real? Do you have any idea what these ten years have been like for me? I've been in hell, Ria. Do you know what I was doing when you walked into the basement that day?"

She slumped against the trunk behind her.

"I was trying to make another woman you. I was trying to feel alive by pretending to be with you when I was with someone else. I was doing that to another human being. And it wasn't the first time. Do you know how that feels?"

Mira's lovesick face flashed in her head, and a sick nauseated feeling swirled inside her.

"Do you know why Mira and I broke up?"

"Please, Viky. Please don't."

His fingers tightened on her shoulders. "I said your name when I was with her. I had been suppressing it, holding it inside for so long, I thought maybe finally it was gone. But then you came back and I had no chance in hell. That day after I watched you read those vows at the temple, after I had you in my arms, there was no going back. I had my mouth on her and I tasted you. I had my hands on her and I touched you. I called out to you. Do you know what her eyes looked like after I said your name? It was like I had hit her, Ria." There was such anguish in his eyes. "You want that instead?"

Mira's heartbroken face swam in her head. Viky stuck in a wheelchair swam in her head. Her own face on her hapless, bruised mother lying in a padded room swam in her head. A horrible coldness closed around her, pulling her under.

"You didn't see Baba, you didn't know him. There was just so much sadness in him. It hollowed him out. I watched it hollow him out. I can't bear the thought of you like that. I could be flinging myself at walls, Viky. I could set you on fire."

"Or you couldn't. You are twenty-eight years old. Your mother, your grandmother, they were in their early twenties when it happened. And you've never shown any signs of mental illness."

She met his eyes, sagged against his hold. "Yes, I have. I spent a year of my life not being able to talk. Even now I struggle not to lose my words. I struggle with sadness, with strangers, with things that happened so long ago."

His hands rubbed up and down her arms. "That was trauma. You were attacked in your own home when you were barely more than a baby. It's probably PTSD and you've lived with it your whole life. And you worked through it on your own. With no professional help. Look at what you've achieved." Love colored his eyes, his voice. His fingers intertwined in hers. "The only thing crazy about you is how you make me feel, Ria, and how you want to protect the hell out of everyone around you. You are the sanest person I know." He dropped a kiss on her forehead and smiled. "Except that day when you jumped on that photographer."

Despite the horrible pain in her heart, she laughed.

"Now, what else have you got? Tell me. Let's end this. You're aging me."

She closed her eyes. If she didn't say it now she'd never be able to say it.

"Really? There's more?" he said, as though he were making a joke, but he stroked her face. "Say it, sweetheart. Please."

She didn't open her eyes, and she let it out. "I can never have children. I won't ever have children. I won't pass this on. I won't risk pushing myself over the edge."

She steeled herself against the resolve she was sure she'd see in his eyes, the sacrifice she had no doubt he would feel compelled to make. But when she opened her eyes he was smiling.

"Viky, are you insane?"

He dropped a kiss on her lips, on her nose. "Sweetheart, this just isn't working out for you, is it?"

She had no idea what he meant, what that stupid smile meant.

"You know how I started V-learn? I was living in Careiro, it's this small town near Manaus in Brazil. The only place I could find a room to rent was in this orphanage. And they let me live there if I taught the kids. It was the most beautiful place." His eyes glowed. She stroked his face.

"I wanted to bring all those kids home. All of them. I was a hardened, half-dead bastard. But those kids, they melted through me like butter." He pulled her hands to his chest. "I always planned to go back and adopt as many as I could. With so many children who need families, I don't want to bring more children into the world."

He flicked a teardrop off her cheek and kissed the edge of her lips, and stayed there until he could speak again.

"Now, what's your next excuse?" he said finally.

She stroked his lips, the thought of ever losing him becoming more and more unbearable with each passing minute. "I feel it coming for me, Viky. It's in my blood."

"Or maybe it isn't. We'll find the best doctors, do everything we can to prevent it, or even treat it if we have to. Your mother might have had a chance if she'd had the right treatment. Drew works with all forms and levels of psychosis. He says treatment has changed drastically in the past decade. It's an illness, Ria. People spend their lives researching it. We'll get help. Chances are we'll never need any of it."

"You don't know that."

"You're right, I don't. But I do know that it doesn't matter. I want you, exactly the way you are today, the way you'll be tomorrow, and fifty years from now. And I want you to want me enough to deal with whatever happens. I can't promise you'll be okay. But without you I will never be okay. And I know that without me you will never be okay either."

She wrapped her arms around him, his words sinking deep into her marrow. He pulled her close, sensing the change, and threw his head back in relief.

His eyes brightened and she followed his gaze to the tree they were standing under. He let her go with a meaningful look. A branch shot out of the tree like a miniature version of their bridge. He pulled himself up onto it and held out his hand.

Wordlessly, she took his hand and let him pull her up on the branch next to him. He snuggled close and kissed her ear. "It's time to stop fighting, Ria. Please."

Shivers of pleasure raced down her neck, making her press into his mouth. He always knew exactly where to touch her, how to touch her. He sucked her earlobe into his mouth and pure, untainted joy bloomed inside her. He had removed her earrings that first night they'd made love and hidden them away and she hadn't worn earrings since. And she never wanted to for as long as she lived.

She grabbed his denim-clad thigh to keep from tipping back. Strong, warm muscle bunched beneath her hand. She stroked it. "That thing about the wheelchair was a lie, wasn't it?"

"Maybe." He smiled against her neck and found every sensitive spot up and down the column of her throat. She had to laugh. Her incorrigible, irrepressible Viky.

"How can I be with a person who lies to me with such ease?"

"You think that was easy?" he said between kisses. But he'd done it all the same. What choice had she given him? "Maybe I can make up for it by giving you a few acting lessons," he said. "You have to admit those are some serious skills." He grinned into her eyes with the full force of that mismatched smile.

She shoved him, but not hard enough for the show he made of almost falling off the branch. "You're a ham. And you're crazy. That's what you are." She held his precious face in her hands.

"Totally. Crazy in love with you."

She kissed him. Overwhelming need flooded through her. Powerful jolts of fear knotted her stomach. He kissed her back with frantic urgency, lazy greed making her wild, out of control. But for the first time in her life, under all the intensity of her feelings, she recognized her well-being, the rightness of it. The way he made her feel, who she became with him. It wasn't a lie, it wasn't a dream, it was who she was, who she loved being, and it was beautiful.

He consumed her with his lips, the sheer force of his will in his kiss. A will that had made it easy for him to get anything he wanted. Except her. Her he'd had to fight for. And he'd fought with everything in him. He always would.

She pulled away from him, searched his love-struck eyes, what they held within them untouched by time. "You're right, Viky, I will never be okay without you."

His smile was all smug arrogance, but the tension in his shoulders eased beneath her fingers. She'd let him down so many times, and still he believed in her. She wrapped her arms around his waist and laid her head on his shoulder, more grateful than she'd ever been in her life. He pulled her to him and leaned his head into hers. They sat like that entwined together in silence and stared at the building that loomed in front of them.

"She looked almost happy, didn't she?" she asked finally, her voice barely a whisper. "My mother."

But he heard her. "Yes, and peaceful. Baba would've been so proud of you, Ria."

And that's why she loved him.

That incredible, imperfect mouth of his—it hadn't driven her crazy for the better part of her life only because it was beautiful, but because it always, always knew exactly what to say to put her together. She reached for his lips and claimed what was hers.

And when he jumped off the branch and asked her if she wanted to go home, she said yes, she wanted to go home.

# Acknowledgments

Publishing your book is a journey that culminates with just one name on the cover, making it seem, horribly erroneously, as though it were a solo flight, when really it was a caravan—a collective of guides and healers, holding your hand through tough landscapes and brutal climbs making sure you reached your destination. Although this is my second book, Vikram and Ria have lived inside my head for a long time and their story was really the first story I started. So this was the story where I most needed my caravan of support and I could never list all the people who helped me nor thank them nearly enough. But here's my feeble attempt anyway.

First, my best friend, Rupali Mehta, for urging me to write what I love and for the many times she had to talk me off a ledge. And for loving and nurturing my books as much as I do. Without you there would be no books.

My earliest beta readers—from my first writing sister, Sally Marcey, who read a painful first draft years ago and told me she thought I'd "got it," to my sister-in-law, Kalpana Thatte, who has read every draft since and championed each one with equal enthusiasm. Without your faith I'd still be dreaming.

My very first published author friends who made me feel like a real writer and then made time to teach me how to be one. Kristin Daniels, Tracey Devlyn, Adrienne Giordano, Robin Covington, Regina Bryant. Without your generosity I'd still be spinning my wheels.

My talented critique partners Robin Kuss, Hanna Martine, Talia Surova, India Powers, Clara Kensie, Savannah Reynard, Cici Edwards, CJ Warrant. Without your eagle eyes and knowledge of craft this would be a very different book.

My writing gurus, whom I unabashedly fangirl, Susan Elizabeth Phillips, Nalini Singh, Kristan Higgins, and Courtney Milan, for writing books I've learned everything I know from and for supporting my debut not just with their amazing blurbs and recommendations, but with personal encouragement that I cherish more than I could ever articulate. Without your example of grace and kindness this would be a very different journey.

My dear therapist friend for sharing her deep and insightful knowledge of trauma and healing. My characters were blessed to have you. Without your facts my fiction would have no anchor. Any errors in authenticity are all my own.

My editor, Martin Biro, for seeing my story's potential and helping unearth it with his trademark kindness; my agent, Claudia Cross, for her wholehearted support from the moment of our first serendipitous meeting; the incredible Vida Engstrand and the wonderful team at Kensington for going above and beyond at every step; and the talented Sam Thatte of Sam Thatte Presentations for producing such a great book video. Without you I can't imagine how I would have navigated any of this.

And finally the people without whom nothing else would mater, my husband and my children, for their pride and love even though the day-to-day pressures of my writing are theirs alone to bear, you are my balance and my reason. And my parents, not just for flying across the globe anytime I need help, but for giving me such vivid living examples of strength of character. Without you I could not write the characters I write.

And of course, to you my dearest readers, my deepest gratitude, you are the destination, the blessing that makes this pilgrimage all the more worth making. Thank you.